THE
DANCE
OF THE
DOLLS

THE
DANCE
OF THE
DOLLS

LUCY ASHE

U

UNION
SQUARE
& CO.

NEW YORK

**UNION
SQUARE
& CO.**

NEW YORK

UNION SQUARE & CO. and the distinctive Union Square & Co. logo
are registered trademarks of Sterling Publishing Co., Inc.

Union Square & Co., LLC, is a subsidiary of Sterling Publishing Co., Inc.

Text © 2023 Lucy Ashe

This is a work of fiction. All characters, organizations, and events portrayed in this novel
are either products of the author's imagination or are used fictitiously.

First published in the UK in 2023 by Magpie, an imprint of Oneworld.
This 2023 paperback edition published by Union Square & Co.

ISBN 978-1-4549-5123-0
ISBN 978-1-4549- 5124-7 (e-book)

Library of Congress Control Number: 2023938520

For information about custom editions, special sales, and premium purchases,
please contact specialsales@unionsquareandco.com.

Printed in Canada

2 4 6 8 10 9 7 5 3 1

unionsquareandco.com

Cover image: Anton Vierietin/Shuttertock.com
Cover design: Melissa Farris
Interior design by Kevin Ullrich

For my sisters, Jo and Suzie

Glossary

Adagio–the opening dance of a traditional pas de deux, e.g. the "Rose Adagio" from *Sleeping Beauty*.

Ballets Russes–one of the most influential ballet companies of the twentieth century, led by the impresario Serge Diaghilev. The Ballets Russes performed across Europe, North and South America between 1909 and 1929.

Cecchetti method–a rigorous style of ballet training devised by the Italian ballet master Enrico Cecchetti.

character shoes–heeled shoes used for dancing based on folk or national dances, for example the "Mazurka" in *Coppélia*. The heel protects the dancers' feet from the frequent stamping movements in character dancing.

Coppélia–comic ballet originally choreographed by Arthur Saint-Léon with music by Léo Delibes. The production staged by the Vic-Wells in 1933 was the Petipa version, with just the first two of the three acts performed.

corps de ballet – a group of dancers performing non-leading roles; literally "the ballet company."

Serge Diaghilev (1872–1929)–the founder of the Ballets Russes.

rosin–a powder byproduct of turpentine used by dancers on their shoes to prevent them from slipping.

Nicholas Sergeyev (1876–1951)–regisseur of the Imperial Ballet at the Mariinsky Theatre, he fled Russia after the 1917 Revolution. He took with him trunks containing the written records of many of the great ballets of Marius Petipa and Lev Ivanov. The classical repertoire of ballets, including *Coppélia, Giselle, Swan Lake, The Nutcracker,* and *The Sleeping Princess*, are known as the Sergeyev Collection.

The Sleeping Princess–a classical ballet choreographed by Marius Petipa in 1890, now known as *The Sleeping Beauty*.

Stepanov notation–a notation system for recording dance movements, named after the Russian dancer Vladimir Stepanov. His book, *The*

Alphabet of Movements of the Human Body, was published in 1892. The notebooks that Sergeyev smuggled out of Russia recorded ballets notated using the Stepanov method.

Dame Ninette de Valois (1898–2001)–the founder of the Vic-Wells Ballet, which evolved into Sadler's Wells Ballet, then the Royal Ballet and Birmingham Royal Ballet. She is known in the ballet world simply as "Madame."

Ballet movements

adage–section of a ballet class with slow movements of the legs to improve balance, extension and coordination.

allegro–section of ballet class with jumping steps.

arabesque–one leg extended behind the body with the knee straight and the foot pointed. In arabesque *allongée*, the line of the body is almost horizontal to the ground.

attitude–the working leg is lifted either in front (*devant*), side (*à la seconde*), or back (*derrière*), with the knee bent.

balancé–a swaying, rocking step in any direction to a waltz rhythm.

barre exercises–in the first part of a ballet class, dancers run through a series of exercises. These take place at the barre, a bar on which the dancer places their hand while dancing. These exercises include, in the order in which they are carried out:

> *pliés*–to bend and stretch both legs at the same time;
>
> *battements tendus*–one foot slides out smoothly along the floor to a full pointe of the toe;
>
> *battements jetés or glissés*–with tendu but with the toe just lifting off the floor;
>
> *ronds de jambe*–the leg makes a circle, front, side, then back, either on the ground (*à terre*) or lifted off the ground (*en l'air*);
>
> *battements fondus*–smoothly unfolding the leg into the air, with the supporting leg bending and then extending;

battements frappés–a raised, flexed foot touches the ankle then springs out with great energy to a pointed position;

petits battements–the foot moves quickly around the ankle with the knee bent;

développés–drawing one foot up to the knee and then unfolding the leg into the air; and

grands battements–exercises that usually finish the barre work; throwing the leg high and controlling the movement as it lowers. For *grands battements en cloche*, the leg is thrown forward then back alternately.

bourrée–steps *en pointe* in tiny movements that make the dancer appear to float or glide.

brisé–a small traveling jump in which legs assemble (*assemblé*) and beat together.

chaînés–quick, traveling, half turns with the feet in a tight first position.

demi-bras–arms held low, extended either side of the body.

échappé–the legs spring out at the same time to either the side, front, or back. *Sur les pointes* is on to the toes.

épaulement–turning the body from the waist so that one shoulder comes forward and the other goes back.

en pointe–dancing on the tips of the toes while wearing pointe shoes.

grand jeté–a large jump with the legs split in the air.

pas de deux–partner dancing, traditionally where the female dancer is supported or lifted by the male dancer.

port de bras–arm movements, literally meaning carriage of the arms.

pirouette–a full turn on one leg. They can be performed *en dedans* (inward) or *en dehors* (outward).

relevé retiré–drawing one foot up to the opposite knee, the supporting foot rising to the toes, the heel coming off the ground.

Prologue

He wheels her out into the road. He should stay hidden, but part of him wants to be seen: he deserves her. He has waited long enough, worked hard enough. She belongs to him, dressed forever in the same red skirt with the same pink shoes tied around her ankles. Lace and net graze against her motionless thighs. Her skin is smooth porcelain and her lips are pink. Never has there been a lovelier figure, unchanging, unbroken by the pace of time. Her sightless eyes will not fade. A beautiful statue, preserved forever. He has watched her for so long, holding her in his gaze, locking her into position like a photograph.

He imagines dancing with her, the two of them arm in arm under the stars. Silent, of course, but that is no matter. It is better that way. She is a dancing doll, his Coppélia, created at last. He can finally believe it, now that he has her in the wheelchair. Pausing at the end of the street, he reaches down to her wrist and lifts her arm above her as if she is waving to a crowd. Ice-cold. He drops her arm in fright. Life lingers, like a promise; but he is afraid of what will happen when she wakes.

He needs to move quickly.

London, 1933

Act One

CHAPTER 1

Samuel

It is Thursday, the day Samuel Steward delivers the pointe shoes to the theatre. He has been looking forward to it all week, even as he sits at his workbench, stills his mind, focuses his eyes on every stitch of satin and leather. Now, he walks hurriedly up through Covent Garden to Clerkenwell. His arms ache under the weight of those pale pink shoes, the satin smooth over the paper, hessian, paste, wax thread, all hidden of course when he stretches it right side out and inserts the sole. A perfect arc of a shoe. Arched like her feet when she rises up, weightless. Olivia Marionetta. He whispers her name, his voice too human, too rough, for a name that dances above him.

Familiar piano notes guide him up the stairs toward the ballet studio. He can hear the dancers' feet, their tapping across the floor, lighter now that the ballet mistress has been granted her wish, a wooden floor rather than the cold concrete that made the shoes echo through the room. It was the proudest day of his life when Mr. Frederick touched his shoulder, nodded his approval and knocked against the workbench the shoe that he, Samuel, had made. An entire shoe made from start to finish with his own hands. He has worked steadily these past two years, making the progress from mixing the paste to cutting the leather, from labeling the regular customers' shoe lasts to stamping the latticework across the sole of the shoe. He has mastered each stage, perfecting the shaping, the molding, the stitching, the exact number of hard hits needed on the shoe jack to produce the pointe shoe's mesmerizing arch.

He imagines his rose, that tiny engraving he has cut into the bottom of her shoes. When he realized that his shoes were going to Olivia Marionetta, he knew he needed to honor this privilege. Writing her name in pen across the sole of the shoe was not enough; he did that for all the dancers. He needed something more for her. And of course he chose the rose. There was nothing else he could see when he closed his eyes, felt the smooth block of the shoe, imagined his mark. Her face, her eyes, the perfect bun she wears at the nape of her neck, her hair parted at the side. And the little white rose she pins into the top of the bun.

Samuel reaches the studio, his bags heavy with the shoes. The door is open, a small window into an imaginary world, a world he would like to trap forever in his mind, transcribe to his sketchbook, mark on paper with pencil, chalk, charcoal, his forever. But he knows he is not welcome. He is for the shadows, basements with dusty workbenches, his hands moving strong and fast over satin and paste, molding the shoes that these dancers from another world will take from him. The turn-shoe method, all the work and sweat hidden inside. When he strains his muscles to wrench the shoe into shape, all that love is tucked away, out of sight. The dancers, they will make them their own. They will stitch them, cut them, wrap ribbons around their ankles, break the shoes, soften them, pummel them against hard concrete steps until they can move silently, softly, like butterflies across the stage. They do not even know he exists.

He knows how to make himself invisible. From the dark, where the shaft of light through the high windows of the studio cannot reach, he watches. He doesn't know what any of the steps are called and cannot keep up with the music of those names when the ballet mistress sings out the words in French, the dancers mimicking them with their hands until the music starts again and they fly across the floor.

And there she is. She flies higher than the others, he thinks. A vision in a bright white leotard, a thin skirt tied around her waist. She wears his shoes, the ones he has crafted with extra special care, adjusting the width, the length, the vamp of the toe box as she needs it. When he pencils her name onto the paper note that he pins onto her bag of shoes, it feels like a love letter. *For Olivia Marionetta.*

The dancers travel across the floor on a diagonal, ending their routine with a spin, their heads whipping around, their eyes steady. Olivia rises up on her toes, his shoes holding her strong. Her body is perfectly poised, and yet she turns and turns, one more rotation, and then a moment of stillness, before running to the side of the room. She watches the next set of dancers repeat the steps. Samuel realizes he is holding his breath.

He looks again. There she is, her legs strong as she jumps. But no, it is not her, not this time. He looks away, steps back further into the shadows. Clara Marionetta scares him. At first glance she is her sister's double. She has the same face, same dark brown hair with the shimmer of red, same long sloping neck, same thin body with strength that defies its suppleness. The same feet, with those high arches that seem to command his shoes to dance. But in every other way they are different. He can tell them apart instantly; he just needs to see their eyes, the edges of their mouths. Clara looks in the mirror as she dances, with a fierce flame in her eyes: she owes the world nothing. She wears her shoes with a careless ease, the soles black and worn, a streak of dirt rising up from her heel. When she finishes her turn, she directs her gaze right at the ballet mistress and smiles; she knows she is beautiful, worthy, outshining the other girls. The ballet mistress calls out a correction; Clara turns away and rolls her eyes.

But Olivia does not dare meet the teacher's eye, hardly glances at herself in the mirror, leaves the dance floor with a little frown. Samuel wishes he could go to her, like he has seen those men do who wait at the stage door after performances. He would tell her how beautiful she is, how perfect, how the whole world must adore her. But of course he could never do that.

The teacher calls for them all to come to the center; for the reverence, he thinks she says. The chords from the piano are familiar, like an ending. He watches the dancers step sideways, their arms wide, and he knows he must hurry. He doesn't want them to find him lingering. Mrs. Dora gave him clear instructions to place all the shoes in the correct cubbyholes in Wardrobe before the class ended. For those ballerinas not yet converted to Freed shoes, he is to leave a little postcard, hand-signed by Frederick Freed himself: *We make shoes bespoke to you, the perfect shape and size for your foot.*

Wardrobe, as he has heard the dancers call it, is a chaotic room with no windows. It has none of the order of Mrs. Dora's shop, the neat cubbyholes of pale pink pointe shoes all paired and ordered by size. Samuel likes to be in and out before the wardrobe manager, Mr. Jack Healey, arrives. He has heard Mr. Healey nagging the ballerinas to remove their piles of pointe shoes, reams of ribbons, the leotards and practice skirts that spill from every corner.

Samuel pushes aside a row of long white skirts, the net catching on his coat. It is quiet here, just the faint hammering from the carpenter's workshop where the set is being prepared for the next ballet. He stands in front of the rows of cubbyholes, the names of the dancers and actors and opera singers chalked in lightly on little slate boards. He places his bag at his feet and lifts out the shoes, protected in their cloth sacks. Scanning the chalk names, it is easy to tell which are the dancers, their names transformed into Russian, French, Italian words, exotic, beautiful sounds that elevate them far from the likes of him, plain and simple Samuel Steward. Beatrice Appleyard, Anton Dolin, Stanislas Idzikowski, Lydia Lopokova, Clara Marionetta, Olivia Marionetta, Alicia Markova, Toni Repetto, Antony Tudor, Ninette de Valois. He would like to know if these are their real names. Perhaps that would make them more tangible, more human; perhaps that would give him the courage to speak to her: Olivia Marionetta. He leaves her shoes until last. Taking them out of the cloth bag, he checks each shoe, rubbing his thumb over the little rose he has engraved into the sole. Each one is perfect.

With his heart beating fast, he lifts out of his deep coat pocket the white rose that he bought for three pence on his way out of Covent Garden that morning. He had almost been too nervous to buy it, the flower seller's smirk following him as he lingered by the stall. But he had been determined and now here he is, a rose in his hand, slightly crumpled but still flawless, smooth silky petals. He places it in Olivia Marionetta's cubbyhole, on top of her new pointe shoes. She does not know the hand that crafted them, but maybe she will feel herself dance lighter, taller, brighter, and she will know that she is adored.

CHAPTER 2

Olivia

I look for luck everywhere. Today, I need to calm my nerves, soothe the anxieties that keep jumping to the front of my mind, refusing to be kept at bay. My porridge stares at me this morning; I can't eat it. It would be unlucky, a curse, to fill my belly with such ordinary, heavy-looking food. Today I need to shine.

We are all superstitious. We thrive on routines and good luck charms. They give us certainty, focus the mind, take us to a magical place where we can leave the real world and become the dancing apparitions the audience want us to be. We need our muse, our Terpsichore, to lead us onto the stage. Changing our names was the first step. Clara and I used to be plain old Olivia and Clara Smith. But we changed it to Marionetta when we left ballet school and ascended to the ranks of the company, joining Miss de Valois at her brand-new Vic-Wells ballet company, rebranding ourselves to match. It was our mother's idea to take her name, Marion, and weave it into something better than Smith. Clara was reluctant, but I persuaded her that Mother needed this, some recognition of the role she had played in getting us this far.

At Sadler's Wells Theatre, the home to our Vic-Wells Ballet, we have a specific dwelling for our superstition: an old monastic well that lurks in the center of a dark and shadowy storage room underneath the auditorium. We traipse down there when we need luck, our visits punctuating the rhythm of our lives. Each day starts with morning ballet class, those essential ninety minutes that keep our bodies supple and strong. No one is allowed to miss class, though the principal dancers often do, somehow avoiding Miss de Valois's disapproval. If we have time, we hide ourselves in the gloom of the well room for a few minutes before afternoon rehearsals, finding a dark spot to massage our feet. We visit it before performances, at least three shows a week in the October to May season now that our company's reputation is growing. And then finally, if there is no post-show party to dress for in a mad, ecstatic rush, we reach down and dip our fingers into the well before we go home to sleep, to recover. My sister will always choose the party, while I prefer the quiet of home. I like to rest my aching limbs for the next day's work.

I spend longer than usual at the well this morning. There is a cool darkness to the room, lit faintly by a single light that hangs beneath green enamel and wire frame from the low ceiling. The well sits in the center, a stone rectangle three feet wide and rising a couple of feet off the ground. I like to sit on the stone edging, my feet pressed into the cool stone wall. Toward the corners of the room, four steel beams rise up from the concrete floor, giving the room a cramped tightness. If there are more than a few of us down here at once, it is easy to bump into something, or even someone, lurking quietly in the privacy of the shadows. The old stone well cover rests against the side wall of the room, a dust sheet draped over the curious carvings that I like to run my finger along when I have the room to myself. It has a long history, dating back to when a monastery must have stood on the site, perhaps as far back as the twelfth century, surrounded by fields and gardens. It is hard to imagine now, with the New River closed over and buildings springing up all over Islington. Our theatre is number five of all the Sadler's Wells that have drawn the London audiences. Miss Moreton, in the rare moments we can distract her from her relentless pace through class, tells us about the theatre, how when Richard Sadler built the first one back in the seventeenth century, he made it popular by playing on this watery attraction. The wells were closed over, but the superstitions remained. We have gladly rebirthed them, all of us dancers ready to pounce on the first sign of magic and mystery.

The stone well cover, found by builders nearly three hundred years ago, has been preserved, protected from destruction every time the theatre is pulled down and built again, emerging from the ashes with new ideas for new entertainments. Even the builders, it seems, were superstitious. Our theatre isn't perfect. But I still love it, despite the tiny dressing rooms and the terrible acoustics in the auditorium.

It seems darker than usual this morning, shadows dancing slowly between the steel beams and the low, still water of the well. I can barely see to the end of the room where a storage cupboard is hidden in the corner and a wooden crate of stage props gathers dust. I looked inside the cupboard once, only to be confronted with mops and ropes, as well as a strange display of tennis balls and cricket bats. The theatre is gradually filling with the debris of productions, each show leaving behind its mark. A stack of photographs that didn't quite make the walls of the theatre foyer is leaning against the back wall, frozen moments of *Les Sylphides*, *Narcisse et Echo, Les Rendezvous, Nursery Suite*, the monochromatic figures blurred and faded. It is wonderful to be part of Ninette de Valois's growing company, the ballets we put on works of art to rival even the legendary days of the Ballets Russes. I do not miss those long nights that Clara and I have spent shivering in cold dressing rooms waiting for our performance in variety shows and revues, squashed between singers, comedians, even Cochran's pretty young ladies who gave us no space in the mirror to do our makeup. Our little ballet numbers were divertissements, instantly forgotten. But not anymore, not with our Ninette de Valois and Lilian Baylis and the Camargo Society propelling us forward.

With cold and frigid air, this is not a place to linger before class. Coming here alone, without the sweat and heat of the other dancers' bodies to fill the space, the room smells damp, like laundry that has been left wet too long. But I have wishing to do this morning. I need some luck. Nicholas Sergeyev is coming to class today.

His arrival has sent whispers around the theatre corridors for weeks, and I am sure the cafés of Bloomsbury and Covent Garden are spreading our excitement even further. Regisseur of the Mariinsky Ballet, Nicholas Sergeyev escaped in the aftermath of the 1917 October Revolution. Somehow, among all the panic, he smuggled out tin trunks holding all his notation books. The records of the great Russian ballets were preserved.

And now he is coming to us. He is to teach us the ballets that made Russian dance so famous. There is to be *Coppélia, Lac des Cygnes, Giselle* and even *Casse-Noisette*. I have heard so much about these ballets. I long to learn the choreography, to lift the notations off the pages of those old books and transform them into living dance. It would be wonderful to see the notebooks, to see the steps Petipa and Ivanov marked onto the page using that devilishly difficult Stepanov notation. There is no way I could understand a single symbol, but I will learn the steps faster and more accurately than anyone. Even my sister, I think. Clara is not very good at sticking to the choreography. It drives Miss Moreton mad. Me too, to be honest. It is one of the reasons I always wear my hair in a low bun, in the romantic style. It sets me apart from Clara, who always wears her hair high: one small difference to help people see us as two distinct dancers.

I perch on the stone edging and lean over into the well, dipping my hand into the water. I have to stretch as far as my arm will go, my fingers just breaking the surface. My knees press against the wall of the well, but the distance is too far and I slip, my ribs hitting hard against the stone. Then I find my balance again, blinking as I watch the water moving and rippling like a kaleidoscope of grays and blacks, hiding whatever lurks beneath the surface. I lift my arm out, my fingers wet, and let the little drops of water fall onto my pointe shoes. The sharp pain of the stone against my ribs has startled me awake, reminding me of what I need to do today. Without pain, how do we know we are working hard enough? I said that to Clara once and she laughed at me. She didn't understand what I meant.

But this is the luck I need, or at least a gesture to give me the clear focus I want for ballet class. I know it is just a superstition, but this little drop of luck is my counterbalance to something strange that happened last week. It makes me shudder when I think of it, red staining my vision when I close my eyes. The blood remains, like an evil curse. When I went to collect my new pointe shoes from my cubbyhole in Wardrobe, there was a white rose in there, resting on top of my shoes. I picked it up, surprised. I turned to Clara, asking her if she'd put it there. She shook her head, refusing responsibility. I think she was a little bored by it, didn't see it as worthy of her attention. An admirer, perhaps; we all have them, men who come to every show, who linger outside the stage door, who deliver buckets of flowers that irritate the stagehands that have to carry them to our dressing rooms, choking on the strong scents and sprays of pollen. But this was just a single rose, no note or signature. When I turned it over in my hand, my finger caught on a thorn. I pulled it away fast, but the thorn had buried itself too deep inside me and I ripped my skin, a tiny bead of blood spilling out. I sucked it clean, but the blood kept rising to the surface in relentless bubbles. Eventually I thought I had made it stop, but I was wrong; it must have continued to bleed as I packed my pointe shoes into my bag. When I started sewing the ribbons onto my shoes that evening, I saw that I had left a dirty smear of blood across the satin of the shoe. It made me nervous, that blood, like a bad omen, a stain that could not be removed. Even once I had frantically rubbed on a paste of baking soda and water, I could still see the red darkening the satin like a ghostly palimpsest.

This water, our well famed for centuries as cleansing and healing, has set my mind at rest. I run up to the studio to prepare for class. As usual, I am one of the first to arrive. Clara always teases me about getting everywhere so early, but I can't help it. I don't see the point in leaving everything to the last minute, as she does. The Company doesn't share my opinion, I know. They think it terribly unfashionable to show too much effort at anything and would never let themselves be seen actually practicing outside of class and rehearsal. Of course they all do, they must, these goddesses who laugh and joke but still manage to perform the perfect triple pirouette, their legs rising to their shoulders.

Today is the perfect day to be early, because just as I am knotting the ribbons on my soft-block ballet shoes, who should walk in but Nicholas Sergeyev himself. Miss de Valois traveled to Paris to persuade him over to London. The rumors are that she found him in a tiny studio *appartement* in a run-down part of the city, another Russian ballet teacher sharing the room. Seeing him now, taking small erect steps into the room with Miss de Valois at his side, makes me jump to my feet. I feel I should curtsy or something, but he ignores me, instead looking about him in a perplexed and rather lost way. I don't know what he expected; perhaps a corps de ballet to welcome him.

But as the Company gradually arrives, there is a very different mood to usual morning class, an energy and excitement that shows in the way we all warm up, the girls throwing their legs higher than ever, the boys jumping up and down at the barre, their muscles firing. We all watch Nicholas Sergeyev. He refuses to smile, the faint ghost of a gray moustache twitching as he looks anxiously around the room. He is small and upright, his cheeks drawn and thin with age, though he is not yet sixty. His travels, the stress of leaving his home country, seem to have lined his face like the contours of a map. I like his presence here, even though it terrifies me; he brings Russia and the old-style ways of ballet with him. Even Clara seems a little nervous. She stands with me at the barre, which I am glad about. It is easier for teachers to tell us apart if we are right next to each other, the small differences in our dancing and our appearance more obvious.

The class begins and Miss de Valois is at her most fierce. From the very first exercise at the barre, she seems to be performing a role, her terrifying eccentricities exposed. We have all heard stories of the Russian ballet masters with their sticks and their anger and their sharp eyes noticing every finger a millimeter out of place. Sergeyev is nodding as she bangs her stick on the floor. This is how he likes classes to run, with everyone a little scared, the adrenaline keeping our legs high and our toes pointed.

Every dancer in the Company has turned up today, and all on time. Even the new and exciting Helpmann is here. The star dancers have taken the best positions at the barre, where the line of their legs and arms will be shown off to advantage. Lydia Lopokova, Alicia Markova, Anton Dolin, they are all here. Markova's is a rare appearance; usually she just appears onstage, barely even warming up. Her diary is always packed with engagements: dancing with the Vic-Wells, for the Camargo Society, for Marie Rambert's Ballet Club. The Wells Room, as our studio is called, is bursting with dancers, the steam from our bodies misting the windows. Strong smells of sweat and rosin and the leather of our shoes pack the air. Even some of Miss de Valois's favored girls from the school have managed to sneak in, squeezing into the corners where there is hardly space for them to stretch their arms. We all know that this Russian man has the power to elevate us to the top, to cast us in the best roles or to leave our names off the list entirely for the ballets he is reviving. For a moment, at the barre, dancing the slow adage that Miss de Valois calls out, I imagine myself as Aurora, Odette, Swanilda, Giselle. But a hard whack on my calf from Miss de Valois's stick wakes me up and reminds me to stand stronger, keep my leg extending away, in arabesque.

We take a few minutes' break after the barre work, the girls changing from soft-toe shoes into pointe shoes. Usually for ballet class we wear shoes that are nearly ready to throw out, saving our fresh ones for performances. They are expensive, and the company allowance for pointe shoes doesn't even come close to covering how many we need each month. I get through five pairs every four weeks, eking out those last few days with my muscles straining to keep my arches lifted and my ankles strong. But this is our chance, finally, to show what we can do. It is worth the expense. We all want to catch his eye. It is surreal, really, that this tiny man, in a suit that falls from his limbs like those costumes hanging from the rail in Wardrobe, has our full attention; he and Miss de Valois, who has transformed into a demon for the morning.

I go into the corridor and collect my bag, settling down in a corner to change my shoes. Clara is with me, massaging her feet through the pink silk of her tights. There is a ladder under her foot, just starting to spread up the heel, which is gray and stained from hours of dancing on dusty floors. She needs to scrub her tights with a bar of soap, like I do, but I know she's unlikely to bother. The corridor is quieter than normal, despite the crush of sweaty bodies; we all fight for space to stretch our legs in among the medley of warm-up clothes and shoes. Hushed whispers spread through us, punctuated by the quiet tap of pointe shoes as girls stand and press their feet into the floor. From inside the Wells Room, we can hear Nathan, the pianist, playing out some tunes while Miss de Valois stands next to him, beating out the pace with her stick.

I reach into my bag.

I know immediately that there is something wrong, something missing. I can't breathe. Both hands now search through the bag, my body tense as I rise up on my knees, hunched over the too-dark cavern of its opening. One of my pointe shoes has disappeared.

"What's wrong?" my sister whispers.

"I've lost a shoe." I try to keep my voice low, holding down the panic threatening to bubble to the surface.

"Let me look," she says, taking my bag from me. I realize that my hands are shaking. I can't go back in there without my pointe shoes. That would be it for me, my chance at being cast in one of his ballets gone forever.

"I've got a spare pair," I hear Clara say, nudging me back from the abyss my mind has drifted toward. I had got as far as Ninette de Valois refusing to have me back in class, sacking me from the company, not being able to pay the rent and ending up dancing for drunk old men on a cruise ship. But Clara saves me from that nightmare with the offer of her shoes. They are an old pair she hasn't cleared from her bag, far from perfect condition, but better than nothing. I will just have to dance my best, rising out of my hips to stay tall in the shoes. Knowing Clara, she's already worn these for a class longer than she should have done. They are a little torn under the toe, but they will do.

Clara squeezes my hand as we go back into the Wells Room, before fighting her way to the front row and dragging me with her. We line up next to each other, waiting for Miss de Valois's instructions. I feel a hit of remorse for thinking so badly of my sister this morning, her lateness and sloppiness, her carefree attitude to everything. But she is the one who is prepared for class, with her spare pair of shoes. I try not to get distracted as we go through the *adage*, then *grands battements, pirouettes en dehors, petit allegro*. It is difficult, though, with my mind drifting back to the well, trying to remember if I left my shoe down there in the darkness of the basement storage room.

When class ends, I gather up my belongings as quickly as I can. I run down the corridor that follows the edge of the building toward the pit and wings until I reach the entrance to the basement room, that flimsy door that the stage manager has given up trying to keep locked. The light is off and I have to fumble around the wall by the door to find the switch. I walk down the steps, my eyes adjusting to the gloom. All is quiet, just as it was before, and there is no sign of my shoe. I walk to the well and kneel down by its thick stone wall. The famous waters have not given me the luck I asked for today, it seems. I am cross with myself for being so careless. I lean over the edge, my eyes finding shapes in the dark.

There, floating on top of the water, is a pointe shoe. The ribbons are tangled like weeds. And next to the shoe, its petals drifting across the surface, is a single white rose.

CHAPTER 3

Samuel

Samuel has all the parts of the shoes lined up neatly on his workbench, a deconstructed artwork. Hessian, paper, satin, glue, the sole. The welting machine is across the room, where Mr. Frederick is standing in his overalls, his hands working fast, his head down in concentration. Samuel can make more than ten pairs of shoes a day now and is getting faster. The work is physically exhausting, each shoe demanding arm, wrist, shoulder strength to wrestle and bang the shoe into the perfect shape. And then there is the tiny rose he stamps into the soles of Olivia Marionetta's shoe, finding a quiet moment when Mr. Frederick is the other side of the workshop, preoccupied with his own craft. He has finally finished his rose cutter stamp, which makes it faster, a quick press, done in an instance. He dedicates one day a month to making her shoes, ten at a time as well as another five soft-toe shoes. He loves those days. Every stitch feels like a caress. He took his stamp home with him to finish, working under the little lamp on his desk in his tiny one-room flat off Exmouth Market. At least it's the top floor, and bright in the mornings, unlike the gloom of the basement where he works beneath Cecil Court.

He does love the workshop though, the chance to create and shape and fashion something beautiful out of all those malleable, simple ingredients. Sometimes he feels like he could be an artist himself, but then he remembers these designs are not his. He does have his own designs, piles and piles of his sketches of shoes, clothes, hats, all scattered about his room, some in the drawers, some pinned up on the walls. Around his bed, his chest of drawers, his desk, are his pencil and chalk sketches in all the colors of the rainbow, scraps of material pinned against them, velvet, silk, satin, lace. He can't share them with anyone. It would be too revealing, too exposing. Sometimes he imagines himself going up to Mr. Frederick with a handful of his designs, maybe the high-heeled boots he is so proud of, with the soft soles for dancing character roles. But it's no use; they are probably worthless, unoriginal, no good to anyone. He should just be grateful for this job, he knows, and keep making these beautiful pointe shoes day after day. As his father always said, stick to what you know and you won't go wrong. Don't give anyone a chance to laugh at you. His father had laughed at him, though, Samuel remembers so vividly, that day he showed him his sketch of a pair of winter boots, the green leather football buttons running down the ankle, the fur trim topping the lining. He had spent days over that sketch, perfecting the shapes and proportions, searching through his chalks for the exact green he wanted. He never showed his father another sketch, not after his loud mocking laugh followed him out of the living room door, back up the narrow stairs to his bedroom. The silence of his mother, her downcast eyes at the dinner table, he remembers it all. It was easier for her to say nothing, a patient sufferance. His parents still live in that dark, gloomy house in Clapham, his father going out every day to the railway where he works as an engineer, his mother waiting for him at home in a freezing house that he refuses to heat during the day. Samuel will never go back there, not if he can help it.

Mrs. Dora has left the door open up to the shop, a little pool of light spilling down the steps to the basement. Samuel likes hearing the murmuring of the dancers who come in to be fitted, the strong tones of Mrs. Dora as she advises them and instructs them. You'd think she knows their feet better than they do themselves. Perhaps she does.

Mr. Frederick asks him to take some finished shoes up to the shop. It is a brilliantly bright morning, still a little frosty, the cold air drifting in through the front door as it opens and closes. On his walk to work he had sunk his feet into the hard white grass in the little parks that he weaves his way through, enjoying the sound of the crisp crackle of the frost. He likes avoiding the main roads that teem with noisy, impatient people, instead finding small havens of quiet.

They are busy this morning. The fame of these shoes grows through the city. No one notices Samuel as he stocks the shelves, ordering the shoes exactly as Mrs. Dora likes them. Two young girls from Miss de Valois's school are laughing as they raise themselves up and down, pressing the arches of their feet forward, pointing their toes, extending their legs. Everyone likes these shoes, how they seem to meld to the feet, exactly the right support without being too hard, too unyielding.

The door opens again, the little bell above the door tinkling invitingly. Samuel hears two voices, both identical in note and pitch. They call good morning to Mrs. Dora. Samuel recognizes them instantly. Even with his back turned, his whole body frozen as he reaches up to the top shelves of pointe shoes, he knows which voice belongs to Clara and which to his Olivia.

"Samuel, get me two pairs of your shoes, size four," Mrs. Dora calls to him, barely turning toward him as she greets the twins. He moves quickly, pulling himself into action, and nods. It is a pointless action; no one is looking at him. He reaches for the shoes, knowing instinctively which are his. The shoes he has made for Olivia are ready for his next delivery, so he takes a pair of these, as well as a pair from Clara's pile. He is ahead of his work, the shoes ready earlier than Mrs. Dora expected.

"Oh no, don't worry about that," Clara says, smiling; a little impatiently, Samuel thinks. "We love the shoes we have from you already, no need to change anything about them. We just want to put in another order."

"And buy some ribbon," adds Olivia, "and see if you've decided yet about adding to your range. We're all desperate for some character shoes that won't give us blisters."

"Give us time," replies Mrs. Dora gently, gesturing them to the counter, where she will put in the repeat order. "Are you sure you don't want me to check the shoes on you again, while you are here? I would so love to see how they fit you." She pauses and looks to Samuel, who is holding the shoes she requested out to her. He doesn't dare glance at Olivia, even though he is desperate to look. She is so close, the closest he has ever been to her. One quick look, and that is all, then. He takes in everything with one little flick of his eyes: her low-heeled boots so snug around her slim ankles, her thick navy coat that she buttons high, a cream scarf wrapped around her neck. Her hair is in the bun she always wears, but without the rose. He has always thought that seeing her dressed as a normal woman, not in her leotard and dance skirt, would make her more real. But it hasn't had that effect at all. If anything, she seems even less real, as though if he closes his eyes she will disappear.

"All right," he hears her say. "It will be fun to try them on with you, in your beautiful shop." Mrs. Dora looks delighted, emerging from behind the counter in an almost youthful burst. She rarely shows such lightness, her authority and experience making her seem far older than her real age, barely thirty. To Samuel she seems ancient, infinitely wise, despite being just ten years older than him.

The twin sisters peel off their coats, draping them over the wooden and velvet stools that Samuel helped Mr. Frederick to build last year. They unlace their boots, Clara flinging them to the side, Olivia placing hers neatly to the left of the stool. Samuel watches as Mrs. Dora kneels, placing Clara's right foot onto the little ramp. She slides on the shoe, feeling around the width. She repeats this with the left foot before moving to Olivia, gently rubbing the satin around the heel and toe. The sisters stand and turn to each other. They take each other's hands and rise onto their toes, their feet strong in the shoes. They draw their feet together into a tight position, legs crossed from the top. Samuel watches, staying as close as he can to the edge of the room. He looks down at his own feet, large and heavy in his boots. He is not delicate or dainty; his feet cannot move like theirs, fast and light little pitter-patters into the ground. Samuel is not graceful, but he is strong. He has to be to make these shoes. Since working at Freed his muscles have grown, his shoulders broadened. Even Mrs. Dora commented the other day, marveling at how he'd changed, his forearms thickened from all the bending and banging. But still no one notices him, standing there in his overalls, gray and brown against the glowing pink of the shoes behind him.

Olivia is bending and stretching her legs. He's heard Mrs. Dora request a plié over and over to the girls she fits, her commanding voice matching that of the terrifying ballet mistresses he encounters at Sadler's Wells. Now plié, and stretch, she says as the girls try out the different shapes and sizes of shoe.

"They feel wonderful," says Olivia, sitting back down on the stool and stretching her feet away to admire the shape of the shoe. Samuel stares as she brings one leg up toward herself, twisting her foot so she can see the sole. She rubs the pale leather with her finger, tracing a line from toe to heel. For an instant he thinks she is looking at his rose, his symbol that marks the shoes as just for her. He feels a sudden panic, deep in his stomach. What if she realizes he put the white rose in her cubbyhole; what if she is offended, or worse, laughs at him for daring to make such a gesture? If he moves now, he can get down to the workshop before she turns to see him. But Mrs. Dora is in the way, blocking his exit route.

Samuel feels his heart beating fast, his face starting to burn. He tries to imagine what he will say if Mrs. Dora reveals him to be their pointe shoemaker. His hands are clammy. What if they want to shake his hand, he thinks, panicking, trying to wipe them on his overalls.

"They are perfect shoes," Clara says, smiling down at her feet. She does a little turn, spinning on one foot then the next until she comes back around to face Mrs. Dora. "You make us dance like swans." She laughs, throwing her hands above her head and crossing her wrists.

Olivia stands and looks about her, taking in the walls of shoes stacked neatly on the shelves. She has taken off the shoes and is holding them in her hands. Her feet are bare, the long thin bones that stretch from her toes to her ankle pressing against mottled pearl skin. Finally she notices him, his large mass blocking a column of shelves. "Do you help Mr. Freed make the pointe shoes?" he hears her say.

He doesn't trust himself to speak. All he can do is nod.

"Well, they are lovely, as Clara says." She turns them over in her hands. "I get through them very quickly, so you'll have to work hard to keep us in our shoes." She is teasing him, he realizes. But all he can do is nod again, pressing his hands against his thighs. She waits a moment, looking up at him. In her bare feet, he sees how small she is, at least a foot shorter than him. He reached six foot when he was sixteen, six foot three when he was eighteen, and over the last two years his body has been slowly catching up and filling out.

He doesn't know why she is still standing there, smiling. Maybe he has paste on his face from making the glue, or maybe she can't believe that someone as large and inelegant as him could work in a shop that makes such a shoe. But then he realizes she isn't looking at him. She is looking behind him at the rows and rows of shoes and the spools of ribbons that Mrs. Dora measures out and cuts with such precision.

"The perfect color of shoe," she says, almost a whisper. She looks like she is in a dream, imagining herself onstage, that burst of applause when the curtain rises.

She finally gathers herself and glides back to join her sister. He is fascinated by how thin and sinewy her feet are, every step revealing muscles, tendons, bones he has never noticed in his own.

And then they are gone. They disappear around the corner, the bell sending out its ripple, like an orchestra has suddenly packed away leaving just a triangle whispering its final notes. That is how he feels, with her gone. It is as though an imaginary world has vanished, leaving him awake and staring at his large, sweaty hands.

CHAPTER 4

Clara

My sister is asleep when I get in, later than I should. She rolls over in bed, murmuring. I reach down and gently ease her hair out of that tight ponytail she insists on keeping in at night. It isn't good for her, all that tension. She almost wakes, but I rest my hand on her shoulder until she is calm. I like to look at her, the smooth skin of her neck that she always manages to carry with such elegance even in Miss Moreton's most painful *petit allegro*. I catch myself staring and feel a little guilty, vain, seeing myself mirrored in her face.

In the bathroom are the bowls of water she has left out for me, two deep chamber pots we found in an antique shop behind Sadler's Wells when we moved here and tried to make these tiny Bloomsbury rooms our home. I refuse the cold salt water, not tonight with a freezing wind seeping in through the walls and windows. And the water is no longer hot. My feet will have to cope, even if they are tired. Hours of dancing in those pointe shoes straight into an evening of dancing through the clubs of Fitzrovia has not been kind.

Olivia will be cross with me in the morning, asking lots of questions which I shall not want to answer. I suppose I should regret not pressing her more determinedly to come with us, but it would have been no use. Nathan always tells me not to bother; he prefers having me all to himself. And besides, Olivia has no time for frivolities that take her away from soaking her feet, stretching her muscles, sewing the ribbons on her shoes, darning the ends with that long, curved needle that I always manage to prick myself with. And sure enough, her shoes are ready, piled neatly on top of her bag. Mine is next to hers, the contents spilling out as usual, in a mess. I know I will find a dozen hairpins scattered among my tights. As I peel off my dress, which is sticking to me with a sour sweat from the heat of the tavern, I catch sight of my own pointe shoes piled against the wall. The top pair has been prepared exactly as I like them, the ribbons angled back toward my heel, the toes darned just around the edge. Olivia. She did this for me, tonight, while I was out dancing, drinking, flirting with Constant, Bobby, Pat, Nathan, a crowd of us wild, restless girls from the company. If only I had her discipline, or even her kindness, though sometimes I think she does these kind things for me in case someone mistakes me for her; she has to work doubly hard, keeping me up to the standards she expects of herself. It must be frustrating for her, especially when she sees me with rips in my tights or cheating the Cecchetti footwork: she is always whispering to me to get my heels down, as if it is her own feet I am somehow neglecting to use with the precision she always manages to achieve.

I return to the bathroom and scrub my face with cold water, feeling even more guilty now. I splash water hard against my skin, shivering as it drips down my arms. I look up into the mirror and stare. Ballet dancers are surrounded by endless mirrors: all morning in ballet class and rehearsals, in the dressing rooms, our bodies and faces straining to match each other's. We train to become identical, perfect, classical, while all at once trying to shine brighter than the others. But me even more so than most. I am mirrored every time I turn to Olivia, every time we follow the instructions of the ballet mistress, our feet moving in time. Sometimes I think I am seeing my sister; sometimes I wish I was more like her, that I could work hard, return home for a good night's sleep, rest my body, save the money that I know she is so determined to bank up for better rooms, warmer walls, a proper kitchen perhaps rather than the sink and stove that are tucked away in the alcove behind the curtain. But I would prefer to dance and party and live my life everywhere, not only when the curtain lifts and the audience applauds, when Constant lifts that baton and the orchestra begins. I love those moments, of course I do, but they are not enough.

* * *

Tonight, when Miss de Valois and Miss Moreton left the Café Royal, it was as though a layer of respectability had been stripped from our little group, leaving us raw and ready for misbehavior. We adore them both, but it is adoration tinged with fear. I couldn't face our ballet mistresses in the morning class if they saw what I really get up to after a few drinks.

Constant had us all roaring with laughter. I joined in the drinking and the incessant chatter as I always do, though I could sense Nathan's disapproval when my laugh spilled out too loud. Constant commandeered the piano, blasting out loud notes of jazz, glasses glowing with Tokay wine never far from his side. We ended up, finally, in the Fitzroy Tavern on Charlotte Street, dancers, musicians, even the stunning young Florence Lambert with her perfectly arched eyebrows and those huge eyes. I still remember the day they married, Constant and Florence, two years ago. It was a hot August day with Florence clutching carnations still wrapped in their paper. She was a child, really, just sixteen, though she claimed to be eighteen. Two years with Constant has sophisticated her, lost her that wide-eyed doe look, that innocence. Now she has a permanent look of mischievous disapproval, enjoying her husband's loud drinking and storytelling so she can hit him playfully over the shoulder. And he had a lot of stories to tell tonight, gossip elevated to myth. He can spin a simple encounter into a legend and reduce a hero to ridicule. He takes great artists and makes them human: Pavel Tchelitchew's painting looks like a *Daily Mail* exhibit for the best design in the sand at Margate; the ballet mistress's love of Schubert worse than listening to a hyena screeching; and so on. It is only when, after too many drinks, he starts his lampooning of the great Diaghilev that Miss de Valois gives a little shake of her head and he clams up with a naughty expression on that childlike face of his.

We exploded into the tavern, full of wine and a little food, ready for music and more drinks to fuel our loud, fast laughter. It was busy, a wall of sweat and steam rising against the bitter February weather outside. Right then I felt like a film star, slipping my coat from my shoulders, my backless dress revealed to the room. Nathan bought the coat for me; he insisted on it one day in October last year when we were roaming the streets of Fitzrovia. I remember it had started to rain, a misty, autumnal drizzle that settled onto our skin like dew. Nathan pulled me into a crowded little shop on Percy Street and rummaged along the rails until he found it, holding it up against me and pressing the fur against my cheek. Second-hand, of course, and rather ragged, but it is still the most glamorous coat I have ever owned. It is dark green, long, nipped in at the waist with a belt, and has a huge fur collar that rises high around my neck. I felt awkward taking it home that night, knowing Olivia would look at it with envy. We share everything, exchanging dresses, blouses, hats, even our bandeau brassieres that Olivia somehow manages to keep in perfect crisp white condition. It's cheaper to share, giving ourselves new outfits by delving into each other's half of the wardrobe. But Olivia never comes out with us, and I have to work hard to convince her she can wear the coat too. She always blushes when I suggest it, changing the conversation as fast as she can.

At first I loved seeing it hanging next to all the other beautiful coats in the cloakrooms of the cafés and restaurants and bars, its velvety thickness, its collar pressing against the others to establish its place, its belonging. But gradually over the past few months it has started to sit differently, weighing heavier on my shoulders. Every time Nathan wraps his arm around my waist, pressing the belt into my stomach, I want to shake him off. I want to throw the coat into the dirty puddles in the road, walk into the restaurant alone, free. But I can't do it; every time I meet him in the theatre foyer, I take his arm and let him lead me to the party, the café, the exhibition, the concert that he has chosen.

Tonight we played silly word games, huddled as we were around a corner table in the already heaving tavern. Nathan was next to me; he was next to me all night in fact, finding the seat right beside me before the others could claim their places around the many different tables we soaked in wine and whisky. At each one, Nathan was a little closer, his shoulder touching mine, his hand brushing against my back as I reached forward for my wine glass, his leg pressed against my thigh under the table. The ballerina and the piano player, all of London ours to charm; I smiled all night.

Nathan Howell is our company pianist. He plays for our lessons, relieving Constant of a duty he can only fit in once or twice a week now that our Vic-Wells Ballet is starting to grow. Constant found him. Or so his story goes, a story that he repeats regularly on our post-performance nights out. Nathan doesn't really like it, I think, though he pretends to laugh along with the rest of them. I have learned not to laugh, not anymore. Attending a concert on the other side of the river, Constant walked in late, exhausted from a busy day, fully prepared to leave after five minutes, to head home and fall into a deep sleep. But there on the stage was a boy playing the piano with such skill. When the concert ended, he marched up to the front, pressing against the shirt fronts and fur collars of the departing crowd. In fact, the performer was twenty-one years old, an accomplished pianist with years of childhood experience playing for packed crowds, a child prodigy, rushed from one concert to the next. But that night when Constant found him, Nathan had very little money left, the concerts were running out, and he needed to pay the mooring fee for the boat where he lived on the canal in Islington, a narrowboat loaned to him by a retired boatman who could not bring himself to sell up. And it was Constant Lambert standing before him. Who could resist the man who had been commissioned by Diaghilev, himself barely an adult when he composed his *Romeo and Juliet*? Nathan said yes immediately. The next day he was perched on a piano stool in the barely finished studio at Sadler's Wells, learning the difference between pliés and *grands battements* as fast as he could. It was that or giving up his strange home on the canal, a lifestyle that turns the heads of the radicals and bohemians and undergraduates he tries to emulate. Nathan, it seems, will do anything to avoid succumbing to a life of dreary ordinariness.

※ ※ ※

I get into bed at last, stretching my legs away from myself and flexing my feet. Olivia's bed is pressed against the wall, barely two feet away from me, but she sleeps so silently and still that I have to check she is there. My calves are tight from the heels I wore tonight and the walk home across cobbled streets behind the British Museum. Nathan walked me home, waiting until I was safely inside before he continued the journey up to his boat on the canal. I am very curious to see it one day. Olivia and I have walked along the towpath a few times, but we get strange looks from the men who heave crates in and out of their barges and the workmen who lean lazily against the large doors of the warehouses, cigarette smoke drifting toward the water. I have never known anyone who has lived on a boat before, but I can imagine Nathan there, the cramped walls decorated no doubt with his piles of sheet music, the programs from all those concerts he has performed in since he was a little boy. But on a night like tonight it is probably freezing. Though maybe no more freezing than our rooms, I think, pulling the blanket higher around my neck.

* * *

I close my eyes, but sleep doesn't come easily. I remember those scraps of paper that littered the table, sticky with wine. It was Constant's idea. He loves games, especially word games where he can build nonsensical epics and ballads. Nathan insisted we play together, and we tried our best to come up with something that made sense. Pat chose the words we were to use for our heroic verses, confounding us all with his wicked wit. He winked at me as he read out the words: doll, phantom, alcohol, crawl, annum. Nothing any of us wrote made much sense, but Nathan used the distraction to turn the paper and scribble out a note, a line of verse.

A lovely apparition, sent to be a moment's ornament. I felt a little lost by it, confused, like I was reading something familiar but with the meaning just out of reach. Nathan does this sometimes, his mind going somewhere I don't quite understand. Sometimes it makes me feel stupid, unable to match his genius, whatever that word really means. But tonight it was as though the words were dripping on to me like candle wax, catching me in the romance he knows how to spin, a secret, intimate gesture. I couldn't place his meaning, but I knew that the words somehow bound me to him against the noise and chaos of the others. I turned to him and smiled, shifting as I untucked my foot from between his shins.

*　*　*

The note is inside my coat pocket. Maybe one day, if I have the courage, I will ask him about it, what he really meant. But for now I am exhausted. And a long day of ballet class and rehearsals is not too many hours away, topped off with a triple bill of performances in the evening. Olivia will be furious if I make us late.

Act Two

CHAPTER 5

Clara

The theatre is silent tonight. There is no show, no audience driving up in their loud motor cars, no rustle of silks and furs, velvet and tulle. Outside, Rosebery Avenue is quiet, as though London has forgotten we are here. Tonight, dressing rooms that are usually packed with dancers have fallen still. It is just me and Nathan, with the lights on low in the Wells Room. We will be thrown out soon, the theatre caretaker doing his nightly rounds to check none of us are sleeping in our tutus, dreaming of tomorrow's class.

We have been rehearsing *Coppélia* for several weeks, Nicholas Sergeyev banging his stick, somehow deciphering the chaotic notations in his books, calling out the steps, the mime, the rhythm. When he finally realized that there were two Marionetta girls, he couldn't get enough of us, searching through his notation books and character lists to see how he could spin the illusion of two identical ballerinas onto the stage. But Olivia looked disappointed when the cast list went up. We are to dance two of Swanilda's friends, good roles certainly, but not what she wanted. But I don't know what she expected. Swanilda was bound to go to the top. Lydia Lopokova and Miss de Valois will be sharing the role. Though when Lopokova arrived at the studio for the first rehearsal, dressed in comically out-of-fashion rehearsal clothes, a little woolen shawl around her shoulders, a baby pink cross-over cardigan making her look even smaller and rounder than she already is, we had to work hard to lower our raised eyebrows. But it didn't take long to see how suited she was to the role, comic, brilliantly expressive, a burst of energy. It's hard to believe she is forty-two. In Act Two, teasing Dr. Coppélius into thinking she is his doll come to life, she had us all in hysterics. Even Nicholas Sergeyev gave in to a brief smile.

Miss de Valois was a more obvious choice, we all felt. It always amazes me how she can go from business all day, running the school, rehearsing us, to then changing into her ballet shoes and practicing at the barre. Then, to top it all, giving a wonderful performance onstage at night. She is a beautiful dancer, with strong, fast legs and an even stronger sense of character. She can bring a part alive, transporting the audience to the dreamland of the stage. Perhaps it is the glass of sherry we know she sneaks in before every performance that helps her to move so easily from all the papers on her office desk to the lights of the stage.

Nathan plays the notes of Delibes's waltz from Act One on the piano and I dance what I can remember of Swanilda's variation. It is not my role, of course, but we all learn everything, just in case we get called up, someone breaks an ankle or there is a sickness that spreads through the principal dancers. Highly unlikely, but we can all dream. I know Olivia has learned every step of every role. She could be Swanilda tomorrow.

I am tired and don't really want to still be dancing. Every rise en pointe is an effort, my legs slow in the *pas de bourrée*, the *relevé retiré* sluggish and low. The air in the studio lingers with the smell of sweat and rosin and the strong cheap perfumes of the dancers;

I want to leave it all behind for the night, escape into the streets. I long to be at a café with the other girls, a glass of cold cheap wine in my hand, but Nathan insisted on rehearsing. He, too, is a little afraid of Nicholas Sergeyev. They argue over the score like children fighting over sweets. When it doesn't fit in with his notations, Sergeyev simply deletes bars of notes from the score that Nathan and Constant have to squeeze back in the next day. Temperaments are fragile, these grand masters shooting each other sharp looks across the studio.

Nathan must feel playing for ballet class is a little beneath him, the child prodigy now banging out tunes for pliés and *battements tendus*. Playing for Sergeyev was to be his big break, I expect he thought, a chance to ascend out of the daily grind of the Wells Room. But it is usually Constant Lambert who plays for rehearsals, or Ippolit Motcholov, Sergeyev's own pianist, who is always happy to make the musical score fit the notations. I rather like Motcholov, the faraway look in his eyes and his gentle manners. But I'll never admit this to Nathan, who sees him as a direct threat to his success. The dancers like him, though, and we find many opportunities to draw him into conversation at the end of rehearsals. He brings us memorabilia of Russia, always carrying a photograph of the Czar, Czarina and their daughters in his coat pocket. It is romantic, like we are recreating the past.

Finally, I flop to the floor, my legs stretched wide. My eyes graze tiredly over the photographs that line the walls as I rest back on my hands, opening out my ribs in a vast yawn. Nathan stops, mid-bar, and looks over to me.

"Had enough?" He sounds a little impatient. He knows I have been rehearsing all day, that my feet will be killing me, my muscles aching, my stomach empty.

"Definitely," I reply. I don't need him to be another ballet master right now. I need him to say that we've been here long enough, that we can leave, go home. I am desperate to get out of here. But I know even then it won't be over. He'll want to find a café, drink wine, talk and talk until I can barely keep my eyes open.

"Let's do Swanilda's solo one more time," he says, looking back at the score. I sigh and pull myself to my feet. I've had enough and I don't see why I should perform for him, rehearsing a dance I will probably never have the chance to do onstage. He starts playing, the music suddenly irritating and fussy, like a fly buzzing around my ears. I refuse to dance, instead walking up to him and putting my hands on his shoulders. Leaning down, I press my head against his, one hand sliding down his chest. His hands falter, missing a note. I kiss his cheek.

"Just one more time, Clara," he repeats, moving his head away from mine. I stand straight and take a step back, looking down from his golden hair to his long, elegant fingers that stretch over the keys. My tiredness is starting to rise inside me, a little hysterically, tears just held at bay. This is what happens when we dance for too long without enough rest. And I haven't eaten for hours. I hate feeling this way, like my body is slipping from my control.

I pick up my clothes and shoes from the corner and head to the door. I just need to get out and home before I say something I regret, my nerves itching with irritation. Even the thought of food has faded from my mind.

The notes fall away and the piano is silent. I turn and he is right there, his arms catching me.

"I'm sorry," he says, pulling me toward him. "You're right. We've been here long enough." I don't want to give in to him, to forgive him so quickly, but I am exhausted and can feel myself letting go.

It is not only rehearsals for *Coppélia*; we are in the midst of a busy season of performances with *Pomona*, *The Lord of Burleigh* and *The Birthday of Oberon*, the latter being a huge production with a chorus of forty, Miss de Valois's first choral production. We have to wear masks, which some of the critics objected to, and I have to say I agree. Dancing with my face sweating under a mask only adds to the exhaustion. And a one-act version of *Le Lac des Cygnes* keeps finding its way into triple bills, the exacting precision of the choreography demanding that we stand for what seems like hours in swanlike poses, our necks and backs stiff. Our days are packed with class, rehearsals, performance, on repeat.

I don't want to cry. It is not the version of myself I let anyone know. Only Olivia sees me cry, but I've been hiding tears even from her recently. She is so self-absorbed, focused only on class and rehearsals, sewing ribbons on her shoes, exercising her feet every night before bed. Sometimes I want to shake her, convince her to come out with us after performances and let herself relax, just for an evening.

But I don't know why I am thinking about Olivia right now. Perhaps because when I catch sight of myself in the mirror that runs along the edge of the room, I see her staring back at me. It startles me, a cold breath of air rushing around my ears. I don't like it, this stern, determined young woman who will give up anything to dance on that stage. That isn't me, and I refuse to let Nathan push me more. Perhaps he should be with Olivia, I think, as I pull away from him, twisting my arm out of his hand. In the corner of my eye I can see myself replicated in the mirror. For a moment, my reflection seems to stay entirely still, a ghostly statue with her arm still gripped by Nathan. Then time speeds up again and she finds me, matching my fast march through the door.

He follows me to the dressing rooms and waits while I get changed. The roots of my hair ache as I release the tight knot on top of my head. It feels glorious to massage my scalp, reversing the direction of my hair. A headache that has been brewing for hours, just under the surface, starts to disperse.

I can see him in the doorway through the reflection of the mirror; he is looking around him with a curious expression, as if this chaotic mess of costumes, hairpins, greasepaint, ribbons, is a toy shop. My eyes narrow as I watch him move through the room, picking up objects we have left on the dressing tables: a brush, a makeup sponge, a lipstick, a tiara made of cardboard and sequins that should have been cleared away to Wardrobe. A layer of powder coats the bottom of the mirrors, transforming the reflection into the impasto strokes of an impressionist painting. It is a little figurine that holds him. A tiny ballerina, the type you might find in a music box. The legs are in arabesque, a long romantic tutu stiff in porcelain. That doll could turn forever and ever and still her skirt would never droop, her arms would never dip with tiredness, her feet would never blister.

He doesn't think I notice when he slips the dancer into his pocket. She is not my dancer; I won't miss her. It probably belongs to one of Miss de Valois's students from the school, who try to tiptoe in here to spy on our costumes. They have so many trinkets and good luck charms. Dolls, jewelry, photographs they have persuaded the goddess Alicia Markova to sign, feathers fallen from costumes that they sneak into their bags, a discarded pointe shoe worn by the leading dancers, as if placing these shoes on their feet will conjure talent and fame. Olivia and I, we just have the well, that shadowy water that promises us nothing. I have found Olivia down in that gloomy basement too much recently, staring into the water as if there is something hidden under the surface. I shouldn't encourage her, but I like the routine too much, dipping my hand into the water before each performance. We all have our obsessions.

As we get out onto the street, the lights in the theatre thud dark behind us. I can breathe easier now we are outside, the sound of a bus slowing at the end of the road a comfort after the echoing silence of the empty theatre. But as Nathan walks with me on my way home, I can't stop thinking about that little doll hidden inside his pocket. When he leans against me, I can feel the sharpness of her legs digging into my hip. He adjusts his coat, moving his pocket so she doesn't press into me anymore. He must realize I felt her tiny foot prodding me through the leather.

We walk quickly, fighting off the cold and the dark. I have refused the offer of a meal, but Nathan persuades me to let him walk with me just as far as Great Ormond Street. We cut along Exmouth Market, the stalls empty and still, just a few tired men in overalls glugging back the last of their pints before they stumble home to bed. A woman sweeps outside the public house, calling out angrily as a man pushes past her, his legs wobbling as he finds his path home. The only lights spilling out on the street are above the shops in those tiny flats that must be noisy from before dawn until the pubs close late at night. I have walked this route so many times, but I find I am glad of Nathan right now. The darkness is unsettling tonight, deep and wide, as though it might swallow me whole.

Something makes me stop, a sudden change in the light.

"What is it?" Nathan says, pulling on my arm. I look up at the row of windows that line the street. A light has vanished on the top floor, leaving a gaping hole like in a smile of broken teeth. I stare up, focusing my eyes. In the darkness of the window, I am sure I can see a man. He is standing very still, almost hidden by the shadows. But I can see him. And I know he is looking right at me.

CHAPTER 6

Olivia

Ballet class ends with Sergeyev appearing clutching a notation book, his pianist Ippolit Motcholov trailing behind him. The pianist winks at pretty little Molly Brown, one of the young dancers who has just made the transition from the school to the corps de ballet, before ushering a scowling Nathan off the piano stool. Miss de Valois cuts the *allegro* short, the men falling away to the sides of the room, sweat staining the cotton fabric of the shirts that they tuck into their black tights.

"*Le Lac des Cygnes* rehearsal, swans only," calls out Miss de Valois as Sergeyev impatiently taps his cane at the front of the room. Already Motcholov is playing the notes of Tchaikovsky's Act Two and already we feel ourselves transforming into one unit, a perfect corps de ballet. The boys slowly leave the studio and the girls line up, our bodies finding the exact alignment mirrored by the others. When I glance up into the wide mirror that wraps around the room, it strikes me how we could be one long paper doll chain, every angle and curve the same. We cross our arms above our heads, holding them there. It is a relief when we step out into an arabesque, returning in a *balancé*, our aching arms now lowered. We *bourrée* en pointe, our legs striking fast into the ground with our bodies still and serene. We can feel every detail of each other, the slant of our necks, the quiet pace of our breath. We must not stray out of line. Sergeyev watches us with a tight glare, his eyes narrow. He keeps shaking his head, the black frame of his round glasses sliding dangerously down his nose.

The moments of stillness are the hardest. We stand in *attitude à terre*, our eyes gazing at a point on the ground away from us on a diagonal. I can feel my toes pressing uncomfortably inside my shoes and the back of my legs are starting to cramp with tiredness. Clara is in the row to the right of me and I look up, finding her reflection in the mirror. She seems to feel my eyes on her and she looks up too, a smile floating over her lips. We hold each other's gaze for just an instant before Sergeyev bangs his stick, spitting out a torrent of angry Russian exclamations. The music cuts mid-bar and we start again, the tension spreading. I can see the strain in our necks, the muscles around the sharp shoulder blades of the girl in front of me tight with nerves. No one wants to be noticed. In the corps de ballet, to be different is to fail.

It is Miss de Valois who stops us this time, her voice sharp in the sudden silence.

"Hermione, your knees are flabby in arabesque. Start putting in some effort." She walks among us and I instinctively pull in my stomach and straighten my back. We are all holding our breath. "And Joan, you aren't in line. I don't want to see you." She turns back around and walks to the front. "I do know you are pulling that face, Joan," she calls out, her voice accusing. "You'll need more talent if you want to get away with an attitude." I turn to see Joan blushing bright red, her eyes fighting back tears.

We repeat the opening five times before finally being allowed to reach the end of the dance. All expression has been beaten out of us until we dance as one, even the set of our faces frozen into an unreadable blank. When, at last, Miss de Valois and Nicholas Sergeyev leave the studio, we collapse onto the floor, a low murmur of sighs spreading through us. No one wants to speak, at least not until we are in the safety of the dressing room. I untie my ribbons and gingerly pull off my shoes. My toes are painful to touch, bruising spreading along the joints.

Alicia Markova and Anton Dolin appear in the doorway. Two stars. They don't have time for us.

"We need the room," Anton announces, marching in and throwing his bag under the barre at the front. They will be rehearsing the *pas de deux*: Odette, the swan princess, and Prince Siegfried. Usually I would want to stay to watch. But not today. I can't hear that music again.

※ ※ ※

Morning class and rehearsals finally over, and no performance tonight, I have an afternoon to myself. The dressing rooms empty out quickly, the girls stripping off leotards and taking down their hair. The differences between us seem to reveal themselves as we wipe down our glowing skin: the shapes of our naked calves, the curve of our breasts, the thickness of our hair as we brush out the kinks. A palette of reds and pinks and burgundies is smudged across our lips. By the time we are dressed again, it is only me and Clara who are still trapped in the repeated image of our face.

The corps de ballet is important, essential even. Especially in *Le Lac des Cygnes*, where the swans drive the entire movement of the dance. But I want more. I don't want to become invisible, an exact replica of everyone around me. Even the direction of our gaze must be identical, which is especially hard for me, I think, for already I am denied absolute uniqueness, Clara sharing my every feature. And so today I am going to do something for me, just me. I have an important mission, a journey across London that may bring me one step closer to principal dancer, prima ballerina; perhaps the assoluta part is a dream too far. Sometimes, if I try very hard, I can imagine myself back in time as one of Marius Petipa's ballerinas, dancing for the Mariinsky Ballet, wrapped in fur that tickles my nose as I leave the theatre, surrounded through Theatre Square by admirers.

I need something to set me apart from the others in ballet class. I want to be noticed, and not only because my mirror image is dancing alongside me. There is such a fascination with identical twins, even more so identical twin performers. It is as though we are a trick, an illusion. Sometimes, though, I worry that if Clara didn't exist, then I wouldn't be enough. I really would be entirely invisible at the back row of the corps de ballet, uninteresting without a double.

The practice tutus we wear for rehearsals are cheap and itchy. They rustle and scratch, hardly the illusion of ethereal magic we are striving to achieve. I look enviously at Alicia Markova, her perfect costumes made at her own expense, replacing the cheap, noisy taffeta for the lightest tulle. She even has two bodices for each costume, a matt one for performances and a shiny satin for press photographs. Of course, she has enough money. Unlike the rest of us, she is paid a proper salary for her performances, while we make do with just £2 per week. We need her, though, her reputation carrying us all with her at our fledgling Vic-Wells. There are rumors she is to be appointed prima ballerina any day now. It would be a sensible move for Miss de Valois, celebrating the fame of Markova.

Today I am going to find the costumier Madame Manya. If I can persuade her to make me my own practice tutu, I can stand out in rehearsals. I can be more than just a replica of my sister and the other girls in the chorus. And besides, I've earned it. While Clara has been out spending her money on champagne and fancy meals across London, I have stayed in, saved up, darned the ladders in my tights rather than spending and spending on luxuries we cannot afford.

I was so nervous when I approached Markova in her dressing room last week. She was wiping makeup from her eyes with cold cream, leaving greasy smears across her cheeks. Even like this she looked beautiful, her eyes shining like a creature from another world. I pretended that Miss de Valois had asked me to collect a package from Madame Manya but that she'd forgotten to give me the address. Although Markova narrowed her eyes at me in the mirror, she scribbled it down all the same, thoughtfully adding some instructions and road names along the way. This is the best way to get there, she told me. Don't risk the back streets; don't go through Regent's Park in the dark.

It may as well be dark, I think, as I make my way through London to Maida Vale. The day started with a heavy mist that refused to lift and by now the sun has entirely given up, a thick fog settling over everything. I have to keep stopping to check the little scrap of paper, a smear of cold cream and blusher from Markova's finger coloring the words. Street signs are not easy to see, but I know where I am for the most part, Regent's Park just to my right. Buses crawl past, their lights struggling to break through the gloom. The light is slow and treacly, like our legs in *battement fondu* when we rise up out of the plié. Pausing as I cross over the wide road above the canal, I peer over the black iron railings into the water, watching as a dirty cloud of smoke swirls below me, ghostly fingers beckoning from under the bridge. They creep into my lungs and I shudder, speeding on along the pavement. Eventually I find the road I need, Markova's light scrawl on the piece of paper matching the street sign that appears and vanishes as the fog floats by. I walk slowly along, counting the houses, the fog so dense with smoke that the numbers are hard to read. Aware that I am a strange woman lingering outside homes, I try not to get too close to each door, but soon I think I must be about there.

I stand in the street for a moment to compose myself. The whole walk here, over an hour of marching through the damp fog, has made me anxious, as though I am being watched and scrutinized. As though someone might jump out at me and demand to know what I am doing. Why do I think the great Madame Manya would make a costume for me?

Madame Manya isn't expecting me, which makes me nervous. I have practiced what I will say, how I will introduce myself: a dancer at the Vic-Wells, a colleague of Alicia Markova. I think about saying she is my friend, but that is simply not true and therefore a risk. I will have to rely on my own credentials and hope Madame Manya is willing to create a tutu for me. She is retired, but I know she still takes on occasional work for deserving dancers.

There is a light net curtain in the window of the front room; it makes me think of the white gauze of our practice skirts, just revealing the shadow of our legs beneath the fabric. I blink, trying to decipher the shapes and colors hidden inside. It is too faint, smudged like a spoiled painting. I squeeze my eyes shut and then open them again. There is something there, a woman, white skin, black lace, her arms held out by her thighs in *demi-bras*. Suddenly, the fog seems to fade in front of me and I see her more clearly, her eyes locking sightlessly into mine. A scream escapes my lips, a weak whimper that is immediately drowned in the rolling, persistent fog. There, through the mist and the glass and the gauze, is my face. I can see myself inside the room, dressed in the velvet and tulle of a deep black tutu. I take a step back, grabbing onto a dark unlit streetlamp. I watch, horrified. The face, my face, is changing, blotting itself out into a white blank. I blink and it has gone, just an oval shape, featureless and bland. It is barely there at all.

Just my reflection in the glass, I tell myself firmly, finding the courage I need to step toward the front door. My knock sounds timid, dulled by the fog, and I shift anxiously from foot to foot as I consider trying again. But just as I reach up to the brass knocker, a young woman opens the door, dressed in an elegantly cut black dress. Her hair is sleek, pressed down at her temples. It is only a white apron, tied at the side, that softens her. A maid perhaps, or a secretary.

"Can I help you?" she says, looking at me sharply. I must look damp and cold, the gray fog drifting behind me.

"I am here to see Madame Manya," I reply, forcing out the words and a smile that I know is far from convincing. "I would like to commission a tutu."

"I see." She waits, looking me up and down. Finally, she says, "Well, you had better come in then."

She leads me through to a small parlor. It is the room I saw from the road. She goes to the window and draws closed heavy red curtains, shutting out the street. Just a small slither of pavement still shows, like the dark shapes of the auditorium in those first few minutes of a stage call. "Wait here, please. I will see if Madame Manya can see you."

The woman leaves me, closing the door behind her. I hear the echo of her heels as she moves down the hallway into the back of the house. I am too afraid to look about me, to see if the woman I saw from the street is still there, watching me with her blank face. I glance quickly to my left. There is a double sofa, old-fashioned but in good condition, the fabric soft and plush. I don't sit. I am too anxious. Slowing my breathing, I listen for any sign of movement. There is nothing, so I try to relax, looking up at the muddle of memorabilia, paintings, sketches, photographs, costumes, that crowd the room. I am surprised the woman has left me alone. There must be a fortune of treasures in here, a delicious temptation for a young ballet girl.

When I see it, I laugh. A mannequin with a featureless white face poses in the corner, dressed in a black tutu with a velvet bodice. A motif of gold thread dances across the skirt and the neckline is woven with a delicate sprig of golden wire. Jewels hover around the hips. They look bold and bright, but I know they will be as light as lace, the dancer never even knowing they are there as she twists and turns across the stage. The mannequin is oblivious to her costume, arms stuck at jaunty angles. The tutu is wasted on her.

I turn, brushing my coat over my hips, imagining wearing such opulent black netting. My fear has gone now, and just a longing remains. Then, surely, Nicholas Sergeyev would notice me, Olivia Marionetta, not just one of those pretty identical twins.

And that is when I see it, arranged with a fascinating mix of care and chaos. There is no mannequin for this, just a pole and a base, no doubt with a fabric torso hidden within. White feathers are layered over tulle, a light sparkle shimmering from the tiers of the skirt. I reach out, my fingers hovering by the bodice, the white and cream goose feathers in perfect condition. A green glass stone centers the costume, like the eye of a swan gazing sorrowfully back at me.

"She never wore it more than twice," a voice behind me says. "Then, she'd be back to me, weighed down by the tulle and tarlatan, demanding the skirt to be renewed. A dying swan, brought back to life."

I turn, my heart beating fast, pulling my hand back from the tutu. Madame Manya is older than I expected, frail too. I suddenly feel a fool, barging in here and asking for my own tutu. Especially now that I am faced with this: Anna Pavlova's costume for her famous dying swan. We have all danced the solo, on our own in dark empty studios, in our imaginations, in our sleep. Saint-Saëns's haunting music hovers at the edge of our consciousness every time we see a white dress, a feathered tutu, a swan arching its long, graceful neck. Before Pavlova died two years ago, Clara and I would creep up to her garden in Hampstead, desperate for a peek at the swans that she kept in her ornamental lake. Ivy House was a beacon for us when we were children; whenever we walked on the Heath and out to Golders Hill, we were drawn to it. Our feet took us in one direction only. We imagined the dancers she auditioned and coached in her studio, the productions she discussed for the Ballets Russes, the costumes she had delivered and prepared. Once, we had been certain we'd seen Enrico Cecchetti appearing at her door in black tie, but really it could have been any white-haired old man with a terrifying look in his eye. We heard that he died not long after, collapsing in the middle of a ballet class. All that ghastly *épaulement* finally did away with him, I remember Clara said, shockingly, when our ballet teacher told us. We were just fourteen then, all of us little girls putting on the perfect expression of loss for the passing of the great ballet master. Not Clara, though. Nothing and no one were too big for her to joke and prod, make a little human.

"Four thousand performances, can you believe," Madame Manya says, her eyes moving quickly over the costume, as though searching for snags and tears.

I take a step back, suddenly feeling trapped in the crowded room. Signed photographs of ballerinas loom down at me from their frames, their smiles too sleek and poised. Madame Manya has reluctantly turned her attention to me, dragging her eyes away from her shrine to Pavlova. She must find me lacking, a dancer that no one has heard of standing among her museum to the greats.

"Thank you for seeing me," I mumble. "I dance at the Vic-Wells Ballet. With Ninette de Valois and Alicia Markova," I add, pointlessly. Of course she knows about the Vic-Wells. She gives nothing back, her hands clasped and still at her waist. I grapple for something that may impress her. "We are rehearsing for *Coppélia*. Nicholas Sergeyev is here in London."

A small smile appears at the edges of her lips, the wrinkles around her cheeks deepening. Her collar is high, little scallops edged in white embroidery, and it makes her head look as though it is floating above her dress. There is more material than there is woman, I think. Maybe this is what happens when you create costumes for ballerinas.

"And you don't think the practice tutus at Sadler's Wells Theatre are good enough for you," she says, tilting her head to one side as if to get a better look at me. I don't know what to say. She is right, of course. But I can't say it out loud. "What did you say your name was, dear?" she asks, moving to the sofa and taking out a little notepad from a drawer in the low table at the center of the room. She keeps the drawer open and I can see inside. A treasure chest of ribbon, buttons, threads, a measuring tape, pins, pencils. It gives me a little confidence, as if this might not to be so strange a request, that she is, perhaps, still working.

"Olivia Marionetta," I reply, relieved at my balletic name, far better than Olivia Smith. "I would love to commission a tutu from you. Nothing too elaborate, just a white practice tutu that will be a little quieter and firmer than the skirts we wear for rehearsals."

I hold my bag close to me. I have the money I have saved up with me, but I have no idea if it will be enough. Surely £3 will buy a tutu; it has taken so long to save it up and I have agonized over whether to spend it. Our salary is so unstable. We are only paid for the season, and there are weeks on end when we have no regular income.

Madame Manya, too, seems hesitant. She takes a notecard from a small pile on the table and hands it to me. There is a sketch of a romantic-style tutu on the front, the end of the long skirt disappearing into the page in light pencil strokes. I turn it to see a list of prices. They start with the most basic practice tutu, no bodice, just the skirt that ties at the back. The list has eight options, the most expensive being a specially designed costume, complete with ornamentation. I don't need that, and besides, it is £20. I run my finger up the list, scanning the prices. The practice tutu is £5. It is a shock, how expensive they all are. It would take me months more to save up another £2. I can feel my cheeks start to burn, the color rising uncontrollably. I feel stupid, turning up here with such high expectations, and now I will leave with nothing. There will be a long walk home through the fog to our cold, draughty flat. And tomorrow I will pull on the same scratchy tutu with no hope of setting myself apart from the others.

The dressmaker is watching me. For a moment I have an insane vision of her asking me to dance for her; I perform the dying swan, my feet *bourréeing* around the room, my arms wrapping around me in those poignant final breaths. A tear comes to her eye; it falls down her cheek like a drop of rain, and she thinks of her Pavlova, how much she misses her, how Pavlova would have wanted her to make this tutu for this special girl, lovingly cutting and sewing the twelve layers of tulle.

Neither of us moves. Eventually she stands, gesturing to the door. "Why don't you have a think, and come back to me next week if you want to go ahead?" She is kind, saving me from the embarrassment of explaining that I cannot afford her.

Of course she wasn't going to ask me to dance for her. Sometimes I think I live in a fantasy world.

She disappears without saying goodbye, and I am let out by the woman in black. Her apron has gone, revealing a long thin body stiff inside her dress. She says nothing, closing the door firmly behind me. Just like that, I am shut out of their world, Pavlova's dying swan costume safe and hidden.

I walk quickly to the end of the road, pulling up my coat collar around my neck. What little light there was has now been consumed by the fog. I am grateful, in a way, my face dissolving into tears. I bump face first into the chest of a large man as I turn the corner too fast, which makes me cry out. The shock of it is what I need to pull me back into reality. I apologize without looking up.

Following the same route home, my spirit is a little crushed, like that feeling after a cast list goes up and I am, once again, in the corps. But I am no longer anxious, and as I walk back I feel a strange sense of safety, as though those judging eyes that were watching me on the way here have turned into guardian angels, following me home and back to where I feel safe. When I really think about it, I don't know if I would have the courage to appear before the company in a practice tutu made by Madame Manya. It would be too bold, too real, too self-assured. Perhaps, after all, I am better off without it.

CHAPTER 7

Samuel

He must speak to her. Something, anything. He feels his cheeks redden right up to his temples when he thinks of how he just stood there, like a dumb oaf, in the shop that morning three weeks ago. They could have so much in common, if he were just able to find the courage to start a conversation. He knows she loves dancing and costumes and ballet shoes. Perhaps she would like to see his sketches. Perhaps he could even design a costume for her. He lets himself daydream, there at his workbench, imagining her running onstage dressed in the lace and net that he has created.

Thursday again. He plans every moment he will spend in Sadler's Wells, how he will go straight to Wardrobe, rushing to get in and out before the dancers or Mr. Healey need the room. Just before he makes his daily commute to the Freeds's workshop, the morning light still reluctant to creep in from the waking street, he writes a note. He is going to put it in Olivia's cubbyhole, just under the shoes so it is hidden from anyone but herself. He hasn't signed it. That would be a step too far. He considers drawing a small sketch of a rose in the corner of the page, but even that feels too much. What if she realizes it is the same as the imprint marked onto the bottom of her shoe? What if she takes the note to Mr. Frederick, demands to know what it means?

Dear Olivia Marionetta, he writes, his hand hovering before the *M.* Should he just write her first name? Would that be too informal, too presumptuous? In the end, he decides it would be. *I am writing to express my admiration, not only for your perfect, beautiful dancing, but also for you. I love your kind smile. I just wanted to write to tell you this. I love watching you.* (Samuel crosses out the sentence and starts afresh, carefully tearing a new square of paper. He tries again.) *I love the moments when I am able to watch you, and one day I hope I will be able to tell you in person.*

Just as he is about to press the note into his pocket, he changes his mind. She doesn't know what the rose means on the bottom of her shoe; surely it will be safe. And so, with a faint hand, hardly there at all, he signs with a rose, drawn carefully in pencil then filled in with a light pink chalk.

✳ ✳ ✳

He delivers the shoes before lunch, listening out for the familiar sounds of piano music punctuated by the tap of the pointe shoes on the studio floor. The music stops and starts, angry striking of a stick on the floor accompanying the heavy silences. He doesn't go near the Wells Room, not today when he can feel the tension spreading out through the corridors of the theatre. When he leaves, he walks down the road to the little stretch of garden further along Rosebery Avenue. He feels exhausted, as though he's just accomplished some great feat. He hardly notices the group of boys who chase each other through the garden, their breath transforming into mist. It is cold, a fog settling over London like a thick pall, claustrophobic and chilling. His hair is damp from the air. He gets out from his coat pocket the sandwiches he made that morning. White bread with cheese and the pickle his mother gave him last month, one of the occasional gifts she delivers when she feels a pang of guilt at how long it is since she's seen him, the house in Clapham too cold and quiet all day.

Mrs. Dora has given him the rest of the day off. He is ahead of his targets, and they are waiting for a delivery of satin before they can begin the next order. With the thick fog creeping around him, his first idea of walking to the river seems less appealing. He doesn't know what he would like to do to fill this rare time off. He should have asked Mrs. Dora if she knows of any free exhibitions, or any art classes he might be able to attend. But he'd been afraid she'd look at him strangely or laugh at him. Why would an apprentice like himself want to go to such things, she'd think.

Just as Samuel is about to give up and go home, he sees a woman speed past him, her head held still, her arms wrapping her coat tight around herself. Olivia. She walks with purpose, her feet making small, fast steps along the pavement. He gets up from the bench, rewrapping his remaining sandwich.

He follows her. The fog threatens to eclipse her, so he stays close. He panics as she turns the corner onto Euston Road, a cloud of dirty fog swirling before him. Samuel thinks he has lost her into the noise of the road, the people in their dark coats and scarves who weave in and out of one another, appearing and disappearing like ghosts. But then a bus groans past, its lights on and sending murky spotlights ahead. She appears again, a dark wool hat fitting closely, just revealing her signature low bun at the nape of her neck. Olivia, he thinks, has no problem dancing between people, sidestepping with hardly a change in her posture. It is harder for

Samuel, whose large shoulders take up half the pavement. They walk in tandem for over an hour, Olivia occasionally stopping and taking out a scrap of paper before starting on her way again, peering at street signs through the haze.

They are in Maida Vale, having walked far along Euston Road, Regent's Park lingering to their right, surrounded in ghostly mist. When they cross over the canal, the water is hidden in dull clouds of fog. He watches from the corner as she stands outside a house, a slender figure moving lightly from foot to foot. Eventually she takes a step forward and rings the bell.

He creeps a little closer to the house she has entered. The curtains to the front room are ajar, leaving a small gap of low, warm light that spills out before it is submerged by the fog. Crouching down on the pavement, he looks through the gap. A low hedge of holly pricks him through his trousers, but he is oblivious to the pain.

The room inside is like a vision from one of his dreams, where his mind drifts as he measures, cuts, stitches the shoes. It is exactly what he wants in his own room, his dark room with the cracked plaster walls above Exmouth Market. His sketches, postcards, scraps of materials: they are all replicated here but on a much grander scale. In this room, lit up like the stage on Sadler's Wells as the curtain rises, there are full costumes, mannequins, framed photographs, not the faded scraps that he has stuck into the wall with pins. Just two nights ago he finished a design of a tutu, a rough sketch chalked in midnight blue and gold. He had, however, been precise with the measurements, writing in the amount of tulle, satin and ribbon it would require. It was a pointless task, really, as he could never afford even half of the material it would need. He'd enjoyed it, though, imagining Olivia's face as he presented it to her. The tutu she is gazing at now is not too dissimilar to his design.

And yet the distance between his sketch and the life-size mannequin's costume in there is an insurmountable gulf.

Olivia is back outside far quicker than he expected. Samuel just has time to run to the end of the street. He turns back once he is around the corner, lingering for a moment. Building up courage, he thinks he could speak to her, as if in surprise at finding her here, a coincidence that they are both on the same street at the same time in this eerie London fog. He has just decided to do it when she flies around the corner, colliding with him heavily. She seems to bounce off his chest with a cry. He is about to speak, but she is too quick for him. She doesn't look up, muttering a quick sorry before continuing along the pavement.

Samuel follows. He waits until she arrives at her flat and the little light from her window illuminates a small square of the night sky before he turns north to his own rooms.

※ ※ ※

At his desk, he stares at his sketch, willing it to lift from the page, transform into twelve layers of tulle. Of course, it does nothing of the sort. He crumples it up in one hand, disappointed in himself. He resents his cowardice, his timidity and his doubt that holds back his ambitions, his fear of being scorned. Olivia had been crying when she left that house. And he could do nothing about it. More than anything he longs to deliver a tutu to her door, handcrafted by himself. But it is not to be. They are both alone in their small, cold rooms. And nothing can be done to bring them together.

CHAPTER 8

Clara

We must visit Mother. It is our penance, the last Sunday of every month. Sunday, 26 February 1933. I have lost count of how many times we have visited. This must be almost the fortieth time. It never gets any easier, and today is one of the worst sorts of days to visit. There is heavy cloud cover, an endless drizzle. We will be stuck inside in a claustrophobic visitors' room the color of puce. We will be suffocated by it on the walls, floors, sofas that sink worryingly low. There will be no chance of a walk through the gardens.

Colney Hatch mental hospital, in certain lights, looks like a palace. But today the sky is a slate board that weighs on the towers and brick of the hospital. Olivia tells me off when I call it an asylum, but that's what it is. We are quiet on the short train journey, getting out reluctantly at the little station in Friern Barnet. We have gifts, as usual, but we know not to bring food. Once Olivia made little cakes, carefully iced with pink ballet shoe shapes. Mother stared at them in horror. She'd turned to me and asked, spitefully, how many I'd eaten on the way here. So now we stick to flowers, a card, a photograph from our latest show, an old pointe shoe of Markova or Lopokova that we manage to sneak out of the dressing rooms before they throw them away. Mother likes the flowers best. She gathers them in her arms, drawing them to her and smelling them with a look of utter delight on her thin face. The nurse always tells us off. We are only exacerbating the depths of her delusions.

Mother is waiting for us in the visitor room. She is draped in a navy shawl dotted with silver thread that sparkles a little in the bland light. Her long gray hair is wrapped above her head with a silk scarf that trails down over her shoulder.

"My girls," she calls to us as the nurse shows us in. She holds out her arms and we go to her, forcing smiles on our cheeks. It comes a little more naturally to Olivia, Mother's favorite. We sit either side of her, all three of our foreheads pressed close together as she squeezes us to her. I can feel her hands, her long thin fingers, grappling and digging into my skin. This is her way, feeling our collarbones and scapulas, testing out the boniness of our spines. I know Olivia can't eat in those few days before we visit Mother. She stares at herself anxiously in the mirror, terrified she won't be thin enough for Mother's discerning grip. But Olivia is always thin enough, and Mother strokes her cheek gently.

"The perfect ballerina," Mother sighs as she turns away from me, Olivia still held in her arms. I sit back, the sofa sinking under my weight. I will wait for Mother to talk to me, I think stubbornly. I know I should be more understanding; she is unwell, anxious, depressed, on heavy medication that just about keeps her on the edge of sanity. But she infuriates me, and if I could, I would leave her here and never visit again. It is Olivia who always gets us to the train station on time, collecting up the little parcel of gifts, putting on the smile Mother requires.

"A little bird tells me Nicholas Sergeyev is in London," she says, a sly smile creeping around her eyes. She grabs both our hands.

"And what roles has he given you? When am I to see my girls as Giselle, Odette, Aurora?" She is getting carried away, her imagination taking her to the only place where she can cope with reality. When Olivia and I started showing talent after those early years of ballet classes, she threw all her energies into our dancing careers. She lived for our classes, signing us up with the best ballet mistresses in London. She forced her way into the lessons when she could, watching us dance with hawklike eyes. She lectured us on the bus journeys home: our legs had been dull, our heels weren't touching the ground in *petit allegro*, our elbows had drooped in pirouettes. Or, when her mood was vicious and triumphant, snarling about how terribly another girl danced, how much better we were, how she couldn't tear her eyes away from us. She seemed to know more about ballet than we did, following the reviews of the Ballets Russes like a religion, knowing exactly who was to be cast for each role, the choreographers, the new dancers rising up the ranks. She hunted down retired ballerinas who could teach us privately, giving over vast portions of our father's salary as a bank clerk to pay for the lessons. When we joined Ninette de Valois's school in 1927, we were thirteen years old and already very accomplished dancers, thanks to our mother's relentless pursuit of the best teachers in London.

Those two years before de Valois opened her school had been challenging for all of us. Our father died when we were eleven, a slow and painful cancer that dominated our non-dancing lives, Mother moving frantically between hospital appointments and ballet classes. When he died, she filled those free hours with more ballet, setting up the front room as a studio for us to practice, taking us to shows, writing charts on the wall of our progressions. Father had known he was dying for months and had prudently organized his finances so that we could cope without him. He knew Olivia and I would become dancers and could make a little money that way, but Mother would never be able to get a job. The few jobs she could be qualified to do would be beneath her. But even so, money once Father died was always tight, and the little we earned dancing small roles in operas at the Old Vic theatre barely covered our costs of pointe shoes and tights.

Colney Hatch costs us very little. But the money Father left behind has nearly run out, and Olivia and I try to avoid drawing down any of those few remaining pounds. I don't like to think of how sad he would be to think that the money he saved for us so carefully has been spent on keeping Mother in comfort at a county asylum. She has a small allowance which she spends on trinkets and worthless jewelry when, on her calmer days, she is allowed to join a supervised group of patients on shopping trips to the local town. She is wearing some of her purchases now, bracelets clinking against each other as she moves her long, wiry arms.

Olivia is telling her about Sergeyev and the rehearsals, spinning it out into a magical tale. Mother is enjoying it, closing her eyes as Olivia hums the music. She opens them again, sharply, when Olivia pauses.

"So which one of you is Swanilda?" she demands. Olivia pauses. I don't care if we tell the truth or lie. Olivia can decide whether it is easier to pretend one of us has the role, or to persuade Mother that Swanilda's friends are worthy, enviable roles.

"Well, Ninette de Valois and Lydia Lopokova are the first and second casts for Swanilda," my sister replies. She sees the look on

Mother's face change; quickly, she adds that we are both also learning the roles, as understudies. Not strictly true, but I suppose we do know every step.

"I remember dancing for Diaghilev," she says, rising to her feet in what she must think is a graceful swoop. "He wanted me to perform as the Firebird, but I was too petite. The costume nearly drowned me." Here we go, I think, glancing at Olivia with a grimace. It has started earlier than usual. Every visit we have to sit through her delusions, her fantastical version of her past where she was a ballerina in the Ballets Russes, dancing for Diaghilev, Fokine, Nijinsky. They all adored her, but she gave it up to have her twins. It is a complete fabrication, of course. She has never set foot on the stage, apart from when she used to linger too close to the edge of the wings at the Old Vic when we were dancing in an opera or play. The stories started after Father died. I think she must have been living them in her mind, fantastical escapism from all those awful hours she held his hand in the hospital bed. He was too ill to be looked after at home and so the small amount of money that his parents had left him when they died years ago was spent, tragically, on his own death. He was moved into a cottage hospital in Finchley and never left.

Once Father was gone, she couldn't resist repeating those inventions out loud, capturing us at the kitchen table while she went on and on about these strange, inconsistent, ridiculous stories.

She sways from side to side, her shoulders so delicate beneath the navy shawl. She has shrunk visibly these past three years. She could be blown away by a strong wind.

We were fifteen years old when Mother stopped eating. Our bodies were changing, both of us developing in mystical synchronicity. It happened so quickly. One day we were these tiny little waifs, our chests washboard flat, our hips narrow and straight. The next we were growing and shifting, our white cotton leotards no longer decent. It was Christmas Day 1929 when we started our periods. Both of us woke with tiny spots of blood in our knickers. Olivia looked terrified, but I hugged her and we laughed and crept into the bathroom to search through Mother's drawers for her Kotex sanitary napkins.

She found us in there, our bloody knickers from the night discarded on the bathroom floor. Her face was frozen, staring blankly at us. It was as if she'd forgotten we were normal girls. I think she wanted us to stay as we were forever, thin, delicate, androgynous nymphs who were immune to the changes of puberty.

I'll never forget that Christmas Day lunch. Olivia and I were in high spirits, giddy with the excitement of becoming adults. We were both piling food onto our plates, tomato soup then the slices of ham that Olivia and I had charmed the butcher into cutting extra thick, potatoes, bread sauce, plum pudding at the end. Mother had a headache that morning so had left us to cook, which was preferable as she never let us add enough cream to the soup. She was in her room, coming out every so often to fill up her glass with the brandy that we were adding lavishly to the butter. She joined us for lunch but picked at her food, occasionally bringing her fork to her lips then setting it down again with a sigh. We tried to ignore her, making our own conversation, laughing about a dance we'd seen the younger class do at Miss de Valois's school that made them look like ungraceful chickens.

Finally Mother snapped. She stood up, knocking into the table and making the lit candles shake ominously.

"You two continue filling your faces until you explode. See how you like it in the morning when your stomachs poke out of your leotards. And do not think I am going to sew another hook onto your skirts, young ladies."

We watched her in silence, our mouths still full of food. My chewing sounded volcanic inside my head. She left us, retreating into her room with another glass of brandy. Olivia looked at me, uncertain. So I picked up my fork and kept eating. Olivia did the same.

And so, for the next three months, Mother shrank and shrank. She lost pound after pound, obsessively checking her ribs and hips in the mirror each day. One morning there was a delivery of weighing scales, far more expensive than we could afford, Mother ushering the man into her bedroom, where he set them up. It was a point of pride for her when she stepped off those scales each morning and announced her new, diminishing weight. She tried to make us get on them after her. She wanted to shame us, two slim and healthy ballerinas who weighed nearly a stone more than their mother. I watched Olivia carefully. It was contagious, this obsession with weight, and I refused to let it catch us.

When Mother fainted at Miss de Valois's studio, that was when we knew something had to be done. A nurse came to see us, then a doctor, then a psychiatrist. Nothing would help. Finally, she was deemed dangerous for us to be around. She had locked the kitchen and hidden the key. For a week we had to sneak out to eat, spending all our pocket money from the shows at the Old Vic on pastries and buns at cafés.

We were sixteen when she was admitted to Colney Hatch. Our house in Highgate was rented, so it had to go. With the returned deposit we moved into the rooms in Bloomsbury, gradually making them our own. Holidays, when there were no performances for us to audition for, were spent in Brighton with Aunt Alice and Uncle

Cecil, who were appointed as our guardians, but we always escaped as fast we could, getting back to the busy schedule of class, rehearsals, small parts in revues in London. The Brighton house was noisy and chaotic and the only space to practice our pliés and *tendus* was in the garden. We did our pointe work on the tiny paved terrace, avoiding the white and green splats from passing birds, and we did *allegro* across the grass, scouting out the ground first to avoid the holes our cousin Benjamin had dug with his spade. A horrid little boy six years younger than us, he found great delight in pelting us with acorns, pine cones and twigs whenever we thought that we had found a quiet moment to dance. They were all happy to let us go when we asked to be driven to the station, to return to our lives in London. Our aunt and uncle would visit regularly to begin with, checking we had food, were paying the bills, were looking after ourselves. But the visits soon dwindled, the train journey in from their home in Brighton too long and inconvenient when they had their own children to look after. Mother's sister, Alice, did not get on with our mother. She agreed to keep an eye on us as a kind of penance, a self-imposed punishment to reassure herself that she had done enough. If she visited us, she could make herself feel better about never going to see Mother in Colney Hatch. Aunt Alice brought her son and daughter to watch us at the Savoy Theatre in June last year, but I think they were shocked by the performance, the jazz of Frederick Ashton and Buddy Bradley's choreography in *High Yellow*, far from their expectations of how ballet dancers moved. They left before we could come out from our dressing rooms at the end, leaving a brief note about needing to catch the last train home.

It is only these monthly trips that drag us back to the past. I long for the day when the doctor calls us in and tells us that it isn't good for our mother's mental stability for us to continue visiting. But he has not done so yet, and so here we are.

We leave when Mother starts shouting at us. She has a surprisingly loud voice for someone so tiny.

When we get home, I go straight to our miniature kitchen. I am prepared, as always after visits to Mother, with the ingredients for one of our favorite meals: cod with potatoes, in a butter and leek sauce. I bought the fish yesterday, so it is now swimming in melted ice, the skin glimmering in nacreous clouds in a bowl by the window. As I chop the potatoes, Olivia comes up to me and wraps her arms around me. I kiss her cheek and we stay like that, reminding ourselves how to love, until the vegetables are ready for cooking.

CHAPTER 9

Nathan

Nathan Howell likes to think he was one of the greatest child piano players of the first few decades of the twentieth century. He has kept all the programs, his name in bold letters, followed by the titles of the most complex of piano solos and concertos. It was a point of pride that he could play anything, even Beethoven's *Hammerklavier* sonata, Ravel's *Gaspard de la nuit*. Stravinsky was easy for him, the rhythms bouncing through his child-size hands. It worried him, as he got older and he no longer looked like a strange little pixie barely able to reach the pedals, that his audiences would lose interest. And he was right. As soon as he reached adulthood, it was as though the enchantment he had conjured as a child had been switched off. The concerts dried up, one after the other, until he was grateful to accept the job with Constant Lambert at Sadler's Wells. Now, he plays in the orchestra when there is an opening, but usually he is in the Wells Room, hidden in the corner, subjected to the loud tapping of Miss Moreton's cane on the floor.

Clara Marionetta noticed him, though, when she came into the studio to rehearse one day over a year ago, her pointe shoes flung carelessly over her back, held by the ribbons. Neither of them, in the end, had managed to rehearse anything that evening. Instead, they found themselves talking for over an hour, drawn to each other, until the caretaker had kicked them out.

They found that they shared a love of exploring, finding out what was new and exciting in London. Together they have visited science exhibitions at museums, art galleries, jazz shows, clubs, tiny wine bars and loud cafés, fashion shows, the zoo, illusionists.

Nathan likes the way it feels to introduce Clara to places she would never go on her own; it reminds him of his importance, his status, the celebrity life of his youth, especially when someone recognizes him from his concert days and comes over to reminisce about one of those great juvenile performances. Once, Clara's sister came with them to an art exhibition opening in Chelsea, but she drifted uneasily on her own, refusing the glasses of champagne that waiters in black tie balanced effortlessly on silver trays. She left early and didn't come with them again. It was just as well, Nathan thought; he did sometimes find it very difficult to tell the twin sisters apart. He always had to work out who was wearing which outfit and secure it to memory so he didn't muddle them up for the rest of the day. In ballet class it was easier, with Clara wearing her hair high and Olivia's in a low bun at the nape of her neck.

He waits for Clara outside Sadler's Wells. It is the first Saturday of March, and a brightness is appearing in the London sky. The opera is performing *Cavalleria Rusticana* and *Pagliacci* tonight, so the dancers have a free weekend now that ballet class and rehearsals are finished for the day. Nathan has decided they will visit the National Gallery. A new work is to be unveiled. Or rather, exposed from under a great sheet that has been hiding the art for weeks. For this is not the usual wall-hanging painting. This is a mosaic commissioned for the portico of the gallery.

At last Clara appears from the dressing room and Nathan takes her arm impatiently. He hurries them forward through the London streets, keen to arrive before the crowds get even heavier. It is busy, this first sighting of early spring sun drawing people from their homes. They pass through Covent Garden, weaving in and out of the bustling energy of men transporting crates, sacks, barrels, boxes, all labeled in the thick black letters of their trade name. The clatter of wheels and the shouts of the workmen ring out through the streets, and Nathan has to pull Clara to the side to avoid a tottering tower of onion bulbs that threatens to spill over into their path. Trafalgar Square is full of a different energy, couples and families parading around in the sun in their best outfits, the light spraying through the water of the fountain. Two little girls play under the translucent mist of the water, screeching joyfully as they find rainbows above their heads. Clara watches them, lingering to dip her hand into the twinkling water as they walk past, a crowd of fat pigeons parading territorially about her feet. Nathan turns to her impatiently, gesturing for her to stay close.

They climb the steps to the National Gallery, Clara readjusting her hat to stop her hair tumbling down around her shoulders. They have walked so fast that they are both breathless.

Inside, men and women move like dancers in slow motion across a ballroom floor. All eyes are down to the ground. "It could be an exhibition of people's ugly brown shoes," Clara whispers to Nathan.

"Shush," he replies. "Let's find a good spot."

The portico has an air of studied quiet, calm and concentrated after the busy chaos of Trafalgar Square. Boris Anrep's mosaic is larger than Nathan expected. This is the second set, *The Awakening of the Muses*. The first set, *The Labors of Life*, was completed in 1928, but Nathan hardly remembers its opening. It portrays so many of life's roles he simply knows nothing about: engineering, farming, science, family. Especially family. This new set of mosaics fires his imagination. Bacchus and Apollo stir the muses awake, revealing the faces of the celebrities of his youth. There is Osbert Sitwell, Clive Bell, Diana Mitford, Virginia Woolf as Clio, Greta Garbo as Melpomene. Anna Akhmatova, the great Russian poet, is Calliope. And then the one Clara is straining to see through the crowds of people: the ballerina Lydia Lopokova as Terpsichore, the goddess of dance and chorus.

※ ※ ※

When Nathan took the job at Sadler's Wells, he imagined he would be quickly snapped up to join the Camargo Society. He was young, talented, had performed at all the great concert halls of Europe. He knew what audiences wanted, where the Arts could go if they took the right steps. He could be an asset to the society, he thought, speaking at their committees and helping with the ambitious programs of dance and music they financed in London. When he was a child, his parents told him daily that he was special, that he was talented, that the world was lucky to have him. They whispered this mantra to him in the green rooms before concerts, at his bedside when, exhausted, they tucked him up and he fell asleep dreaming of scales and chords, his own inner metronome sending him to sleep. He grew up believing the world owed him applause and gratitude, that he would be welcomed with open arms in any theatre or concert hall.

He looks over to the little crowd of people who peer down at Anrep's mosaic. The Camargo Society at large, he thinks, enviously. They have a basket with them, tucked between their feet, which holds a bottle of champagne and glasses. Maynard Keynes reaches for it, laughing as a museum attendant rushes to him, shaking his head.

"But my wife is at our feet, cast forever in marble," he objects, politely and indulgently. His wife smiles, dipping her chin a little, posing. She is Terpsichore, the great muse, her face etched in Byzantine colors on the ground, a vision of greens and pinks and ochre. Nathan watches them, Lopokova and Keynes admiring the art, the champagne bottle now returned unopened to the basket. Constant Lambert is there too, and Ninette de Valois. Edwin Evans arrives and joins their group. He is the Camargo Society's musical adviser and recently music critic for the *Daily Mail*. Nathan turns away, angry. He regularly encounters Evans in the corridors of Sadler's Wells, but he always avoids him. He doesn't trust himself around him, not after what happened all those years ago. He's convinced it is Evans's influence that is keeping him from the exclusive meeting rooms of the society.

Edwin Evans had followed his music career, writing up marveling, exuberant reviews when Nathan was very young. The dazzling Nathan Howell was a child star, a musical genius, performing virtuoso piano work with extraordinary skills. Then, in 1925, when Nathan was fifteen, by now starting to look like an adult and playing the piano no differently to how he had played it for the past five years, Evans changed his tune. He came to see him in a concert of Elgar's piano music, a gala at the Philharmonic Hall that Elgar himself was attending. Nathan was still at his peak, astounding audiences and taking in a good salary. Of course, it was harder for him and his father by then, with his mother gone and his father struggling to keep up with Nathan's busy and complicated schedule, but this was a highlight, a concert they had both been looking forward to. Nathan's father still whispered the mantra: he was special, he was talented, the world was lucky to have him. He built Nathan's already inflated confidence with those words of praise, but Cedric Howell's heart was no longer in it. Since his wife had gone, some part of him had gone with her, and he could no longer find the enthusiasm to lead Nathan around Europe, waiting in gloomy green rooms, signing contracts in dusty offices and sending endless letters reminding producers that they were yet to pay his son for his performance. Cedric had lost his sense of purpose, that drive to make certain his son was the best. And more importantly, to fulfill the endless expectations of Nathan's grandparents. From the moment Nathan was born, Cedric's parents had hovered close by, asserting their authority with advice and gifts, paying for piano lessons, tutors, clothes, anything that would make Nathan stand out above the grandchildren of their friends. As Nathan's talent started to reveal itself, they followed his career with the type of pride that can only be crushing in its insistency. But when everything started to slip after that fated performance at the Philharmonic Hall, they vanished too, preferring to tell stories of a family at the summit of success, ignoring the downward direction of their son and grandson's life. It was a brutal departure from their lives and Nathan's father coped by a relentless reliance on his little pot of sleeping pills, barbiturates that knocked him into a fast, deep sleep earlier and earlier each night.

The review that came out in the *Evening Standard* the day after the performance was cruel. It would have been cruel for anyone, but for a fifteen-year-old, even one as self-assured as Nathan, it was a blow. He read that he played with the emotion of a rock and the charisma of a fish. While his fingers performed all the right notes at the right tempo, there was nothing in his performance that couldn't have been performed by a diploma student who had diligently worked through their exams. In short, Nathan might have been a child prodigy, but now he was well on the way to becoming a mediocre adult.

Musicians, critics, audience members, they all rallied round to complain about the harshness of Evans's words. But the die had been cast and slowly, gradually, almost imperceptibly, Nathan's invitations to play dwindled. Over the next six years, he made a slowly declining living as a struggling concert pianist, his father too old and tired to help, until one day he was found by Constant Lambert and the new stage of his life began.

Clara returns to him, full of energy. "What do you think of them?" she asks, putting her arm through his. She guides them around the mosaic, pointing out little details that Nathan hasn't even started to notice. "Look at Woolf," she demands. "Her silver dress is so alive, like it might fall off her if she stands up. Let's hope it does," Clara laughs, pulling Nathan in toward her. "Clive Bell doesn't look like he's indulged in much wine, does he," she continues. "He's got grapes in his hair, but he's a very somber Bacchus."

"Is that Greta Garbo?" Nathan asks, pointing at a golden mosaic of Melpomene, her hand held out with a wreath of flowers suspended in the air above her. "Isn't she supposed to be the muse of tragedy?" he continues. "She looks far too happy for that. I rather like the idea, though, of her fixed forever in the ground. I didn't enjoy *Mata Hari*; all that crazed exotic dancing was vulgar."

"Don't be ridiculous, Nathan," Clara replies, digging her hand into his ribs and making him double over in unwilling laughter.

"Greta Garbo as Mata Hari is my absolute idol. An exotic dancer and a spy, entirely unafraid of her own desires. Why would you want to condemn her to a life of stone, being trampled on daily by all these visitors? One day, they'll hardly notice she is here." She moves them on, pointing out details in the art that bring the figures to life, enjoying the strange contrast of stone and energy. "And there is our Lydia," she cries out at last. "The muse of dance. How funny that she is holding a squirrel."

"Surely you would like to be immortalized in art, fixed forever in perfection?" Nathan asks, more serious now, almost talking to himself instead of Clara, who is crouching at the edge of the mosaic. "There is the great Lydia Lopokova, the perfect muse of dance, never changing, a goddess."

"Like your mother, you mean?" says Clara, forgetting herself, letting a touch of resentment creep into the words. Nathan has told her many times about his mother and her tragic departure from his life when he was twelve. He has described his mother as perfection, shown Clara photographs of her, a stunning woman with bright blonde hair and a long, elegant neck. In one photograph, the one he carries with him always, she looks like a film star, glamorous and ethereal.

"What has my mother to do with this?" he replies.

"I'm sorry," Clara says, seriously, standing up to face him. "But don't you see what Boris Anrep has done here? This is not a fixed memorial of lifeless art. This is a conversation, a moment's breath, a celebration of all the varieties of life. These aren't gods in stone, they are people, alive and breathing who reassure us we can find art and beauty in every corner of life.

"Look over there." She points. "Lydia Lopokova in the flesh, trying to persuade her husband to pour her a glass of champagne. And in three weeks she'll be onstage as Swanilda in *Coppélia*, teasing Dr. Coppélius into thinking she is his precious doll come to life. And we can, forever, dance and run and skip over this mosaic. This makes me think of life, modern life, not memorials to perfection."

"Well, let's agree to disagree on this one, my beautiful ballerina," Nathan says, taking her arm again, finding control. "Personally, I would like to be fixed in time at my most glorious. But for now, let's try to get a table at the Café Royal and drink far too much wine to art and beauty and to getting on Anrep's list for his next instalment of muses."

He tightens his grip on Clara's arm and leads her to the exit. As they pass between the columns of the façade, Nathan looks back and casts a grim stare at Edwin Evans and the rest of the Camargo Group, desperate for them to notice him here, the once-famous child prodigy still in the midst of art and culture, still walking among them, this time with his very own ballerina. But none of them even notice he is there. Nathan Howell has been forgotten, a passing footnote in the records of the gazettes and journals of his childhood.

CHAPTER 10

Olivia

The studio at the top of the theatre where Miss de Valois runs her school is empty this morning. The girls and boys are down at the Old Vic for the day to audition for chorus roles in a new opera. I take a step inside, at once remembering the relentless exhaustion of those ballet classes, the repetition of each exercise until Miss de Valois was satisfied. I remember standing in fifth position en pointe until my legs shook with the effort. A long mirror reflects my image back at me, my face thin and tired, my hair tied tight off my face.

I walk to the front of the room and place my bag down at my feet. Looking back at the door to check no one has followed me, I take out a pair of pointe shoes from the depths of my bag. They are not mine. Alicia Markova left them behind after a rehearsal for *Le Lac des Cygnes* yesterday, two discarded satin shoes in the corner. I stole them when she had left the Wells Room, tucking them away in my bag.

Turning them over in my hand, I try to find some secret clue as to her fame, her certain status as prima ballerina. The satin is scuffed more on the outside edge of the foot than the rest and the sole is soft and pliable with a sweet smell of glue and sweat and baking soda. She has burned the edges of the ribbon with a match to stop the fraying and her stitching is neat and even. I place them on the ground in front of me and reach again into my bag, a nervous thrill spreading through my toes.

It wasn't only her shoes that I took. She had tucked away a little makeup pouch in the corner of the studio, packed with cold cream, powder, lipstick, a stub of a kohl pencil. I stole the lipstick, hiding it within the folds of my warm-up layers until it was safe to transfer into my bag. Now I take it out, pulling off the lid with a satisfying pop. The end has been worn down into a smooth red round. Stepping toward the mirror, I lean in until I am just inches from the glass. It takes a few attempts to paint the color onto my lips, dabbing with my finger to tidy the glow of red that threatens to dance outside the bounds of my mouth.

I put on her shoes, tying the ribbons securely around my ankles. They are too narrow around the toe, the wing soft but still pressing uncomfortably into the arch of my foot. When I stand they feel a little better, the supple satin and leather bending to me. I rise en pointe, drawing my feet into a tight fifth position. The shoes are far too soft and it takes all my strength to stay tall. With small shifts of my weight, I try to find balance. Taking my arms into a round first position in front of me, I start to turn, little *chaînés* that take me around the edge of the room. My head finds a spot in the direction I am traveling, whipping around fast every time I turn. The room becomes a broken collage of cubes, the black-and-white photographs on the walls, the hard straight back of the piano, the dark brown line of the bar. But then my vision starts to falter, the lines blurring and bleeding as I turn and turn, my balance breaking and the shoes unsupportive underneath me. They know I am not their mistress; they care nothing for me. I catch sight of my shape in the mirror but all that I can decipher is the red of my lips like a wound.

And then I see him. In the doorway a man is watching me, his body heavy and dark, with shoulders that threaten to break through into my space.

I fall, the shoes slipping and dragging me down to the ground. A bolt of pain shoots through my wrist and my hip smacks hard against the floor. But when I look up, there is no one there, just a gaping emptiness leading back out to the corridor. And yet I am sure I recognized him. A hulking man who lurks behind his bags of pointe shoes, his unsettling eyes following our feet as we dance.

When I take off the shoes, blood stains my tights, a red and brown mess that is wet and fresh. I gently feel through the tights, wincing at the raw skin on my toe. Seeing myself in the mirror, I shake my head angrily. This is what happens when I try to rise above my level, when I try to be someone I am not, overreaching myself and falling hard. Hurriedly, I pack away the shoes and the lipstick, wiping my mouth with the back of my hand. It looks like a rash, a red slash that has started spreading through my skin.

* * *

Downstairs, I quickly find my balance again. When I go to collect my new set of pointe shoes from Wardrobe, there is a frantic energy in the room, a frisson that spills out on fitting days despite the sharp pins that the costumiers fasten precariously around our ribs. My previous pointe shoe delivery is just starting to run out now, so I haven't been in here for over a week. After my trip to Maida Vale, I have been avoiding rooms that remind me of my misguided Promethean failure. Stealing Markova's shoes did nothing to help. Mr. Healey is shouting at a girl from the school who has knocked into his stand of tutus, their frills poking up indecently into the air. Two women from the company are being measured for costumes, and a large pile of colorful shoes for the men in *Coppélia* is slowly collapsing into the middle of the room, a red heeled boot making a daring dash toward the door. I hover at the edges, keeping out of everyone's way. Miss de Valois is also in here, with a new girl I have only seen once, when she came for an audition. I had been walking past the Wells Room and was shocked to see that the girl hadn't even brought her practice clothes or shoes. Miss Moreton made her remove her outdoor shoes and stockings and stand at the barre in her bare feet. She must have had something special, because within days she was enrolled in the school, joining "the bombs," as we liked to call them, in their make-shift changing room in the dress circle ladies' cloakroom. Clara and I had been there once, and yet we were all quick to forget how intimidating older, more established dancers could be.

When I reach into my cubbyhole and place my pointe shoes in my bag, a little square of paper falls to my feet. All theatre post is delivered to our Wardrobe cubbyholes, our pointe shoes stacked among letters from admirers, cuttings from newspaper reviews that one of the girls thinks we might like to read, the season's contracts. But this little note feels different, the edges of the paper thin as though torn from a larger sheet. I pick it up, turning it over twice.

Dear Olivia Marionetta, I am writing to express my admiration, not only for your perfect, beautiful dancing, but also for you. I love your kind smile. I just wanted to write to tell you this. I love the moments when I am able to watch you, and one day I hope I will be able to tell you in person.

It is signed with a rose. No name. On the other side is a simple sketch of a ballerina in a long white romantic-style tutu, little wings floating out from her arms.

Holding the note to me, I smile. I long to get out of Wardrobe and somewhere quiet where I can turn this over in my mind, work out who it is that has written this for me. It is too noisy in here, with Mr. Healey shouting louder, the musical lilt of his accent ascending into hysterics. A headdress for an Act Two doll in *Coppélia* has disappeared from Wardrobe and he is furious. Even Miss de Valois is starting to look flustered, ushering the new girl out of the door. The girl looks terrified, her wide eyes staring at Mr. Healey in amazement. Miss de Valois never brought me in here for a fitting when I joined the school, I think, a little resentfully. Clara and I had to be resourceful, begging older girls for their discarded leotards, resewing ribbons from worn-out shoes onto each new pair. I wish I had been adored by Miss de Valois, taken under her wing and protected. But there were two of us, two Marionetta girls who could look after each other. We carried our mother's name, Marion, and we carried her anxiety and stress and fear, but we left as much of her as we could in that hospital a train ride away. Perhaps wishing for a replacement mother in Miss de Valois is misguided. One mother hasn't helped us make a smooth transition into adulthood; why would a second be any better?

I go straight to the well, nodding politely at the new young stagehand I encounter on my way along the corridor. He looks back at me as I open the door leading down to the storage room:

he is too new, I think, to realize how regularly we like to come here. I make my way down the steps, relieved to see that there is no one else here. It is cold, as usual, but the stillness of the water and the dim, quiet light is soothing. There are no shadows reaching their gray ribbons around the edges of the well, no whispers from the low chill that reaches up from the water. I feel safe in my isolation.

With my eyes straining in the low light, I read the note again. There is something wonderful about a note like this. The writing is round and firm, the words clear but artistic, as though the writer has taken care that every letter is beautiful as well as legible. I lower myself on to the stone wall surrounding the well, easing my legs out in front of me. My muscles ache, a dull tiredness that spreads all down my hamstrings and calves. I lean forward, stretching luxuriously, the note balancing on my feet. Too many *brisés* today; I've been trying to match the same rhythm and energy as Lydia Lopokova, who seems to fly across the stage. She has a wobbly knee, as she calls it, an injury from overuse throughout her long career. I've seen her speaking firmly to herself, doing her funny little warm-ups before launching into the most bouncing and brilliant arrangements. But when rehearsals end she walks with a limp, the jarring bursts of pain streaked across her smooth round face revealing her as human. I shouldn't be complaining about tired legs, the right sort of tiredness that signifies I will wake up stronger and faster in the morning. Getting old and injured feels so far away, like a tiny gray cloud hovering benignly on the horizon.

Bending forward further, I press my hands into my thighs. I know exactly who I want the note to be from. And yet that would be impossible. Nathan Howell's affections are firmly fixed elsewhere. I have watched him with Clara. The two of them are always out together, exploring London, experiencing so much in a world that doesn't include me. I tried once to go with them, to visit an art exhibition. I hadn't realized it would be an opening, and I felt underdressed and uninteresting compared to everyone else there. They were all either glamorous or bohemian. I was neither, just a little tired and too nervous to approach anyone. Nathan and Clara hadn't wanted me there, not really. So I can cross Nathan off the list. Or maybe not, I think, turning the note once again and checking it really is addressed to me and not my sister. Yes, it is definitely to me. Perhaps it could be from him, a secret message to signal his desire. And I have, often, seen him staring at me, his gaze lingering as I finish a *grand allegro* right next to his piano.

I know it is the coat that makes me think more hopefully of Nathan today. When Clara got in from a day out with him this weekend, she threw off her coat, casting it in a crumpled green pile in the corner. Nathan bought it for her last year and she wears it whenever she goes out with him, the fur thick and elegant around her neck, her waist neat beneath the belt. I imagine him holding her there as he kisses her, his hands pressing into the soft green fabric. Picking the coat up off the floor, I gently smoothed out the creases as I hung it up.

"Just leave it," she said, waving her hand dismissively. "I'll deal with it later." It was so strange, I remember thinking, to talk about the coat that way, as if it was a problem to be solved. "In fact, why don't you wear it," she said, a little tiredly. "I'm sick of wearing the same thing every time I go out." She paused and added, "It'll look lovely on you."

"Won't Nathan mind?" I asked, anxiously. I was longing to wear it, the thrill of feeling the same wool against my skin that Nathan had touched and admired. It would make him feel closer, more mine. I could feel the heat rising in my cheeks as I imagined walking to the theatre in Clara's coat.

"He'll probably just think you're me, same as everyone else." She turned to me, more focused now. "Honestly, you'd be doing me a favor."

* * *

I lean down, finding my faint reflection in the water. Perhaps he does admire me, not just as the mirror image of my twin. But of course I am her double, every contour of our faces replicated, captured in the other like a daguerreotype. Clara and I find it hard to avoid the stares of men when we walk together outside, two identical young women side by side. Sometimes, when we walk through Regent's Park, they call out to us, harmless admiration I suppose, but I hate it. It always feels like an attack, even though, technically, the words are kind. I fold into myself, moving closer to my sister, letting her laugh at the men, sending them away with a quick comment and a toss of her head.

There is a man who sends me flowers before every Tuesday night performance. But he is old, a regular patron who takes the same seat every week. And he would definitely sign his name on a note such as this. He is a lover of the ballet, the art of it, the music, the choreography. He doesn't hunt for pretty young dancers to seduce with rich gifts and generous payments. Mr. Ilya Abelman is his name, a Russian émigré who now lives in Primrose Hill with his very bossy daughter, or so he tells me when he finds me in the foyer after a performance and talks until I am half asleep and longing for my bed. He always has a little box of Carson's fruit pastilles with him, sold for sixpence by attendants at the auditorium doors, that he takes home to his adult daughter. He moves from theatre to theatre each night of the week, never missing a ballet show. He told me once, when I found him waiting outside the theatre to present to me the most elegant box of chocolates, that he had followed the Ballets Russes across Europe—*Swan Lake* in Monte Carlo, *The Firebird* in Lisbon, even *The Rite of Spring* in Paris. He loves the ballet, purely and devotedly, and would never write a note like this. His words would be bold, indulgent, describing his favorite divertissement in a performance. I am fond of him, especially when he catches me leaving the theatre and folds my hand in his, kissing it chastely as though I am a princess. Clara has no time for him. But he is one of the few men that seems to be able to tell us apart, and I love him for it. Perhaps he can sense that I belong to another time, that I would be more suited to the glamour of Imperial Russia than this penniless London life where we have to search the audition lists for roles to occupy us out of season. Our Vic-Wells season runs from September to May, so there are three long summer months to find employment, and more importantly payment. It is an exhausting time, and I don't relish the hours spent standing in stiff poses for the opera or for plays, dressing the stage with my body. Some of the other girls have found themselves rich patrons, men who linger after each performance, pressing gifts into their hands: jewels, clothes, expensive meals at hotel restaurants. My Mr. Abelman isn't like that; he never expects anything from me, never invites me out to late-night dinners in the corner of secluded bars. The girls come into class the morning after these dinners, a new fur stole on their coat, a new bracelet circling their wrist. They smirk and smile, but I don't believe them when they say they enjoyed themselves. If I catch them when they think no one is looking, I can see another look clouding their eyes. They stare down at their new jewels with a fascinated horror, as though struggling to comprehend what it was their body did to get it there.

* * *

Despite the first signs of spring, it is cold, especially down here by the well. Eventually, I stand, stretching my arms up to the low ceiling and rolling my neck. With stiff fingers, I release my hair from its bun, spreading it across my back. I hardly ever wear my hair down now. It feels exposing, like I am giving away a part of me that I prefer to tidy away and hide from sight. The note is a mystery and will have to stay that way for now.

As I walk back up to the Wells Room, I hear piano music trickling down from the top floor. It is coming from the boardroom, a small room at the top of the theatre that we use for solo rehearsing. It can barely fit a piano, a dancer and a teacher. Sergeyev has been coaching the leads in there, and we can hear him sometimes, even from the floor below, calling out instructions in broken medleys of French, Russian, English.

I make my way up the stairs, the warmer air of the top floor reaching me with its distinctive smell of damp, like wet fur. I avoid looking into the school studio, the rip of skin on my toe still too fresh, the humiliation too sharp. The door at the end of the corridor of offices and small rehearsal rooms is ajar, and I peer around to see who is rehearsing. The blood rises fast in my cheeks, color spreading uncontrollably up from my neck. It is Nathan, his face fixed in concentration, his hands moving lightly over the keys as he plays the familiar notes of the bolero.

Before I can stop myself, I have taken a step into the room, propping myself up against the door frame. He looks up at the end of the piece, noticing me for the first time. His face softens into a smile.

"You sure you don't want to rehearse?" he says. "I don't think Sergeyev needs this room for another hour."

I am confused. He has never asked me to rehearse with him before. That has always been a privilege reserved for Clara, the two of them secreting themselves away whenever Nathan can find a piano free in an empty rehearsal room. It only takes me another second to realize that he thinks I am Clara. My hair is loose and I have the green coat over my arm. I had taken advantage of Clara's offer this morning. It might not be too long before she changes her mind and takes it back.

Our voices are similar, nearly identical, and to someone who doesn't know us well, they would be impossible to tell apart. I don't know if Nathan will be able to tell I am not Clara if I speak. Something makes me think not; he is not the sort of man that really listens to a woman when she speaks. And yet here I am, wishing he loved me, wishing he looked at me with the same admiring, even proud way he looks at my sister. Recently I've noticed her dismissing him at the end of rehearsals when he comes and puts his arm around her. She shrugs him off, making up an excuse about needing to cool down, to stretch, to get to a costume fitting. I wouldn't treat him like that, not if he looked at me with the same pride as he looks at Clara.

My heart beats hard as I take one step into the room. I want to go to him and kiss him. It would be like a dare, like when Clara and I were little and we would challenge each other to creep up to Pavlova's Ivy House, to touch the wall, to clamber up on the tree by her garden and look over at her pet swans.

I can't risk it. I am not prepared. Instead, I stop after just a few steps and smile at him, trying to mimic Clara's wide smile, showing her teeth, so different to mine, which is guarded, closed. "I've got to get ready for the Act I rehearsal now," I say. "But maybe tomorrow."

I turn quickly, almost running out of the room.

"See you later then, Clara," I hear him call after me, more a question than anything else. And I don't correct him. This isn't new, being mistaken for my sister. But this time it feels thrilling, adventurous, like I've slipped into a role where I can do whatever I wish. I feel stronger, a little dangerous.

Later in rehearsal, my hair back in its low bun, I enjoy watching Nathan staring at my sister. This time it feels as though it is me he is looking at, that I too am the recipient of his gaze. It is an opportunity. And one that I will not let slip, wasted, through my fingers.

CHAPTER 11

Clara

Rehearsals for *Coppélia* are picking up pace. We are all excited about the first night, but it is still over two weeks away. Costume fittings are frantic and there is the constant sound of sawing and banging coming from the carpenter's workshop behind the stage. They are creating a set of an Austrian village, influenced by the tradition of the Bavarian harvest, complete with pretty flower displays, wooden benches, rustic door frames. And of course there is the workshop of Dr. Coppélius, the eccentric dollmaker who makes a mechanical doll so lifelike that Franz, Swanilda's fiancé, is convinced she is a real woman, perpetually sitting in the window reading a book while lace frills sit stiffly around her neck. The perfect image of dull, idealized femininity. Franz is an idiot. He should be able to see that fun, lively, alive Swanilda is a much better choice. I am glad we are not performing Act III, in which Swanilda forgives Franz for preferring a lifeless doll to her. They marry, a joyful celebration with the whole village coming out to dance. I am not sure it is realistic. Would Swanilda really forgive him? It seems unlikely.

It is a wonderful ballet, full of comic energy and fun. Lydia Lopokova has become quite friendly with us all, enjoying our attentions, it seems, the opportunity to share little scraps of stories and choreography from her days at the Mariinsky, the Ballets Russes, touring in America, dancing with Fokine and Diaghilev. I watch Olivia hanging on her every word. If she could, my sister would transport herself back in time to the early twentieth century, to the dormitories of the Imperial Theatre School in St. Petersburg. She would be entirely suited to the prison-like routine, a convent of precision and order. The chance to dance alongside Bronislava Nijinska and Tamara Karsavina would make it all entirely worth it.

I prefer listening to Lydia's stories of Fokine and Isadora Duncan, how they broke all the rules of classical ballet, determined that they could do something better than the rigid poise of the Russian school. Isadora Duncan is so entrenched in myth and magic that she barely seems real to me. I remember when the news of her death was plastered dramatically across the papers in 1927. It had seemed like the loss of a dream: how much I would have loved to have met her. But even her death was glamorous to me, her long silk scarf caught in the wheels of the motor car on the Riviera in Nice. She was thrown onto the road, strangled by the scarf. Her last words, *Adieu, mes amis. Je vais à la gloire*, seemed so romantic; but then I was just an impressionable child in love with the stage, desperate to find my own chance of glory.

It is the glamour of America and the experiments of dance, film and theatre that truly excite me. I long to be as bold and outrageous as Isadora Duncan, who shocked Russian audiences by dancing on the stage with her hair loose and flowing, her feet bare, once even exposing her naked breasts. I smile when I think of how shocked Mother would be if I got on a boat to America and broke from the traditions of classical ballet. But there is no chance of that happening, not when I have the comparative safety and security of the

Vic-Wells, my sister by my side, Ninette de Valois steadily expanding our world, the promise of a growing British ballet. And yet I would love to leave London. The furthest I have ever traveled is on a ballet tour to Manchester.

* * *

Hanging back after rehearsal today, I linger at the barre with my pointe shoes still on. I feel restless and I don't want Olivia by my side. She is at her most intense right now, driven only by the ballet. She left the studio without me when she realized I had no plans to hurry. Nathan isn't here either, his absence giving me permission to dream and imagine, to feel lighter without his gaze fixed upon me. It was Ippolit Motcholov who played for the rehearsal today, Constant Lambert seething from his chair at the front as he tried to work out how he was supposed to reconcile Sergeyev and Motcholov's version of the score with the expectations of the orchestra. It is usually the dancers he has to worry about, grumbling when they refuse to keep up with the pace of his baton. Though to be honest these dress rehearsal altercations thrill me, ballerinas shaking their heads under the glowing light of the stage while Constant angrily throws his arms around from the orchestra pit.

Nathan isn't here today and I feel no guilt that I am glad. I need a rest from him and his constant watching and expecting. He always has to be doing, achieving, finding purpose in every stage of the day. So frequently, he makes me rehearse with him, which is tiresome, especially when I can tell that he is watching me as he plays the piano, stopping when he can sense me faltering. Let's start again, shall we, he'll say, waiting for me to get in position. Or we are out in London, searching for exhibitions and concerts, tracking down the best new restaurants, walking briskly through the cold night air to find the new wine he knows we absolutely must try. He always has to be first, fully immersed in London culture, shaking hands with composers and conductors, artists and actors, the top chefs and sommeliers. He is used to it, from his days as a child star, and I can tell he still yearns for that attention, to be the most admired person in the room. That is what attracted me to him at first, I suppose: this relentless drive and pursuit of the best. His unapologetic entitlement. Often I think he still achieves this attention, especially with me on his arm, a beautiful young ballerina in a backless silk dress. I know I look different to the other women, my glamour coming not from expensive jewels and furs but from the way I hold myself, my elegance, my ballerina poise. He introduces me as his ballerina from the Vic-Wells and men look at him enviously, their eyes grazing over me. It is easier to smile and shake their hand, but I don't know how much more of it I can take.

I tried to make it very clear to him the other night that I am tired of being treated like a prize, paraded in front of the men he wants to impress.

It was the night after the opening of Anrep's *The Awakening of the Muses*. We were on our way home from a Sunday night Ballet Club performance at the Mercury Theatre in Notting Hill. It had been a glorious evening of dance, with a triple bill of *Lysistrata*, *Les Masques* and *Le Spectre de la Rose*. With a trio of choreographers, Antony Tudor, Frederick Ashton and Michel Fokine respectively, this felt like we were at the center of something exciting. Alicia Markova, Pearl Argyle, Walter Gore, even Ashton himself, were dancing. I loved *Les Masques*, the glorious costumes by Sophie Fedorovitch with Markova in a white chiffon ballgown with a long train, carrying a transparent mica muff, a white gardenia in her hair. The story is daring, sexually heightened: a wife and husband meet each other at a masked ball, each with their lover. After some changing of partners, the wife and husband are reconciled and the mistress and lover go off together.

"I prefer the Russian classics," Nathan said on the way home, as we squeezed ourselves through the crowds leaving the packed Mercury Theatre. "Petipa and Ivanov, they knew how to create a perfect line of corps de ballet. This was just an excuse to flaunt sexual promiscuity under the guise of art."

"You're wrong," I replied bluntly. "There was more art and drama in *Les Masques* than in an entire row of *Lac des Cygnes* corps." We walked in silence, a deep frustration building inside me. He had ruined the evening, somehow, by not understanding that ballet was so much more than lines of dancers standing in perfection across a large, open stage. Eventually, with the silence widening between us, I had to speak.

"If you don't want to see the new ballets, why do you agree to come to these Sunday nights at the Ballet Club? No one is forcing you to. I'd rather go alone than have you whining about the dancers being too expressive for you."

"I don't have to like it to want to see it, Clara," he said, a note of smug intellectualism creeping into his voice. This is how it always seemed to go when we disagreed. My enthusiasm was childish, undiscerning, whereas his critique was founded in knowledge and experience. I had thought, when we first met over a year ago, that I would enjoy having someone to talk with about art and dance and music, and maybe I did to begin with, when I thought I was in love with him, impressed by his past, his confidence, his certainty that he belonged. But now it grates with me; I find him supercilious, condescending. It is only when we are both a little drunk on wine and glamour that I find myself drawn to him now. There needs to be champagne flowing, a band playing, the loud laughter of friends, for me to find him attractive.

"I didn't like the way you introduced me to Charles Lynch," I say, bolder now. I am in the mood to argue.

"What do you mean? The pianist? How did you want me to introduce you?"

"Not in that patronizing way you always do it."

"You're going to have to more specific, Clara."

"And this is my ballerina," I mimic. "It's as though you are offering me up on a plate. Can't you just say my name, or, even better, let me speak for once."

"I didn't think you'd be interested in speaking to Charles."

"And why not?" I demand. "He's Marie Rambert's pianist; he set up the Ballet Club with her. I might want to talk to him about the performance, maybe even tell him how much I enjoyed *Les Masques*. You didn't say anything at all to him about how well he'd just played. You just wanted to show off your ballerina."

"Don't be ridiculous, Clara."

We were silent in the taxi home. I asked the driver to drop me at the end of my road. If Nathan had apologized to me then, I might have forgiven him. If he had invited me back to his boat, then the evening could have ended very differently. But he'd never asked me to come back there with him. I'd hinted, frequently, about how much I wanted to see his home, how romantic it must be living on the canal. I had visions of us wrapped in blankets, a candle burning, the water glistening in the moonlight. He never responded to my suggestions, though. At first I thought he was being chivalrous, protecting my honor. A year on and he still has not broken, no matter how much I want him to. All I get are kisses, his lips pressed against mine, his hands wrapping around my waist. We kiss in the dark behind Sadler's Wells, our bodies pressed into each other. I have felt him harden, my body responding, pulsing and wet. But even then he has resisted, turning away and returning home alone, leaving me frustrated, disappointed, frozen with longing.

* * *

Lydia Lopokova is still in the Wells Room, pulling on her pink cardigan again and rubbing her knee. She sees me by the barre and comes over.

"Are you all right?" she asks, her face kind. She has a wonderfully expressive face, with big eyes and smooth round cheeks. Lopokova is not at all sculpted with the angular sharpness of so many of the other great ballerinas. I nod and smile back. I like talking to her. She has so much personality, breaking the myth of the mysterious ballerina.

"I have watched you," she says, putting her hand over mine on the barre. Her skin is warm, alive. I can see veins throbbing across her wrist. I have heard her playfully complain in the dressing room that hands are the first to betray a dancer's age. It is an insult to show veins in the theatre, she has said, laughing a little but also conscious of her age, forty-two compared with my nineteen.

"You remind me of myself when I was younger," she says. "You dance like an actor, full of passion and fire. You need to keep it, nurture it. Never let anyone take it away from you." I feel a lump forming in my throat. No one has ever said this to me before. "When I was at the Imperial Russian Ballet," she continues, "they tried to stifle us. At my graduation from the school to the company, I was told I should immediately divert myself from my overemphasized affectation and mannerism. Thank goodness I didn't listen. If I did, do you think I would have traveled the world, had roles created for me by the best choreographers, had my name splashed across the American and European newspapers?" She stops and looks at me, her eyes narrowed curiously. "Come," she says. "Let me teach you one of my favorite moments of ballet from all my many years of dancing." She smiles as she says this, hiding how she must really feel about her age behind a charming laugh.

Lopokova takes both my hands and pulls me into the middle of the room. "Now, fold back your arms like this," she instructs, throwing her head back. "The Firebird. Diaghilev was worried I wouldn't be able to do it, but I proved them all wrong. I was just eighteen years old and taking on the most challenging of Fokine's creations."

She chants the music, its strange rhythms and beats, Stravinsky's clashing collage of wild sounds that make me feel on edge, at the precipice of some painful passion. Her voice is discordant and labored, her uneven breathing a bass to the familiar tune.

"Imagine the red silk, the flames of your headdress, jewels flashing at your wrists." She continues singing the music, her voice rising and falling in chaotic cries. I follow behind her, my arms fighting against imaginary chains, moving in and out of arabesques and jumps that shine and then hold, frozen like a bird watching, waiting.

"Use your eyes," she calls to me. "They must look down your arm, then up, sharply. Feel the anger of the bird, refusing to be entrapped by the prince. Resist him, find power in your arms."

We dance, our legs fast, changing directions, jumping high *jetés* across the room, pirouettes in *attitude* that hardly end before we jump again. Every turn ends with a staccato pause, our heads moving in fierce stares. Finally, we both collapse, exhausted, onto the floor. We lie side by side, our breathing heavy. I can feel every nerve in my body tingling, alive and used. Awake. She turns her head to me, smiling.

"This can be you, always," she says. "Look outwards, beyond this room." She gets up slowly, pushing herself to her feet with her hands. "I'm going to pay for this tomorrow," she laughs.

She is at the door before I can stand to join her. I call out to her, to thank her, but she is already gone.

CHAPTER 12

Samuel

Samuel has had an idea. It is bold and potentially futile, but he has been working himself up to it all week, making himself promise that he will not let the weekend arrive without seeing it through. Finally, on Friday morning, he finds the courage.

The workshop feels alive this morning, the machines buzzing and the benches spilling over with tools and satin. Beauty stripped down to its first construction. Samuel has his sketches rolled up, tied with a piece of string. He has been carrying them around with him all week, in to work and then home again, a constant reminder of his promise to himself. And now they balance on the workbench, just clear of the shavings of leather and the dust of the paste flour that settles around him.

He eventually manages to speak when they are standing by the urn where they make their mid-morning tea.

"I heard some of the dancers talking about needing character shoes."

He pauses. Mr. Frederick nods, listening as he stirs the sugar into his cup. Samuel waits to see if Mr. Frederick wants to speak.

There is nothing, just another nod as he pulls the teaspoon out of the cup.

"I was delivering pointe shoes last week and caught the end of a rehearsal of Ashton's *Façade*, the tango I think it was, and I noticed that the heeled shoes Markova was wearing were not as well-made as our pointe shoes. Perhaps if we branched out, made character shoes as well, there might be some demand from the dancers." Samuel shifts nervously from one foot to the other.

"I am not sure we can fit them in right now," Mr. Frederick answers. "We have so many pointe shoe orders coming in. And I'd need to hire a designer for the shoes, which would take time."

This is Samuel's moment. He takes a deep breath and unrolls the sketch, holding it out to Mr. Frederick. "I wondered if you might like to look at my designs."

He waits as his employer takes the sketch, holding it open at the top and bottom. The drawing is neat and precise, measurements written around the edges with a list of materials penciled in at the bottom of the paper. Samuel knows he only has one chance to make an impression, to convince the Freeds that he is serious. Mr. Frederick reaches into the top pocket of his overalls and pulls out a pair of glasses. He doesn't laugh or grimace. He doesn't pass the paper back to Samuel with a shake of his head. He doesn't speak harsh, dismissive words, all the things that Samuel has imagined each morning when he runs through scenarios in his head.

"This is very interesting. Very interesting indeed." He taps the paper lightly. "Where did you learn to do this?" He doesn't wait for a reply. "Why haven't you shown me this before?" Frederick Freed looks up then, his forehead dimpling with lines that speak real interest and real, unfeigned pleasure.

"I've been designing shoes and costumes since I was a little boy," Samuel replies, a little louder now, strength coming into his voice. He surprises himself by being able to say the words he has practiced; he didn't think it would be possible. But he doesn't tell Mr. Frederick the full story, how it was his schoolteacher, Miss Frances Luck, who first showed him the women's magazines with the pages full of patterns and designs and haberdashery advice. There was *The Needlewoman, The Lady, Woman's Life*. Samuel was fascinated by them and his teacher let him flick through the pages each morning while he waited for the rest of the class to arrive. He was always the first one in, his father marching him out of the house far earlier than necessary every day. Then there was the school production of *Peter Pan*. Miss Luck asked him to help with the costumes and he spent many happy hours after school sewing a headdress for Tinker Bell and a little red smock for Peter. That was until he made the mistake of asking his father if he wanted tickets to the performance. There were no more afternoons staying late at school after that. His mother was given strict orders to collect him immediately after lessons. She was not to let him indulge in such frivolous nonsense ever again. Miss Luck had no opportunity to persuade his parents otherwise. She left the next term to get married, taking her pile of magazines with her.

He forces himself to stand still and firm. "I love creating the sketches and the designs, imagining the materials that would work best. It's what drew me to applying for a job with you and Mrs. Dora in the first place. But I've never actually created any of my designs, not the shoes anyway. I don't have the tools at home. I've created cheap versions of some of the costumes, but I don't have a sewing machine, so it's slow work. I've just made a few headdresses and ballet tunics, nothing special."

Samuel has still not told his parents exactly what he does for a living. He doesn't like to think how his father would react if he knew he was creating pink satin pointe shoes, a far cry from the train engines and railway tracks his father maintains. They think he works in the bookkeeping department of Selfridges, still a disappointment but at least an acceptable employment. And he hasn't lied to them as such. He did have an interview at Selfridges; he just didn't mention to his parents that this was not the job that he ended up accepting.

"Well, these are certainly very special, lad," Mr. Frederick says, filling the silence that has replaced Samuel's words. The two of them look back down at the paper, Samuel tilting his head, seeing the sketch as though it is the first time. The shoes are cream-colored with a small heel and the shape is all curves and smooth lines, an embellishment of petals cut into the toe in a fan design. He can see them now on the stage, worn by a dancer, Olivia maybe, the debutante in Frederick Ashton's ballet *Façade*, the village dancers in the *Coppélia* mazurka.

"I'll talk to Mrs. Freed about it, I promise you that," Mr. Frederick says, rolling up the sketch and placing it on the workbench. "We might not be able to get started on these right away, what with all the pointe shoe orders, but you can rest assured that we will come back to you for designs when we can." He picks up his tea and starts to walk back to his stool by the welting machine. "You've got talent, my lad. And make sure you remember that."

* * *

Samuel finishes his order of shoes by lunchtime. Mr. and Mrs. Freed have a wedding to get to and are keen to close the shop early for the day so they send Samuel out, wishing him a happy weekend.

"And you'd better not be thinking of selling those sketches to anyone else," Mr. Frederick calls out, cheerfully, as Samuel walks up the stairs from the basement workshop. "I should make you sign a contract," he laughs. It is the most animated Samuel has ever seen his employer, usually such a quiet, reserved man, reluctant to emerge from the privacy of his workshop.

Samuel laughs back. But inside he is overjoyed, too happy for mere laughter. This is serious, life-changing even, the first time he has ever been handed such praise. Praise for something that he and only he has created. His father's harsh, cruel laughter doesn't even enter his head. He knows he should be more understanding, that his father became a different man when he came back from France, how it affected every decision he made as a father, a husband, a man. But Samuel is glad he has left that house, even if he does worry every day about his mother, who has to manage those cruel dark moods alone.

※ ※ ※

When he delivered the pointe shoes to Sadler's Wells yesterday, there was a poster on the noticeboard reminding dancers of the *Coppélia* stage call. Someone, probably Miss de Valois, has scribbled across the bottom of the notice in thick black ink: "Do not make dinner plans." They all know these rehearsals can go on for hours. With just one week until the first night, the energy at Sadler's Wells is bubbling, a flurry of costumes arriving, the last parts of the set constructed, the props gradually building within the properties room. Wicker crates packed with lighting foils and new metal brackets for the sidelights pile on top of one another in the foyer, waiting for someone to clear them away to the correct department. Stage calls are exciting, and Samuel knows he will be able to sneak in to the auditorium without any trouble. He is a regular, part of the scenery, accepted without being noticed. It is to the theatre that he will go on this unexpected Friday afternoon off.

Samuel walks fast, enjoying the early signs of spring. He notices everything today: the light on the grass, the bright yellow of the daffodils that have sprung up in the most unlikely places on the roadside, the blue gems of the grape hyacinth hiding among the base of trees. As he walks through Exmouth Market, he looks up at his rooms. Even they look less gloomy today, and he can just about make out one of the walls with its patchwork of sketches, designs, colors, tiny pieces of fabric. He is proud of that wall, a museum of his ideas. Even the people of London look less miserable today as they move briskly along the market stalls. There is a brightness to the noise as the sellers call out their prices: the market is full to the brim with breads, fruits, vegetables, cakes of soap made in the warehouse down by the canal, wooden figurines handcrafted by the old man on Meredith Street. Newspapers are packed together like stacks of ironed laundry, the mesh-covered news boards announcing horror in Germany, but no one seems to notice. Not today. A boy is selling white roses from a trough at the end of the market. He is calling out in a loud, high voice, like a song. Samuel cannot resist. He has some coins in his pocket, enough to buy one rose. The boy takes his money quickly, pocketing it away with fast hands, in case his customer changes his mind. Samuel carries it with him to Rosebery Avenue. He feels bold today, certain that nothing can happen to make this feeling go away. It reminds him of when he was very young and it was his birthday, the promise of the day's specialness acting as a barrier from the threat of sadness. His mother always made an extra-special effort on his birthday, baking a cake and cooking his favorite meal of sausages in batter. His father usually managed to make it through the day without saying anything cruel, once even taking him outside and playing a modified game of cricket until he grew tired and left Samuel alone to throw the ball up and down into the air.

He won't think about his father today. The theatre promises excitement, transportation to another world. Olivia will be dancing. He read the cast list; he knows she is one of Swanilda's friends, dancing in the square in Act One, sneaking into Dr. Coppélius's workshop in Act Two. Entering by the Pit door on Arlington Street, he moves solidly and silently through the dim light. The rehearsal has not started yet, but there is a quiet energy, a low murmur of activity, the set being adjusted into place, the orchestra gradually filling the pit and warming up their instruments, the muffled banging that he recognizes as ballerinas pounding the noise out of their pointe shoes on a hard concrete step. He pauses, looking down the corridor that runs toward the pit and backstage; the door down to the well is open and he peers in to see nothing but a dark set of steps that fall steeply to the basement room. The light is too dim to make out who is down there but there are voices coming from below, the sound now growing and coming closer toward him. Suddenly, a group of six dancers, men and women, burst out, running in single file up and then along the corridor toward the entrance to the wings. He stands back against the wall, watching them as they fly past. They are not in full costume, just a few fragments that he has seen building up in Wardrobe: floral headdresses, colorful boots, bright sashes, wigs. Mostly they are in practice tutus, two in the long romantic style, one in a stiff, doll-like classical skirt that extends straight out from the hips. They have to practice in the more challenging costume elements, checking they can still dance the role with the addition of headpieces and bows. It is Olivia and Clara who are the last to appear up the steps. They are laughing together; Samuel feels a pang of envy at their intimacy.

Olivia stops at the top of the steps, turning back around in the dark of the doorway. "You go on," she says to her sister. "I've left my cardigan down there."

Samuel waits in the corridor, still pressed against the wall. He hears her feet tapping lightly, then silence, then they are tapping again on the way up. She is in her pointe shoes. He knows the sound of those blocks, the supple leather sole that he has formed with his hands.

"This is for you," he hears himself say.

Olivia jumps, crying out. "Goodness, you scared me." She looks upset, irritated. He is imposing on her preparations, ruining the calm and control that comes from dipping her hand in the magical waters of the well, her good luck charm.

"I'm sorry," he stammers, holding out the rose. A thorn is digging into his thumb.

"What's this for?" she says, looking at the rose suspiciously.

What is it for, thinks Samuel, panicking. This isn't working as he imagined it would. On the short walk from buying the rose and arriving at the theatre, he had visualized her drawing the rose to her and smelling it, perhaps rising up on her toes and kissing him on the cheek. Looking at her scowling face now, that doesn't seem very likely.

"It's to say good luck, for the stage call," he comes up with. She takes the rose reluctantly, turning away from him immediately as she does so, her bag spilling open at her hip. Inside, he can see two more pairs of his shoes, both a little worn, the ends gray with the dust of the floor. Her darning is neat, small U-shaped patterns adorning the satin. "I hope the pointe shoes are working out well for you," he adds.

Her face softens a little but Samuel can sense distrust, a barrier she has fixed between them. "Of course, you work for Mr. Freed." She is smiling politely, nodding to herself as she remembers where she has seen him, why he seemed familiar but distant, a face she simply couldn't place. "Well, thank you. This is very kind of you. The shoes are marvelous, and I shall dance even better knowing I have the luck of Frederick Freed's magical pointe shoes."

She is acting, he thinks, turning on the role of the gracious ballerina. He wants to mention the note, tell her it was from him, but he can't. It doesn't feel right.

"Goodbye then. Enjoy the rehearsal if you decide to stay," she calls out as she turns and starts running along the corridor. Her bag is still open, ribbons and ballet shoes exposed. A soft-toe shoe balances precariously on the top and at the moment she starts to run it falls out, hitting the ground with no sound at all. She doesn't notice and keeps running away toward the stage.

Samuel waits, listening to her steps disappearing and merging with the growing moans of the orchestra. He walks toward where her shoe lies on the ground, the ribbons splayed wildly about the upturned leather sole. Kneeling, he picks it up, turning it over in his hand before going to the top of the steps. He has been down here before, to the sacred well that he knows the dancers obsess over, their good luck routine. It is cool and quiet, making him think of the Freed basement workshop at the start of the day, before the welting machines start up their whirring. Some of the same smells linger too: wood, dust, the musk of satin and leather. But there is something else drifting through the damp air, the salt of sweat, grit, passion. It had been strange to see the dancers emerge from here, their faces bright and their costumes sparkling as though sprinkled with a magical, unearthly dust. There is none of that brightness by the well: it is a monster's cave, the water shadowed like those gloomy children's books he remembers from school, with their illustrations of Hades dragging his victims across the river Styx. Kneeling by the stone that surrounds the well, he looks down into the water.

He holds it in his hands now, feeling the darned edges of the toe, the satin scuffed and stained from dancing on dusty floors. This is not the first time he has stolen one of her shoes, and it occurs to him that he is locked in a strange cycle of creation and destruction. It feels ritualistic to him, lowering the shoe into the water, spreading the ribbons out on the surface. The water darkens the satin, slowly filling the shoes and turning it on its front. She will need to return to him for more, and each shoe will give her luck, strength. He soaks her shoe in the water she trusts. She will come back here later; she will see her shoe dancing in the dark water; and she will believe, truly believe, that her luck can come true.

CHAPTER 13

Clara

I don't hang around after the stage call. It has gone on all afternoon, stopping and starting, constant readjustments of the placements of the corps de ballet on the stage, Miss de Valois calling out orders which are then reversed by Sergeyev, who creeps up onstage and twists props and furniture as he sees fit. They argue over the position of the dolls in Dr. Coppélius's workshop in Act Two, and there is a tense silence after Miss de Valois absolutely refuses to let the hay bales from Act One stay visible onstage in the second half. And the orchestra is all over the place, having had not nearly enough rehearsal. It is such a musical ballet, every step working in a precise marriage with the music, that the pressure to get it right is immense. I thought Constant was going to explode during the mazurka. He isn't supposed to be conducting. It was going to be Geoffrey Toye. We rather depend on our Uncle Geoffrey, as Lambert affectionately calls him. He has an air of complete experience, which of course is entirely to be expected after his years working with Lilian Baylis at the Old Vic before she renovated our Sadler's Wells and expanded her management to these two theatres, each on opposite sides of the river. Uncle Geoffrey has been a governor at Sadler's Wells since its conception two years ago and there are rumors he is composing a wonderful ballet about a haunted ballroom for us, which Miss de Valois will create. But he was in a car accident last week, the news of which has shaken us: I overheard Constant say to one of the orchestra that he barely escaped with his life. So Constant is conducting, which is only increasing the tensions between the musicians and Sergeyev.

By the end of Act Two, we are all very relieved that we are only putting on the first two acts. I know I should stay and wait for all the notes, but I am exhausted, we all are. The ballet is held together by the corps de ballet, with some big dances in Act One that require strength in the legs and light smiles on the face. I have smiled enough for one day. Once I have changed out of my practice clothes, I join the rest of the cast in the auditorium. I take a seat at the back of the stalls, half hidden in darkness, hoping to find a moment to sneak out unseen. The other girls are huddled together near the front; a mistake, I think, but at least they can distract each other. I could go to join them, but I don't have anymore energy left to move. Instead, I stare up at the ivory panel above the proscenium arch, staying awake by attempting to make out the features of the Finsbury coat of arms that glares down at us. A fish and a winged bull peer angrily at one another between arabesques of running water.

After the Act One notes, I have had enough. It is late and I just want to get home to bed. I catch Olivia's eye and gesture to the exit, but she shakes her head. She will wait, of course, committed to the bitter end. I have almost made it, my bag over my shoulder, my old woolen coat wrapped around me with a scarf right up to my chin. I leave via the Arlington Street exit, the cold air a shock after hours inside the busy theatre.

I feel a heavy hand on my shoulder. Turning abruptly, I pull myself away. It is Nathan. He doesn't have his coat, just the Delibes piano score under one arm.

"Where are you going?" he asks. I look at him blankly.

"Home. It's late and I'm done here."

"They haven't given the notes for Act Two. You can't leave yet."

"Nathan, it will be fine. Olivia will tell me if there is anything I need to know."

"Are you going to walk home on your own?" he asks. He might be concerned about my safety, walking home late in the dark, but right now it just irritates me, a paternal pressure that goes beyond what I want from him.

"I'll see you in the morning, Nathan," I give in answer, turning to walk away from him.

"There's the exhibition tomorrow, at Olympia," he calls after me. "Shall I meet you in the foyer after morning class?"

I stop, sigh, turn back to him. I had forgotten about the exhibition. I really want to go, and Nathan has already bought the tickets. There is a special dance sketch by Penelope Spencer that the Vic-Wells girls are all desperate to see, and I don't want to miss out. I just wish I hadn't agreed to go with Nathan. More than anything, I want to dress up for the outing with Olivia, meet the other girls after class, travel on the bus with Beatrice and Hermione, Sheila and Nadina, all of us graduates from Miss de Valois's school who have been working hard together all season. I have been spending so much time with Nathan that I've rather neglected my friends, and I realize how much I miss them. Right now I feel on the outskirts of their group. We are all village girls in *Coppélia*, rehearsing together, complaining about our sore feet together, laughing behind their backs about the strops our ballet masters and mistresses throw. But somehow I don't feel like I belong; I'm left out, not quite getting all the jokes. And it is because of Nathan. He takes so much from me, all my energy, everything I have to give.

"Yes, of course," I reply. I do want to go, and Nathan has bought the tickets for us. "I'll meet you after class, but I think lots of the others are coming too, so we can get the bus with everyone." This is my attempt to prepare him, ease him into the fact that I do not want to spend the entire afternoon by his side. I want to watch Penelope Spencer's sketch with a laughing group of girls by my side; I want to enjoy the fashion parades and the garden shows without Nathan's commentary in my ear.

"See you then," he calls out as I walk away. "And I've got a surprise for us," I hear him add. My heart sinks at that; this will be his way of getting me alone, a romantic gesture that I don't want, not when it takes me away from my friends and my sister.

* * *

The next morning, we all get changed after class with an excited buzz, the girls revealing new dresses and hats for the occasion. We add lipstick and rouge, all of us hustling for places in front of the mirrors, pinning our hair into place. Gradually, the familiar smells of sweat and powder sweeten into new perfumes of citrus and vanilla. When we left the flat this morning, Olivia asked if she could wear the green coat. I wish I could find the words to tell her that she really doesn't need to ask. She can keep it. When I wear it I feel trapped in its folds, the fur choking me. I feel the expectant weight of Nathan's eyes on me, transforming me into a woman I do not want to be anymore. I have started trying to tell Olivia so many times, but I never get very far: I just don't think she would understand. We share everything, have experienced every moment of our lives together. That is until Nathan came along and made a little world for me that was mine alone. I know I shut Olivia out of my life with Nathan, presenting her with a curated and limited version of our relationship. The morning after an evening with him, all she wants to hear about is the music, the champagne, the dresses and jewelry of the women we encountered, the dancing, the walk home through a moonlit London. All she sees is romance.

Today, I manage to feel elegant in my new dress and stockings, a navy hat with a twisted knot at the side adding a modern look. These, I bought for myself, and I love them all the more for it. I have unpacked my old woolen coat out of its hibernation at the back of our wardrobe; I never thought I'd feel so pleased to wear it again. There is a copy of the latest *Woman's Own* on the dressing table, and Hermione flips through it as she waits for the rest of us to finish getting ready. Hermione Darnborough sets the style for all of us, bringing in her discarded blouses and skirts, leaving magazines for us girls to read with avid attention between rehearsals. She is a year younger than me but seems much more mature, helped of course by her wealthy family keeping her in the best new fashions. She looks like a model, tall and lithe, and leaves an absolute mess behind her wherever she goes: makeup, hairpins, tights, ribbons. Miss de Valois once shouted at her for being so slovenly. But she is very beautiful and we all rather look up to her. Though sometimes I feel she takes those matronly words of advice in magazines such as *Woman's Own* a little too seriously: I do not only look after my appearance as a duty toward myself and some hypothetical man I am to marry. All this talk of marriage and duty and creating the perfect home makes me wants to laugh, loudly and rudely. I remember an article in *Miss Modern* last year: "When a man looks for a wife, she must have a nice taste in dress. Clothes are important to a man's success." This secretly horrified me, the idea that what I wore was more relevant to a man's success than my own. But some of the girls read these magazines as gospel, hanging on to each word of advice.

* * *

The *Daily Mail* Ideal Home exhibition is not to be missed. We all love it and Olivia and I have been attending every year since Father died, dreaming up ways we too could transport the modern furniture and gardens and linens and fashions into our own little lives. The trick is not to take it too seriously, not to be drawn into the advertisements and model homes that pronounce how to live, the ideal role for a woman, how to be happy. I admit that sometimes it looks tempting, a husband, a large home in the countryside, two cheerful children, a dog. But then when I really think about it and imagine myself in that life, a life without the theatre and Olivia and the freedom of living right in the center of London, I feel a sense of dread. What I really want, I suppose, is change. Constant, exciting, exhilarating change that makes me feel alive. The last few years at Sadler's Wells have given me that, the joy of growing with this new company, seeing our audience numbers build, reading the reviews in the newspapers. I worry, though, that this feeling isn't going to last, that soon I am going to be looking for something else.

Nathan is waiting for me in the foyer. It takes him a beat to work out who I am, his eyes instead following Olivia in my green coat as we walk through the entrance together. Perhaps I could persuade her to swap for the day, like we used to when we were little, tricking Aunt Alice into muddling us up. But I couldn't do that to her; Nathan is my burden to manage.

I tell myself to be cheerful and pleasant, but I don't take his arm. I keep hold of Olivia's and call out to him to hurry up or we'll miss the bus. He follows us, our growing group of young women, a few of the men joining too. In the bus we are noisy, Bobby Helpmann entertaining us all with his comic stories of astonishment at all our British ways. He is Australian, only arriving in London this year, and he finds us very strange. We find him strange too, but in a lovable curious way. Just last week he had us in fits of giggles as he argued with Lilian Baylis over how much brilliantine he uses in his hair. He argued none at all, that he had his own concoction of Vaseline and paraffin. You wouldn't want to light a match too close to him. Now, he is up at the front of the bus, getting Hermione to point out London landmarks, which he deconstructs, scandalously. Even the grandeur of Buckingham Palace is a joke to him.

Turning, I look back at Olivia. She is sitting with Beatrice, the two of them talking intently, their heads close together. I long to know what they are talking about, but I don't think I would be welcome. I am with Nathan, and everyone expects me to enjoy his attentions. But I can't, not when all I can think about is how much I used to love taking the bus with Olivia and how far away from her I feel right now. When we were younger, we'd run onto the bus after ballet class, our slim shoulders easing effortlessly through the press of men with their briefcases and the women clasping their shopping bags. We'd make up stories about the people passing by, our faces pressed against the window, curiously watching as cyclists plaited in and out of the taxis and pedestrians marched onward, everyone finding the tempo of their day.

Today London feels on edge. I notice policemen stationed outside Green Park and on the edges of Hyde Park Corner, their faces alert and wary. I watch them as the bus stops and starts on our way to Olympia, a restless light bouncing off the silver star on their helmets. Along the side of the road is the debris of a march that took place yesterday, an anti-fascist protest that wound its way from Commercial Road to Hyde Park with determined energy. A cloth sign has been discarded on the pavement, the large bold letters that call for a boycott of German goods still showing through the dirt smeared across the fabric. The Vic-Wells dancers dominate the bus with their talk of it as we pass by Hyde Park, several of the boys giving their accounts of the crowds that had packed the streets yesterday. I wish I had been there, joining in as the protesters swept through the city. Olivia and I had read in the papers back at the start of February about Hitler's power. It had unsettled everybody, the dressing rooms noisy as we repeated the phrases we'd lifted from the stacks of newspapers we walk past every day on the way to the theatre. But we'd all moved on with our day quickly, forgetting as soon as the first bars of the piano heralded the start of ballet class.

As the rest of us chat loudly, Nathan is quiet. I have noticed that he prefers it when it is just the two of us. That is when he is at his most confident, talking endlessly, giving his opinions on everything. But now, when Bobby makes a comment about the czardas in *Coppélia* being played so slowly yesterday he thought his legs were going to fall off, Nathan says nothing. If it had been just me, he would have started a long lecture about why the piece had been played at exactly the right tempo. I try to ignore Nathan and his silence, instead taking part in the loud energy of the others. But when we arrive at the Olympia exhibition center, I have to stick with him. He has our tickets.

The exhibition is vast, growing every year. This year's main attraction is a "Rainbow City," and it is just as brilliant as advertised. In all the colors of the rainbow, the giant domed roof is lit up by a gigantic scheme of neon lighting. I look up, dazzled by the lights reflecting from the glass of the Grand Hall. I imagine our lighting designers at Sadler's Wells will be stealing some ideas from here. There are still the same categories as last year, the show homes, working-class housing, child welfare, "homes fit for heroes," the results of the reader "ideal homes" competitions. But there is also a series of "Rooms of the Scientists," which apparently will show us the history of inventions from Newton, Faraday, Marconi and more. There is a section on the home cinema, one on the telephones of the General Post Office, another on modern sanitation and heating. I long for better heating, but Olivia and I will never be able to afford the luxuries on display here. Saturdays are the busiest days, of course, and we are immediately thrown into the crowd. I watch as Olivia disappears with the other girls, and I am left with Nathan. Reluctantly, I put my arm through his and decide I will have a good time, whatever the situation. I lead us toward the fashion area, past the "ideal dinner party" displays, through the common-sense kitchens, along the village of ideal homes. It would be a shame to miss the fashion pageant.

There are displays set up either side of the central walkway, and I stop at a few of them, taking a mental note of the new styles and shapes of the clothing. Nathan follows, dutifully, stopping when I stop, moving again when I do. I am fascinated by a set of removable dress shields that apparently can be sewn into clothing to prevent the dress or blouse staining from underarm sweat. This is absurdly exciting to me, and I wish Olivia was with me so I could share this. We have to throw away so many clothes far too soon because of stained underarms. I turn to Nathan.

"Now this would be useful," I say, smiling.

"What exactly is it? It's hardly pretty."

"It's not supposed to be pretty, Nathan. It's to stop sweat stains ruining clothes."

He looks horrified. His eyes widen, and then he turns away. "Don't be ridiculous. You don't need that."

I refuse to let this go. It both amuses and alarms me that he thinks I might not be susceptible to the same bodily functions as himself. He's seen me sweat in ballet class; perhaps he thinks it is some sort of magical ballerina glow.

"Nathan, women get exactly the same sweat stains as men. It's foolish to pretend otherwise." I see a cosmetics stand across the aisle and I drag him over. "Look at this powder," I say to him, firmly. "Do you think my nose and cheeks stay this smooth matte color without it, especially in ballet class when I'm hot and sweaty?" I hold him by the arms, turning him to look at my face. Today I spent longer than usual on my makeup after class and I know my face looks flawless. "This isn't my natural skin," I repeat, laughing now at how uncomfortable he is looking. I remember a hilarious article in *Miss Modern* last year where a man was complaining about the Bank of England banning its female employees from wearing makeup. Little did they know that they might be surprised when the women did not look quite as perfect and polished as the men were used to. Yet I remember not being entirely enamored by the male writer objecting because of his desire for women to introduce glamour and romance into "our humdrum routine." I had felt very sorry for those poor female office workers with the men ogling them in some fantasy world of romance.

"Come on, let's find the pageant."

The fashion pageant is extremely popular. Already the hall is full, women vying for the best positions. I see Olivia has found a spot near the front, so we push our way through and join her. It is

Penelope Spencer we have all come to see. She is famous in our ballet world, a great comic dancer, her choreography modern and daring. Olivia and I danced in some of the pieces she choreographed for operas several years ago, the most memorable being *Cupid and Death* at the New Scala Theatre on Tottenham Court Road, for which she made us go to the zoo to get inspiration for some of the characters. She is very bold and gets exactly what she wants. The theatre manager for the opera claimed he had no money to pay us, so she threatened to pull us from the night's performance. And lo and behold, we were suddenly paid in advance, the dance going ahead.

This sketch is called "Ladies, Sigh No More!" and it features thirteen women as mannequins and one dancer. It is advertising five brands of stockings by I. and R. Morley, a comic display of the woes of finding the right stockings that won't tear, stretch or fade. The music starts and the "mannequins" find their positions. It is wonderfully funny. I glance at Nathan and see that he too is lost in the comedy. He looks entirely transfixed by the mannequins, their long legs clad in the smoothest, sheerest of stockings. When it ends, I have to drag him away. I think he enjoyed it even more than I did; I am surprised by how warm it makes me feel toward him, the great Nathan Howell finally showing a sense of humor about something frivolous and playful. I had expected him to be stuffy and boring about it, making some comments about how lowbrow it all was. But he did nothing of the sort.

Olivia walks with us to the next hall and then heads off to meet the other girls. But before she goes, she turns to Nathan and says the funniest thing.

"Have a lovely afternoon with my sister. I hope you don't muddle us up this time."

Nathan doesn't reply, just splutters some sort of mumble half-way between a laugh and a cough. I raise my eyebrow at him, but he just shrugs. "I would never muddle you two up," he says to me once she has gone. I am not sure that I believe him.

Olivia looks lovely today, but a little different to normal. It takes me a moment to realize what it is, but then I see it. She has styled her hair exactly like mine, loose around her shoulders, with just the front sections tied back in a low twist. With the green fur of the coat around her collar, the coat Nathan bought specifically to dress me and show me off to his friends, anyone would think she was me. Or I was her. It is confusing sometimes, and not altogether pleasant, trying to work out whether people think I am her double or she is mine. I suppose it depends on who you ask.

"Don't you want to know the surprise?" Nathan says, interrupting my thoughts. I had forgotten about this. Part of me is curious now that we are here, ready to be spoiled and treated to afternoon tea or champagne or a show. It is easy to get swept up in the exhibition. Everyone here is looking to escape into an imaginary world of idealness, visualize themselves in a new home, a new dress, owning a fancy refrigerator, illuminating their bedrooms with the glass light shades that hang, resplendently, around the Grand Hall.

I let Nathan lead us out of the main hall and into the Pillar Hall, a smaller space with rows of ornate marble Corinthian pillars and an elaborate ceiling emblazoned with rich decorative plaster-work. Little tables are laid out with crisp white covers, arranged with crockery and champagne coupes. A waiter comes to us, takes Nathan's name, and then leads us to a table at the edge of the room. It is a relief to be out of the noise of the Grand Hall and I enjoy looking around me at the other couples, the sprays of flowers at each table, the cakes and tea and wine that waiters in black tie are spreading through the room. It looks choreographed, a dance of nodding and smiling and order.

"My mother would have liked this place," Nathan says, dragging me back to attention. I would be perfectly happy to sit without talking, to watch the varieties of life around me. But I agree; I can also imagine his mother here, the beautiful dead woman with the bright blonde hair, always perfect, her makeup never smudged. She has no need for powder and undergarments that protect her clothes from sweat stains. I find myself wanting to be cruel again, to say something harsh and unnecessary to Nathan, but I stop myself. He has organized all this and he wants it to be special.

"She loved everything to be dainty and elegant," he continues. "Anything loud and vulgar upset her. Afternoon tea was her specialty, the tea just right, the cake light and airy. We always had to have cotton napkins, bright white and pressed."

"She sounds like a perfect mother," I say. "My mother would have taken to the bottle if she'd seen me or Olivia eating cake." He frowns. I know he doesn't like it when I talk about my mother. She is too real and upsetting, a wild, mad woman that doesn't fit into his ideal.

"I found another photograph of Mother the other day," he says, reaching into his jacket pocket. "I was clearing out papers in the boat and I found this one hidden among some programs from my concerts, the ones I played at before she . . ." His voice trails off, unable to say the words. Blowing gently on the photograph, his breath cleans off the lint from his jacket that has clouded the picture. It looks like he is sending her a kiss. He passes it to me.

There she is, standing next to a grand piano. A very small and wide-eyed little boy is seated on the piano stool. Nathan. It is hard to imagine that he is about to give a concert to a packed audience. He looks perfectly calm. But it is his mother who I can't stop looking at. She has very white hair, soft like a cloud, and her eyes are large with long, even eyelashes. It is her youth that really strikes me. She looks barely twenty, but of course she must be older. And just a few years after that photograph was taken she would be dead.

"I still can't believe she's gone," he says. "I remember the day it happened, when my father broke it to me, so gently, I simply couldn't understand what either of us had done to make her leave us."

"You were a child, Nathan. You were too young to understand death, how no one can control those things." I give back the photograph and take his hand. "There was nothing you or your father could have done to keep her alive."

I have tried asking him how his mother died. He doesn't like to talk about that, though. Instead, he likes to keep her memory alive with stories of how wonderful she was, how caring, how she made him feel like the most loved little boy in England. I envy him this. When I think of my mother, it is with guilt and anger. Guilt for hating every second of those monthly visits to Colney Hatch; anger at having to go in the first place. But then another feeling creeps in, slyly, cruelly. I am glad she is there, locked up, drugged too heavily to complain. It keeps her away from us; it gives me and Olivia the freedom to live our lives as we want.

When I look up from my plate, my mouth full of cake, I freeze. Nathan is holding out a ring. Silver, a dark red ruby encased in diamonds.

"This was my mother's engagement ring. She left it with us, a memory of how happy we were together. I want you to have it." He is looking at me with very earnest eyes. "I want you to be my wife."

The noise of the room seems to vanish and all I can hear is a loud whooshing inside my head. At the edges of my vision, the waiters appear to have slowed down, performing a long and fluid *adage* as they dance across the room. I look down at my plate, transfixed by a gem of pale pink icing. I need to say something, but the words are stuck in my throat. Finally, I raise my eyes.

"Nathan," I say. "I can't marry you."

All at once, I am afraid. His hands have clenched into tight fists and the skin on his neck is throbbing a mottled red. I know he is used to getting his way. But he gathers himself, readying for the next attack.

"It's too soon? You want to dance, I get that. I wouldn't get in the way of your career." He is trying to keep his voice calm, but I can hear the strain in the words.

"No, Nathan. It's not just that. I can't marry you." I push my chair away from the table. "Please don't ask me again."

He reaches across toward me, his hand finding mine. I pull away, standing abruptly. He looks shocked, and for a moment I feel a terrible guilt. I know I am supposed to say yes to him; this is what the girls in the dressing room gossip about, dream about. We have all imagined the scene a thousand times: the setting is perfect; he has surrounded me in idealness, an ideal home, an ideal life. But the feeling passes as soon as it arrives, and I know I need to get out of here.

I start moving, pressing my bag into my chest, weaving in and out of the waiters and the guests, avoiding a tower of cakes, a tray of champagne coupes. The crowds in the Grand Hall seem to bear down on me, the model homes and ideal kitchens looming large in a grotesque nightmare. A row of mannequins in silk evening dresses point their wooden arms at me as I run, the cloying floral smell of perfume thickening the air. It is only when I get outside, when I've run through the street and made it onto the bus, that I can breathe again.

Act Three

CHAPTER 14

Olivia

I never sleep the night before a first performance. I don't think Clara did either last night, judging by all her tossing and turning. She came in very late, out with the musicians, no doubt. At one point, I opened my eyes to see her at the window, the curtains drawn, looking out in to the night. I mumbled something and she returned to bed.

Coppélia has finally arrived and Sadler's Wells feels alive, delivery men going in and out, posters pasted onto the walls, the press sending their runners to collect first night tickets from the box office. This is the biggest production our Vic-Wells company has attempted, and Miss de Valois knows the pressure is immense. It is not only the cost of the production, which is significant and has required the support of the Camargo Society, but the knowledge that the critics will be out in force, waiting to pass judgment on Miss de Valois's success or failure in bringing one of the great Russian classics to London.

The whole cast take ballet class together this morning, packed like sardines along the barre. Miss Moreton leads the class, calling out the exercises with fast precision. There is no time to get left behind. Thankfully she keeps the barre simple today. There are too many of us to risk the *battements frappés* and *grands battements en cloche* flying off in the wrong direction, legs clashing and crashing. We work through our pliés and *tendus*, our *relevés* and *ronds de jambe*. It calms us all to follow this daily routine, establishing order through our legs, reassuring each muscle and tendon that tonight will go as planned, that our bodies will know exactly what they need to do.

Clara has a furious, focused expression on her face all class. She looks hardly present, as though she is fixed in some labyrinthine internal battle. But when we get into the center, she doesn't dance with her usual brightness, and it worries me. Her *adage* and *port de bras* droop a little and I notice that she hides herself at the back. Miss Moreton sees everything, though, and calls out sharply to her to lift her elbows. Clara seems to wake up and the next exercise is better, her pirouettes showing her usual sharp head and strong lifting out of the hips.

Nathan is playing the piano this morning. I have noticed a tension between Clara and him this past week, ever since our trip to the exhibition. She doesn't wait for him after class or rehearsal anymore, and she avoids his eye completely. He still stares at her though. It frustrates me, all this attention he wants from her, when she is clearly not interested. He should have known he couldn't catch her, couldn't keep her. My sister has always been restless. She used to sigh loudly and naughtily whenever she was bored in ballet class when we were younger, despite knowing Mother would tell her off on the bus journey home. She resented having to repeat an exercise over and over until the ballet mistress was happy. Clara was always ready to move and on and try the next step.

At the end of class, Miss de Valois wants to rehearse the Act One mazurka one last time. We change into our character shoes, the heels feeling strange after a class in soft blocks followed by pointe shoes, our toes moving more freely when released from the tight pink satin. We line up, finding our partners, and the music begins. I love the mazurka, the strong rhythm reflected in the stamp of our feet and the swoop of our arms into *épaulement*. Clara is always the best, though, her musicality finding the exact notes to rise and fall. We are a chorus, a corps de ballet, but still she stands out.

After a few counts of eight, Miss de Valois bangs her stick. Nathan stops playing and we all fall out of our movements.

"Clara, come up here," she calls. I turn to watch my sister hurry to the front of the room. Even Clara would never dawdle when our ballet mistress summons. But she doesn't look concerned; instead, there is a sharp look of defiance behind her gaze, as though she is daring us to challenge her.

"Watch how she does it," Miss de Valois tells us. "Listen to the music, watch how she finds the beat, becomes part of each note. The rest of you are not listening."

Nathan plays the introduction again and Clara starts dancing, on her own this time. Miss de Valois is right. None of the rest of us can become the music the way my sister can.

"Now everyone," she summons, and we join in, breathing into the steps, listening to the accent of the music. We watch Clara at the front the room as we dance, matching the stamp of our feet to hers.

"Better," Miss de Valois tells us at the end, when we are all sweating from the effort. "Costume call at five o'clock," she announces as we leave. It is no change from usual that the costumes are only just ready. We've had productions before where we were pinning ourselves into our tutus with minutes to go before the curtain rose. There are nearly always missing items, a headdress, perhaps, or a lace armband. I have two costumes in *Coppélia*, first the villager dress with a white frilly blouse underneath and the soft leather boots with a little heel. Later I change into a romantic-style tutu, white with a red sash, for one of Swanilda's friends.

I love the choreography at the end of Act One where we all hold hands in a line and sneak into Dr. Coppélius's house. He drops the key in the square and we have no qualms about breaking into his home. Lydia Lopokova is a very bold and lovable Swanilda, bossing us all around and enjoying the fun of her naughtiness. I am surprised Swanilda goes for someone like Franz. Stanley Judson is brilliant as Franz, all doe-eyed and pathetic, looking up at the doll Coppélia who sits in the balcony reading all day. I don't understand how Franz thinks she is real. Perhaps a more entertaining—albeit darker—version would be if Dr. Coppélius really did steal Franz's life and transfer it into his doll. It would serve him right.

The afternoon is rehearsal-free for most of us. Everyone seems to disappear, so I go for a walk through Clerkenwell, dropping down to the canal at Duncan Terrace Gardens. I walk as far as Sturt's Lock, turning around after watching a barge and tugboat slowly rising and falling through the barriers of the lock. I enjoy looking at the boats, some of them packed with crates, deliveries to be dropped off at London pubs and markets. As I walk, I like to imagine the journey they have made along the canal networks of the country, like veins and arteries, ending up here in the heart of our city. A few of the boats clearly haven't moved in a while, flowerpots resting on the roofs, laundry hanging out to dry. I remember Clara telling me that Nathan lived on one of these boats, renting it far more cheaply than he could find a flat. He made a deal with a retired old boatman whose wife wouldn't agree to live on the boat anymore; the old man had spent his life traveling the country along the canal, from warehouse to warehouse, and couldn't quite bring himself to sell this physical, nostalgic memory of his life. He installed a new engine, prepared it for sale, but at the last moment couldn't go through with it. Renting it out, keeping it close by, was a compromise. I hope I will feel like that about a home one day, somewhere special that I can build memories with Clara.

It is good to get out of the theatre, to calm my nerves. Sturt's Lock is eerily quiet, just the low clangs of metal and the hisses of steam whispering from the chimneys. It is hard to imagine the factory workers hidden inside the brick walls of the blackened buildings that line the water. The only evidence of their existence is a barge loaded up with stacks of wrought-iron bars ready to be carried along the web of waterways. But as I turn and start to walk back, the broken sound of boys fighting, their voices loud and rough, breaks into my path. I look toward the noise, strangely unsettled by the intrusion. Two young boys are in the water, their chests naked as they wrestle, their thin arms grabbing at each other in the slime of the cold and dirty water. I slow down, watching the way the water washes over their skin, hair sticking to their foreheads in greasy clumps. A green finger of mare's tail root clings to one of them, wrapping its tendrils around his arm. The two boys look feral, dangerous water nymphs emerging out of the muddy water. They seem entirely oblivious to the cold, their bodies alive and unafraid. It only takes me a second longer to realize this is just a game to them, their cries morphing into laughter. This is their affection, bold and physical; they grab at each other without shame, a primeval display of unapologetic power.

A whistle blows from above me, followed by the angry shout of a policeman. People drown in the canal all the time, foolish swimmers who think they are invincible to the dark swells and depths of the locks. Even walkers like myself are discouraged from the paths, seen as nuisances getting in the way of the trade and transport of the waterway. I watch as the boys swim fast to the edge of the canal, hauling themselves out and running, laughing, to where their clothes lie in the dust. They run with identical strides, throwing their shirts over their shoulders. They look like brothers, even their slim calves springing in exactly the same taut way as they move.

The policeman has walked away, and I hurry back toward the Islington Tunnel. It is the image of the two boys that stays with me as I get back to Sadler's Wells. There is something about the ripples of energy that danced from them, the green weeds of the canal that clung to their skin, the tangle of their limbs in the water, that makes me long for something unknown, something visceral and animal, something I can't quite define.

❄ ❄ ❄

When I return just after four o'clock, I don't take long to get into costume, but when I try to dance a few steps in the corridor outside the dressing room, the heeled boots for the villager dances feel stiff. They need dancing in a little more, breaking in until the leather is supple enough to move. I walk up to the Wells Room, but it is already being transformed into a reception room, high round tables with white cloths laid out across the space. I try the board room on the top floor. That is all the space I need to dance a little, to knead the shoes up and down in *relevés* and *retirés* until they soften.

I hear piano music coming from the room. I suddenly remember the last time I came across Nathan in there, how tempted I had been. Now that I have seen my sister's dismissal of him, I don't feel so guilty. Perhaps I too can have a moment of love; I deserve some affection, some admiration. I've worked for it, danced for it, starved myself as my mother told me I would need to do if I wanted to be beautiful. I need some recognition of all the sacrifices I have made.

Standing outside the door, I look down at myself. I am wearing a costume already; I've taken on a role. I haven't done my hair and makeup yet, but that is no matter. Pulling out my bun, I redo it, piling my hair on top of my head as Clara does. I close my eyes and try to imagine myself as my sister. What would she do? How would she talk to him? Would she wait for him to acknowledge her, or would she just walk straight in, go to him, kiss him?

I step into the room.

It is gloomy, the only light coming from above the piano. Nathan is staring down at his hands as he plays, shadows dancing across his face. He looks up as I reach the piano, and I see a look of surprise and then fear move through his eyes.

"We worked well together earlier," I say. I cannot falter. This is just a performance, I tell myself. I know how to do it. "It must be all that practicing we've done. You've taught me how to find the music in my movement."

I continue walking to him and then crouch at his side, leaning my arms across his legs.

"Clara," he falters, his voice uncertain.

My eyes widen nervously as I wait to see if he has realized who I am.

"Does this mean you've changed your mind?" he says, reaching for my hand.

I don't know what he means, but he sounds like he wants me to say yes. Looking up at him, I smile. He stands then and lifts me up with him, wrapping his arms around me. My lips have never been this close to anyone's before, not even in the ballets where we fold and bend from the waists, our partners holding on to our hips, drawing us close as we rise up from arabesques. Nathan's hands feel so different to the hands of the men in class, their grip firm and safe around our waists and thighs. His hands feel hot and alive, moving down my back, gripping my buttocks. He pulls me in tighter and I feel him moving, hard against my pelvis. I lift my chin and he kisses me, his lips rough, his tongue finding its way into my mouth. He tastes stale, like old coffee, and his teeth clash against mine. But I try to transform every moment into the fairy tale I was expecting, closing my eyes and imagining that this is me, and not my sister, who is being kissed and adored.

His breathing is faster now. I have an urge to pull away from him, to get his tongue out of my mouth. But I don't. I have dreamt of this and even though it is not exactly as I imagined, I will not waste it. He hands move between my legs, lifting up the weight of my skirt. There are layers of net, topped with a red apron, and he struggles to find my skin beneath all the material. I am not wearing tights, but as I feel his hands brush my thighs, his thumb reaching up to the edge of my knickers, I wish I had put on the full costume, with the tights and the leotard to protect me. I flinch, but then tell myself not to be stupid. This is what I have asked for; I am in control.

But then he moves my knickers aside and pushes his fingers inside me. I gasp and jerk away from him. My mouth is wet and there is a line of saliva running down my chin. I don't think it is mine.

"Clara," he says, reaching for me. "I thought that's what you wanted."

I don't know what to say. I push his hands off me. "I did. I do. Just not right now. I . . ."

"Yes?" he says, his hands returning again to my hips.

"I need to get ready for the performance." Extracting myself, I walk to the door, trying to stay calm. I want to run, but it would look strange, over the top. Right now I feel so foolish, my cheeks burning hot.

I open the door, the faint noises of the theatre downstairs returning. It is reassuring to hear the sounds of the stagehands and the musicians, even from a distance, muffled as though at half speed. A window out onto the street must be open nearby. I can hear a bus go by along Rosebery Avenue, the hard groan of the wheels. But then it disappears and the claustrophobic murmurs of the narrow corridor return, as though a door has been slammed shut and locked me in.

Nathan has caught me by the hand. I turn back to him, trying to pull away, but his grip is strong. He pushes me into the door frame, the lock digging into my back. Even with his breath steaming against my neck, all I can think in that second is that I hope my dress doesn't rip.

"You haven't answered my question, Clara," he says, his body pressing against mine.

"What question?" I say, turning my head to the side.

"You know what question. What is this? A test to see if you really wanted me?"

"I don't know what you mean." My voice is rising.

We both freeze. There is a sound of footsteps coming toward us. Nathan takes a step away from me and I run.

I go straight to the well, even without thinking: my feet guide me. I can't go back to the dressing room immediately. Clara will know something is wrong.

The heels of my boots echo against the steps down to the well. Thankfully no one else is there. I get down onto my stomach and dip my hands into the water. It swells then stills against my skin, giving away nothing. I haven't turned on the light, so just a faint glow spreads down from the top of the steps, fading until the corners of the room are plunged into darkness. It is a relief to see that none of my pointe shoes are floating across the water. I have found them here twice before, each time putting my nerves on edge, as if I am being followed. That same feeling lingers now and I keep rubbing my hands together in the water, washing away what I have done.

Then, with the cold traveling through me, I find stillness. I spread my fingers into the black, claiming this darkness, a hidden secret world where I can cleanse myself, wipe away the pretense, become Olivia once again. As the water cools me, I imagine green weedy fingers climbing up my arms, wrapping tendrils and twists and coils up and up until they find my throat. It should be terrifying, the darkness hiding the smooth porcelain of my skin. But I am not afraid. As I feel my body returning to me again, I know that I am different, stained inside with a new pattern, as though if you opened me up I'd be a painting of my desires. Unique. Spreading away from the identical design of my sister.

When I finally stand, my hands cold and sore, I realize that my costume is creased, the netting crumpled. I smooth it down as best I can and make my way back up the stairs, trying to find the composure and the focus that everyone expects of me.

* * *

Clara's gaze catches me in the mirror when I return to the dressing room. She raises her eyebrows, momentarily distracted from putting on the makeup that is scattered around her. "Got into a fight with your costume?" she asks.

I mumble something about my shoes being too stiff; I got carried away breaking them in. The cold suddenly hits my body, but I need to stay in costume until Miss de Valois has been to do her checks. Clara's green coat is further down the row of dressing tables, draped over a chair. I reach for it and wrap it around my shoulders. But as I curl up on my chair in the corner, making a start on my hair and makeup, I feel the heaviness of the coat pressing down on my shoulders. Clara may have said I can wear the coat as much as I like, but it isn't mine. Nathan gave her this coat, bought it for her, chose it specifically for her to wear. The guilt of what I just did chills me and I shiver, even in the warmth of the fabric.

When I am finished on my makeup, I tentatively put my hands into the pockets, trying to warm my fingers, which are still cold and stiff. The coat is indulgently soft, but I can't get warm; it is as though the fabric refuses to accept my skin. Slowly, as I dig my hands deeper, I touch the sharpness of two pieces of paper, a small scrap and a card. They are right at the bottom, almost hidden in the folds. One of them feels like a business card. Clara is at the other side of the room, talking loudly to Hermione and the others. Something tells me these are not for me, so I alter my position, leaning forward over the dressing table as I pull them out. The scrap of paper is just a line of poetry: *A lovely apparition, sent to be a moment's ornament.* The words make me shiver. *Lovely, apparition, moment, ornament.* These words are haunting, a little terrifying. They remind me of my mother when she was at her thinnest, less than eighty-four pounds. She thought she was beautiful, admiring the bones and sinews on her back in the mirror, the cords of her neck twisted so she could see herself.

I turn over the other piece of paper, a card, feeling the sharpness of the edges against my fingers. It is addressed to Clara. The handwriting is bold and round, the pen pressed deeply.

Call me at my hotel when you have made up your mind. I can make you a star.

Jacob Manton, the Atrium Suite at the Hotel Great Central

P.S. America will love you.

I slip the poetry and the card back into the pocket, my heart thumping. When Clara returns to our dressing table, I look up at her, scrutinizing her face. But there is nothing, no sign that she is hiding anything from me. Not even the giant revelation that she might be leaving me. I think of everything we have done together, right from the instant we were born, when we were children constructing elaborate games around the fallen trees in Hampstead Heath, when Father died, when Mother turned from us and forgot how to treat us like the children we were, when she was admitted to Colney Hatch. I can't imagine going forward without my sister. There is no part of my life that exists separate to Clara.

As I watch her finish her makeup, I feel another more complex uncertainty. Part of me wants her to leave, to let me be more than one of those identical twin ballerinas, the pretty Marionetta girls. But another, deeper, part of me is scared. What if she leaves and people realize that I am nothing without her? I don't know if I can be talented enough, strong enough, beautiful enough, without my sister to reflect back at me. Without her I might just go back to being ordinary Olivia Smith.

CHAPTER 15

Samuel

The orders are coming in even faster than before and there has been no time for Mr. Frederick to consider Samuel's sketches. Samuel, too, has hardly been able to think of them, rushing as he does between home, the workshop and the theatres and ballet schools where he delivers shoes. A new ballet company is forming, Les Ballets 1933, and they, too, are in need of shoes. They will not be in London until June, Samuel has been told, but the Russian-born George Balanchine has heard about Freed and has given them advance warning of his needs. And dancers for the Ballet Club have been asking for more shoes, so Samuel has been busy creating shoes, labeling the soles with the names of more and more ballerinas, traveling across London to deliver them. They have a new shop assistant, Milly Bell, who works with Mrs. Dora upstairs, sorting the shoes, cutting the ribbons, learning how to fit the dancers who come in. She has had to learn quickly to keep up with the growing numbers of dancers who seek out their shop. He has heard Mr. Frederick say to his wife that they also need to hire a delivery boy; Samuel is needed in the workshop. Samuel isn't sure how he feels about that. The deliveries are exhausting, but how else would he get to see Olivia, to watch her dance in class and rehearsal when he arrives at a lucky moment?

Tonight is the first night of *Coppélia*, and he longs to be there. He has seen enough snippets of rehearsals to excite him, and he loves the comedy, the joyful peasant dances, the angry Dr. Coppélius who wants nothing more than for his creation to come alive. Samuel has some sympathy. But he is unlikely to get a ticket for tonight's performance. It is the talk of the town, and all the seats will have been taken. He will wait, he tells himself as he sits as his workbench, his hands moving securely over the shoes. One of the later performances will have some tickets still available. He might be able to afford one of the cheaper tickets, just over a shilling for a seat in the amphitheater.

Halfway through the afternoon, Mrs. Dora calls him up to the shop floor. He stands there, blinking in the light that reflects from the mirrors and the sparkling pink of the shoes.

"Do you like ballet?" she asks him as she rolls the pink ribbons into a tight spool. It seems like an absurd question. Of course he likes ballet. How could he not like watching his shoes come alive, the costumes that he would like to design one day, Olivia floating across the stage? He nods.

"Yes, I always like to watch when I have a chance." He hopes he hasn't said the wrong thing, that this isn't some sort of test to see how much time he wastes when he delivers shoes at the theatres. But Mrs. Dora isn't like that. She doesn't speak in riddles. If she had a problem, she would just ask, directly and clearly.

"Good," she replies, looking up at him. "Frederick and I have tickets for tonight's *Coppélia*, a gift from Ninette for all the shoes we've delivered for the production. But we don't really like going to the ballet, not after a long day here. Frederick is too tired; he'll just fall asleep."

Samuel feels suddenly very awake. He doesn't speak, just in case he says something to make her change her mind.

"So, here is a ticket if you want it." She hands it over to him. It is just a little piece of paper, but it has immeasurably changed his day. It should be edged with gold, not this flimsy white and red card. "Milly is taking the second one, so perhaps you two can go together."

He looks over to where Milly is sorting shoes into size order on the shelves. She turns to him, a shy smile on her face. Samuel is confused by her wary expression. He doesn't know whether she is nervous he'll say yes, that she'll be duty-bound to stay stuck to him all night. Or maybe she's afraid he'll dismiss her and go on his own, or not go at all. Samuel has no experience with these things.

"Well, that's settled then," cuts in Mrs. Dora. She makes the decision for them. "Samuel, you'll meet Milly outside the theatre at 7 p.m. You both need to go home first, to get changed, so you can leave early today."

"Thank you, Mrs. Dora," Milly says, her cheeks blushing prettily. Samuel has never really looked at her before. The clean and shining world of the shop floor is not for him. She is very small but soft and round, her face a smooth circle. Her blonde hair is neatly curled, short and pinned up around her face like a frame. The collar of her white shirt is high, a navy ribbon tied loosely underneath, and her skirt sits neatly over curved hips. Even her hands are small, Samuel notices as she turns back to stocking the shelves: small but soft and smooth, the skin plump.

✳ ✳ ✳

Mrs. Dora closes the shop early, sending him out at three o'clock with a final delivery of shoes to Sadler's Wells which he must drop off before he goes home to get changed. He notices that Milly has already gone. Perhaps she lives further away than him or needs longer to get ready. Samuel doesn't know what he is supposed to wear, as he can't possibly match the smart suits and evening dress of the audiences he has seen going in and out of the theatres. He considers asking Mrs. Dora for her advice, but he doesn't want to seem inexperienced, uncultured.

She seems to read his mind.

"Do you have a jacket you can wear?" she asks as he walks through the shop to say thank you once again. "It doesn't have to be an evening jacket. Times have changed, you know. Many people turn up at the theatre in exactly the same clothes they've been wearing all day at work. It's a good thing, in my opinion. We can't be expected to spend all that money on both a ticket and a dress. So, don't be embarrassed if the person you end up seated next to is looking all fancy in evening dress. A day jacket will be fine."

Samuel nods. He has a jacket. He wore it to his interview with the Freeds. And he has a clean shirt, a waistcoat, and a tie that he made himself from scraps of silk that were being sold for pennies on Exmouth Market one day last year. He thinks he can make himself look respectable if he asks the landlady to let him borrow her trouser press. He'll need to give his one pair of smart shoes a good polish too.

✳ ✳ ✳

He arrives at Sadler's Wells just after four o'clock, weighed down by the bag of pointe shoes. Hopefully they don't need the shoes for tonight's performance, he thinks. It will be tight timing for the dancers to sew on the ribbons, darn them, wear them in until they are soft enough to be quiet on the stage. The main door on Rosebery Avenue is busy with deliveries of wine for the reception. Samuel has a ticket for the stalls, the best seats, but he knows he won't find the confidence to go into the Wells Room for the reception. They will all be far too finely dressed in there. And what if someone recognizes him, the pointe shoemaker apprentice lingering where he is not invited.

Samuel walks around to Arlington Street, avoiding a pile of bricks abandoned by one of the builders who occasionally show a reluctant commitment to continuing with the renovation. The theatre may have been rebuilt two years ago but the rest of the street remains tired. Samuel finds a door open. Discarded cigarettes are scattered about the pavement where stagehands have escaped to find a moment's peace before the chaos of first night. Inside, the corridors feel alive, the preparations for the show building and building to the inevitable climax when the curtain opens at half past seven this evening. For any passerby walking past the worn and sagging buildings on Arlington Street, it would be impossible to imagine the scenes of creation and preparation going on inside the theatre walls.

He goes straight to Wardrobe and delivers the shoes. It is busy in there, a seamstress stitching on last-minute additions to the costumes and dancers searching through the cupboards for hairpins and makeup brushes they can spirit away to their dressing rooms. When he has finished, he lingers outside the dressing rooms, imagining Olivia is in one of them, preparing for the night's performance. He doesn't hear anything, so he moves quietly through the theatre, unnoticed, peering into the Wells Room, which has transformed for the refreshments. Samuel keeps on moving up the stairs to the top floor, drawn by a desire to find her, to glimpse her just once before she appears before him onstage. He is oblivious to the closeness of the air, the smell of damp and musk, as he moves steadily forward through the narrow upstairs corridor that houses offices and small rehearsal rooms.

There are voices at the far end of the corridor. He stops and listens. One of the voices is familiar: Olivia Marionetta. But the man, the other voice, speaks to her. He calls her Clara.

"You haven't answered my question, Clara," he hears the man say. But it is not Clara who replies; it is Olivia. Her voice is rising. She sounds afraid. Samuel takes a step closer toward them. There she is, his Olivia, pressed against the door frame, her face turned to the side. He thinks he recognizes the man: it is the pianist, the one who plays for their ballet classes. Samuel has seen him often with Clara, the two of them leaving the theatre together, sometimes hand in hand when they think no one is looking. He doesn't understand what is happening. Surely the man doesn't think it is Clara in front of him now, that it is Clara he is pressing into the door like that, breathing into her neck?

He takes another step toward them, the tread of his feet louder now. They seem to freeze, the pianist pulling away. Olivia runs past him, not looking up, the lace of her skirt flying behind her as she moves. The pianist turns and sees Samuel. He narrows his eyes and sighs in frustration, running his hands through his hair. For a moment, neither of them moves, but then he walks toward Samuel, his shoulder knocking into him as he pushes past.

Samuel wants to grab the man and shake him. He wants to shout at him how stupid he is. How can he think Olivia is Clara? Does he really, properly, see either of them? How he can he love when he is blind to who they both are? But of course Samuel doesn't do any of these things. He watches the pianist walk away before he heads back down the stairs and leaves.

* * *

Milly is waiting for him outside the theatre when he arrives just before seven o'clock. Samuel is distracted, upset about what he saw, but he smiles nervously when he sees her and tries to be friendly. He doesn't know how to behave. This isn't a date: Mrs. Dora wouldn't have thought of it like that and would never put Milly in that situation. He still feels an expectation, though, a nervous tension hovering between them. It would have helped if they knew each other a little better, but they've hardly spoken, just a few nods as they pass each other in the shop, Samuel holding the door for her, Milly bringing him a cup of tea a few times when she is making one for Mr. and Mrs. Freed. She has dressed up for the occasion, wearing a plum-colored crimped chiffon dress with frills around the hem and the collar. Her white fur stole sits high around her neck, her bright blonde hair resting above in tidy curls. Although she is too small and round to look fashionable, not at all like those glamorous photographs of Hollywood stars, when she smiles at him he relaxes a little. He has never been on a night out with a woman before, but this arrived so suddenly and unexpectedly that he hasn't had the time to get anxious.

Although Milly loves ballet and theatre, she has never been to Sadler's Wells before. She tells him about the theatres she has been to with her mother: the new Mercury Theatre, Drury Lane, the Old Vic. As the two of them walk in, get their tickets checked at the door, she talks with a natural cheerfulness, filling Samuel's silences and nervous replies. She went to ballet classes when she was younger, but stopped when she was fourteen, accepting that her body wasn't suited to the movements. Samuel finds it hard to tell how old she is, her round rosy cheeks giving her a youthful doll-like look. But she must be at least eighteen for Mrs. Dora to have given her a theatre ticket and sent her out with just him, unchaperoned. Samuel feels a weight of responsibility toward her, and offers her his arm as they walk in to the crowded foyer.

"My ballet teacher said I would be more suited to cabaret or musical halls. I guess she meant I wasn't really elegant enough to be a ballerina. It's okay, though. Fitting the dancers for their pointe shoes is exciting enough for me now." She says this with a bright smile, not a hint of regret.

They walk straight to their seats in the stalls. The foyer is too busy and there is nowhere to stand without feeling awkward or getting in the way of the attendants who sell little packets of Hunter's fruits and nuts, their harnessed wicker trays packed with sweets, chocolates and cigarettes. Already the auditorium is filling, a noisy medley of voices, instruments, the rustle of dresses as women shuffle their way down the rows of seats. Men and women light up their cigarettes as they wait for the performance, ushers politely reminding them that there must be no striking of matches once the performance starts.

Samuel buys them a program from an usher who walks along the rows, and the two of them read it together, Samuel pointing out names of dancers he makes shoes for, Milly asking him questions about the ballet, the rehearsals, the costumes. He tells her everything he knows and she is fascinated by the story of Swanilda and Franz, how they plan to be married at the Harvest Festival, how she shakes an ear of wheat to her head to see if he loves her. If it rattles, then he truly is in love with her. However, she hears nothing. And perhaps the wheat tells the truth, for Franz is enraptured by the doll Coppélia, who he thinks is a real woman. So much so that he creeps into Dr. Coppélius's house to try to woo her. The old man drugs him and tries to steal his life-energy in order to magically bring his precious doll to life. Poor Dr. Coppélius is tricked by Swanilda, who has dressed up as the doll and pretends to be Coppélia coming to life. It all ends happily, with Swanilda revealing the trick and forgiving her fiancé. It has taken a lively, naughty young woman to teach the men that there is more to women than dull, passive beauty.

Milly laughs at that. "That should be a word of warning for all those young men who stare at photographs of movie stars all day. Greta Garbo, Joan Crawford. My brother has a whole stack of them that he buys from Woolworths: Mae West, Katharine Hepburn, Bette Davis. I don't know how any woman is ever going to live up to his standard now. Even those actresses don't look like that when they've taken off their makeup each evening."

Samuel is thrilled to hear her talk this way, dissecting the beauty of these women just like the construction of a pointe shoe. For him, the shoe is just as beautiful before he turns it the right way out, the folds and stitches and glue hidden underneath the perfection of the satin. When he says this to Milly, she laughs again, a jolly, light sound that he enjoys. He is glad to have her here with him. They are surrounded by very smart-looking men and women, many of them in silk dresses and black tie despite what Mrs. Dora had said. Without Milly he would have felt out of place, too large and too common for these seats. But her bright smile, her brilliant blonde hair, her fascination for everything around her, makes him start to relax.

Finally the conductor, Constant Lambert, walks to the pit and bows to the audience. As he dips his head the energy in the theatre changes, as though the air is charged with electricity, pulsing dangerously as it waits for the curtains to open. The clapping is loud and hard around Samuel, and he can imagine the dancers bending and stretching in the wings, pounding their feet into the ground, using the volume of the applause to disguise the final sounds of their warm-up.

* * *

The rest of the evening passes in a dream, a story brought to life. And of course it is Olivia whom he watches most of all, waiting for each moment that she returns to the stage. He is impatient during the opening dances from Swanilda and Franz and he is overjoyed when the friends of Swanilda enter. Olivia is among them, smiling so brightly as she dances. There is so much jumping, he notices, her feet moving fast in his shoes. He doesn't know how she manages to do it all without her face showing any effort. It is as though her legs are moving by magic, conjured to life by a spell.

At the end, as he walks Milly back to her home in Islington where she lives with her parents and brother, he finds it hard to concentrate on her chatter. He is still back there, in the stalls, watching his Olivia.

CHAPTER 16

Clara

I linger in the dressing room at the end of the performance, waiting until there is no one left but me. There is a party in the Wells Room, and I know I should attend. All the dancers will be there, as well as the usual critics and photographers. We know we are more likely to get a mention in the next day's papers if we make an appearance at the party afterwards, dressed in our evening best. The trick is to find Arnold Haskell, one of the Camargo Society founders, and let him maneuver us through the heaving room of mustached men. But I need to make a decision. I have a choice to make, the biggest choice of my life. I could continue as I am, dancing with the Vic-Wells, enjoying the opportunity to be part of this fast growth of British ballet. Or I could take this gift that Jacob Manton has offered me, and leave. Now, more than ever, it feels right. It frightened me how Nathan's proposal made me imagine my life. How easy it would be to slip into mundanity, Nathan controlling every decision.

Mr. Manton approached me last night after the second dress rehearsal for *Coppélia*, and I have to say that I was impressed he had worked out which of the Marionetta twins he was looking for. This season he has been a regular presence, watching us in *Pomona* and *The Birthday of Oberon*, even coming into class one day. Miss de Valois did not look so delighted about that, but she couldn't exactly say no when he is a friend of the Camargo Society and promising to donate some large sums. He has been clever, gradually making himself familiar around Sadler's Wells. So when he came up to me, I wasn't affronted. Quite the opposite, in fact. All I could think about was this is my chance. This is how I escape Nathan. This is how I stop hating myself every time I join him in the theatre foyer, smiling absurdly as he leads me to the evening he has planned.

Jacob Manton is an agent from America. He represents movie stars and dancers, actors and comedians. He finds models among the masses, draws them out and makes them shine. He can spin gold from straw, he told me last night, which made me slightly worried that I am the straw. But apparently gold is just around the corner if I want it. And he knows the ballet world: he is currently working on George Balanchine, persuading him to set up a dance school and company in San Francisco.

He was waiting for me in the foyer, his coat folded tidily over his arm. I was struck by the neatness of his trousers, the way they fell in sharp lines down to spotless black shoes. We took a taxi to the Hotel Great Central in Marylebone and a waiter found us the best table in the courtyard, an indoor extravaganza of shining glass, exotic plants, a grand piano, opulent golden seating. I had never been there before last night, this vast atrium with warm lighting reflecting off the marble, and wished I had dressed more smartly rather than just throwing on my green coat over my dress in an unthinking rush. Olivia had worn it earlier in the day on the way to the theatre, but I doubted she would object to me taking it back just for the evening.

Manton ordered us champagne with a pretty selection of cakes and sandwiches as well as jams in the brightest of colors. The waiter looked a little surprised by the order, but Mr. Manton laughed.

"I'm American. I need to try all these funny British delicacies before you kick me out for breaking all the rules." He was quick to put me at ease, with his wide smile and comic mannerisms. Everything entertained him.

He gushed about the ballet, the Vic-Wells, everything Ninette de Valois is doing to put British ballet on the map. And he gushed about me. My artistry, my musicality, my eyes, my legs, my stage presence, my *allegro*, my pirouettes. It was exhausting listening to him. I kept trying to interrupt, to at least thank him for his compliments, but he wouldn't let me. He had to get to his climax.

"And so I want you to come with me to America. I have watched you perform, and I think you need more. You need to dance, yes, but you also need to act, to model, to shine on Broadway, to be delivered into the hands of the best Hollywood directors. You can make your career your own in America, and you can be central to the development of American ballet. We need more dancers like you, dancers America will adore."

He was sitting forward in his seat, his dark eyes boring into mine, his hands pressed firmly into the table. I held his gaze; there was nothing in it to intimidate me, just the promise of change and excitement.

Slowly, he sat back, crossed his legs, his eyes finally leaving me. "And you'll be paid twenty times what you're paid now."

"You don't know that," I said, laughing a little at the extravagance of it.

He looked at me again, totally serious. "Yes, I do. It would be my agency paying you. We'd represent you, and for the first year your contract would be fixed. Sixty pounds a week."

I almost choked on my sandwich. That was more than twenty times what I was paid here. It seemed absurd that I could arrive unknown in America and make that sort of money.

He continued, graciously pretending to ignore my reaction. I tried to regain my composure, taking small sips from the champagne coupe. American women were probably far more sophisticated around discussions of money. "After the first year, we'd renegotiate payment. It may be you're doing so well by then that you prefer the agency to take a percentage of each engagement's pay. We'd put you up in a lovely apartment in New York, though you're likely to be on the road a lot for tours, so I can write in a guarantee of first-class hotel suites wherever you travel. Something like this, eh?" he said, gesturing around him at the brilliance of the courtyard bar.

I hesitated, unsure how to frame my first question. I wasn't sure what I wanted the answer to be.

"And it would be just me you wanted? I would be going alone?"

Manton tilted his head to one side, studying my face. He was definitely observant. He knew this wasn't a straightforward question.

"Look, obviously I've thought about it," he said. "I've imagined bringing the two of you, introducing America to the two identical twin ballerinas. It would be exciting. We would make headlines. There would be a real media thrill, the type you just don't get here in England. But it wouldn't last. Not if that was how we sold you, advertised you. One of you would get sick of it and want to go home. And then we'd have blown it. No," he said, leaning forward again, "we need to do this differently. We need to start with just you, make you a star in your own right. Then maybe, if your sister is interested, she could join you for a few seasons."

I nodded slowly, liking this idea. For the first time in my life I felt as though something was being decided that was for me, just me. I had another question, though, one I was longing to understand.

"And why me? Why did you choose me and not Olivia?"

"Clara, your sister's gorgeous, obviously. She dances like a dream. But I've watched her too, and I don't think she'd last a week in America. She wants ballet and only ballet. She wants to do her morning class, rehearse, perform, repeat it all again. She's a purist, living for the ballet. But you, I think you're different. I think you want to try everything and be everywhere. I think you want fame. Your sister, well, she wants fame too, but in a different way. She wants a mysterious, aloof kind of fame. She wants to be a prima ballerina."

He was right; we both knew it. But what I didn't know was whether I could leave her. Could I get on that boat and know, for the first time, that I would be drawing my own path, one that didn't involve Olivia? I did want to say yes, I really did. But it was too big a question to decide at eleven o'clock in the evening after a glass of champagne.

Mr. Manton could tell what I was thinking. He took out his card and scribbled a note, handing it to me across the table. "Think on it. I don't need an answer until the middle of April. If you said yes, you'd join me in the summer."

"That's just a few weeks," I said, biting my lip anxiously. It felt ridiculous that I was to make this decision so quickly. All I could think about was how I was going to tell Olivia. And there was

Mother. I didn't know if I could leave Olivia to brave those monthly visits alone. It would be irresponsible, dangerous even. Mother had always had a stronger hold over Olivia, her words eating away at her, worrying her. Without me there to balance out those stinging criticisms, I didn't know if she would cope.

"You'll be surprised how quickly you make up your mind," he replied. "Take a day and imagine yourself in a year's time. For half the day, imagine you have stayed in London, with your sister, with the Vic-Wells. For the other half of the day, imagine you have decided to come to America. That you have a schedule set out for the next month: performances on Broadway, modeling for a fashion brand, perhaps a screen test for a movie role, an appointment with a group of dancers to help set up an American ballet school. Try to work out how you feel about each future. Which one makes you anxious, nervous, depressed? Which one makes you excited?" He stood up and offered me his hand. "Call me here when you've made up your mind."

I wanted to stuff those remaining cakes into a handkerchief to take home to Olivia, but I didn't. Making a good impression mattered so much to me, and I longed to emulate the sophisticated mystery of the dancers he must have assumed I could be.

He walked with me to the lobby and asked the concierge to call me a taxi on his account. There was just something about him that reminded me of my father, a steady certainty that had surrounded him until the last weeks in the hospital when he could barely recognize us. But Mr. Manton was different in every other way; loud, confident, his hair shining from brilliantine, a big smile that showed his large white teeth. He was a neat man, his suit perfectly pressed and tailored, his shoes so clean that they shone. I enjoyed watching him flirt with the concierge, as he had with the waiter, a kind, warm flirtation. He made you want to be part of his circle, as though his hands lit up everything he touched.

* * *

Wiping away the bright stage lipstick and then reapplying a softer shade, I decide that I can't sit here all night, waiting for some revelation to fall upon me. I get changed into my evening dress, the last one left on the rail now that all the other girls are already at the party. My reflection gazes back at me. There I am, looking like a bolder, more beautiful version of myself, my dress a bright blue silk, falling in a bias cut over my hips. With my dark makeup still bold around my eyes, I look like one of those postcard pictures of movie stars, otherworldly, untouchable. Right now, I can imagine myself in New York, Hollywood, on the screen, in a magazine. This dressing room, with its chaotic piles of old pointe shoes, feels too small.

There is music and the busy hum of voices coming from the Wells Room, and I join them. The room is transformed from the sweaty studio of our morning ballet class into this party of beautifully dressed dancers, musicians, patrons, rich old women with jewels hanging from their wrists and fingers, pearls encircling their necks like collars. It is still sweaty, but now with the heavy musk of scent and powder. I join Olivia and the other girls who are standing in a cluster, not yet finding the courage to start weaving their way between the guests, smiling for the critics and photographers. None of our dresses are expensive, except Hermione's perhaps, but we know how to wear them to make them work. That is our reward for all those hours of exercises at the barre.

I glance around the room, trying not to fidget with the hair that I have re-pinned in a more fashionable shape after the tight bun required onstage. I see that Nathan is here, talking to a group of men by the drinks' table. He is nodding, listening to an older man go on about something, but I can tell his attention isn't quite there. Instead, he keeps glancing into the room as though he is looking for someone. It is probably me he is trying to find; I have been avoiding him since his proposal, terrified of a repeat. I know I should have ended it with him weeks ago, but I couldn't find the courage to shake him off; it was easier to accept his gifts and attentions. And now he wants to trap me, to bind me to him with a ruby ring. I cannot give up everything I dream of to settle down to a life of marriage. He said that I wouldn't need to give up my career, but I've seen it before, dancers determined that nothing will change when they marry but who are pregnant within months and picking out linens for their nursery. Thinking back to Jacob Manton, his advice of living half a day imagining each alternative to my future, I know I don't need to live half a day imagining a marriage to Nathan. I know it would be impossible. When I remember all those nights spent rehearsing together, his desire to make me perfect, his control over every weekend's plan and night out, how much he kept me for himself, I feel sick.

I know I should at least speak to him. I don't want to be cruel; he has done nothing wrong except want me to love him. But his just isn't the type of love I can let into my life.

Excusing myself from the girls, I squeeze my way through the room. "Nathan, how did tonight go for you?" I ask, coming up to his group and nodding to the men around him. They seem to understand that he is to be released from their conversation, that the company of one of the Vic-Wells ballerinas trumps theirs. He walks with me to the edge of the room. I repeat my question, something easy and neutral to start us off.

"It was fine. Constant kept us all together and that rehearsal after class today really helped you dancers keep to the rhythm." Already I am finding him irritating, his commentary on the dancing unnecessary. I don't think he means to annoy me; that is the problem. Increasingly, though, I am finding that everything he says jars, as if we are shouting at each other from different rooms. It is sad, really, considering how many hours we used to fill with our endless chatter. Maybe this is what happens when you fall out of love.

"And you," he says. "Did you enjoy yourself?" His tone surprises me. It isn't a kind question; it has bite, as though he is trying to make a point. I ignore it as best I can.

"Yes, it was wonderful. And Lydia was hilarious, even more so than in rehearsal. You must have heard the audience. They were in stitches when she pretended to be the doll, rolling her eyes at Dr. Coppélius."

He doesn't smile. "What do you want, Clara?"

I sigh. This is more difficult than I imagined.

"Nathan, you know I am fond of you. I am sorry I can't marry you. I can't marry anyone right now. But I had hoped we could move on and be friends."

"Really? You want to be friends. And what was that this afternoon then?"

"This afternoon?"

But he isn't looking at me anymore. He is staring at the door and his face has gone an awful white. I start to turn, to look where he is looking, but he grabs me above the elbows and stops me.

"Just make up your mind, okay." And then he leaves, pushing his way through the crowd and disappearing into the gentlemen's bathrooms. I turn to look toward the door, to see who it is that made him go that ghastly shade. But the space has already filled again with new guests, the room shifting and changing as each group divides and reunites, and I walk back to find the girls, grabbing a glass of wine on the way. I move too fast through the crowds, wine spilling over onto my hand and splashing dark shadows onto the silk of my dress.

Nathan asked me to make up my mind. But I am already entirely decided on that question. I will not be marrying Nathan Howell, or anyone for that matter. I don't know how he could possibly have interpreted me any other way. Something keeps stopping me from telling Olivia about his proposal. Maybe because I don't like to think about it. If I don't mention it, perhaps it will all go away. I will tell her tonight, I think, once we are both home and in bed.

"Where's Olivia?" I ask Hermione when I join them again. Hermione, I notice, is looking radiant in a long silver dress, the back scandalously low. She always has admirers, but there are more than the usual number of stares tonight, a musician from a film company lingering close by.

"Oh, she left a moment ago. Probably gone home. You know how she is."

I do know how likely this is. But tonight I am disappointed. I want to walk home with her, like we always used to do before Nathan started to monopolize me; I want to open up to her about all these strange changes in my life. I know I have been distant recently, and I need to remedy that before I decide on America. She cannot think it is because of her. It would horrify me if she misinterpreted my journey toward America and all its promises as a desire to leave her. I know how sensitive she can be.

* * *

Somehow, I arrive home before Olivia. It is late, almost one in the morning, and I have been thinking up ways of explaining everything to her the whole way home. But she gets in just after me.

"Where have you been?" I ask her, surprised.

"Just out, walking. I couldn't sleep." She looks exhausted.

We get ready for bed quickly, splashing water on our faces. Although we both still have dark eye makeup staining our skin, it is too late for us to care. I try to start a conversation, but she is so silent, her eyes glazing over. Now is not the time.

I am almost asleep when I hear her get out of her bed. In an instant, she has climbed into mine, tucking herself in, pressing herself against my back. She is warm, and I nestle closer to her. We fall asleep like that, wrapped up together as we used to do every night when we were younger, before Mother went to Colney Hatch, before we found that we could breathe easier when it was just us. Two sisters, together. I don't know how I will be able to break that apart.

CHAPTER 17

Nathan

Nothing goes right for Nathan Howell today. Miss Moreton snaps at him twice during ballet class. He is playing the wrong type of polonaise for the *petit allegro*; his tarantella is too fast for the pirouettes. And then there is Clara. She dances the mazurka demonstration perfectly, every tiny movement an extension of the music. How can she dance like that, finding the heart of his music with such ease, and for them not to be made for each other? When she comes into the boardroom later that afternoon where he is practicing, he is overwhelmed. Finally, after this week of silence, she is responding. He has the ring still; he carries it everywhere he goes. As he kisses her, he thinks of it there in his jacket pocket. But he doesn't have the chance to offer it to her again, for almost as soon as she arrives, she is gone again. She leaves him frustrated, cold, angry.

He dresses for the performance with a full mind that darts from place to place. Slowing his fingers as he buttons up his shirt, he focuses on every little movement: he needs to force himself to calm down if he is to be ready to play. Nathan loves the music, the choreography fitting better than so many of these modern ballets where the score and the dance have to be forced to work together with no care for the nuance of the rhythm. He is angry that he is going into the first performance feeling so unsettled. It is not as he planned it. He has imagined a very different scenario, him confident and assured, kissing Clara in the wings, reminding her to take off her engagement ring before going onstage. She was to have looked down in delight at her hand, hardly bringing herself to slip off the ring. But, reluctantly, lovingly, she would have done it, holding it briefly to her lips before giving it to him for safekeeping while she danced.

But now she has made him feel lost, disoriented. Nothing is going as he had so carefully and indulgently imagined.

※ ※ ※

Settling at the piano in the orchestra pit, he finds the pace of his breathing. He looks over the score, not that he needs it; he knows the entire ballet by heart. The piano sits behind the harps and from his position he can see out into the auditorium. It is filling quickly and he is calmed by watching the seats changing from uniform red to a portrait of richly dressed benefactors, colored in furs, silks, pearls.

Suddenly, as though a memory were surfacing hard and fast from the depths, he is hit by another wave of panic, the day's onslaught of confusion and stress never-ending. He feels his heart racing, a shock of sweat breaking out under his armpits.

He catches sight of a woman ushering her two children, a girl and a boy, along the rows of the dress circle. A man follows. Then they are out of his sight, too far stage right for him to see. But her face is still clear in his mind, imprinted there like a flash from a camera. Tall and slim, bright white hair, a long sloping neck, dressed in the sort of simple elegance he remembers. And she has the same quiet beauty, her hand on her children's shoulders with a light touch, a reassurance that she is just behind them.

But of course it can't be his mother. That is impossible. He has conjured up visions of her funeral so many times since she left, the details shifting and changing. Sometimes it takes place on a bright summer's day, the coffin showered with huge white lilies. At other times it is inside a dark and gloomy church, mourners following the coffin, black veils covering their faces. But there is one constant, no matter how the images align themselves: his mother is dead and his father and grandparents weep by her grave.

He has kept all her cards and notes, the little words of encouragement she would write to him before each performance. They are packed neatly into a box that he keeps safely in his boat on the canal. He had to fight to get them out of his father's hands in those early weeks when the house felt like a silent tomb. His father tried to burn everything, every last memory of his wife. Any object that could remind him of her was too painful; he could not bear to keep those remembrances alive. But Nathan reacted differently, grabbing everything he could and storing it safely in a large trunk under his bed. That was one of the reasons he moved out of his father's house in Richmond when he was nineteen years old and he knew he would go mad if he had to stay there a day longer. He needed the space to remember his mother as he wished, and, to make matters worse, his father was drawing further and further away from him. Once Nathan's piano career started to lose the star quality it had attracted when he was a child, his father's interest began to wane into a tired indifference. He died two years ago, alone, miserable, too bitter to find the courage to write to his son. The words of apology never came.

Perhaps he knew that it was too late to ask for forgiveness: to Nathan for giving up on him; to Elizabeth for his cruelty. From the day Cedric and Elizabeth married, their relationship was broken. The damage continued to fester every year, fueled by Cedric's ever-present parents and their insistence that they knew best about how to run a home, look after a child, obey a husband. And Elizabeth was so young, her parents too far away to offer any support. They had moved to Shanghai for her father's work as soon as their daughter was married. If they had any idea of the life into which Elizabeth was walking, they chose ignorance over truth.

Between Cedric and his parents, every minute of Elizabeth's life was controlled. She could only go to the hair salons approved by her mother-in-law, shop at the same dressmakers, feed her child the same meals Cedric had been given as an infant. When Elizabeth was pregnant, it had been unbearable: regular trips to the family doctor with Mrs. Howell hovering at her side, a notebook recording every detail. During Nathan's birth, she had been there, instructing the midwives and ignoring Elizabeth's tears of frustration when she refused to place the child in her arms. Elizabeth had found herself relieved when war began and Cedric went off to France. Finally, she thought, she could have some time with her son, just the two of them playing with the little figurines they liked to buy together, a purchase permitted by the elder Mrs. Howell. But instead, the pressure from her parents-in-law grew, Mrs. Howell swooping in and taking up residence in their home. When she found old copies of the Women's Social and Political Union's newspaper, *The Suffragette,* in Elizabeth's desk, she was apoplectic, accusing her of being unwomanly, loose, a stain on civilized society. She watched Elizabeth even more carefully after that, following her to the shops, keeping track of the household accounts, checking the post as it arrived every day. For Elizabeth, it was only when she listened to her son playing the piano that she found any peace, letting the simple beauty of music transport her far from the claustrophobia of her home.

But then everything shifted like an opera ascending toward the final act of a tragedy, and she could no longer pretend that this was a normal life. It was a year after the war had ended, when Cedric was home and her parents-in-law had finally moved back to their own house in Twickenham. She slipped out one day when Nathan was occupied in a rehearsal and went to watch the crowds outside Parliament: the first female MP was taking her seat inside walls that for so long had been reserved for men. Elizabeth could not bear to stay away, not when Nancy Astor's success reminded her how to dream of a different life. But when she returned home a few hours later, Cedric refused to speak to her. As she closed the door of her bedroom, she heard a key turning in the lock on the other side. He kept her in that room for two days and two nights, ignoring her cries every time he appeared with a plate of food. Nathan spent hours listening outside her door, his face blank and cold as he heard her shuffling around the room, tired sobs fading to an exhausted silence.

It took two more years and then she was gone, disappearing from their lives and leaving every memory of marriage and motherhood behind her.

When Nathan went back to the house in Richmond to organize the sale after his father's death, there was nothing left that even hinted his mother had once lived there. Every dress was gone from the closet, every bottle of scent, every flower she had ever pressed. He searched frantically through the bookshelves, trying to find a book that might hold one of her dried flowers. That was her one eccentricity, bringing in flowers from their little garden and pressing them between the pages of books. His father had not found it so endearing and would fuss noisily whenever a dried daffodil petal or snowdrop fell out from the pages of his book.

Nathan took that trunk from under his bed with him when he left home. He has it still, the items carefully placed around his boat. They are his memories, beautifully wrapped in the pale pink tissue paper his mother saved from department store packages. That was her one brief freedom: trips to the department store on New Bond Street, her purchases studied and approved by her husband at the end of each month. Nathan has transformed these objects into precious relics: her white silk gloves, the feather headpiece she used to wear to the few parties whose invitations Cedric accepted for them both, her bottle of scent that Nathan occasionally sprays over his pillow, sparingly. It needs to last forever. Her silk stockings, her little book of Shakespeare sonnets that, now that he's read them, he finds surprisingly erotic. There is an evening dress, midnight blue with feathers edging the hem. A pair of shoes, silver with little buckles. A white fox fur piece that he stores with blocks of cedar wood to keep the moths from getting to it. And everything she ever wrote to him, all her gifts, the miniature dolls she bought him for the playroom. He has quite a collection: soldiers, princesses, musicians, priests, ballerinas.

Nathan pushes all these memories away, reordering his thoughts around the familiar delusion of her death. And so it cannot be his mother up there in the dress circle, seated with a man and two children. A trick of the mind, he tells himself as Constant raises his baton and the performance begins.

⁕ ⁕ ⁕

He is distracted in the Wells Room at the party. Usually this would be his opportunity to meet composers and musical directors from the top theatres in London, his chance to remind them of the Nathan Howell who impressed them all these years ago as a little boy. His heart isn't in it, though. In a backless blue dress, her slim white arms beautiful like smooth porcelain, Clara looks like a model. She acts as if nothing has happened when she comes to speak to him, as though she thinks he can forget it all and move on, establish some sort of friendship. But it is too late for that. She needs to be his, exactly as he imagined it. He is already regretting what happened in the boardroom; it wasn't supposed to be like that, her body coming too close and then pulling away, perfection tarnished. When she talks to him, he looks down at her hand. He would like to take the ring that even now is nestled in his pocket and slide it over her finger, encaging it in silver and diamonds.

It is then that he sees her again. The woman with the bright white hair. Her children are at her side, a girl and a boy, both around ten years old. They look like her, too, blonde, with big green eyes. A man is just behind her; he has a hand around her waist. Nathan watches as she turns to the man and smiles, moving her hips just a little.

Nathan cannot bear it. He runs to the bathroom, locking himself in the cubicle, but even here he cannot find the quiet he needs. Men walk in and out of the bathroom with noisy laughter, and he wants to scream. But he doesn't; he has enough control. He leaves the theatre, going out the back way onto Arlington Street. One of the stagehands catches him as he leaves.

"There was someone looking for you," the boy says, handing him a note. "She said she was sorry she couldn't wait any longer as she needs to get her children home to bed."

Nathan looks down at the note, his hands shaking.

"She said she's your mother," the boy adds. "Nice of your folk to come to this, give you some support. Usually it's just the ballerinas I'm delivering cards and flowers to."

Nathan doesn't hear him. He is reading the note.

Darling, please don't be angry. I've been trying to find the courage to visit you since your father died, but I didn't know if you wanted me to. All those years ago, I wrote to you so many times in Richmond but heard nothing back. I would love to be part of your life again. You can meet my family. I know you'll get on so well with Lily and Charlie. Please write to me. We live at no. 5 Hadley Gardens, Chiswick.

Yours, your loving mother.

The words swim in front of his eyes. His mother is dead. She died the day she left them, the day she decided that he and his father were not the family she desired. He gave her a glorious funeral in his mind, dressed her body in a white gown, buried her. The letters that arrived regularly at their home in Richmond were not real. He had ripped them up, burned them, expunged them from his mind every time they appeared on the doormat. Until finally they stopped. And he was left in peace. His memory of Elizabeth Howell was preserved, a perfect woman, a goddess, an adoring mother. He has built his shrine to her, a woman who would never leave them for another man, replace them with a new family. Better dead than to have rejected him like that. Nathan never wanted to know who had finally drawn her away. But his father, in that first fit of rage before falling silent and never speaking of her again, railed angrily about the injustice. There was a terrible mockery, he felt, that the man who stole his wife was a manager at the very same New Bond Street department store where he had sent her to shop. He had believed that those regular shopping trips were harmless, easily monitored, a sign of a woman accepting the narrow freedoms he allowed her. But while Cedric had been paying the store account with the smugness of a man in control of his wife's purse, Elizabeth was slipping into the office on the top floor, building a relationship with a young man who could provide her with the new start she desired.

* * *

Nathan starts walking home to the canal. By the time he reaches his boat, he has ripped the note up into little pieces of paper. He throws them into the water and they disintegrate; there is no proof that they ever existed.

CHAPTER 18

Olivia

I decide to leave the party early. My mind is too full of my sister, Nathan, the first night of the ballet. It's too much of too many things at once. I don't know how I feel about any of it, other than that I feel like an imposter. Maybe Sergeyev should have cast me as the doll in Act One, the immortally passive Coppélia sitting immovably at her balcony. If Clara goes to America, if she says yes to that note in the pocket of her coat, will I finally find out if I am enough, if I can make it by myself? I might have found the note in a coat that Clara is insistent we share, but the words from Jacob Manton are very clearly for Clara only. A thought keeps creeping, insidiously, into my mind. Why did he choose her over me? Is she better than me, a more talented ballerina, performer? Even today it was Clara who was pulled forward in class to demonstrate to us her perfect timing in the mazurka. She shines, while I fade into the background. But even as I think it, I know it isn't true. I am a better ballerina; my technique is more precise; I take direction, adapt my movements to the demands of the choreographer. Clara isn't designed for the corps de ballet. She should be in America, on Broadway, in films. Jacob Manton was right to choose her.

As I leave, hugging my goodbyes and congratulations to the other girls, I notice Nathan over in the corner with Clara. It scares me to watch this conversation from a distance, hearing nothing but seeing the tension spread across Clara's back. I hadn't even considered whether Nathan might mention what happened in the boardroom. I don't know what Clara would do if she knew I had pretended to be her. She would never suspect me of something like that, which makes me even more terrified about how she will react if she finds out.

Nathan isn't even looking at her. He is staring right past her at the doorway. I turn to look, following his gaze. There is a woman framed by the entrance to the Wells Room, her two children at her side, a man behind her with his hand on her waist. Her hair is very white but it doesn't make her look old; quite the opposite, it lights up her face like a crown. She looks around her, then turns back to the man and shakes her head.

I follow her and her family out of the Wells Room. Without really intending to, I end up standing behind them in the queue to the cloakroom. I had taken my coat and bag with me to the Wells Room on my way to the party earlier, thinking there would be somewhere to put them, but it had been so busy that I'd asked the cloakroom attendant to look after them for me.

"Do you know how I can find one of the orchestra?" I hear the lady ask. She has a light, sing-song voice.

"They are probably all at the party in the Wells Room, ma'am," the attendant replies, handing over a stack of coats. I watch as the woman passes them to her husband. He helps the children into their coats, tickling them under their arms and making them giggle as they wriggle out of his way. The boy is tired, his eyes glazed as he stares about the foyer. They look contented, like sleepy little cherubs.

"I tried in there, but I couldn't find the man I was looking for."

"Who is it you are after? I might be able to tell you if he's left already."

"Nathan. Nathan Howell, the pianist."

I stiffen, listening more intently now.

"I haven't seen him leave," the attendant says. I see her notice me. She is fairly new here, and we've only spoken a few times, but she knows I am one of the dancers. "She might know," she says, nodding to me. She probably knows I am either Olivia or Clara Marionetta but hasn't got a clue which one. Safer to stick to "she," it seems. The lady turns to me and smiles.

"Do you know Nathan?" She pauses and smiles even more, drawing her hands to her chest. "Oh, you're one of the dancers, one of Swanilda's friends. You were just wonderful tonight. We loved every moment." She turns to her daughter, who is staring up at me with wide eyes. "Lily, this is one of the ballerinas. Isn't it exciting?"

Lily does not seem able to speak, despite her mother's coaxing. Her eyes are fixed on me with intense curiosity. I remember looking the same way at ballerinas when I was even younger than her, when Mother would take us to the theatre and fight her way backstage, bullying the poor stagehands into letting us through.

I lean down slightly, smiling at the little girl. "Do you like ballet?" I ask her. "Have you started lessons?"

She is shy, shuffling a step closer to her mother. But she nods, blushing.

"Oh, she adores ballet," the woman replies for her. "We haven't been to many shows yet, but now the twins are a little older we're going to be more adventurous."

I reach into my bag. It is stuffed with shoes, tights, hairpins, my wool leg warmers. The pointe shoes I wore for Act Two are already a little worn out. They might get one more ballet class out of them, but that will be it.

Taking out the shoes, I kneel in front of the girl. "Have you ever held a pair of pointe shoes?" I ask her. She shakes her head, looking at the shoes with nervous excitement. "Well, you can have these, if you would like," I say, holding out the shoes. "They're too big for you now, but one day maybe they'll fit and by then your feet will be ready. If you start ballet classes soon," I add. "These are the shoes I wore tonight; so you will always remember your first performance of *Coppélia*."

"How generous!" exclaims the woman, kneeling down by her daughter. Lily looks up at her mother, seeking permission to take the shoes. She nods, and so the girl reaches out and takes them. The girl turns them over in her hands, so gently as if she were holding a bird. It is lovely to watch, a shy little girl dreaming of wearing such shoes herself one day. She has a pink bow in her hair and her dress is covered in frills and froth. I was the same at her age, transporting myself forward to the life I wanted to live.

The woman whispers something in her ear. Lily turns to me, more confident now.

"Thank you very much." She blushes again. "I love them."

"You are so kind," her mother adds. "She won't stop talking about this for months, I can tell already." I think she is right; Lily is swaying from side to side, lost in her own imaginary performance. "Please will you sign our program?" The woman holds it out to me and I take the pen that the cloakroom attendant offers. I lean against the counter and sign my name next to the cast list. *Olivia Marionetta.* I might not be at the top of the list, but it is only my name that is drawn in pen across the page. And it is my name that Lily will remember.

As I return the program, the woman looks anxiously at me. "Sorry, one more thing. You have been so kind, so I hate to keep asking questions, but do you know the pianist Nathan Howell?" I nod and her face lights up. "Oh, wonderful. I don't suppose you know if he is still here?"

I think back to that moment in the Wells Room when I saw him across the crowded room with Clara, that strange, shocked look on his face. He had bolted out of the room through the side door.

"He left the party, but maybe he's still backstage. I can try to find him for you?"

I really don't want to; I can't face the thought of speaking to him now, of trying to behave as though nothing has happened between us. The woman is looking uncertain and her son is nearly asleep, leaning heavily into his father's waist. "Or I can ask a stage-hand to deliver him a message, if that would be easier?"

"Could you? That would be a great help. We need to get these two home to bed."

"One moment," I say, moving quickly toward the auditorium. A young stagehand is sweeping, and I call to him. He follows and joins us in the foyer.

"This lady would like a message going to Nathan Howell. Can you take it?" He nods and we wait while she scribbles a note on a piece of paper that the cloakroom attendant hands her. She gives it to the stagehand, lingering a little as she passes it over.

"Tell him it's his mother."

I look at her in surprise. She seems too young to be his mother. And surely these can't be his brother and sister. I have a vague memory of Clara telling me his mother was dead. But I must have been mistaken.

Her husband takes her arm. It is a gentle movement, kind and patient. She looks up at him and nods.

"Time to go before we all turn into pumpkins."

I wait until they have left, the children bundled out through the doors and into a cab that lingers on the street. Although I leave too, I am not tired. I can't go home just yet; I know I wouldn't be able to sleep.

It is too early in the year still for the nights to be mild and I shiver as I stand on the corner of Rosebery Avenue and Arlington Street, deciding where to walk. A bus goes by and I feel myself tempted to get on, see where it takes me. But even that is too daring for me, even tonight when I am feeling strangely wild, as though I have transformed into a different person. Perhaps it was the girl, Lily, her obvious admiration and excitement at seeing a ballerina so close-up. Giving her those shoes had been just as thrilling for me as it was for her. Or maybe it was meeting Nathan's mother. I had been afraid of him after that kiss, when he had pressed his hand between my legs. But there is something about meeting someone's mother that brings them back to the realm of the human; it normalizes, takes away mystery. It makes a person seem just like the rest of us. And besides, I don't even know if I want Nathan anymore. I thought I did, but in that moment with him in the boardroom, I had not felt the joy and exhilaration I had been expecting. Instead, there had been guilt, disappointment, disgust.

Turning north, I start walking away from my usual homeward direction. Arlington Street is dark and quiet, the walls of the theatre windowless on this side. They loom high over me, a faceless stare of shadowy brick that seems to swallow the sounds of the street. There is an old pub further up, but it is shut and boarded, the chipped harlequin sign fading. I walk quickly past a narrow alleyway on my left that disappears into the gloom, piles of discarded bricks, crates and wooden pallets cluttering the entrance. Building work on the street started last year, catching up with the renovated theatre that has emerged, gloriously, from its ruins, but it is painfully slow, the debris of bricks more common than the sight of a workman. When I reach the end of the street, I continue without thinking into the narrow passageway that leads onto Owen Street. Usually, I would be afraid to walk this way at night, avoiding the warbling calls of the drunks who spill out from the public houses. But tonight I am not afraid. When a man turns at the end of the passageway, I instinctively press myself into the wall, hiding myself in the shadows of the building. I see his face, partly lit up by a street lantern, one of the old gas lights dimly fighting their yellow rays into the night. Even with half his face in shadow, I can tell it is Nathan.

I feel an urge to follow him, as though tracing his journey home will purge the fear I felt when he touched me, will give me the power to move unnoticed and unafraid. Landing each step lightly on my toes, I keep my distance. It is not difficult to keep up this dance; I am used to balancing my weight forward, always ready to jump and leap and turn across the stage. But now I must be silent.

He continues north, crossing Goswell Road and then the city road. These roads are wide and open, and I feel anxious for a moment that he will turn and see me, but he seems intent on his direction now, surging forward with a certain step. He cuts through the gardens alongside Duncan Terrace and Colebrooke Row, and I follow. In the darkness it is hard to tell where I am going, the trees reaching up and out of the ground either side of me. A few squares of light from the windows above the two roads taper in through the tree cover, but they are not enough to provide a guiding path. At the end of the gardens, I look about me, trying to spot him again. And just as I think I have lost him, there he is, disappearing down a slope to the right.

I wait, unsure. I can see down to the canal, Nathan marching along the towpath. The water is a yawning black, impossible to tell how deep it is. It both frightens and rouses me, this water that sits so still like spilled ink. It reminds me of my well at the theatre, but without the luck that comes from dipping my toes into its mysterious waters. This water, here, looks cruel and heavy, as if it might stick to me if I dared to lower myself into its blackness. I walk down to the canal, touching my fingers against the brick wall on my left for support. The brick feels cold and wet, and I draw my fingers away hastily as I feel something moving beneath my touch. Just moss, I tell myself sternly.

Standing at the bottom of the slope, I look out along the canal. To my right is a tunnel, its mouth gaping wide with darkness. I turn back to the open canal, the rows of boats set neatly against the path. And then, suddenly, the dim glaucoma of the clouds clears and for a moment there is a brightness from the sky. The moon is large and whole. It looks like a searchlight, scanning the area for intruders.

I can see him. He is standing on the front decking of a narrowboat, holding his hand out above the water. As he opens his fingers, white fragments flutter down into the water, twirling as they do so. At first, I think they are pieces of satin, like the scraps we cut from the end of our pointe shoe ribbons. But as the last wisp of cloud disappears from the face of the moon, I see they are paper, torn and shredded in his hand.

There in my mind is his mother, the beautiful woman with the bright white hair, anxiously scribbling her note onto the scrap of paper. Nathan watches the water, the pieces of paper disintegrating on the surface of the canal. Once the last one has vanished, he crouches down, lowering himself inside his boat.

* * *

I get home late and I am too tired to talk to Clara. I don't tell her where I have been. There is nothing I can say. But still I can't sleep. It is only once I have crawled into her bed and wrapped my arms around her back that I feel my mind relaxing, and sleep finally draws me down into a quiet rest.

Act Four

CHAPTER 19

Clara

Miss de Valois calls me and Olivia into her office after class. There is a telephone call for us. She leaves us alone, and I see her look back at us strangely as she closes the door. It isn't quite sympathy, nor is it concern. Instead, it is almost a nod of reassurance. She knows we can handle whatever the telephone call will reveal.

We both know it will be about Mother. We've been expecting a call like this ever since she was admitted into the hospital three years ago, both dreading and wishing it in equal measure. It is the senior doctor waiting for us on the telephone, Dr Morris, a man we have only met twice before. First, when he came to our house, coaxing Mother out of her bedroom, leading her by her skeletal arm toward his car. Then, in his office at Colney Hatch, about a month after Mother was admitted. I remember that a bar of light had been shining across his face and he kept blinking, as if he could make it go away. All I could think about was why he hadn't just closed the blinds.

And now we hear his voice again. I am holding the receiver, but Olivia has her cheek pressed to mine, listening in to the call.

"Miss Smith?" the voice asks. It is a while since anyone has used that name. The nurses know we are Marionetta now, instructed as they are by Mother, who talks about us endlessly, boasting to the other patients about her ballerina daughters. Not that any of them care, I expect.

"Yes, speaking," I reply.

"It's Dr. Morris, from Colney Hatch. I am calling with some bad news about your mother." There is a fraction of a pause on the line, but then he continues, his voice steady. Dr Morris is too busy to do this slowly, though I imagine many of the patients have no relatives to call, none who would be interested anyway. "I am sorry to have to tell you that she passed away this morning."

Olivia and I reach for each other, our hands clasped together. I feel her press her cheek into mine more firmly, her skin hot and damp.

"Was she ill?" I say. It is a stupid question: of course she was ill. But it seems strange that she would die so suddenly, without any word of warning. Even as I think it, I know it is an unreasonable thought. Death, especially for someone like Mother, would not be a slow easing away from life. Nor would it be a long painful suffering, like our father's. Mother's death was always going to be dramatic, a sudden burst, a grand finale.

"Not as such," he replies. "She was doing well, in fact. I know you visited a few weeks ago, and she has been very positive and cheerful since then. The nurses thought she had turned a corner, fewer outbursts, more polite to the other patients. They were so confident in her behavior that she was included on the morning walk today, to the park across the road from the hospital." He pauses now, and I can hear a faint buzzing from the telephone line. It seems he is uncertain about how to continue. "Would it be better if you came in to the hospital? It might be easier to explain in person."

"Yes, okay. We'll come in this afternoon," I reply. This is not how we should be finding out about our mother's final moments, with our faces stuck together, sweating as we both struggle to hear Dr. Morris clearly.

"You can collect her belongings then, too, if you would like. There is no obligation to do so; we can dispose of them here. But you might not want to return too many times. And there is the funeral to arrange, if you feel able."

It is too much to think about. "Yes, fine. We'll do that this afternoon when we are there. It makes sense to do it all in one go." I realize I sound harsh and unfeeling. And maybe I am, just wanting to process it quickly and move on. But I am sure the emotions will come later. There is only so much one can think in half a minute.

When I put the phone down, I forget where I am. The walls decorated with photographs of ballerinas, a pile of pointe shoes in the corner, a set of glasses with decanted sherry in an ornate bottle on a side table: for a moment I could be back in our family home in Highgate, in Mother's bedroom. But this room, Miss de Valois's office, is too tidy, too ordered, a professional office, not Mother's chaotic world of make-believe.

*　*　*

Miss de Valois gives us the afternoon off rehearsals, and we take the train to Colney Hatch. Olivia is quiet, her hands anxiously turning and turning on her lap. I reach across to her and she stills.

"It's going to be all right," I whisper. And I truly believe it. As the train brings us closer, I feel more and more certain that we can survive this. More than survive this; perhaps it is what we need to move on with our lives.

A nurse is waiting for us at reception, and she takes us straight to Dr. Morris's office. I peer down the long corridor to the right. It is quiet, ghostly even. It always surprises me how empty the hospital feels, even though I know it is packed with more than two thousand patients. The corridor goes on and on, the end just a tiny dark speck in the distance. It must be nearly five hundred feet long, an endless tunnel of rooms and wards and offices, all hiding madness and pain.

Dr. Morris stands when we enter, and gestures to two chairs across from his desk. He is a short man, stocky, with a wide neck that seems too large for his shirt. I remember this from the first time, how solid and sturdy he looked compared to our frail, birdlike mother.

"I thought we could take a walk," he says after repeating the condolences he expressed on the telephone. "I can show you where your mother died. It may be easier for you to understand that way. First a few papers to sign. This for next of kin and this one to confirm that your mother died while living here." He nudges some papers across his desk toward us.

"Shall I sign, or would you like to?" I ask Olivia.

She shakes her head. "You do it."

He waits for me to look over the papers, then stands. "Shall we?" We follow him out of his office and back outside into the driveway. Another nurse is waiting for us by the gate. I notice how nervous she looks, her eyes flitting up and down as we approach her.

"This is Nurse Sarah," Dr. Morris tells us. "She was there when your mother died." The nurse nods at us, a sympathetic smile spreading anxiously across the width of her face. She is all large angles and lines, thick, straight ankles rising out of her brown shoes. Her white cap sits firmly on the back of her head, strangely at odds with her restless eyes.

We leave the premises and cross the road into a park.

"The nurses take the patients here for a change of scenery, if we feel they are sufficiently stable. It is good for them to get out and feel a little less cooped up. They always go early in the morning, before too many locals are out and about. And the patients are often more receptive in the mornings, before they have worked themselves up into tiredness and hysterics. Everything seems a little clearer in the mornings, don't you think?" he says, a friendly smile on his face. He is trying to engage us in conversation, but neither of us are in the mood.

"As I said on the telephone, your mother was doing very well. We thought she might start getting agitated if we didn't give her a little outing. But we misjudged her condition. She was clever, your mother. She knew what she was doing, I think."

I turn to him sharply. "What do you mean?" I don't like his suggestion that she somehow manipulated the nurses into thinking she was getting better. But of course that is exactly what she would have done. I don't know why I am surprised.

"Just that she knew she could control her behavior in order to get what she wanted." He stretches his hands out in front of him, his thick wrists too wide for his cuffs. "That is not unique to a mental hospital, Miss Smith."

I nod and he continues, leading us toward a large pond, almost a lake, that appears as if by magic out of the ground. It is lined with reeds, the grass merging into the water. A bank of swans swim across the surface, their long necks still and serene. Another group is resting by the edge of the water, looking around them with territorial suspicion. Nurse Sarah walks a few steps behind us. When I turn to look back at her, I catch her letting out a sharp sigh. This is hard for her, I realize.

"There were two nurses and four patients, which should have been fine. But one of the patients, a young woman with a nervous disorder, was upset. Something your mother said, apparently. The patient wasn't clear on what happened, but it was something about her feet. Your mother kept calling them lumps of clay. It wasn't really anything serious."

I can't help smile a little and I turn to Olivia to see her, too, struggling to suppress a laugh. That was exactly what Mother used to say about the other girls in ballet class, especially those who had been given more attention than us by the ballet teacher. "I don't know what she was looking so smug about," Mother would snarl on the way home. "Lumps of clay, her feet were. Absolute lumps of clay."

Dr. Morris continues. "While the two nurses were calming down the other patient, your mother slipped away and ran off into those trees." He points to a little copse of woodland just behind the pond. With the afternoon sun lighting up the leaves, it is hard to imagine them hiding Mother.

"When they finally located her, she had stripped off all her clothes and was walking, naked, toward the water."

He shows no embarrassment at telling us this story. No doubt patients taking off all their clothes is not an uncommon occurrence at Colney Hatch. But now he turns to Nurse Sarah and gestures for her to join us.

"Perhaps you could explain to the Miss Smiths what happened next?" he asks, but it isn't really a question. He shows no sign of noticing the nurse's discomfort at being brought here to relive our mother's death. She must only be in her mid-twenties but her solid, sturdy frame makes her seem older, masking her nervousness from anyone unwilling to look too closely.

Nurse Sarah shakes her head as she speaks, as if she can negate the story she is telling us. "Your mother kept heading toward the water and suddenly started speeding up. We were on the other side of the lake so couldn't get to her. She was taking quick, dainty steps and her arms were flapping all over the place. It looked as though she thought she had wings. She just kept going, bending her body up and down, her arms above her head, sometimes wrapped around her, sometimes flapping frantically. She went right through the middle of a group of swans and they weren't very happy about it. They kept hissing at her, beating their wings and winding their necks toward her, but she didn't seem to care. In fact, she started to move a bit like them, writhing her neck and shoulders in this very swanlike way. It gave us all rather a shock to see her like that."

Olivia has moved closer to me and we both stare across the lake. I can picture Mother, her tiny naked body, her fading bones jutting out, her fragile skin draped with creases and folds. It was always her frustration, her flesh dissolving but leaving loose folds of skin that she could pinch between her fingers. I imagine her dancing toward the water.

I know what she was doing. This was her dying swan, her final performance. She always had a fascination for Fokine's *Dying Swan*, Saint-Saëns's music, Anna Pavlova's famous solo. She sought out opportunities to see it performed and when she returned home we would find her dancing around her bedroom, her arms twisting and turning, her feet trying to mimic the little *bourrée*.

Nurse Sarah cuts through our thoughts. "I ran around the lake toward her, but my colleague, Nurse Lizzy, had to stay with the three patients who were by now beside themselves, crying and screaming. Your mother walked right into the water and kept going and going until she was beyond her depth. I called out to her, but she sank down into the water and was not able to find the strength to rise out of it again. Perhaps she could not swim, or perhaps she was too weak from anorexia. By the time I had waded my way in and gone down under the water to find her, she had drowned. I dragged her out and pulled her onto the bank, but it was too late."

I turn to Olivia and hug her. Neither of us are crying, though somehow I feel I should. Maybe the doctor expects it. Or maybe not. Perhaps no one cries when someone dies in Colney Hatch. It is a terrifying, haunting death, but it is also exactly as Mother intended. Of that I am sure. Finally, our mother found a way to become not only the ballerina but the muse itself. A dying swan, dancing to her death.

✳ ✳ ✳

Dr. Morris leaves us with a different nurse once we are back at the hospital. Nurse Sarah disappears immediately, before we have a chance to thank her. It must have been awful, running into the water after Mother, searching for her body among the reeds.

The nurse takes us to Mother's room. It is both disappointing and a relief to see it already packed up, her belongings neatly placed into two boxes.

"Sorry that we couldn't leave everything as it was. But this room is needed for another patient, and we couldn't wait."

"Not even a few hours for us to visit?" Olivia says. She is upset, I can tell. This is all moving too quickly for her.

The nurse looks apologetic. She is young and pretty, just the sort of woman Mother would have courted. "I fully appreciate that would have been better. But we had no choice. It was that or making a vulnerable patient in a busy ward wait until tomorrow to get a room of their own."

Olivia looks down. "Of course," she says. "The living take preference over the dead."

There is an uncomfortable silence before the nurse gestures to the two boxes. "There's no need for you to take any of this if you don't want to. We can dispose of it here if you prefer. But I'll give you some time to go through them and decide."

"Thank you," I say. "We won't be long."

I take the first box and open the lid. Mother's scarves and jewelry, her colorful headbands and trinkets that she must have convinced the doctors it was safe for her to keep. I close it quickly. "I don't think there's any need to look through this one." Olivia nods. She isn't touching anything, just standing there with her hands behind her back, hardly even looking at the box.

Then I open the other one. In it are the letters we have written to her over the past three years, stacks of photographs, programs from theatre productions, memories of the days before Father died. I take them out and start to leaf through them. There are signed photographs of Pavlova, Lopokova, Nijinska, Massine. There are old reports from the many different ballet teachers Mother persuaded to train us over the years. There are a few photographs of me and Olivia, one from our first ballet class, one of us before performing in an operatic play at the Old Vic, dressed in little sailor costumes. There are a few more recent ones that we have sent her since joining the Vic-Wells. It is interesting that in every photograph she has of us, we are in ballet clothes or costumes. Any image of us as ordinary little girls does not exist.

Olivia has joined me now, looking through another pile of papers that she lifts out of the box. She holds a photograph out to me. It is Father. He looks so young in the photograph, dressed in an army uniform with his hair swept across in a side parting. An inscription on the back of the photograph says it was taken in 1915. Just one year after we were born.

He was in France then, fighting in the war. Mother would tell us the story regularly in those earlier, happier days before Father died. Apparently, as the two of us were fighting our way into the world, Father was escaping death by a matter of inches. He would take over the storytelling then: he was in the trenches that night, the night before a big offensive at the Marne. He was instructed to join a group of men to creep out into no man's land and cut through German barbed wire. Out in the field, mud creeping up around his boots, he heard the man beside him drop his wire cutters. Father reached down into the mud to pick them up and reached out to hand them back. As he did so, there was a blast of gunfire. The cutters were blown clean out of his hand, sending shards of metal into his arm and fingers. In agony, he was rushed back to the trench by the men around him, finding help in one of the dugouts. The metal shards had missed a major artery in his arm by millimeters. He spent six months recovering at home, during which time he got to meet his beautiful twin daughters. Then he went back to the front. He avoided death throughout the war with his three lucky charms, his wife and two daughters, protecting him. But it was cancer that got him six years after the end of the war. His luck had run out.

* * *

In the end, we take just a few photographs. The memories of everything else belong to another time, when we were a different family to what we became. We find the nurse and let her know.

"And the funeral?" she asks. "What would you like to arrange?" I feel lost by the question. How is anyone supposed to know how to arrange a funeral?

She must notice my look of confusion. "Come and sit in reception and I'll talk you through the options."

We decide on a small ceremony in the hospital chapel next week, followed by a burial in Highgate. Mother will be buried next to Father. The extended family in Brighton will be invited, but it seems unlikely they will attend. That will be easier, really, avoiding their stares and undisguised disapproval. Aunt Alice will overcompensate for her guilt at neglecting us so entirely and it will be unbearable.

"What happens to those who have no family to arrange their funerals?" Olivia asks.

"We organize it all for them," the nurse replies. But she says it quickly, a little dismissively. It sounds as though she doesn't want further questions.

"Where are they buried?" I push her. I've heard rumors of large, unmarked graves in the grounds at Colney Hatch, forgotten and unloved people left here to die by their indifferent relatives.

"There is a graveyard by the chapel," she says, smiling and standing. The conversation is over. I feel glad that Mother has us, that we never neglected our monthly visit. I am glad too that we got to visit the place she died, to pay tribute to those final moments. She died as a swan, a dancing swan, and she will be buried with Father, her great love, the only person who could relieve her terrible anxieties. There, under the ivy and stone of their grave, they will be together again.

CHAPTER 20

Samuel

If Milly Bell hopes Samuel will ask her out again, properly this time, without Mrs. Freed to orchestrate it all, she is to be disappointed. While she longs for Samuel to take the next, obvious step, it doesn't even occur to him that she might like him. Perhaps if he wasn't so wrapped up in replaying Olivia's dancing in his head all night and all morning as he walks to work, he might notice the smiles and friendly attentions Milly gives him every time she finds an excuse to come down to the workshop. For days now it has been the same painful routine, Samuel oblivious while Milly tries her hardest to get his attention. Mr. Freed, of course, notices nothing. Mrs. Freed is more observant and feels for Milly every time she comes back up from the workshop, her face uncertain, disappointed.

The morning after the two of them had such a wonderful time at Sadler's Wells, Milly is filled with excitement. Getting ready in her little bedroom feels like preparing for a night out; even the morning light spilling in between her pink curtains takes on a different hue. Everything has a thrill to it: choosing her skirt and blouse, which shoes she is to wear, the pearl necklace she knows looks good against her skin. She takes longer with her makeup than usual, a light blusher on her cheeks, a new lipstick. Milly graduated last year from a tiny women's college next to Regent's Park. She was taught the importance of dressing beautifully and neatly every day for work, but sometimes she rushes her face in order to get to the shop on time. Madame Clement would be proud of her today, she thinks. The other girls at the college had been envious when Milly got the job with the Freeds. Several of them had applied, attracted to the glamour of ballerinas and pink satin shoes. It was preferable to a dull job typing up letters and making diary appointments for boring men in gray suits.

Downstairs in the kitchen, she hurries with her breakfast. Milly wants to get to Freed early, to be already behind the till when Samuel arrives. She thinks forward to when she can make him a cup of tea and take it down to him mid-morning. What she will say to him, how he will respond, how easy and friendly it will all be, she imagines it all. She refuses the egg sandwich her mother offers to make her, instead putting together her own plain roll and some thin slices of beef. Everything is deliberate this morning: she imagines Samuel watching her, eating with her perhaps out on the little bench in the square close to the shop. An egg sandwich would be too messy, too smelly.

Her brother Jonathan comes in, yawning, his hair a mess. He seems to drag himself awake as he notices his sister, searching lazily for something to tease her about.

"You came in rather late last night, Milly," he begins, leaning forward on the kitchen table and picking pieces of beef from the plate. His mother pushes his hand away from the meat, passing a cup of steaming hot tea into the other. He is spoiled and he knows it. They all know it, but they are too fond of him to do anything about it.

"Not so late," Milly replies, packing her roll into her bag. "I was at the ballet, if you must know."

"Who with? Go on. Tell us. I saw you coming back dressed up all fancy in that ghastly fox piece."

"Hey," she cries, hitting him on the arm. "I like that fox piece."

"I'm not sure the fox agrees with you," he smirks.

"I went with a friend, a colleague actually."

"That giant I saw at the end of the path? He's a colleague?"

"He's not a giant. He's a pointe shoemaker. They need to have very strong . . . arms." She can feel herself blushing and turns away.

"Strong arms, eh," he laughs. "I bet he does."

"Oh be quiet, Jonathan," his mother scolds. "He was a gentleman and walked Milly all the way home."

"I'd hope so too. It's not like he could just leave her stranded in the middle of London."

Milly cuts in, her face gradually returning to its normal color. "So you've walked every girl home you've ever been out with, have you?"

"No, of course not. But not every girl is worth walking home," he laughs, pinching her waist.

"Well, clearly Samuel thought I was worth walking home."

"Oh, Samuel," he teases her.

✳ ✳ ✳

Milly leaves her mother and brother arguing over what sandwich he is going to take to his office for lunch. All the way to work she thinks about the route Samuel might take, whether they will bump into each other before they arrive. She'd like that. It would be almost as though they'd walked the whole way together, which of course they haven't, and she knows that would be an outrageous and shocking suggestion. But it is only inside her head, so it doesn't really matter.

She is disappointed when she arrives at the shop to find that Samuel is already there, stationed at his workbench downstairs. It will be several hours until she can find an excuse to go downstairs. Mrs. Freed asks her about the ballet and she replies at length, going through every little detail she can remember. Talking always calms her nerves. She knows it is ridiculous to be nervous; she has seen Samuel every day for weeks and not thought anything of it. And yet one evening with him at the ballet has set her on edge, as though an entirely new person is downstairs crafting those shoes. She likes him, and she is longing to know if he likes her too.

* * *

After several days of awkward and polite exchanges, Mrs. Freed decides something must be done. She cannot bear to watch Milly making a fool of herself day after day while Samuel is oblivious to it all. Samuel comes up to the shop floor just before lunch, carrying piles of pointe shoes in his arms. Immediately Milly blushes.

"Hello, Samuel," she says, smiling at him from where she counts out a delivery of spools of pink thread. "How was your morning?"

"Very good, thank you, Milly," he replies, nodding in her direction as he continues unloading the shoes into the shelves.

Mrs. Freed cuts in. "How about you show Milly your ideas for the character and ballroom shoes?" she says. At least they will have something to talk about, rather than skirting around each other. What Samuel needs, she thinks, is a chance to really notice Milly. And men, in her opinion, notice women most when that woman is praising them, complimenting them over something brilliant that they have achieved. Milly surely won't be able to look at those stunning designs without giving him lots and lots of praise.

"Only if you're interested?" he says uncertainly to Milly. But he looks happy, his chin lifted.

"Bring them up here and you can have lunch with Milly behind the desk while you look."

He returns in a few minutes, some of his drawings wrapped up in string while others, the ones Mr. Freed is thinking they might be able to use soon, are held flat between two pieces of leather. It was Mr. Freed who bought him the leather case, dark brown with a strap inside to hold the designs. Samuel lays it open across the desk, unrolling the other sketches alongside it. He arranges them neatly while Milly leans over his shoulder. She gazes down at them, making little cooing sounds, pointing out her favorites: the green boots with the fur trim, the fur collar for a coat that clasps at the side with a beautifully cut felt button, the high-heeled dancing shoes with petal shapes cut into the toe. Milly can't believe that this man, this giant man, as her brother would say, is capable of creating such delicate and beautiful drawings. She imagines herself in the shoes and the fur collar, heading out on his arm to a restaurant. These are shoes to wear while drinking champagne.

"So, are you going to make these?" she says to him. "You should set up your own dressmaking shop." She blushes again when she says this, seeing the eyes of Mrs. Freed on her. It wouldn't do to suggest Samuel should leave the Freeds, set up on his own, not when they have given him all his training. But why should he stay here making the same pointe shoes day after day? Not when his head is filled with the most glorious and varied designs.

He shakes his head firmly. "Maybe Mr. Freed will make some of the dancing shoes, the character ones, soon, when we think we'll get enough of a customer base to make it worthwhile. The others are just a bit of fun, something I enjoy doing as a hobby."

"One day maybe," Milly says, almost a whisper. Mrs. Freed is the other side of the room and Milly is feeling bolder now, their hands close as they look through the drawings. "Perhaps I could join you and run the shop. We'd have every woman in London coming to us wanting these," she says, nodding to the designs. "You're very talented."

Samuel looks down at his designs, Milly's soft, plump hands grazing them. She has placed a seed in his mind, something he had never dared think before. Starting his own shop is a wilder idea than he has ever imagined. But of course it is what he wants. One day.

"Like Mr. and Mrs. Freed, you mean?" he says, stopping as abruptly as he began. He didn't mean it like that, not the Mr. and Mrs. part. But it's out now, and there is nothing he can do to take it back. As he looks down nervously at Milly's bright blonde hair bopping prettily at her shoulders, the little smile on her lips, he thinks perhaps she isn't offended. She turns her face up, her eyes directly on him.

"A little like that, perhaps."

* * *

Mrs. Freed watches them from the other side of the room, where she sits with her tea and her sandwich. She doesn't want to lose these two; they would be very hard to replace. But she doesn't think there is any risk of that just yet. They remind her of herself and Frederick when they first started working together, Frederick's shyness, her leading him subtly to every step forward in their courtship. While he might have been the one to propose, she had got him there. She wonders if he has any idea how much she had to do to make it happen.

Milly is full of chatter all afternoon. When she is ready to leave, the shop packed away neatly and the blinds down, she calls down to Samuel.

"Are you finished yet? I'm going home via a new fabric shop on Percy Street. Do you want to come too? I hear they have lovely new colors you could build into some of your designs."

Samuel is just walking up the steps, his coat over his arm. He had been planning on working on his tutu design, the one for Olivia that he knows he will never be able to afford to make her. But he decides that can wait.

Mrs. Freed watches them leave the shop, Milly a few steps ahead. She smiles before turning away to finish checking the till.

CHAPTER 21

Olivia

The second performance of *Coppélia* is a whole week after the first, which gives Miss de Valois plenty of time to respond to the reviews and work us hard in rehearsal. Critics were, however, very positive. They enjoyed the chance to comment on our revival of a Russian classic, this story ballet so different to the choreographic experiments of Ashton and Miss de Valois. Clara and I collected all the newspapers after the first performance, laying them across my bed and poring over them indulgently. We read that it was a "sparkling performance," that Swanilda danced with "superb grace, ease, and vitality." We quickly glossed over the news report immediately next to the review: a man murdering his girlfriend on the towpath at Barnes hardly seemed in keeping with our joyful ballet. Of course we were both disappointed that our names weren't mentioned, but we hadn't really been expecting it. And then the next day Mother died. We forgot to look out for reviews after that. It didn't seem to matter.

I have been avoiding Nathan. He pays no attention to me, so it isn't difficult. It is my sister he desires. She still hasn't mentioned America to me. Sometimes I catch her looking thoughtful and I try to imagine what is going through her mind. Can she leave me here alone right after Mother has died? Does she want to give up her place in the Vic-Wells, just when it is getting started? Is America and all its promises worth it for all she would lose? If she would just speak to me about it, I could help her. Ever since I read that note in the coat pocket, I've been thinking about it more and more. And now I know, or at least I think I do: I want her to go. I want to make a name for myself here in London on my own, to prove that I am good enough just as me. And now that Mother is dead, well, I am even more certain. I don't need Clara to hold my hand anymore, not now we don't need to suffer those monthly trips to Colney Hatch, Mother making me feel like a child again, her searching eyes checking that I still look like the ballerina she expects of me.

With the second performance finally here, the energy in the dressing room is high. It is different to the nerves of the first performance, instead a more certain, entertaining mood, with the girls making jokes about the ballet, mimicking the mime sequences with exaggerated movements. By now we are all experts at playing at being dolls, copying the stiff *port de bras* that Swanilda performs while pretending to be Coppélia, bending forward from the hips, turning our heads abruptly from side to side. We open our eyes very wide and blink in time to the beat, two slow and three fast, our dark eye makeup framing the movement. Some of the men have decamped to our room to share makeup tips, William Chappell drawing an extra line of pencil under our eyes: "A miniature Clapham Junction," he says, leaning back to admire his artwork.

When there is just an hour to go, we traipse to the well, the steps down to the storage room becoming congested with dancers who search for their luck. We need to dip our fingers into the water, our lucky charm to send us on to the stage with certainty.

It is our moment of transition, resetting the muscles and the mind from an afternoon of rehearsing other ballets to the performance of the evening. Clara is already down there. I am surprised to see her there before me. She doesn't always bother with the ritual of the well; she has never been as superstitious as me. I am even more surprised to see her dressed in the costume for the doll Coppélia, the red tutu with the frills. That part is usually played by one of the students from Miss de Valois's school; there is nothing more to it than sitting in a chair on a balcony, reading a book. It requires utter stillness, but that is all.

"Oh, hello," she says, looking up at us all as we fill in the cold gloom around the well, the men leaning against the steel beams, their dressing gowns, dirty with makeup grease, draped over their costumes. "Miss de Valois asked me to put this on for some press photographs. It's all done now." She stands and starts to move toward the stairs. "I had better hurry if the girl performing Coppélia tonight is going to be ready in time. Is it Molly Brown tonight?"

I ignore her question. "What photographs?" I ask. None of the rest of us were asked, and I feel let down that she has been chosen for this over me. Or, at least she could have told me about it and I could have gone along to watch. It would have been fun seeing her onstage, posing for the camera.

"They were mostly of Lydia, but they wanted the doll in the background, to set the scene. I just had to sit completely still, trying not to wiggle my nose when I had an itch." She is trying to trivialize it, I can tell, reducing it all to a joke, a nuisance. And in that pretty costume it is hard to be cross with her. She really does look like a doll, her costume all frills and dark pink scalloped ribbons. In her hair she wears a crown of flowers, and there are more red ribbons around her wrists.

"See you onstage soon for a warm-up." And then she is gone, running up the stairs and pulling the flower crown from her head as she does so. She is late as usual.

* * *

We drag the portable barres on to the stage behind the thick red curtain and warm up to the rhythmical clapping of Miss Moreton as she instructs us in a quick routine of pliés, *tendus, ronds de jambe* and *grands battements*. Raising our legs onto the barres, we fold forward to stretch out our hamstrings; we listen to the tones of the orchestra as they tune their instruments, their own warm-up that does not need to be hidden from the audience like ours does. We have a magic to preserve, one that relies on mystery and illusion. The stagehands hurry us off the stage as we get closer to the beginners' call and we continue our preparations in the wings, spilling further into the scenery docks. I notice a door is open out onto the street, a faint smell of cigarette smoke drifting toward me: someone's last minute attempt to calm their nerves, I expect.

As soon as the music starts and the audience settles into silence, I forget about everything else and just focus on the performance. The familiar smells in the wings center me: the musk of the curtains, the heat of the lights warming the stage, the sweet sweat of the dancers, our bodies supple and warm. I love this ballet, the drama, the story, spinning a whole tale through dance. But in the interval there is chaos. Mr. Healey is furious, storming in and out of the dressing rooms in a rage. The headpiece for the doll, Coppélia, is missing. So the girl from the school who was performing the doll had to wear the second one, the one that Swanilda needs in Act Two when she pretends to be Coppélia. I look over to Clara, who is redoing her lipstick in the mirror. She doesn't look at all concerned, shrugging as Mr. Healey shouts at us all.

"This room is an absolute disgrace," he cries, his arms flying about him as he gestures to our chaotic piles of coats, warm-up clothes, practice skirts, pointe shoes. "And what is that ribbon doing on your dressing table, young lady?" he shouts at poor Gwyneth Matthews, who has left her face cream open right next to part of her costume. She goes bright red and gathers up the ribbon into her hand.

He sees Clara. "You," he says. "You wore the Coppélia costume earlier for the photographs. Where did you put the flower crown?"

Clara turns to him, coolly, without the panic of the rest of us. She doesn't stand, just crosses her legs and leans back into her chair. "I returned the costume to Wardrobe for whichever one of Miss de Valois's students is performing the role tonight. I can't be responsible for whatever happened to the costume after that. I put the flower crown back on the mannequin head on the shelf above the rail. Have you checked there?"

"Of course I checked there." Mr. Healey stares back at her. He looks as though he might explode. We all sit very still, trying to avoid his eye as he starts rummaging through the dressing room, lifting up our piles of coats and bags. But he doesn't find the crown.

He leaves and the tension slowly dissolves, but we have to force ourselves to find the same ebullient mood for Act Two. Lydia looks sternly at us when the movements turn her away from the audience, which wakes us up and reminds us that we need to be performing with much greater energy. When Swanilda mimes to her friends to wind up the clockwork dolls positioned around Dr. Coppélius's workshop, I think she is really telling us all to brighten up our performance. By the time we take the curtain call, I feel better again, but I go down to the well at the end anyway. I need a moment to settle myself.

The light bulb, shaded in its enamel frame, is just strong enough for me to see after the darkness of backstage. I am still in costume, a shawl around my shoulders for warmth. It is quiet and relaxing down here, strange after the raucous applause from the audience, and I stretch my arms up to the ceiling, shifting my weight from side to side as I reach up and up out of my hips. I let my head lower and I roll forward, stretching out my hamstrings. It feels glorious to hang my head upside down like this, letting the weight of my body pull me down. I wrap my hands around my ankles and touch my lips to my knees.

As I draw my body slowly upward, I catch sight of something in the water behind me. I pull myself upright immediately, so fast that my head spins and my vision blurs. Kneeling to center myself, I creep slowly, nervously, toward the edge of the well. My legs feel heavy, dragging behind me, and I can hardly bear to look down into the water. But I do look, my hands gripping the stone.

I throw myself backward, drawing away from the water in horror. I think I must have screamed, because I hear concerned voices coming down the stairs. It is Clara and Hermione.

"What's wrong?" Clara cries, running down and kneeling next to me. I must look a sight, thrown back against a beam, breathing hard.

"In the water," I whisper.

"What, this?" Hermione says. She is reaching down in the water. I watch, transfixed, as she pulls out the head of a mannequin, one of the light, hollow ones that we use for storing wigs and headdresses. In her other hand she is holding the flower crown. "How on earth did that get in there?"

"I thought . . ." I begin, but then I stop. It sounds too ridiculous. When I looked into that water, I was sure I had seen the head of a woman, floating there in her floral crown. But I was mistaken. Just the costume Mr. Healey has been searching for, thrown into the well by someone mischievous.

I look up at Clara and Hermione. They are staring anxiously at each other. It might only be a costume, but it's enough to scare us.

Another image comes to me: a pointe shoe drifting among ribbons, rose petals wilting in the dark water. A suspicion lingers, just enough to make me shudder. That large man with his bag of shoes, his ungainly tread as he moves through the corridors of Sadler's Wells. I remember him watching us at the shoe shop, his heavy body blocking the shine of the pale pink shoes. Ever since he gave me the rose before the first night of *Coppélia*, I have been wary of him. A disturbing, reluctant feeling has been lingering at the edge of my mind recently, a feeling that it might have been him that wrote that note. I have tried to push the thought away, preferring to think that the rose and the note are from a worthier admirer. Now, I feel disappointment, but worse than that, dread, as my suspicions of the pointe shoemaker's apprentice grow into something solid, menacing, real.

CHAPTER 22

Nathan

When Nathan goes into the orchestra pit a few hours before the performance to check his music is in place, he is surprised to see Clara on the stage, dressed in the Coppélia doll costume. She is entirely still, up on the balcony of Dr. Coppélius's home, book in hand, staring down at the pages with large eyelashes that rise up slowly. For a moment he thinks she really is a doll. Someone has created a doll of Clara Marionetta, he hears himself think, absurdly. Nathan is envious of whoever had such an idea. He would like to lift her out of that chair and take her home to his boat. Then he could have her forever, in doll-like perfection.

But then she moves, just a little flicker of her eyes. Of course, she isn't a doll. There is a photographer on the stage, kneeling as he holds up the camera. Lydia Lopokova is moving in and out of a low arabesque and the photographer is straining to capture the image. Clara is part of the backdrop, setting the scene for the ballet. Nathan watches from the pit, leaning against the piano. He doesn't care if Clara can see him; why shouldn't he stare at her? She never minded before. They were so close, Clara grateful for his love and admiration until he proposed. Since then she has been drawing away and then pulling in close, confusing him with her rejection and advances. It has unsettled him. But not only that: seeing his mother surrounded by her new family, her pretty children, has turned everything upside down that he thought was straightforward and simple. It is harder to make himself believe in her death now that he has seen her. But that isn't her, not the mother he remembers. That mother is dead, preserved forever: she would never leave him for someone else. It was easy, he found, to bury all memories of the way his father and grandparents treated her. His vision, instead, is of a perfect happy family.

Clara is utterly still again. It amazes him how long she can go without blinking. Perhaps she is testing herself, some sort of personal challenge. That would be just like Clara: to turn this into a game. Some of the other musicians have joined him in the pit. They are checking the angle of their seats, the height of their music stands. One of the flautists starts playing snatches of the music, breaking the silence of the auditorium. Clara shifts, just a little note of surprise. She has awoken from her doll-like sleep, Nathan thinks. The photographer stands, pressing his free hand into his thigh. This is the cue for the world to begin again. Clara rolls her shoulders, opening her lips a little. It is as though she has started breathing again, a doll come to life.

As Nathan stares down at the flawless ivory and ebony of the piano keys, he has an idea, or less an idea than a vision. It reminds him of when his mother first left, and he knew that he wouldn't accept it. He remembers sitting on his bed after his father told him what had happened, remembers reimagining the entire conversation, changing the words, changing it all. After that he couldn't go back. And now, with Clara, he thinks he knows how he will get her back. He will make her his again.

* * *

The auditorium starts to build in noise and movement, ushers checking there are no old programs lying around, the stagehands sweeping the stage before the dancers emerge to start their warm-up. Nathan can predict every movement in that hour before a performance, the ushers, the stagehands, the dancers, the musicians: he knows exactly where everyone will be, the routines and rhythms of the theatre ingrained into him like clockwork. He follows Clara at a distance, watching her tutu bob up and down as she walks. She goes down to the well; the dancers' daily ritual. Although he is fascinated by their superstitions, he understands. Nathan has his own routine before performances: he whispers the mantra to himself, even though the words have become hollow and meaningless. He is special, he is talented, the world is lucky to have him. When his mother said these words, he believed them. But now they do nothing except trick his brain into preparing for the ballet. As he whispers them, he touches every black key on the piano lightly with the tip of his finger. Then he visualizes himself in the prelude of performance, the conductor raising the baton.

Dancers are coming the opposite way along the corridor to the well, their voices loud and fast. The second night is always easier on the nerves than the first, everyone a little more relaxed. Nathan pulls back and waits for them to disappear down the steps. He doesn't want them to wonder why he is hovering in the corridor.

Clara runs up a few moments later, pulling off the headdress. She dashes along the corridor away from him, the crown of flowers hanging down from her hand. He smiles bitterly. It is just like her to rush through life treating everything with careless disregard. He is angry with her. Why can't she slow down? Why can't she be more like that doll Coppélia, content to sit, passive, with a book in her hands?

As he follows her along the corridor around to the dressing rooms and Wardrobe on the other side of the auditorium, he feels his anger growing. He wants to get hold of her and keep her still. But she moves so fast, she always has. He doesn't know why he ever thought he would be able to have her.

She is in Wardrobe for a few minutes. Nathan waits in the shadows behind a properties storage container; if anyone sees him he knows it will be hard to explain why he is hiding there, but he feels compelled to stay and wait for her. When she comes out again, he finds himself gripping the edge of the storage box.

She is naked. Not quite, he realizes, the blood pulsing hard in his neck. She has taken off the costume and is wearing only her pale pink tights and pointe shoes. Although she has pulled her tights as high they will go, they do not cover her breasts. She looks around her guardedly before dashing down the corridor to the dressing rooms. Her room is only a few doors down, and he hears peals of loud laughter coming from inside as soon she enters. The musicians love to joke about what goes on in those dressing rooms, some of the men making dirty jokes about the ballerinas' flexible legs and hips. It seems that perhaps they weren't so wrong after all. Naked dancers daring each other to run through the corridors: he can imagine the leering laughter if he tells this story to the other men. But he won't. This is just for him.

It is quiet inside Wardrobe. There is no one else there. He sees the Coppélia doll costume back on the rail, hanging on its side with the netting sticking out. He goes to touch it, feeling the softness of the bodice, sticking his hand inside the net knickers. He rubs the tulle between his fingers, where it has been resting against Clara's thighs. He wants to take it, but he knows that would create an uproar. Someone will be coming in to put this on soon. He looks up. The flower crown is resting on a mannequin head. Before he thinks about what he is doing, he has reached up and grabbed it.

✳ ✳ ✳

The well is quiet now, all the dancers warming up onstage. He holds the mannequin head in front of him. There are no eyes, no features, just the shape of a head molded out of hollow plaster. He tilts it to one side and bows a little in response.

"Clara Marionetta," he whispers, "may I have this dance?"

The mannequin head nods in return, the flower crown dipping down over where the eyes would be. Nathan starts swaying from side to side, the head held level with his eyes. He hums a tune. It is the waltz that his mother used to put on at home before she left: "The Blue Danube." His father didn't like it though. He'd always turn off the gramophone whenever his mother tried to dance; he had no time for such frivolity. And now Nathan thinks of those notes drifting across mourners. It is easier to conjure a picture of her coffin down here, in the quiet gloom of the well room, dancing with plaster and paint.

He presses the head to his shoulder. They are dancing closer now. He dips his forehead against her, the flower crown tickling his cheek. Nathan closes his eyes and sees her again, as she was when she appeared out of Wardrobe. The pale pink of her tights and pointe shoes merge into her naked torso. She could be entirely naked. He sees her breasts, small and high, her nipples like raspberries. She doesn't even try to cover them with her arms. He pulls the head into him, even tighter now. There is a heat within him and his breath is faster, the tune of the waltz distorted. They dance together, around and around.

"Nathan, is that you?" A voice is calling down the steps.

In shock, Nathan wakes from his dance, his tune cut short. He hears footsteps coming down the stairs.

"I thought I saw you coming this way. We want to rehearse the bolero, the Spanish dance, before the House opens."

He panics. Constant Lambert is coming down the stairs, every step bringing him closer to finding Nathan there holding the mannequin head. Nathan has seconds to spare. He throws the head into the well. There is a small splash and he watches as the head dips and then bobs up again, floating on the water's surface. Flowers spread themselves across the darkness of the well.

"What are you doing down here?" Constant asks, suspiciously. "You've not fallen for those same good luck charms as the dancers, have you? What are you going to do, anoint yourself with holy water?" He is laughing and Nathan laughs too, joining him on the steps.

"I just needed some quiet. I've had a headache all day," Nathan lies. It comes easily to him.

"Try smoking. A cigarette before a show usually sets one up all right."

"Yes, maybe I'll do that." Nathan nods and follows Constant up the stairs.

* * *

It is one of the girls from the school as the Coppélia doll tonight. Nathan, at the piano, keeps finding himself turning toward the stage, studying the contrast between the fast, dancing feet and the calm stillness of the doll up in the balcony. When Swanilda and her friends creep into Dr. Coppélius's workshop, he glances around and up at the stage. Clara is in the middle of the line of girls, her white skirt moving smoothly as she places each foot firmly onto the stage. Nathan is almost late with his cue and he turns back to the piano swiftly, sensing Constant's stare on him from the conductor's stand.

He knows what he must do. He just needs to find the perfect opportunity.

CHAPTER 23

Olivia

Mother's funeral is a small, quiet service. It is a bright April day and we squint in the clean light of the chapel at Colney Hatch, the glare exposing the smallness of our group. There is just me and Clara and some doctors and nurses who come to pay their respects. It seems Mother was rather a celebrity around here, which doesn't surprise me.

Aunt Alice and her family do not come. She sent us a note yesterday, written in a neat, careful hand. She is too shocked, too upset. Her presence would be a hindrance and we will, she tells us, be able to mourn for our mother more appropriately without her there. It is just an excuse, of course. Aunt Alice never could cope with Mother's madness. She blamed ballet more than she blamed the stress of war and of loss. We were a reminder of everything she could not endure. She preferred to keep a stiff lock on emotion, pain, memory: life must go on.

After the service, the chaplain offers us a lift in his car. We follow the undertakers as they drive Mother to Highgate Cemetery. The chaplain is young and fresh-faced, new to Colney Hatch. When we ask him questions to fill the silence of the drive, he tells us that it is different to his previous post at Edgware hospital. There he had administered to the sick in body, the elderly, the frail, easing them gently toward an acceptance of death. He had comforted families and helped them prepare funeral services. At Colney Hatch, death comes suddenly and when you least expect it. No one thought our mother was going to die, not for many years. It was a shock to them all. I nod, make soft noises of sympathy. But then I stop and stare out of the window at the passing cars, buses, an old man bent double at a bus stop. It is my mother who has died. The chaplain does not need my sympathy.

We get out at the gates of the cemetery while the chaplain finds parking down the street. The porter lets us through, nodding politely. Clara and I have visited the cemetery every year since Father died. For the first few years it was always with Mother, the three of us standing very close at the foot of his grave, laying a small bunch of flowers by the headstone and then leaving after a few silent, strained minutes. In recent years it has just been me and Clara. Each year we stay a little longer, kneeling in the grass, reading the stories Father used to tell us, the ones he had been so drawn to after the war. Tales of Rat and Mole, the Wild Wood. They were glorious escapism for us all, a brief respite from his memories of those awful years in France. Now, each year on the anniversary of his death, we spread out a picnic blanket on the patch of grass by the grave, on the top of a little slope less populated than other areas of the cemetery. A large canopy of trees shades us, ivy and ferns creeping up around the tombstones. The Western Cemetery, where Father is buried and Mother is about to join him, is dark and wooded, trees packed tightly together around the graves. Every year it is a little wilder, more and more moss and ivy taking over the graves. Even the imposing Egyptian Avenue is fading under the growing green of the wood, the old cedar tree looming darkly over the graves. Father's grave is at risk of being swallowed by the neglect, but we make sure to clear the tendrils of the ivy, wiping the headstone free of moss.

As we reach the grave, the undertakers are already there, waiting silently by the open hole in the ground. It is a shock to see the grave disturbed like this, and we stand a little further off, waiting for the chaplain. When he arrives, he smiles at us and nods. We follow him toward the grave. Mother, Father, the two of us: it is strange how close we all are right now. There is so much I want to say to them both, my anger at Father for leaving us when we needed him, my disappointment at Mother for failing us. But I will never be able to say these things. And perhaps it is better that I don't. I have blamed them too long for every anxiety, every self-doubt, every fear. It is time I start taking responsibility. Time to move on.

The ceremony is short, and I don't think I am really listening. It is only when they lower Mother's coffin into the grave that I reach toward Clara and take her hand. She squeezes mine in response. I turn to her, looking straight at her profile. She is gazing up at the tree in front of us, her eyes still. Neither of us can cry.

* * *

The walk home is well over an hour, but it is preferable to taking the bus. We don't want to go inside just yet, don't want to face the stillness of our flat and the quietness of loss. Out here in the streets, with London hurrying by, it is easier. We talk of tomorrow's performance: the third night of *Coppélia*. There is significant cast change and we have been rehearsing for the past few days to prepare. At the end of the last performance, Lydia Lopokova gave a curtain speech, curtsying low to the audience and then holding out her arms to quiet their applause. She teased them, laughed and bowed, saying that while this was her final performance in this run of *Coppélia*, she would not promise never to appear again. I expect she cannot bear to give up; to retire is to be old, acknowledging the frailties of the body. We have all seen her struggling with her knee in rehearsals, hobbling back to the dressing rooms between Acts. But onstage she is wonderful, full of the wit and joy that makes her so perfect for the role.

Ninette de Valois is to dance Swanilda for the final few performances. When this was announced, Miss de Valois called me back at the end of class. I am to take on her old role of leading peasant girl. It is wonderful news, and I have been working hard outside of rehearsals to prepare, going over and over the steps, the music, the rhythms. I was surprised it was me she asked, to be honest. After Clara had demonstrated the mazurka in class, I was convinced that she would be the one to be promoted. I worried that Miss de Valois had made a mistake in asking me to take on the role, that really she had meant Clara the whole time. I couldn't bear it if it was taken away from me now. But she had definitely asked for me, Olivia. She had used my name several times. No matter how strong my self-doubts, I could not deny that it was me she wanted.

Clara stops suddenly. It takes me a moment to realize that she is no longer walking by my side, and I have to turn and walk back to her. The pavement is narrow and getting busier as people start leaving work, the early April sun still bright. Clara is blocking the path, her shadow merging with the commuters who are walking fast and determined in each direction. They are yet to adapt to the warming weather, a block of browns and grays and blacks, coat collars rising high around their faces.

"What is it?" I say, avoiding the sweep of a satchel from a man charging past me. My voice is carried away by the grinding wheels of a delivery truck that rocks unsteadily past us.

"Let's keep walking," she says eventually. She looks unsettled, nervous. "I need to talk to you about something, but it's too noisy here."

"When we get home, then?" I think I know what this will be about. Or at least the different options start playing anxiously through my mind as we continue the walk home. I too feel nervous all of a sudden. It could be about the peasant girl role, though that seems unlikely. Clara has shown no signs of caring about that. Or maybe she has found out about what I did with Nathan, how I pretended to be her for that brief moment. I feel sick when I think about that. Or perhaps she is finally going to tell me about America, the note I found from Jacob Manton, whoever he is.

When we are nearly home, she suggests we stop in Gordon Square. The gate to the garden is open, and we find a bench under a tree. We love this garden, how quiet it is, the residents of the square the only ones to use it, and us when we can find a gate that has been left unlocked. Sometimes Lydia is here, dozing under a blanket, reading a book, even practicing her conditioning exercises, her white feet stretching and flexing in the sun. She likes to escape from the intellectualism and pretensions of her husband's Bloomsbury Group friends who haunt Gordon Square. They don't understand her, she tells us; they complain about the noise of her *allegro* on the wooden floors of the flat but really believe her an unsuitable wife for a man like John Maynard Keynes.

She always leaves the gate open for us if we ask her.

"Olivia," Clara says, turning to me but not quite looking at me.

This is hard for her, I think. It has always been this way; the longer we wait to tell each other something new, the harder it becomes. When we were children, it was so much easier, our whispered confessions binding us together against the paranoid stares of our mother.

"I have been trying to find a way of talking to you about this. I haven't made up my mind yet, as in I don't know if this is what I want, but I've been offered a really exciting contract."

I nod once but say nothing. She continues, a little more certain now that she has begun.

"It's in America. I'd be working for an agent and performing on Broadway, modeling, maybe even doing some film work. And he wants me to help set up an American ballet school. It's a really exciting opportunity for me."

"Who is he?"

"Jacob Manton. An agent. He's been watching performances at Sadler's Wells this season and noticed me."

This hurts a little. If he noticed Clara then he noticed me too. There is no avoiding the two identical twins. I just didn't stand out for him. He didn't want me too.

"How long would you be gone for?" I ask, holding back the lump settling in my throat.

"A year to start with. But maybe longer if it goes well and we want to renew the contract."

"And what's holding you back from saying yes? You seem really excited about it." I try to keep the bitterness out of my voice, but I can hear myself failing.

She sighs. "You know what's holding me back. I don't want to leave you, to be without you. Would you be okay without me here?"

I don't like this. I don't like her assumption that I can't cope on my own, that I need her by my side to survive. Perhaps there was a time when that was the case, when Mother had first been admitted into Colney Hatch, when our monthly visits took their toll. But not now. Now I am a different person from that anxious, afraid little girl.

"Clara, I'll be fine. If you want to go, you should go. I can manage by myself." I struggle to keep the harshness out of my voice. I want to say something cruel, to shake her confidence, her certainty that she has a brilliant career mapped out for her in America while I languish in the corps de ballet in London. But there is nothing I can say.

"Will you stay living in the flat on your own?" she asks.

"I have no idea. You only told me you were leaving about a minute ago, so there have been other things to process first."

"Sorry. Of course."

"Have you told Miss de Valois?"

"She already knows. Jacob Manton went to her first. She gave him her blessing, as long as he promised to give me access to daily ballet classes."

"And Nathan?"

"What about Nathan?" I notice an impatience in her voice.

"Have you told him? Surely he deserves to know. You are so close."

"We're not that close. Not anymore, not really."

"What happened?" I am wary of asking too much. It seems like dangerous territory. But I need to know if it was my fault, if what I did pushed them apart.

"He proposed to me," she replies. Then she laughs, rolling her eyes. "Can you believe it? As if I would marry anyone right now. I'd go from independence, a career, doing what I love, to folding his pocket handkerchiefs and making him dinner. It's laughable really."

I nod. It is making more sense now, why he behaved the way he did in the boardroom that afternoon.

"I thought you liked him?"

"I did. I do, I think. But he's changed. He wants me to be this perfect woman and I'm just not prepared to fit into his ideal. We've never even done anything more than kiss, you know. I used to be so frustrated by it. It was as though he would only love me if I was held at a distance, chaste and innocent. I can't take any more of that."

An image comes to mind of how he pushed himself against me, his hands hot against my thighs, his tongue hard. What was it about me, how I behaved, that made him do that to me? I had assumed that he and Clara had slept together, or at least got close to it. Finding out now that they haven't, that there was something about me that pushed him to do that, even if he did think I was Clara, makes me feel ashamed.

Clara is staring at me, looking concerned. "What's the matter? Why does it matter what happened between me and Nathan?"

I shake my head. But there are tears threatening.

"Do you like him?" she asks, her voice shaking a little with laughter. "I've seen you looking at him. If you want him, don't let me stop you."

"How can you say that?" I cry out, standing abruptly and stepping away from her. She spreads out her hands, tilting her head.

"Don't get upset, Olivia. I don't know what you want. It was just a suggestion. Perhaps you'd be suited. You're exactly the kind of perfection he wants."

"I am not perfection. Don't say that as if it is some sort of compliment. We both know you think I am dull. I don't break the rules like you do; I just get on with what I'm asked to do. Of course your Jacob Manton didn't ask me to come to America too. I don't have the personality and the charisma for such a privilege. I should stay in London, dancing in the back row, waiting for someone like Nathan Howell to propose. Is that it?"

"Olivia, no. Why are you being like this?"

But I don't wait to reply. I press my bag to me and run to the gate, nearly colliding with a couple coming into the square. They exclaim indignantly as I barge past them. When I get home, I rip off my clothes and get straight into bed. Clara gets home soon after and I pretend to be asleep. I hear her padding around the flat, hanging up my clothes, making dinner. Eventually she comes into our bedroom and sits on the end of my bed. I can feel the weight of her as the mattress sinks, but I don't move. My eyes are tightly shut. I hear her voice, barely a whisper.

"Olivia. I don't know why I said that about Nathan. I guess I've been feeling bad about turning him down. And I'm feeling bad about going to America and not telling you about it straight away. I don't know why I kept it from you. I suppose I wanted to have a clearer idea of my answer before I told you."

She pauses. I can feel the heat under her hand as she rests it against my shoulder.

"Maybe I thought that if you wanted Nathan and Nathan wanted you, I wouldn't have to feel so guilty. I could even make you both feel guilty about it, about taking him from me, and then I could go to America without feeling so wretched about myself. But I know that's unfair, more than unfair. I should have been honest with you. I'm so sorry, Olivia."

I shift a little under her hand. She knows I can hear her. I turn and open my eyes. She doesn't know how close she is to reaching some sort of truth. But any longing I have ever had for Nathan has vanished. It started fading away in the boardroom when he reached up between my legs. It vanished entirely this evening when Clara revealed the truth about their relationship. I don't want to become her replacement, a second-choice Marionetta.

Reaching up to her, I pull her in toward me, kissing her on the cheek. I hear her sigh. It is a sigh of relief, I think, that she can go to America without the guilt she was waiting for me to absolve.

Act Five

CHAPTER 24

Clara

Final nights are bittersweet. And this final night more than most. *Coppélia* is my last performance at the Vic-Wells, at least for the next year. I sent a note to Jacob Manton last week accepting his offer and within hours a giant bouquet of pink flowers had arrived at our lodgings. Olivia put on a delighted front, laughing as we tried to find a vase big enough. In the end we had to separate them into several vases and jars, decorating our flat with pastel pinks and hot shocks of red. She struggled for the first few days after I told her, but she gradually eased back to me, accepting it, seeing it differently from that first angry reaction. I imagine she is coming around to the idea, realizing that we could both do with some time apart. Now that Mother is dead, we have the space to be who we want to be, to be different, to be ourselves. And we need to find a way to let that difference flourish.

Olivia left before me this morning. She has a rehearsal to get to: *Les Sylphides* at the Ballet Club, a Fokine revival, and she will take ballet class at the Mercury Theatre. I did feel a little sadness that I couldn't be involved, but preparations for my departure are building, Jacob sending me schedules and performances and bookings he's sorted for me almost daily. It will be so busy when I get there that taking it a little quieter now is probably good.

I leave the flat mid-morning, stepping out of the downstairs front door into a warm block of bright light; the April weather promises to behave today. I lock the door, first letting the little tabby cat who belongs to our neighbor upstairs run out into the street. When I turn back to the road, the light has changed. I give an involuntary cry of shock as I realize it is Nathan standing there, his shadow stretching up the steps.

"What do you want?" I ask him. But I realize my voice is hard, suspicious, and so I smile, trying to be polite. And yet this is difficult when he is the last person I want to see right now. I know I need to talk to him, to tell him about America before he finds out from someone else. It isn't fair on him. I may have fallen out of love, but I still owe him an explanation.

"I thought I could walk with you to the theatre," he replies. "Like we always used to do."

"All right." I am irritated. I had planned to walk slowly, taking in the spring air, the flowers springing up around the grass verges, dotting my way through the little gardens and parks there for anyone who bothers to look for them. It won't be the same now that Nathan is with me, looking at me in that wounded, expectant way.

I set off at a fast pace, taking the most direct route. The morning has been ruined, so I might as well get to Sadler's Wells as fast as possible. Nathan keeps up with me, taking large strides.

"No Olivia this morning?" he asks.

"No, she's already left for Notting Hill Gate."

"Is she rehearsing at the Mercury today?"

"Yes, she's dancing for Marie Rambert at the Ballet Club in May. She's joining them for class this morning."

"And not you?"

"No, not me."

We fall silent, the sound of the road and the breeze too loud in my ears. Nathan's footsteps echo on the pavement. I am tense, waiting for the moment I can find the courage to tell him. When we reach the New River Head garden, I know my time is almost out.

"I don't think I've mentioned to you about America, have I?" I begin. It is a coward's approach to trivialize it, to pretend I don't realize this will be upsetting for him. But it's all I can bring myself to do right now.

"What about America?"

"I have a contract to go over for a year, maybe more, to perform. I leave next month."

"Next month." He stops now, turning to me. A bus lumbers by and we have to wait until it has passed for the road to be quiet enough to speak. I stare up at him, determined to hold his gaze. I cannot read his expression. It is not as I expected, instead a strange mix of confusion, hostility, defiance.

Finally I can speak again, the noise of the road fading as the bus continues its journey toward Angel. "Yes, it's come around so quickly."

"And you've only just told me now?"

"I don't understand. Why should I have told you earlier? Surely you see that I wanted to wait until it was all confirmed?" Of course, I know exactly why I should have told him earlier, but I'm not going to admit that right now. I turn away from him and catch the eye of a small boy who is crouching down in the grass on the other side of the road, waiting for his mother. A worm is struggling to escape from his determined grip.

"Clara," Nathan says, reaching across to me and taking my wrist, "I proposed to you. I thought you might say yes, that you'd think about it and decide you wanted me too. The least you could do is tell me. I think I deserve a straight answer."

I pull my arm away from him and take a step back. "I'm sorry. But I thought I'd made it very clear I didn't want to marry you, or anyone. I don't know how you could think I would change my mind."

"That's not how it seemed to me."

We stand there on the pavement, neither of us knowing what to say, neither of us moving. I watch his face as it starts to shift and change. At first I think he is about to cry. But he doesn't. His lips twist into a smile and he laughs. One loud, hard laugh. I look back at him, confused.

"You really think you'll make it to America?" He drawls his last word, contorting his voice into a parodic attempt at an American accent. "Well, good luck to you." He turns and resumes his loud, long strides until he reaches the stage door.

"What do you mean?" I call to him. But my voice is drowned out by another bus. I follow him toward the stage door, gazing up at the large poster advertising *Coppélia* on the side of the theatre. Lydia Lopokova, smiling in a low arabesque. And there, in the shadows behind her, is me, dressed as the Coppélia doll, gazing down at a book with complete stillness. I give an involuntary shudder and enter the theatre.

CHAPTER 25

Nathan

The first thing Nathan does when he enters the theatre is steal the Coppélia doll tutu. It is even easier than he thought it would be, with the dancers all in their daily ballet class and Wardrobe empty and quiet. Constant is playing for class today, his weekly duty that gives Nathan time to practice for performances. There is just the gentle hum of the stagehands cleaning, the carpenters preparing for the next production, the deliveries of drinks for the interval. If he closes his eyes, he can picture the entire theatre like a dolls' house, each occupant precisely where they should be. They will shift and change and shuffle between rooms exactly as he predicts, like the clockwork dolls' houses his mother took him to visit when he was performing in Nuremberg as a child. All Nathan has to do is walk into Wardrobe, lift the tutu from its rail, and walk out again. He lingers a little, feeling confident no one will find him, and identifies the headdress, the ribbons for the wrists, the heart necklace. These he takes too, pressing them tight to his chest as he walks quickly down the corridor toward the well. If anyone sees him, layers of tulle pressing against his chin, he will have a lot of explaining to do. But the corridors are clear.

Down in the well room, he makes his preparations. He is relieved to find that the cupboard at the back of the room is not locked. The door opens easily, and he carefully lays out the tutu and the accessories among the pipes and brooms and mops. Bundles of rope that look as though they were once used by the stagehands for securing scenery are coiled in piles on the ground, gathering dust. Stacked against the wall, looking strangely out of place, is an assortment of sport equipment: a set of tennis balls, a racket, golf clubs, a cricket bat. Perhaps props from a production that never found a permanent home. He takes out the cricket bat, blowing dust away from the edge. It is covered in little flecks of paint. Nathan has always marveled at the strangeness of theatres, the medley of items that pile up in dressing rooms and scenery docks. He thinks of his boat, his home, his own museum of the past, a carefully curated selection of items that center him, write the story of the life he wants to remember. Soon there will be a major addition to his collection. He places the cricket bat in the corner of the room, hidden in a patch of shadow.

There will be chaos when they find out that the costume is missing. But they have spares for the second cast performers; and perhaps Swanilda and Coppélia can find a way to double up, the woman and the doll sharing the same tutu. He finds it quite comical that he is concerned about this: the show must go on, even among his plotting and planning. It has always been this way, this irrational desire for the production to succeed despite his deep-seated resentment at being consigned to secondary importance, the piano player accompanying the dancers as they rehearse. When they arrive for company class each morning, it is as though he is invisible, Miss Moreton only speaking to him to give instructions for the *allegro*, whether she wants a tarantella or a mazurka for the pirouettes, the type of waltz she requires for the *grand allegro*. It never used to be this way, not when he was a star and his dressing rooms became confectionery shops of treats and toys, offered indulgently by the wives of the other musicians who fawned over him backstage. From the moment he arrived at each theatre, concert hall, grand mansion of a wealthy patron, he was treated like a prince. He didn't have to think of anything but placing his hands on those keys and performing.

Once all is set, he walks back up the stairs and goes to find Constant. Ballet class will have ended but he knows where he will be, and he is right. He bumps into Constant as he is coming out of Miss de Valois's office, a cigarette balanced between his lips.

"Constant, I've been looking for you. I need to talk to you about tonight's performance."

"Yes, what is it?" Constant replies, preoccupied as he digs through his jacket for a lighter.

Nathan coughs heavily before taking out a handkerchief and wiping his brow. "I'm not well. A horrible cold, and I don't want to risk ruining the performance with this cough all night. I'm really sorry. Could you ask someone else? Charles Lynch maybe? He'll know what he's doing."

Constant lets out a long exhalation of smoke and then grimaces. "Fine. But you've got to make sure Charles is up to speed."

Nathan coughs again, a great racking cough that vibrates through the corridor. "Actually, don't worry about it. I'll sort it out," says Constant with a sigh. "If you stay here a minute longer you'll infect us all. Go home and get better."

"Thank you. I really am feeling very rough. I'm sure a day in bed will sort me out."

"Perhaps if you lived in a real house with real walls, this wouldn't happen. It can't be good for you to live among all that damp."

Constant takes a long drag on his cigarette and walks off, shaking his head.

* * *

Nathan has one more job to do before leaving the theatre. He waits until he knows the backstage crew will be on their lunch break and then makes his move. It throws him a little to see that a new stagehand has stayed behind. The young man is sitting alone in the scenery dock with a sandwich and a newspaper, easing his nerves on his first day at Sadler's Wells, but he doesn't notice Nathan.

Once he has completed his task, Nathan enters the building again via Arlington Street and makes his way through the theatre to the main Rosebery Avenue entrance, nodding at the dancers who have spilled out onto the street for fresh air between class and rehearsal. A few loud coughs announce his departure to anyone who cares.

Walking quickly toward Duncan Terrace and down the slope to the canal, he imagines the next time he will do this walk home. On his way he checks the pavements, the roads, the height of each drop between the two. He will need to plot his route carefully. When he gets home, he sits for a long time at the front of the boat. People walk by, making the most of the warm spring weather, but he ignores them all, even the dog that barks up at him, trying to jump on his boat. There is a new narrowboat moored just above him, its hold stacked with crates, an awning protecting them from bad weather. It is rare for anyone to stay long, so he doesn't worry about it. Most boats are working boats, gliding through the country's canal network collecting and delivering goods. Using it as a home, as he does, amuses the boatmen, who like to salute him on their way out of the tunnel's mouth under Duncan Terrace. They are entertained by him, why he would choose a boat when he has no connection to the water, no history of traveling through the waterways, of striking deals at the locks, of searching for the best pubs, of haggling with suppliers. He is a pretender, they think, but a harmless one, especially when he offers them a whisky as they come to peer at him in the evenings: the strange pianist with this narrowboat that hasn't left its mooring spot for nearly two years. Nathan always explains to them about the man who owns the boat, his refusal to sell up, his delight when Nathan met him in a pub and offered to live there for rent. One day the old man will find the courage to say goodbye to his boat, but for now he is happy for Nathan to live there, occasionally visiting him and waving from the canal's edge. He never comes in, just pats the boat lovingly, as one might pat a dog.

Nathan doesn't react as the man from the new narrowboat waves at him. He needs to plan and prepare. Closing his eyes, he thinks about the inside of the boat. There is his bedroom at the back with a door leading out to the tiller, the bed not so narrow that it couldn't fit two people. The blanket is navy and white, the same nautical colors in which his mother had fitted out his room back in Richmond, as though it was a boat to sail them far away together. A small bathroom, a stove fitted tightly, a wooden table that cuts out into the room, narrow seats with red cushions. There is a space where he could fit another chair, right next to the gramophone. And opposite is his trunk, surrounded by a wall of photographs, programs, memorabilia of his life, exactly as he wants it. He smiles to think of it all, his shrine, so perfect, now to be added to in such a significant way. The little ballerina figurine is center stage on top of the trunk, her skirt fixed and stiff. He touches her every day when he gets home, a little gesture of luck.

At six o'clock he eases himself up from the front deck and goes down into the boat to do one final check. All is ready.

He starts the walk back to the theatre with a spring in his step.

CHAPTER 26

Samuel

Samuel goes home immediately after work. This is no ordinary Tuesday evening, and he needs time to think. The final performance of *Coppélia* is tonight, and he wishes he could be there. He would like to sit in the stalls; the back row would be just fine. Perhaps he would even send flowers to the dressing rooms for Olivia, maybe write her a note. Of course, any flowers he could buy would be pitiful compared to the huge bouquets he has seen delivered backstage by couriers and chauffeurs. The dancers are not short of admirers. But he has no ticket for tonight's performance. *Coppélia* will have to go on without him; and it will. No one will care that he wasn't there to watch.

In fact, he has other plans, something which surprises even himself. He often has plans these days, a walk after work to a little café Milly wants to try, the cinema with Milly, a Sunday walk through the park, Milly bringing a picnic. He doesn't remember ever actually coming up with any of these ideas himself, but he has a good time anyway, Milly's tireless energy not giving him a chance to be distracted by the eternal doubts that plague him. Milly always has a plan: exactly how far they will walk, when they will stop for lunch, what drinks they will order, what film they will see. He likes her certainty, how easy everything is. She never doubts her decisions.

Tonight, he has been invited to her house for dinner. Her parents will both be there, as well as her brother, Jonathan. He doesn't know who he is most nervous about. Probably the father, Mr. Bell. Milly has tried to reassure him. Her father is an academic at University College London, in the English Literature department. He is close to retirement, Milly tells him, as if his old age will somehow reassure Samuel. Milly's father is writing a book on the absent mother in Shakespeare's plays, and all his conversations will come back to this particular theme, she warns him. Her mother finds it particularly tiresome, but they all humor him. Once the book is published, he will be much easier. Samuel is also nervous of the brother. As an only child, he doesn't know what to expect. Milly talks about Jonathan as though he is a child, naughty but harmless; she is clearly very fond of him and so he wants to make a good impression.

Samuel changes into a clean shirt and tie, peering uncertainly at himself in the small mirror above his sink. Milly has told him what to wear: a jacket and tie, nothing too smart. Her father will be wearing a sweater with holes in the elbows and her brother will strip down to his shirtsleeves as soon as he gets in from work. If Samuel dresses too smartly, they will think him very odd. He is to bring a small bunch of flowers for her mother, a box of chocolates for her father. She helped him pick them on their way out of Covent Garden that evening, telling him exactly which colors her mother would most like, which flavors her father would be pleased by. Not too expensive, of course. Milly knew it wouldn't do to embarrass him with instructions to buy something far beyond his means.

He leaves his flat on Exmouth Market just as the sun is starting to dip toward the highest buildings, a warm glow lighting up the road behind him. The market traders are packing away, just a few stalls left with sad piles of sagging vegetables and stale-looking loaves of bread. He often picks up a simple dinner from here at night: some bread and a few slices of ham from the butcher, who spreads his produce out into the street on long tables, flies congregating as soon as he lifts the cloths from the meat. Sometimes he adds an apple from the greengrocers. They are used to him now, his daily routine. Samuel hasn't brought Milly up this street yet. He is nervous about it. She likes everything, is enthusiastic about even the smallest spot of life in the most mundane corner of London. If she doesn't like his street, his home where he's learned how much more he can be away from the cruel laughter of his father, he doesn't think he will cope. It is silly, he knows, this self-preservation. But still he avoids Exmouth Market when he walks her home, instead continuing along Rosebery Avenue and up to Islington Green.

Sadler's Wells looks alive, the lights glowing in the Wells Room, the front doors to the foyer buzzing with life. He cannot resist going past the stage door, imagining the excitement in the dressing rooms as they prepare for the final night. Cars and taxis pull up outside the entrance and he watches for a few moments as men and women dressed in their finest furs and jewels step out onto the pavement. He feels a warmth running through him as he remembers meeting Milly here those few weeks ago, how lovely she looked in the plum chiffon dress. Even though it was him explaining the story of the ballet, pointing out the shoes he had made, telling her about the dancers, she had made him feel as though he belonged. He had been glad to have her by his side.

He needs to hurry up or he will be late. And Milly told him very pointedly that he was not to be late or her brother would be insufferable, teasing her that she'd been stood up. The road is quiet behind the theatre, just the distant whisper of the orchestra's warm-up that spills out from an open door somewhere along Arlington Street.

As he walks past the end of the theatre, he hears a strange noise coming from behind him; he turns, a brief pause in his journey. A man is throwing his arms around in a narrow alleyway to his left. He seems determined to unearth something, but a layer of broken wooden crates is weighing down whatever it is, bricks wedging it into place. Samuel is about to go and help him when the man stands up tall and pulls something clear from the mess of bricks and crates piled up at the edge of the passage. It is a chair, a wheelchair perhaps. The shadows of the alleyway make it impossible to tell.

There is no need to help, so Samuel continues on his way. It is only when he reaches the end of Duncan Terrace and gets into Colebrooke Row that Samuel realizes he recognized the man. It was Nathan Howell, the pianist. The one he caught pressing his body into Olivia before the first night. The one who could not tell the two sisters apart.

Samuel is suddenly anxious. It has been several days since he's seen Olivia. That pull, that desire to be near her, has started to fade recently. And he hasn't objected. It is easier that way. But remembering that moment with Nathan has brought it back again. He has a sudden urge to turn around and go back for her, to run backstage and check she is all right. Right now she should be waiting in the wings for her moment to appear, pressing her feet up and down in his shoes as she warms up. But the flowers and chocolates in his hand remind him that he has no right to do this. Olivia has never really acknowledged him, not since that day in the corridors of the theatre; she doesn't even know his name. It is Milly who is waiting for him, her whole family there to meet him. He keeps walking onward, not looking back.

※ ※ ※

Milly is right about the flowers. Mrs. Bell looks delighted, giving her daughter a sly smile as she takes them from him. Mr. Bell receives the box of chocolates with genuine pleasure, leading Samuel straight through to the living room, where he offers him a drink.

"Best not to linger in the kitchen too long," he says to Samuel with a conspiratorial raise of the eyebrow. "You never know what you'll get roped into doing."

A young man with wild, floppy hair steps into the room. Just as Milly predicted, his sleeves are rolled up and his tie is loose around his neck.

"This is my son, Jonathan," Milly's father says by way of introduction before turning with mock severity to his son. "How you get away with looking like that at your office, I'll never know." He addresses Samuel again. "Jonathan is training at one of the best law firms in London, but you wouldn't think it to look at him."

Samuel holds out his hand to Jonathan. The boy, for he looks far too young to be a man, offers his own in return. Jonathan is suddenly shy, all the teasing and joking to which he has subjected his sister for the last few nights disappearing. He is, if he is honest with himself, intimidated by this large man whose shoulders look as though they might burst through his jacket. Jonathan is tall but as skinny as a child, his fragile wrists looking even smaller against Samuel's broad arms. He is so different to his sister, who is small and plump, with soft round cheeks; he looks as though he would blow away in the wind.

The two women join them in the living room, the warmth and smells from the kitchen following and spreading indulgently between them. Samuel says little to begin with, just answering the polite and interested questions of the family, Milly standing by his side with a happy smile on her face. But at dinner he starts to relax, the easy familiarity of them all moving through him. It is so different to his own memories of family dinners, his mother nervously offering his father more potatoes, the silence as they ate, just the sound of his father's loud chewing and his mother's nervous gulps as they finished their meal. Here the family tease Mr. Bell, mocking him as soon as he starts talking about the effect of the absent mother on Cordelia, Goneril, Regan, Hero and Beatrice. Samuel is lost by this list of names; it is a world he does not understand.

"No one is interested, Father," Milly says, smiling.

"How sharper than a serpent's tooth it is to have a thankless child!" Mr. Bell replies. The family groan in mock despair.

"So, Samuel," Mrs. Bell says when their laughter has calmed, "Milly tells us you are designing shoes for the Freeds. She says you are very talented."

Swallowing his mouthful, he looks up. He assumes they will be bored by his answer, just asking out of politeness, but he is surprised to see them all looking at him with genuine interest, even Jonathan waiting expectantly for his reply. Samuel imagines his own mother asking him about his work. His father would grunt and say dinner is not the time for such nonsense.

"Hopefully, yes," he manages to reply. "I have some designs, and Mr. Freed is considering whether they will be a popular addition to the pointe shoes we already make."

"They are gorgeous," Milly adds. "One day we'll all be wearing his shoes. And his clothes! You should see Samuel's design for a winter hat. It's got the prettiest trim of navy lace embroidery."

"It sounds lovely," replies Mrs. Bell. "Do you take commissions? You could start your business from home perhaps, just with the occasional item when you have time on the weekends and after work. And then one day perhaps you can open your own shop."

Milly has been suggesting this to him recently, dropping it into conversations as though it is the simplest thing in the world. But he doesn't have a sewing machine, not even close to enough money to buy one, and the costs of starting up would be too immense. It feels like a dream too far off to grasp.

"Not yet," he replies. "But if I can save up enough for a sewing machine, then I can start practicing and maybe be good enough to take commissions one day."

"Why doesn't Samuel borrow our sewing machine?" Mr. Bell says as he pours a thick layer of custard over his pudding. "I don't think I've seen either of you use it for months."

Milly looks up excitedly. "What a brilliant idea. Jonathan and I can bring it over this weekend."

It is all moving too quickly. Samuel feels unsteady, as though the walls are expanding and swelling around him. He doesn't know what to say, but the excited chatter of the others means that he doesn't really need to say anything at all. When there is finally a lull in their noise, he speaks.

"Thank you." And he adds in his head that this is the kindest thing anyone has ever offered him, but he doesn't have the courage to say it out loud. He turns to Mrs. Bell. "Perhaps you could request the first commission?"

The rest of the meal moves between planning Samuel's first design projects and Mr. Bell trying to squeeze in anecdotes from his book. The laughter and the noise do not die down, even when Jonathan and Mr. Bell take to the sink, continuing their conversation as they do the washing-up. Samuel offers to help, but Milly and her mother put their hands on his arm, keeping him at the table. He has never, in all his life, seen his own father do the washing-up after a meal.

When he leaves just after ten thirty, the family press into the hallway to wave goodbye. "See you in the morning," Milly shouts at him as he walks away. Samuel turns back to wave, feeling an immense relief that it is fewer than twelve hours until he sees her again. He will time it so that he arrives just as she does, the two of them appearing at the turning down to Cecil Court at exactly the same moment; he knows her schedule now, as precisely as if it were his own. It will be like they never left each other's side.

*　*　*

At first, he thinks he is hallucinating. But then the figure comes closer, materializing out of the darkness. He knows her run, the shape of her shoulders as she moves, the rise of her breath now hard and panicked. Olivia Marionetta is running toward him. Duncan Terrace Gardens transform, and all his thoughts of Milly, the sewing machine, the laughter around the table in the little home off Islington Green, dissolve and vanish. He is only here, in this moment, waiting for Olivia Marionetta to reach him.

CHAPTER 27

Clara

Tonight, I am the last to go down to the well. I need to do this alone. My final performance, my final routine of getting ready for a show in this theatre I have grown to love so much. The energy in the dressing rooms is high, not even dampened by Mr. Healey's noisy hysterics about the missing Coppélia costume. It is a mystery but probably easily explained. Maybe it was taken to the cleaners a day too soon; maybe someone has stolen it—it could be anyone. The theatre is hardly the most secure place, suppliers in and out all day, audience members who might be tempted to sneak backstage. You could make a lot of money from a costume like that. But we nod sympathetically as he charges around our dressing rooms, and then we get back to our conversations. I have told them about America now. Everyone reacts in different ways. Some of the girls seem envious, while others think I am crazy for giving up all we have created here at the Vic-Wells. I can see them turn subtly to Olivia, trying to gauge her reaction. But she just smiles and gives them nothing.

I haven't finished my warm-up, but the quiet of the well room is what I need tonight. So I linger after all the others have left. I lay my shawl across the ground and lower myself down slowly, stretching out my hamstrings. Then I rub my feet, flexing them, rolling my ankles. I have my pointe shoes with me, hanging over my shoulder with the ribbons loosely knotted. Tying my pointe shoes has become a part of my body, a muscle memory I could do with my eyes closed. But tonight I think about each movement, each turn of the ribbon, how the shoe feels against my foot, exactly how tight the ribbon needs to be around my ankle. Once they are tied, I stand and pad out my feet, walking through the pointe, pushing my arches forward. I know I will need to keep up this discipline, taking class every day, keeping my body in the condition it requires to be able to dance as I expect of myself. It will be hard in America to be strict with myself without Miss de Valois and Miss Moreton pushing us through our barre work every morning. But I am excited about the chance to do more. I long to travel, to meet people, to explore a new theatre every season, to meet actors and dancers and musicians on tour. I long to get away from the still waters of this well. I want an ocean, not a dark puddle that drags me back here every day, reflecting back a face that is not sure whether it has chosen this path. Now that Mother is no longer judging and shaping us, I can re-evaluate every decision I have ever made.

There is a noise from the other side of the room, a rustle and then a bang, as if something has fallen over. I look up with a jump, startled by the intrusion on my preparations. But there is no one there. I start to gather up my belongings, wrapping the shawl around my shoulders. The moment of calm has come to a sudden end and I need to return to the dressing room to do my last few preparations before the performance.

I start to walk toward the steps. But there is a louder noise behind me now, footsteps gaining on me quickly, heavy breathing. I start to turn but then there is pain, darkness.

CHAPTER 28

Nathan

Nathan holds the cricket bat in his hand, suddenly afraid. What if he has killed her? Throwing the bat aside, he kneels beside her, pulling her head into his lap. When he feels the back of her head where he hit her, a bump is already forming. He leans forward, his ear to her mouth. She is breathing, a mist of air hovering above her lips. He lifts her wrist, feeling for her pulse; he can just feel it, faint through the delicate white of her skin.

Lying her on her side, he gets up and goes to the broom cupboard. He has been hiding in there for nearly an hour and his limbs are stiff from the effort of staying so still. Nathan had hoped he would find her alone, but he hadn't really thought it would work out like this. His alternative plan was more complex, riskier, but he'd practiced it enough times in his head that he was convinced it would work. He was going to find that new stagehand, the one who hasn't been here long enough to know what Nathan Howell looks like. Nathan would send him to find Clara Marionetta, to tell her there was an American gentleman waiting for her with some news. The gentleman wanted somewhere quiet before the start of the show and had found out from the dancers that the well was the best place in the theatre for a private conversation. Nathan knew that she would come running, afraid her precious contract was about to be taken from her. But in the end, he didn't even need to do that. She'd lingered. He'd been there to catch her.

Nathan can sense the movements of the theatre around him, even from the secluded darkness of the well room. There are a few minutes until the beginners' stage call and then the corridors will fall empty and quiet just long enough for him to move her. He brings the Coppélia costume from the cupboard and lays it on the ground next to Clara. She looks so peaceful like that, sleeping on her side, her legs stretched out elegantly, one foot crossed over the other. Kneeling, he feels for the clasps on the back of her peasant girl costume. They are tight and firm, but he manages to loosen them. Nathan rubs her collarbone with his thumb as he draws the straps down her arms, pulling the skirt and bodice from her body. He stands and looks at her, casting her costume to the side. The skirt ends up on the stone wall of the well, slipping too close to the water; the netting soaks from the bottom up within seconds. Slowly the costume sinks into the well, floating there in a mess of satin, net, lace.

Now he turns his attention back to Clara. He has seen her like this before, when she ran half-naked out of Wardrobe. But she was moving then, a flash of fast flesh and motion. He can really look at her now, the curve of her breasts, her small, firm waist flat beneath the band of her tights. Her spine is protruding, each vertebra poking through the skin, and he draws down them with his finger, stopping in the middle of her back where one of them is red, the skin abraded. He has seen the dancers doing their exercises, lifting themselves up and down on their backs to harden their stomachs, caring nothing for the pain of their bones against the studio floor.

It is not easy getting the doll tutu over her legs and pulled up to cover her body. For a moment he wishes he had waited until later, instead keeping her in the peasant girl costume, but he knows that wouldn't do. He needs her as Coppélia from the moment he possesses her.

Nathan adjusts the tutu around her thighs, running his fingers around the net gusset, settling the knickers into place. Clara murmurs as he tightens the bodice around her. He freezes, his hands still, but she doesn't wake. The ribbons are easy to tie around her wrists, and the necklace fits perfectly around her neck. He is less skilled with the headpiece, his hands slipping as he tries to pin the floral crown into her hair. The final result is not perfect, a little skewed, making her look wonky, a faulty doll. Not happy with it, he tries again, his heart beating faster now. He needs to hurry.

Finally, she is ready. He lifts her to her feet, groaning with the weight of her lifeless body. She falls forward over his shoulder but he catches her, holding her under her arms. He takes a step to the side and her legs drag with him. It is a dance of sorts, a sleepy, heavy dance of acceptance. She has accepted him at last, he thinks.

The drink is prepared. His Sleeping Beauty. He takes the bottle out of his jacket pocket: water mixed with sleeping pills, crushed into powder. They will take effect quickly, especially after the blow to her head. Her shoulders drop forward, her head lolling over to the side, but he catches her, holding her upright again. He lowers her to an awkward seated position, holding her head back as he tips the bottle toward her lips. Clara is almost awake, but lost in a haze. She resists, murmuring a protest, but she has no strength and eventually he manages to get the contents of the bottle down her throat. A trickle of water has dripped down her chin, and he wipes it away. The skin beneath is paler now, her stage makeup fading.

Nathan dabs at it with his finger, trying to even up the color of her foundation. It unsettles him, this flaw. He needs her to be perfect.

From the quiet of the well, he can hear the orchestra starting to tune up, the hum of the audience filling the auditorium. Someone must have left a door open onto the pit, he thinks; the noises of the stage are louder than usual. There are footsteps above him, at the top of the steps, dancers running to the wings to complete their warm-up. He will need to wait until the performance has started and the corridors are quiet again. Nathan thinks of Charles, the pianist taking his place for the night, and he hopes he doesn't mess up. He thinks, too, of the dancers, the missing costume, the missing doll's wheelchair, their missing peasant girl. They won't think of him though, the pianist who sits silently in the corner, who has learned every beat of the rhythm of the theatre.

Suddenly, a voice at the top of the stairs. He freezes, gripping Clara with shaking hands. It is Olivia, looking for her sister. Her voice carries down to him with unnerving strength, as though the sleeping woman in his arms has sprung into life in the bright light at the top of the steps.

"Clara, if you're down there, hurry up. We're on in minutes." He stays still, not daring to make a sound. If he is silent, maybe she won't bother coming down. And he is right. He hears her sigh, muttering something about where Clara could be, and the tap-tap of her pointe shoes disappearing down the corridor.

Nathan needs to move. The performance is starting and he knows he has just a short window of time in which the stagehands, dancers, musicians will be occupied with those opening moments of the performance, all attention on Constant Lambert making his way to the podium. Already the discordant notes of the orchestra warming up are starting to metamorphose into harmony. Clara is heavier than he expected, her body giving him no help, limbs falling uncontrollably. How do the male dancers make it look so easy, he thinks, envious of their effortless strength at lifting and throwing the ballerinas up in the air. But of course they have help, the women taking half the effort, their muscles taut and strong. Clara is giving him nothing; she collapses like a puppet.

He is sweating with the effort by the time he gets to the top of the stairs, but fear and anticipation keep him moving with a power he did not know he had. The door to the street is not far, and it is easier once he is no longer climbing the narrow stairs from the well. He kicks the door open and looks around him before stepping out in the street. It is still light, too light, and for a moment it feels as though a spotlight is directed right at him, his body lit up as it used to be when he was performing at concerts, the child star. These longer evenings have arrived so quickly, he's missed it, somehow expecting it to be pitch black by the time he leaves the theatre with Clara. The street is empty so he surges forward, his back aching with every step. Sweat drips down his forehead and he can smell the cloying dampness on his top lip.

Nathan reaches the alleyway opposite the theatre, a narrow lane off Arlington Street used as a dump by workmen. Finding a hiding place for the Coppélia doll wheelchair while the stage crew were on their lunch break had not been easy, but he'd been relieved to find the chair still in place when he'd returned this evening, covered by the broken crates and pallets he'd pulled across it. He lowers Clara down behind a pile of bricks, covering her gently with his coat.

As he shuffles about in the alleyway trying to release the wheelchair from its hiding place, a man walks past carrying a box of chocolates and a bunch of flowers. It seems so out of place, this ordinary man continuing along the road for his ordinary evening. Nathan waits for him to get to the end of the road before he hauls the chair out and steadies the wheels. He is grateful for how silently it moves, greased regularly by the stagehands who are instructed to keep it quiet onstage. When he turns back to Clara he is dismayed by the sight: she looks like a discarded china doll, a smear of dirt across her cheek. He wipes it off tenderly before lifting her into the wheelchair.

* * *

It is with reluctance that he places his coat over her, hiding the tutu from view. She looks so small all of a sudden, her body disappearing under his long heavy coat. He wraps a shawl around her hair, very gently so as not to disturb the angle of her floral crown. And finally she is ready. As he wheels her out into the road, he feels calm, in control. Now that he is wheeling her steadily, no longer sweating under the weight of carrying her over his shoulder, he feels better. Reaching the end of Arlington Street, he looks about him, watching as a steady stream of cars, three women on bicycles, a bus, continue past him. A taxi pulls up further along the road, its navy body rocking as four men rush out, the bottles of beer in their hands splashing over onto the pavement. They ignore him. He is just a man wheeling a sleeping invalid back home after an ordinary day. They do not notice the tiny flash of pink satin peeking out under the bottom of the coat. Two young women stop right next to him, waiting to cross the road. He turns his head just an inch to look at them, to see if they are staring curiously at his sleeping doll. But they don't even register the wheelchair. Their heads are close, both of them in matching gray hats, and he sees that they are holding hands. One of them notices Nathan looking and pulls her hand away. They take a step apart from one another, their faces taut. Nathan feels relief. Everyone has their own personal adventure to worry about tonight.

A break in the traffic emerges and he crosses the road, quickly slipping between the warehouses on Owen Street and then into the shadows of Colebrooke Row. A mother and daughter walk toward him and he feels his chest tighten as the little girl stares at Clara with wide-eyed curiosity. But her mother yanks on her arm to hurry her up, and they move on.

It would be safer to stay hidden, waiting in the darkened alleyways until the streets clear, but there is a part of him that wants to be seen: he deserves her. He has waited long enough, worked hard enough. She belongs to him, dressed forever in the same red skirt with the same pink shoes tied around her ankles. Lace and net graze her motionless thighs. Her skin is smooth porcelain and her lips are pink. Never has there been a lovelier figure, unchanging, unbroken by the pace of time. Soon she will be home with him and he can start to preserve this memory, this moment of perfection. Her sightless eyes will not fade. She will be a beautiful statue, preserved forever. He has watched her for so long, holding her in his gaze, locking her into position like a photograph. Now she can join his mother, but it will be so much more real this time. No more pretending. No more fantasy.

He imagines dancing with her, the two of them arm in arm under the stars. Silent, of course, but that is no matter. It is better that way. She is a dancing doll, his Coppélia, created at last. He can finally believe it, now that he has her in the wheelchair.

Pausing at the top of the slope down to the canal, he reaches down to her wrist, which has broken free from the coat. He lifts her arm above her, as if she is waving to a crowd. Ice-cold. He drops her arm in fright. Life lingers, like a promise; but he is afraid of what will happen when she wakes.

He needs to move quickly.

CHAPTER 29

Olivia

I am convinced that Clara will turn up. Just before we are about to run onstage, she will appear, a little apologetic, making up some excuse. And so we delay rearranging the order, the patterning of our corps de ballet, until the last possible moment. When we finally realize she isn't coming, I take charge and give everyone their new places, a little shuffling of the positioning so that the audience won't notice the missing peasant girl. One of the men runs around to the other side of the stage to pass on the message to those entering stage right. Everyone seems to feel it is my responsibility to sort this out. She is my sister after all.

We are all nervous, me more than anyone. It doesn't feel right. Clara has never missed a performance; and besides, I saw her ready in costume just half an hour ago. My stomach is in knots and I can't keep still, repeatedly rising and lowering in *relevé* and *échappé* until my legs feel warm and awake. It is easy to tell when we are feeling unsettled before a performance. The rosin box at the back of the wings is always crowded with our feet, all of us returning too many times to dip our toes into the powder. There will be no slipping onstage for anyone tonight.

It is not only Clara's absence that is strange. One of the Coppélia costumes is still missing. And even stranger is the missing wheelchair. The backstage crew realized it had gone as they were preparing the stage this afternoon. They have had to make do with an ordinary wooden chair instead, which doesn't quite have the same effect, and we are all hoping Sergeyev doesn't notice the small change to the choreography.

I hear the applause of the audience as our conductor walks into position, the moment of silence as he lifts the baton, the first slow notes, like an awakening. Taking a deep breath in, I find the pace of the music, let it wash over me. It is so familiar; I can hear each note, each bar, even before it arrives. The melody, high and strong, comes in after half a minute. Usually this is when I start to picture myself onstage, visualizing each step. But tonight I feel nothing. The music sounds strange, distorted, as though I am listening to it underwater. I watch Miss de Valois onstage, the Swanilda variation that she performs with such lightness, the mime usually so clear it is as though she is speaking the words. Tonight I cannot read the language of her gestures; it seems to me that she is dancing another story altogether. It is just a chaotic mix of waving arms and legs.

All I can think about as I run onstage and start dancing is where Clara could be. The audience are even more of a faceless sea of shapes and shadows than usual, and the swaying movement of the orchestra unnerves me, like a leviathan rising from the depths. In the interval I search every dressing room. I even consider running home, to see if she is there, but I know I won't make it back in time.

Just before Act Two is about to begin, I realize that I haven't checked with Nathan. He might have spoken with her; perhaps they had an argument. I hurry to the dressing room where the orchestra spend the interval. It is packed in there, a crush of white shirts and black jackets. Most of them ignore me as I ease my way into the room, asking them if Nathan is around. But finally one of the percussionists takes pity on me and asks me again who I am looking for.

"Is Nathan Howell in here? Or do you know where he is?"

"Nathan isn't on tonight. He's unwell. A cough or something. Constant told him to go home."

I leave, disappointed. Act Two should be a moment of celebration, our final night. But I can't find the energy and I know my dancing as the mischievous friend of Swanilda is flat. After the curtain call I get changed as quickly as possible, ready to hurry home. The other girls are preparing to go out with feverish excitement, refreshing their makeup, loosening their hair and re-pinning it into glamorous styles, smoothing out their party dresses. A bar in Covent Garden has been booked for the evening, but I can't join them. Not without knowing what has happened to Clara.

"You're not going to know where Clara is all the time when she moves to America," Hermione scolds me, playfully, as I fret with the buckle on my shoe. "I'm sure she's fine. When has she ever not been fine?"

"This isn't like her. She's never missed a show before." I have no patience for the persuasions of the girls. I know they are just trying to help, but I can't focus on anything they say.

As I walk along the corridor to the stage door, I try to remember how she was when I last saw her, what she was doing. It was down by the well, all of us dipping our fingers into the water and trailing the drops over our toes. There was quite a crowd of us, laughing and joking as we mocked ourselves for our ridiculous superstitions; Clara was the last to arrive. I can't remember seeing her after that.

Reaching the door that opens onto the staircase down to the well, I am nervous again, as though I might find something horrible down there. A memory of the night I found the flower crown in the well comes back to me sharply. It spooked me, seeing those flowers floating in the water, the mannequin's head bopping up and down. And now the missing tutu, the wheelchair. I don't know if anyone thought to look down here in the dark corners or the cupboard at the back. Perhaps no one wanted to try.

I turn on the light as quickly as I can, but it offers little clarity, the shadows and shapes of the room lurking. When I reach the bottom of the steps, I move quickly toward the water. At first I think it is her, drowned, the net of her dress consuming her body. I hear my cry, a loud, sharp scream. But the silence of the room swallows it just as I realize there is no body. Just a mess of costume half in, half out of the water, her shawl in a heap on the ground.

I call out for her, but there is nowhere she could be. The room is empty. My sister has vanished.

CHAPTER 30

Clara

I struggle to find myself. Sound comes back first, a strange discordance of familiar music, ripples splashing against a surface, low slapping footsteps, water under a bridge. My head aches, a dull pounding through my temples, a sharp pain near my neck. I try to open my eyes but they feel glued shut, my eyelids heavy. There is music coming from very close by, soft at first but gradually getting louder and clearer. I recognize those notes. Long, slow, a little haunting. The melody comes in with a brightness that hurts my head. The opening of *Coppélia*. That is when I panic. It feels like hours since I was getting into my costume, warming up, putting on my makeup for the start of the performance. I try to think. Has the performance happened? Did I fall asleep? Am I in the wings, waiting to enter the stage? Or am I at home, having some horrible dream? It would make sense, I reason with myself, to be plagued with nightmares about missing the show, a manifestation of my decision to go to America. I try to feel my body, bring it into my consciousness, find its location. No, I am sure the performance hasn't happened yet. Either I am dreaming or I have missed it altogether. My thoughts dance and drift over each other, not grasping anything real.

I try to move, but I can't. My legs feel like lead, and it is as though something heavy is sitting on my chest. My mind jumps painfully to a copy of a painting Olivia and I were obsessed with as teenagers: Fuseli's *The Nightmare*, with its terrifying creature pressing itself down into a woman's body. Right now, with my eyes refusing to open, I feel its claws working their way into my ribs, my lungs struggling to find enough air. The image was in a book Mother kept in her bedroom, an illustrated history of romantic art and literature. We would sneak in and look at it when Mother was out. I can't get that awful image out of my head now; it is imprinted in the dark pink and black behind my eyelids.

My body is slowly coming back to life. I move my fingers, stretching out my palms, though my grip fails me when I try to fold them into a fist. Extending my consciousness down my body, I think about my feet. But they feel trapped, restricted. I register that familiar feeling of tightness around the balls of my feet and realize I am wearing pointe shoes.

I feel a soft brushing on my arm. It moves up and down, gently, rhythmically, out of time with the music that continues to build around me. I try to let it soothe me, like the way Olivia and I would tickle the inside of each other's arms with the lightest of touches when we were tired and scared. But the more I try to open my eyes, the more I think about that stroke on my arm. I don't know what it is and it unsettles me. I want to push it away, brush it off. Eventually it stops. I think I can hear footsteps moving away from me.

It takes great mental effort, but I manage to pry open one eye, just a little, before it closes again. I feel myself drifting in and out of sleep. But what I see when I open that eye stays with me, turning itself over and over until I can decipher some of what is around me. Red, brown, dim golden light, wooden surfaces with red curtains and cushions. Directly opposite me, a trunk. Papers, maybe photographs, chiffons, dresses, a fox fur piece, a pile of hairpins, silk stockings, a little music-box doll. It reminds me of a dressing room. Perhaps I have fallen asleep in the dressing room. Why would no one wake me? I can hear the music, but it doesn't sound quite right; a low crackle stains the clarity of the sound. My entrance is just minutes away. I need to be warming up, preparing my body for the first steps across the stage. I try and try, willing my body to get up. But it does nothing.

I must have fallen asleep again, because I jerk awake this time, my eyes opening and flicking wildly around me. I am in a narrow room lined with wooden seats, a small table that juts out from the wall, a stove in the corner. The light is dim, just a few candles dotted on the surfaces, a paraffin lamp lit low against the wall. I try to stand, pressing my hands down against the sides of the chair to lift myself up. The ceiling is low and I feel breathless, as if the walls are closing in around me. With my feet firmly on the ground, I take a step forward. The ground doesn't feel right, as if it is shifting and rocking ever so slightly. My head pounds and I suddenly think I am going to be sick.

"You'll feel better if you sit down," a voice says from an inner door to my right. I turn my head too sharply and reel. Although I recognize the voice, the pounding in my head is muffling everything and I can't think straight.

He comes into the room, the light from the lamp just reaching the edge of his face. I lean against the chair but don't sit down; my legs quiver with the effort. He takes another step forward, and that is when I realize who it is.

"Nathan," I say, alarmed when my voice refuses to work properly. It is barely a whisper, but it hurts my head, the word reverberating through my skull.

He comes to me and puts his hands around my waist, gently lowering me back into the chair. I murmur a protest, but I need to sit. If I don't, I think I might collapse. The seat is uncomfortable, a hard wood, but it feels faintly familiar. I look down and to the side and notice wheels attached to the chair. I am in a wheelchair; there is a block of wood wedged under one of the wheels. This is the Coppélia doll chair, I am sure of it. I can't make sense of it, this strange mix of Delibes music, the chair, my feet in pointe shoes, this long, thin room. Now that my neck is moving more easily, I can see my body. Red ribbons are tied around my wrists and I am wearing a tutu. It is uncomfortable sitting in the skirt, the netting at the back sticking into my thighs. I will be crushing it. We've been taught never to sit like this in a tutu, but right now it doesn't seem to matter.

"It suits you," Nathan says. He is leaning against the door, watching me with an odd expression. He seems so different somehow, as though the Nathan I know has morphed into someone new. "I saw you wear that for the photographs, for the poster. I'd never seen you sit so still as when you were posing for the photographer."

"But I'm not Coppélia tonight," I insist, moving awkwardly in the chair. I try to pull the back of the tutu out from under me and it fans out behind me, the netting reaching high against the chair. "It's one of the students. Mr. Healey will be needing this tutu. Why am I wearing it?" I don't really think Nathan will have the answer, but I ask it all the same. He should be in the orchestra pit right now.

"You're wearing it because it suits you," he replies. I don't understand him. "I chose it for you. The perfect costume for my doll."

"Your doll." As I speak the words, I start to panic again. There is something about his tone, the way he is looking at me, that I don't like. It reminds me of when he proposed. I think that was the first time I truly felt afraid of him. Before then there had been no reason to, not even when he was at his most controlling, leading me from restaurant to café, dictating the rhythm of my evenings, what I must wear, when I should dance, when I could go home. He had never done anything to suggest he'd hurt me, or anyone for that matter. I had always felt balanced on the edge of control and submission, as though a word from me and he'd give in, let me choose my path. But I realize now that I have never really tested that hypothesis. I always gave in to him, right up until his final demand, the marriage proposal that I finally found the courage to refuse. Looking at him now, he is different. Dangerous, even. I shift uneasily, the bodice cutting into my waist. Someone has done it up too tightly.

He steps forward and kneels in front of me, placing his hands around my ankles. I try to move my legs away from him, but his grip tightens.

"Would you like to see my collection?" he says, smiling up at me with a new hardness I have not seen in him before. "I've got to share it with you, now you're finally here."

"But where am I?" I look around me again, trying to piece together some order to the dull shapes that dance in the candlelight. I hear voices and footsteps close by. We must be near a street, I think, but there are other sounds too that confuse me. The music continues to rise and fall around me, but I see now that it is coming from a gramophone to my left.

"You've always said you wanted to visit my home," he replies. "Well, here we are. My boat. What do you think?" He gestures around him. "Is it how you imagined?"

"But how did I get here, Nathan? The last thing I remember is getting ready for the performance, warming up. I was by the well." And then I remember those footsteps behind me, the pain in my head. Nathan is still holding on to my ankles. I flinch away from him, trying to kick his hands off me. But my feet can barely move.

"Steady, Clara. You're okay now. I brought you here. You needed help."

"Why did I need help? Did you hit me?"

"Yes. Of course I did. As I said, you needed help."

"How was hitting me over the head and dragging me all the way to your boat helping me?"

"Let's not get ahead of ourselves. You're tired. You've had a shock. Just rest a moment, and then we can talk further."

"What is it you want from me? I need to be onstage right now."

"It's a bit late for that, I'm afraid."

"Olivia will be wondering where I am. She'll come looking for me."

"I'm sure she will. But by the time she's worked out where you are, it won't matter anymore."

"What do you mean by that?"

"Hush. It's okay." He pauses and looks up at me, his hands relaxing their grip on my ankles. "Let me give you a guided tour of my boat. That will make you feel better."

I stand up in one strong effort, pushing him as hard as I can from where he is crouched on the floor. He falls backward, letting go of my ankles. I try to step forward, my body propelling itself toward the door at the other end of the boat. But there is something stopping me, a rope perhaps, tying me to the frame of the chair. I fall onto my knees. The chair bucks behind me, knocking into my back painfully.

Nathan stands quickly, lifting me back into the chair. I struggle against him, but he is too strong, his weight pressing into me. He has a piece of rope in one hand and I fight him as he winds it around my chest and arms, pinning me to the chair. My head still aches and my throat is dry. When I cry out, I don't know if I am even making any sound. It feels like I am in a nightmare. I must be making some noise, for he drives himself at me, holding his hand against my mouth.

"Clara, it's okay. I don't want to hurt you."

I shake my head at him. I want to believe him, but I can't. Not now that I am tied to this chair, my head swimming in pain.

"I'm going to tie this around your mouth if you can't be quiet," he says, looking at me with eyes I don't recognize. He has a thin silk scarf in his hand. It looks delicate, a silvery blue with half-moon patterns printed across the silk, but I don't want it near me. It transforms into something terrifying, held like that in his hand. "Can I trust you?" he says, his face close to mine. His hair is burnt gold, fading just a little above his temples. I have never looked at him this closely before, not even when we were out in London, at cafés, restaurants, exhibitions. It is as though I am seeing him for the first time.

I nod, desperate for him to remove his hand. I can feel the wetness of my breath pooling in his hand; the rise and fall of my chest is strained and heavy.

He pulls back, watching me carefully. I move my jaw from side to side, easing out the ache across my face. He's looking at me strangely, critically, as though there is something about me that is not quite right. He reaches behind him toward the trunk and picks up a powder compact. It is an old style, the type my mother had when we were very young. There is a pretty floral design interwoven across the case.

There must be lipstick on his hand, perhaps even some smeared across my face. Nathan wipes his hand on his trousers as he comes toward me, opening the compact. He leans over me, dabbing the sponge against my skin. I twist my head away, but he turns me back again, holding my chin with a tight grip.

"I need you to look just right," he says as he straightens up, staring down at me as though I am a painting. "There." He turns the compact around and holds up the mirror. "Don't you look lovely. Like a doll."

I stare at my reflection. I do look like a doll. My makeup is heavier than usual, rosy cheeks rising up into my hairline.

"I added a bit of makeup once you'd got here," he says, as if reading my thoughts. "The journey didn't do you any favors. But it's okay now. You're here."

"What is this?" I say, my voice rising uncomfortably. "Why have you brought me here?"

He ignores me, instead going to the trunk opposite and starting to tidy up. He puts the makeup back into a box, rolls the stockings into a ball. The hairpins are scattered among the photographs. He draws them all together and tucks them inside a velvet purse. There is a little box on the trunk. I know what is inside: the engagement ring I refused to accept.

"These all belonged to my mother." He picks up each item tenderly before setting it down again more neatly. "This was her favorite fur piece," he says, stroking a white fox fur shawl that is fraying a little around the edges. "And she loved an occasion to wear these shoes."

His hand lingers over the ring box but then he moves on, placing the shoes back on a shelf above the trunk; they are silver with delicate buckles. Hanging from a hook on the wall next to the trunk is an evening dress: it is blue, trimmed with feathers, the sort of dress I remember my mother wearing too. It makes me sad to think of how much he has saved. He has all these memories of his mother, while Olivia and I threw it all away. We took nothing but a few photographs from Colney Hatch. All of Mother's clothes, her jewelry, her makeup, they would be discarded by now, thrown out among the belongings of those patients who have no family to preserve their memories.

"Do you want to try on her gloves?" he says, holding out a pair of white silk gloves. I shake my head.

"Probably for the best. I don't want to muddle up the artifacts." I don't like the way he calls them that, artifacts, as though this is a museum. But looking at the way he handles her belongings, his memories of his precious mother that he has told me so much about, it really could be a museum.

"Do you want to see my toy room?" he asks me, his voice rising in excitement. "Don't you dare say no," he warns. He is smiling, though, like a little child showing his new toys to a friend. I do nothing, just stare blankly back at him. He is a stranger to me, this talented pianist I thought I knew so well, reverting back to some childlike state. "Don't you move," he says, laughing. "I'll bring them to you."

He disappears into the room from which he first emerged. I have never been on a narrowboat before, but there is no bed in this main room and nothing that looks as though it could be converted into one. The other room must be the bedroom, I think, shuddering as I remember all those times I had longed for him to bring me back here, how much I wanted him to run his hands over me, to press his mouth against my skin as we lay on his bed. Now, the thought makes me sick. As soon as he leaves, I strain at the bindings, pushing my arms against them. But all that happens is the wheelchair comes loose from the wooden wedge holding it in place and I roll forward, crashing into the trunk.

"What's going on?" he says, appearing quickly out of the bedroom. "Clara, you have to stay still. This is only going to take longer if you struggle." Nathan wheels me back to the same position against the side of the boat, placing the wedge back under the wheel. He disappears again but this time comes back immediately. In his hands is a tin box.

He collects a few candles from around the boat and places them on the table diagonally across from me. I have a clear view of the space, and I watch with reluctant fascination as he opens the box and starts to empty its contents onto the table.

Nathan starts with the soldiers. With a steady hand, he lines them up in two rows at the edges of the table. They are all standing to attention, painted in bright red and gold.

"These were my first. Mother bought them for me after each concert as a reward. They were unpainted and I would sit the day after each performance and paint them in the finest detail. I still have the workbox, all the tiny brushes and the bright tubes of color. It became a routine, a reassurance I suppose, that I was still a child and could do childish things. Mother found all the best toy shops in London, Paris, Venice, Geneva. It was the first thing she would do when we got to a new city for a concert; find me my next doll."

Gradually, I watch as he fills the center of the table with more miniature dolls and figurines. There is a priest, painted in long robes with a purple chasuble. There are many musicians, some medieval minstrels with lutes and recorders, some in modern dress attached to miniature musical instruments. A little boy plays at a piano, his hair painted golden. There is a woman in a long blue dress playing the violin. A choirboy stands with a hymn book open in his hands.

"I had a princess stage, which amused my mother and horrified my father. Here's Sleeping Beauty." He lays her out on the table, a little doll resting on a bed lined with roses. "I remember painting her, how careful I had to be with her lipstick. I have a very steady hand. Mother said it was because I was so good at the piano. All those scales."

"Why are you showing me all these?" I say. I have been here too long without understanding what he wants from me. These dolls are scaring me, the way they are lined up in perfect rows with the candlelight flickering gloomily over their faces.

He ignores my question. "And finally we have the ballerinas." He places three dolls along the front of the desk, one of which he picks up from the trunk. There is one kneeling, with her arms crossed over her legs. She is wearing the dying swan tutu, the feathers painted with careful precision. Another is in chiffon trousers drawn in at the ankle, a bright red cropped top that is studded with jewels. The attention to detail is remarkable. It is the Firebird costume, recreated in miniature. The final doll is familiar. It is the music box figurine, the one I saw him steal from the dressing room all those weeks ago. I don't know why, but it is this one that scares me most, its stiff skirts and hard skinny arms sending a shiver down my spine.

"And you, Clara, you have just joined them. You are my greatest creation, my Coppélia doll brought to life."

"What do you mean, I have joined them?" I say, trying to control the fear in my voice. I want to ridicule him, show him what a child he is being. "Who do you think you are? Dr. Coppélius?"

"Now perhaps that wouldn't be such a bad idea," he laughs. "For years I've kept Mother dead, convinced myself, convinced you, that she died when I was twelve. I created a story that worked for me. I needed that story, that version of my life. I couldn't let Mother leave me, to choose to leave me. And what is that, I suppose, but being a dollmaker, a Dr. Coppélius, creating someone who would never be able to fight me, hurt me, leave me. And then you came along. We were supposed to get married. You were supposed to love me. You did love me, I thought. But no, you decided you didn't want me, that I wasn't good enough for you. You refused me, you walked out on me. And now you are moving to America. You're leaving me too, just like she did. Well, this time I am not making any mistakes."

He is standing very close to me now, the music box ballerina gripped in his hand.

"I did love you, Nathan," I whisper, afraid of him and the way he is staring at me. "But people fall out of love. It happens all the time. It's nothing to do with you or me or your mother. It's just what happens to people. We love and we stop loving. There is no other explanation. You can't let your happiness ride so entirely on the decisions of others."

"As I said, Clara, I'm not making the same mistake again." His voice has taken on a new grimness, a hard determination.

"What mistake?"

"My mother came back to life. She turned up one day, with her new husband, the children who replaced me. Her very presence reminded me that I was not enough for her."

"So your mother isn't dead?" I whisper, uncertain. "I thought she died years ago?"

"Don't you understand anything I've just told you? It would have been better if she *had* died."

He walks to the end of the boat and opens a cupboard. I strain my neck to see what he is doing. In the gloom it is hard to see what he has picked up. He comes back toward me, holding up a box. At least it looks like a box. But as he gets closer, I realize it is a camera.

"Clara, I need you to stay very still for me. I'm going to take some photographs."

CHAPTER 31

Olivia

I kneel by the well, as I have done so many times before. I don't know what I expect it to give me. Hundreds of times I have reached down into its mouth, straining to reach the magic waters that spring up from the borehole that plunges more than six hundred feet down to the chalk below London. I think of all those people who traveled to visit the spas of London over two hundred years ago. It would have been a countryside retreat, an escape from the censorship controls of the city center. Perhaps not much has changed. Perhaps this theatre is a fantasy world where we get lost in the seduction of dance, music, creation. We search for something outside ourselves to find hope, certainty. But now, with Clara missing, not even the most holy of waters would comfort me. I feel a wrench deep within my body, like there is part of me gone too. I am afraid that if I stand I will fall, a vertiginous descent into the well.

I pull out Clara's costume, a stream of water soaking me as it escapes the netting. As the water runs down and pools around my feet, those other discoveries in the well flood my memory. My pointe shoes, the white rose petals, the flower crown, the manne-quin head. And now this. An entire costume drowned. I try to piece it all together, but it doesn't fit; I can't match the shoes floating there among a bath of petals with this sodden dress. Desperately, I try to think where she could be. I know I need to go home, to check she hasn't gone straight there. Maybe something has happened, some news. I can't think what it would be apart from about her contract to America. Now Mother is dead, we have stopped waiting for the phone to ring, a doctor's voice telling us the news. That chapter of our life is closed. We are both ready to move on.

There is one room I have not tried. The boardroom. I don't really want to go back there, not after last time. Every time I go to the top floor of the theatre, I think of Nathan. It makes my cheeks hot to remember what I did. I don't understand why I wanted him; it feels like madness, an irrationality that I can't connect with myself. But if the ballets and operas in which I have performed have taught me anything, reason is an irrelevance when desire is involved. Yes, I admit it. I desired him. But now when I think of him, it is with horror and shame. I wonder if I really did want him, or whether it was what he had with Clara that dug its way, insidiously, into my heart. It scares me a little to know that I am capable of changing so quickly, from obsession to disgust in minutes. The catalyst for that change: the sudden arrival of reality. The hard, cold, unpleasant reality of his tongue pressing between my teeth, his fingers inside me. Or maybe the reality of how it felt to betray my sister.

The boardroom door is closed but unlocked. Nervously, I fumble for the light switch. I don't know what I expect to find. Nathan and Clara locked in an embrace? Clara alone, hiding from us all? There is no one there, just a piano, an empty stool, a few boxes of music stacked at the side of the room. I walk to the piano, looking around me for any clues that Clara has been in here. There is nothing.

It is colder than usual in here; the window has been left open. I pull the coat around me tighter, pressing the green fur high around my neck. Part of me is glad to be wearing her coat today, a little piece of Clara wrapped around me. But it also makes me think of Nathan, the heat of his hands that have lingered around the collar when he kisses my sister. I shudder. There are some music scores on the piano stand, several of them stacked open on top of each other. I flick through them as if they will miraculously reveal a map to Clara. The end of Act Two of *Coppélia*. Berners's *Foyer de danse*. Rachmaninoff's "Prelude in D Major."

There is something else tucked between the scores. It is a photograph, fallen in among the pages of music. Taking it out, I hold it in front of me to catch some light. I recognize the woman immediately. Younger, dressed in the fashions of a decade ago, but it is definitely her. Nathan Howell's mother, the beautiful woman with the two sleepy children who came to the first night of *Coppélia*. The woman he seemed so determined to avoid. I remember watching him walk home to his boat, ripping a note into shreds.

I turn over the photograph. There is an inscription on the back, written in a hand that looks vaguely familiar.

Mother, died 1922.

I squint at the words. But she isn't dead. I saw her just a few weeks ago, right here in Sadler's Wells. And who writes the date of their mother's death on the back of a photograph? It makes me uneasy, these bold, certain words. There is another note written below the date.

Her beauty shall in these black lines be seen,

And they shall live, and she in them still green.

These lines jog a memory. Clara and I used to love searching through Father's bookshelf, the slim volumes of poetry with his light pencil markings in the margins. His little book of Shakespeare's sonnets, green leather and small enough to slip into a coat pocket, had delighted us. We had pored over those poems, unpicking them like a riddle. We had taken childish joy in laughing at the poet's arrogance, his belief that his lines would remain when the youth's beauty had long faded. It is, I realize now, a chilling thought that he believed his art could triumph over life: and perhaps he was right in some way. But our dance, our ballet, denies art this change; it lives only in the moment, that split second where the dancer flies through the air, spins round and round.

Taking the photograph, I put it in my pocket. I want to show Clara. She should know that Nathan has been lying to her, pretending his mother is dead when I have seen her in this very theatre, alive and well.

There is another note in my pocket, the one I found next to the card from Jacob Manton. I remember how it had confused me, the line of verse strange when taken out of context, alone on the scrap of paper. I take it out now and read those lines again. The hand is identical to the writing on the back of the photograph.

A lovely apparition, sent to be a moment's ornament.

As I stare down at the words, trying to make sense of them, I can feel my chest tightening. *A moment's ornament.* I think of Clara's complaint about Nathan after Mother's funeral. How she didn't want to fit into his unrealistic ideal. How controlling he had become. Now, reading these lines of verse, something feels terribly wrong.

I start to run. Out of the boardroom. Along the corridor. Down the stairs. Out of the stage door, ignoring the waves of the others who are congregating in the entrance, their long dresses and bright red lips signaling their readiness for a night's celebration. I cannot be part of them, not now. Not with my sister missing. And I think I know where she might be.

Turning north, I run up through the back streets, across the two roads, narrowly avoiding a cyclist who shouts back at me angrily. The air is cool on my skin, but I am sweating inside my coat. Clara's coat. Now I am starting to understand why she wanted me to have it, why she was drawing away from anything that bound her to him. I run fast, the heels of my shoes loud against the pavement. The houses on either side of the terrace loom down, lights from the windows dotting on and off; I imagine my footsteps waking up their occupants, a running woman charging through the London streets. I fly between the pools of light that paint the ground underneath each streetlamp, running faster than I have ever run before.

A man has stopped in the street just ahead of me, his large bulk blocking my path. I am aware of him watching me, waiting even. His chest and shoulders seem huge in the shadows from the streetlamps, his face dark.

"Olivia," he calls to me. At least I think that is what he says, but my own breath is too loud in my head for me to be sure.

I need to turn off the terrace and go down to the canal, and he is blocking my way. As I try to push past him, he says my name again, holding out his arms and taking me by the shoulders.

"Olivia, is everything okay?"

I shrug him off me and stand back, finally stopping. He releases me immediately, his arms falling heavily down to his sides. I must look a mess, my hair flying loose around my face, sweat pooling above my lip.

"What do you want?" I manage to gasp.

"I'm just walking home," he says, looking down at me strangely. "Why are you running? Is everything okay?" he repeats.

As I look back at him, I realize that I see this man everywhere. The pointe shoemaker's apprentice. I do not know his name. He is always there, watching our ballet class from the doorway, lingering in the corridors, in and out of Wardrobe. He was there that afternoon when I pretended to be Clara; he saw Nathan kissing me. He knows everything about us, when we take class, when we start warming up for the shows, when we go home, when we come in again in the morning. He creates the shoes we wear on our feet; he understands our strengths and weaknesses. I have ignored him for so long but he has been there all the same, watching me, watching Clara.

I look at him again, really look at him this time. And I am afraid.

CHAPTER 32

Nathan

The first few photographs he takes will not turn out right, Nathan thinks. She looks frightened and angry. In black and white she will appear sinister, demonic. He needs her to be flawless. This is not what he wants, and he places the camera down for a moment, working out how he should proceed. He wishes he could process the photographs immediately, transform his bedroom into a darkroom. Sadly, that is not possible, and he will need to wait until he can access the darkroom off Dean Street, tucked away in the corner of Soho, where no one asks any questions. He has been there before to develop his photographs, the ones he's taken of his toy soldiers and princess dolls, all of them arranged in complex stories and scenarios. They were a little blurred and it was disappointing to lose the vibrancy of their colors, but it was a good test of the lighting in the boat at night. He knows what he is doing now, his hands comfortable with the camera and its functions.

Nathan was fascinated by the darkroom, the men moving in and out of the corridors, their photographs hidden away for their eyes only. And the assistants who took bundled cash payments for silence. Not so secure, though, once one was inside that shabby door at the end of Diadem Court: Nathan walked into the wrong room while he was waiting for his photographs to develop, only to be quickly ushered along by one of the assistants. But he saw a glimpse of those photographs hanging from the line, naked limbs contorted and bound, open mouths like dark tunnels, men and women stripped down to their wildest, barely human. He hadn't liked it; all this rawness, it terrified him. Nathan wants order, precision, perfect lines of the corps de ballet, not a hair out of place. There will be none of that grotesque display of desire in his photographs tonight, he assures himself.

He goes to the little sink and takes out a bottle of champagne. It has been chilling all afternoon on a bed of ice that he bought from the local fishmongers on Exmouth Market. The woman asked him if he was having a party. He supposes he is; this is the closest he is going to get to a party with Clara. But that is her fault, not his. The ice is melted now, the label of the bottle wet and fragile. The cork makes a loud popping noise, the bubbles fizzing over onto his hand. He pours two glasses.

"Just imagine it exactly like it was before," he says to Clara. "When we would go out dancing together after shows, trying every new cocktail we could find. You wanted me then, didn't you? You were desperate for me to bring you back here." He drops more of the crushed sleeping pills into her glass, careful not to let her see. The music is loud, the end of Act One of *Coppélia* singing out from the gramophone, and Clara will not be able to hear him mixing the powder into her drink with a spoon. The bubbles dance against the metal. As the previous dose is still in her system, he estimates it will not be long before it takes effect. He knows all about barbiturates; the little pot of pills by his father's bed became a frequent sight after his mother left them. Nathan knows how quickly they start to work, how long they last, which ones are fast-acting, which ones will keep her asleep. He will need to act fast, persuading her into the poses he wants.

Nathan picks up a knife from the drawer next to the stove and tucks it into his trousers. He turns around to her with a smile. "Champagne?"

"No. Of course not." She glares at him. "What do you want from me? You have to let me go now."

In one tidy sip, Nathan drinks from his own glass of champagne, neatly dabbing his mouth with a handkerchief. Then, he walks to Clara. He leans over her, the other glass held in his hand. Swiftly, she turns her head away, her lips tight. He grabs her face and twists it back to him, tilting her chin back. She struggles to move away from him, but he has tied the ropes too tight.

"Don't fight or you're going to get champagne all down your tutu. Come on, you'll feel better after a drink. You always say that, don't you, when we're finding a table in one of those cafés you like so much. You love this champagne. Pol Roger. I got it especially for you."

She closes her eyes as he forces the glass to her lips, squeezing her jaw and cheeks to press her mouth open. Much of it streams down her chin and neck, but finally he gets her to drink. She coughs loudly. He strides over to the stove and returns quickly with his handkerchief, wiping the spilled champagne from her skin. It has pooled down between her breasts and he gently reaches the handkerchief under the tutu. He hopes the stain will not show in the photographs.

"I'm going to untie you now. But you're not to going to fight me, or scream, or try to run away. It won't be a good idea, I can promise you that. I just want a few more photographs, and then I'll stop."

"And then you'll let me go?"

"We can talk about that afterward. It really depends on how you behave with these photographs."

"You could have just asked me if you wanted a photograph, Nathan. It didn't need to be like this."

"I've already explained to you," he says with a sigh. When he takes the knife from his trousers, Clara shifts in the chair, knocking the wedge from under the wheel again. "You've got nothing to fear if you stay still and do as I ask," he stays sternly, placing the wedge back. "I will only use this knife if you give me reason to do so."

The drugs are taking effect, Clara's head falling to the side. She immediately jerks herself to attention, but Nathan can tell it is a struggle for her. He kneels in front of her and places his hands in her lap.

"As I said, I'm going to untie you now. You don't need to get up. I just want you to take this book. Imagine you are the Coppélia doll, reading in the window of Dr. Coppélius's workshop. Okay?"

Clara nods, her eyes following the knife. Nathan reaches around her and finds the knot, releasing her arms first and then her feet. He watches her carefully, the knife gripped in his hand. She shifts uneasily as he leans over her, the blade grazing her skin. Even though her feet and arms are now free, she cannot find the energy to move. He hands her the book, a hardback of *Tess of the D'Urbervilles*, which he opens to a random page. Clara holds it in front of her, the words swimming. She tries to stay awake and alert, forcing her eyes to travel across the page. But she cannot take in the words, just a sea of Angel and Tess and the fire in the grate and horrible laughter. She blinks and the words do nothing to reassemble themselves. Once Nathan has prepared her feet, maneuvering them up to a tight parallel resting en pointe, he moves away and picks up his camera.

"Just read the words. No blinking now. That's it. Soften your lips a little. No scowling."

He takes two photographs, one from directly in front of her and one from the end of the boat, filling the lens with her body.

"You can stand up now. Put the book down."

"I don't think I can. What did you put in the champagne?" Clara can barely whisper the words; it takes tremendous effort.

"Yes you can. Just a few more minutes, then you can sleep."

Clara pushes herself to her feet, trying to thrust sleep to the edges of her mind.

"One of those low arabesques, please," Nathan instructs her. "One hand to the side of your face, the other stretched out behind you." She slowly eases her body into position, arabesque *allongée*, her shoulders in *épaulement*. Nathan holds out the camera, takes several photographs, murmuring softly to Clara as he does so. Lift your chin, dip it again, open your eyes wider, part your lips. All the time the knife is at his side, back in the belt of his trousers. Clara is just conscious of it, the glint of its edge floating in and out of her consciousness.

Nathan turns to put down the camera. As he does so, Clara forces sleep away for just a moment longer. With great effort, she breaks out of the arabesque, one great *glissé* followed by a determined jump, landing her right by the door that leads out to the front deck. She pushes it open, the music from the gramophone dancing in her ears. It is the gigue from Act Two, the tempo fast and strong. It propels her toward her escape, the cheerful notes so strange against the frightening shadows of the boat.

Nathan grabs her and slams the door shut. She feels the edge of the knife against her jaw, the metal cold and hard. But then even that sensation fades as the drugs take over.

This time, he doesn't bother putting her back on the chair. He drops her to the floor, her legs and arms falling to the side like a rag doll. Looking down at her, he feels a strange, unexpected sensation. He thought he would only want perfectly curated photographs, his Clara preserved forever like a china doll. But there is something about the way she lies now, her tutu rising awkwardly, that reminds him of those secret, sensual photographs in the darkroom on Diadem Court. He leans over, his camera ready to capture the images he wants. Her thighs, her lips slightly parted, the thin slope of her neck, her collarbone. He places the champagne bottle to catch the light, the glass reflecting the flame from the candle. He photographs her feet, their high arches pressed between the pink of her shoes. He travels upward, his camera searching between the folds of her net tutu. A collage of body parts. This is not what he expected, but he feels himself enjoying it, testing the boundaries of his desire.

Eventually the camera clicks empty, signaling the end of his cataloging.

Leaving Clara sleeping on the floor, Nathan goes onto the deck and starts to prepare the boat for departure.

CHAPTER 33

Samuel

"Your sister?" Samuel stammers out in confusion. "Is she here?"

"I'm asking *you* that," Olivia cries, looking wildly around her into the dark of the street and down the slope toward the canal. They are standing above the Islington tunnel, where the waterway disappears under the surface of the streets for half a mile. "She's missing. I thought maybe she was here with Nathan. But you're here instead." Her voice is accusing, afraid. "I see you everywhere, watching us, hanging around. What have you done?"

"I don't know what you're talking about. Please, Olivia, tell me what's happening. Maybe I can help you find your sister."

"You can't deny it. Why are you always there? Why do I see you all the time, in and out of the theatre, always lingering?"

Samuel has been afraid of this moment. His father drilled into him the importance of staying in the shadows, hiding from attention, from ridicule. Why risk being laughed at, mocked for his desires and ambitions. But Olivia has got it all wrong. He never meant to scare her. He didn't even know she had noticed him. And he doesn't know where her sister is; how could he? There is only one thing he can do now, but it terrifies him. He needs to tell her the truth.

"Olivia. I don't know where your sister is. I haven't been following her; I don't know anything about her." He takes a deep breath; the next words will be the hardest. "It is you. I love to watch you dance. And when you started wearing my pointe shoes, well, I think I started to love even more about you. I was drawn to you."

Olivia has taken a step back from him. "What do you mean, your pointe shoes? Doesn't Mr. Freed make them?"

"I make shoes too. I make yours, and your sister's, and ones for several of the other dancers in the company." Samuel pauses. He needs to be honest with her. She is staring at him apprehensively, doubt still creeping across her face. "Your shoes are different to the others. I wanted to do something to make them special. Have you ever noticed the rose engraved into the sole?"

She nods. "Surely they are on everyone's shoe?" But as she says it, she looks uncertain, trying to picture the soles of her sister's shoes.

"No, just yours."

She looks horrified, but worse than that, disappointed. "The note. With the rose sketch. It was you?"

"Yes, I wrote you that note. I wanted to sign my name, but I was afraid you would laugh at me. You have so many admirers, always getting gifts and flowers sent backstage. I am no one, just a pointe shoemaker's apprentice. You don't even know my name."

"And the shoe in the well, the rose, the flower crown, the mannequin head?" She gestures manically around her. "And what is your name?" she adds, her voice accusing.

"Samuel. My name is Samuel Steward. But I don't know anything about a head and a crown. That wasn't me. But I admit that I took one of your shoes and scattered the rose around it in the well. It was supposed to be a good luck charm. I thought you'd like it, part of your routine of visiting the well before each performance."

"Maybe I'd have liked it if I knew who'd done it," she replies, her voice a little softer now though still suspicious and wary. "But I had no idea. You scared me. Why couldn't you just say something to me?"

"I couldn't say anything to you. There is a world between the two of us."

Olivia says nothing, shifting from foot to foot as she thinks. She wants to believe him; but she can't help but feel disappointment now she knows who was leaving roses in her cubbyhole, who wrote the note all those weeks ago. And to think she had believed for a moment that it was Nathan. She feels stupid, so blind to what was going on around her. Samuel is standing before her now, telling her all this, admitting to loving her. As she looks up at him, trying to work out how she feels, all she knows is that her sister is still missing. She still doesn't understand why Samuel is here, so close to where she thought she would find Clara. There is no time to take this all in.

"What are you doing here then?" she snaps at him, her chin lifted in anger. Samuel shakes his head, scared of her and this strange ferocity that he has never seen in her before.

She continues, her words faster now. "You need to explain why you're here. Where is my sister? You need to help me find her."

"I'm not here specifically. I'm just walking home. I was invited to dinner at a friend's house a few streets away and I'm heading home, to Exmouth Market, where I live. I only stopped because I saw you and I wanted to check you were okay."

Olivia nods, not really hearing him. Her eyes are turned to the canal, down to where she was headed so determinedly before Samuel appeared and all she had been so certain about dissolved into doubt. She isn't interested in his dinner, where he lives, what he is doing. She only wants to know about Clara. But still, perhaps he can help her.

"I'm sorry I never noticed you, Samuel." But her words are hollow, spoken only as a way of using him to find her sister.

He realizes he has been holding his breath. Now, hearing her say his name, he lets it go, a long slow exhalation. He is sorry she never noticed him too, but it doesn't hit him as hard as it would have done a few weeks ago. There is Milly. And she has noticed him. He doesn't have to creep around in the shadows, watching her from a distance.

Samuel shivers in the cold. There is the faint ripple of water below them, a boat pressing its bow through the canal. He thinks he can hear music, its notes distorting as the sound moves beneath them, but it is too quiet to be sure. It must be dark down on the water, he thinks, the canal giving up no secrets in the gloom of the night.

"You said that you thought your sister might be with Nathan?" he offers tentatively. "The pianist?"

"Yes, I thought so. He lives down here, on a boat on the canal. That's why I was so confused when I saw you here instead."

"I saw him earlier this evening outside the theatre. I didn't think anything of it at the time, but he was acting strangely. He was dragging a wheelchair out of an alleyway."

"A wheelchair? Like the one for the doll in *Coppélia*?"

"Yes, I suppose so. Now that I think about it, it might have been the same one."

"Why did he take it? The stage crew were losing their minds trying to find it before the show."

"I didn't stay to watch, I'm afraid. I was late for dinner. With Miss Bell, my friend," he adds after a pause. If he says her name, keeps reminding himself of his happy evening with her family, perhaps he can prevent himself from falling for Olivia again. He doesn't know if he can cope with the anxiety, the disappointment, the pain of loving someone who barely acknowledges his existence.

"Will you come down to his boat with me?" she asks, moving toward the canal entrance. "Just in case there are problems."

"Of course."

The two of them start walking down the steep slope to the water, Olivia in front, Samuel pressing his fingers against the mossy wall to secure his footing.

"It's not far," she calls back to him. "I've seen it before. His is one of the only boats that never moves."

They walk in the dark, the dim lights from the moored boats barely spilling their glow onto the path. The warehouses on the other side of the water are closed up like sleeping giants, their shadows pressing down on the water. Olivia pushes aside the branches of a willow tree, continuing up the path to where she remembers seeing Nathan's boat before. She stops before she gets to the bend in the canal, looking around her. The boat was here last time; she is sure of it.

"It's gone," she says, turning to Samuel. "He's taken her." She doesn't know what to do, standing there at the edge of the canal staring into a blank space where the boat should have been.

"It can't have gone far," Samuel reassures her. But he is not so sure. They don't even know which direction it has gone. "Why don't we ask on some of the other boats? They might have seen something."

Olivia nods and they start walking back up toward the tunnel. The next boat along has a long cargo hold with a short living area, boxes and crates packed tightly underneath a tarpaulin. A light burns on the front deck and Samuel can just make out low voices inside. He knocks lightly on the side of the boat and then steps back, waiting.

The voices stop.

"What do you want?" calls out a man's voice. It is not a London accent. Birmingham perhaps, Samuel thinks.

"We just want to ask if you've seen a boat leave here recently? We're looking for someone."

The door opens onto the deck and a man comes out, pressing his cap back down onto his head as he leans against his boat.

"You mean the one who's here all the time?" he says, lighting up a cigarette and exhaling the smoke that lingers around him. "He was here earlier, but I heard him leaving not long ago. You've just missed him." He pauses, scratching his chin. The strong stale smell of cigarettes and old yeast escapes from his mouth. "You know, I've been on these parts of the canal maybe ten times these past few years. Never once seen that boat move. And now you come along just as he does, wanting to know what's going on. Seems odd to me."

Olivia has stepped up to Samuel's side. "Did you see him bring anyone on to the boat? A woman?"

"A woman, eh? What's this about? He your sweetheart?" The man laughs, the smoke from his cigarette drifting further away from him. Olivia says nothing, waiting for him to reply properly. "No, miss. I've been inside for the past few hours. I ain't seen anything."

"How about a wheelchair?" she presses.

"Nope. But as I said, I've not been out on deck. Some people have walked past, I guess, but I didn't look out. Look, he didn't leave long ago. He went into the tunnel. You'll have to go back up to the streets, but if you're quick you might catch him somewhere on his way to King's Cross. It's slow going there, and he'll have to pause at St Pancras Lock."

"Thank you. We'd better get going then," said Samuel, nodding to the boatman. They start walking briskly away, Olivia breaking into a run as soon as the streetlamps from above the tunnel's entrance start to breach the darkness. The man calls out to them.

"You might be able to hear him. He's been playing this damned music all evening. That's how I knew he was leaving. His music faded away into the tunnel."

Samuel waves his thanks and they run toward the edge of the tunnel.

"How far do you think he's got?" Olivia says, just as much to herself as to Samuel. "I wish we could get in there. I don't like to think of him in that tunnel with her. What if something happens in there?"

"There's no towpath. We can't follow. As the man said, it's not far to the other end of the tunnel. If we're quick, we'll catch him coming out the other end."

Olivia presses herself against the mouth of the tunnel, leaning out as far she can over the water. "Perhaps we'll be able to see them?"

"Be careful, Olivia." Samuel comes up to her. "At least hold on to me so you don't fall in."

"Okay. You hold my hand and I'll lean around." Samuel wraps his hand around her wrist, widening his stance to secure his footing. She leans further now, peering down into the tunnel. It is pitch-black, the curved walls and the dark waters merging like paint.

"Can you see anything?"

"Not a thing."

But then there is a moment of complete stillness, as though all of London has held its breath. From not far away she hears the notes of Delibes's *Coppélia*. She can't quite place the piece, perhaps from Act Three, the part they didn't perform. She leans out even further, pressing her arms away from the tunnel's mouth. There it is, the smallest flicker of a light. A candle perhaps, or an oil lamp, its flame reflected against the water and the wet walls of the tunnel.

She pulls back and turns to Samuel. "They're in there. I think the boat has stopped not far into the tunnel. I can hear the music. How are we going to get to her?"

Before he can reply, another noise joins those quiet notes. It echoes and vibrates around the walls of the tunnel. Heavy shunting, a scraping noise, dull banging. And then a splash. One, and then another.

Olivia doesn't stop to take off her coat. She jumps down into the canal and starts wading through the murky waters into the darkness. Her legs move too slowly, so she throws herself forward into a swim. She hears Samuel call after her, but she doesn't stop. Not even when her clothes are heavy, their weight pulling her down, each stroke making her muscles scream. Samuel has no choice but to follow her. The gaping mouth of the tunnel swallows him whole.

CHAPTER 34

Clara

I am trapped in a nightmare where I want to scream but I can't; my throat is stuck, my limbs are too heavy to move. I drift in and out of waking but it is so dark that I cannot be sure when I am asleep and when I am awake. Time is impossible to grasp, the sound of Delibes's *Coppélia* weaving its way into my mind and then vanishing again. For a while I sense that I am moving, a slow steady floating. But then the movement stops and I feel as though I am suspended between two walls gradually filling with water.

Now the sounds around me have changed; they are echoing, cavernous. I am certain I am awake this time. It feels different, as though my body is coming back to life, a sharpness edging around my mind like a mirror gradually clearing of steam. I look up. The darkness is vast, like black paint smeared across my vision. But gradually my eyes adjust, the faint light from the boat casting slow shapes into the air. A curved brick ceiling flickers into view, the walls domed and falling to unseen depths below the waterline. We are in a tunnel, the smell of damp and algae and cold wet brick hovering thickly. Nathan has placed the oil lamp on the floor of the decking and I can see that I am lying on the floor next to it.

Lifting my head off the ground, I peer as far around me as I can; I cannot see Nathan. I try to roll onto my side, to push myself up off the floor. That is when I realize my hands and feet are bound. I strain against the bindings. They are not too tight and I can shuffle my feet against each other, the knots of my shoe ribbons rubbing against my ankle bone. But I cannot get out of them, not with my hands tied behind me.

The engine of the boat shudders and then stops, leaving an eerie stillness. In this stillness, I realize that I am shivering, my arms exposed to the dampness of the air. My tights feel wet, and the netting of the tutu sticks into me uncomfortably.

Although I am afraid, my anger overwhelms my fear. I am furious that I am held like this, prevented from dancing, walking, making my own decisions about what I want to do next. Even the simplest task has been taken away from me.

When I hear Nathan's footsteps coming back out onto the deck, I struggle more determinedly. I can't be trapped here. Not now. Not with my life laid out for me with such promise: travel, fame in a new country, the freshness of change. Nathan has always tried to stifle me, making me adapt to his version of what he wants me to be, a prize possession to make him feel as though he is still a star, beloved by all. And now I fear he is taking this vanity to its extreme. With a slow, nauseating tightening deep within my stomach, I realize what he meant when he said he wasn't going to make the same mistake again. He created a fantasy for his mother, one that suited his inflated ego. It makes sense now, the way he has always talked about her as though she was a goddess, the perfect woman. And she was, in a way: he created her; she was a religion for him. Then she ruined it when she revealed her living, breathing self to him, refused to play his game. He isn't going to let that happen with me.

Those photographs he was taking—I had hoped, prayed, that they were the extent of tonight's madness, his strange obsession needing an even stranger outlet. But of course the photographs weren't enough. Here, in this tunnel, he is going to kill me.

"Stay still, Clara," he whispers, kneeling next to me. "It's almost over now."

"Nathan." My voice comes out high and pleading. I try to calm down, but I can feel the panic washing through my body. "You can't do this. It's insane. Do you really think you'll get away with this?"

"No one knows you're here. And if, as you say, your sister does turn up, she isn't going to find you. She won't even know where the boat has gone. We're halfway along the tunnel, hidden under London."

"She'll look for me. She'll find me."

"Unlikely. And I'll be back in my usual spot by morning, nobody the wiser."

"You don't need to do this. What do you want from me?"

I don't know how to reason with him, not when he has convinced himself of such a wild, irrational plan. And this just makes me more terrified. It is as though the Nathan I thought I knew has transformed into a madman. Part of me, the part that knows I need to fight to stay alive, tells me I should beg him. I should offer him an alternative; I should promise myself to him, a future where I stay in London, marry him, become his ideal wife. But even as I think it I know I can't do it. And it's too late. I can see that he doesn't trust me anymore.

"I have what I want from you now; I have no more expectations. Not from you, not this Clara on the ground in front of me. I'll build a new Clara now, one that lives just in my head, exactly as

I want her. I have learned the hard way. People make promises, they let you expect the world. And then, nothing. They take it all away again. I was loved, famous, the best child pianist across Europe. And now look at me. Even a dancer in the corps de ballet thinks she is too good for me."

"I didn't think I was too good for you. You know that wasn't it."

"No, you were too good for all of us. Even your sister. And your mother, who you left to die in a mental asylum. The Vic-Wells. London. It always has to be the biggest and the best for you, off to America to fulfill some crazy dream." He leans over me. The light of the oil lamp illuminates the gold of his hair, casting shadows across his forehead. "Maybe I should have gone for Olivia from the very beginning. Maybe I still can. When you're gone, she'll need someone to turn to."

"Don't you dare go near her. She won't love you. No one will love you." I spit out the words.

He stands up, dragging me with him. My legs buckle, but he lifts me by the waist. It is a strange, painful dance, my weight falling awkwardly, a pas de deux with no harmony, no connection, no sharing of body weight, the momentum carrying each step. This is ugly, angry, my toes scraping against the wooden decking. I fight him, tossing and turning in his grip. But he drives us forward to the edge of the boat. I see the black of the water, an endless tunnel with no light marking out its end.

And then I am in the air, just for a second, before landing with a hard splash in the water. The cold immediately rushes over me, my bottom sinking first, then my torso, legs, feet, head. Dirty water presses me down, goes over my hair, into my mouth, drenching my skirt. Pushing myself up to the surface, I gasp for air. I try to move my arms and legs to keep me afloat, but it is hard with them tied together, and I have no idea how deep the water is, whether if I attempt to find the canal floor I will sink too far to rise again.

It is the tutu that protects me: a life jacket of tulle and satin. I find myself floating, the smallest of leg movements enough to keep me above the waterline. Turning away from the boat, I start to kick out, propelling myself forward down the tunnel, into the darkness. I need to get away from him. If I can find the end of the tunnel and crawl onto land, I will be safe.

There is another splash behind me. I don't dare turn. Eyes forward, determined not to lose my sense of direction, I swim with as much force as I can, my back and legs aching, my hamstrings on fire. I push the water away with my feet, my neck straining to keep my head above water.

I don't know how far I get: it could be yards or it could just be a few, futile inches. A hand grabs my foot. He pulls me back to him. I try to scream, but the water rises around me, rushing into my mouth.

And this time I do not float back to the surface.

CHAPTER 35

Olivia

I shrug off my coat as I swim. It is so heavy, weighing down every movement I make. As I swim away from it, the cold hits me once again, but I don't stop, even though my arms are in agony. I know Clara is on the other side of the boat; I know that splash was her. I need to reach her.

As I swim further into the tunnel, darkness folds over me. It is terrifying, impossible to tell where the surface of the water breaks into air. I force myself onward, my arms stretching and disappearing with each stroke in the black night.

Eventually, I can make out the outline of the boat. It creates an even block of darkness in the tunnel, framed by a flickering glow that creeps out onto the walls. But I don't seem to get any closer, the darkness distorting my sense of distance. By the time I reach the boat, I am cold and exhausted. I reach up, my feet pressed against the hull. One foot finds the rudder and I rest my knee on a rope fender that hangs wet and heavy over the edge of the boat. In one movement, I propel myself up onto the back of the boat. It surprises me, this strength. I did not know I could lift myself out of the water with such power. But my arms ache painfully, a sharp throb running down my sides and across my shoulders.

Peering into the shapes and shadows, I try and decide on a route, my mind struggling to stay calm when I hear angry splashes intensifying on the other side of the boat. There is space to edge my way between the wall of the tunnel and the side of the boat, but finding a footing will be a challenge; there is only a thin edge jutting out above the hull and I don't have time to take this slow. Instead, I lift myself onto the roof, grabbing a small chimney pipe and dragging myself upward. There isn't much space between the roof of the boat and the ceiling of the tunnel, just enough for me to crawl forward. I know I need to be as silent as possible, but I can do that. I'm used to moving swiftly and silently across a stage, merging effortlessly into the corps. I remove my shoes and leave them on the decking at the back of the boat. My stockings are slipping so I remove them too, throwing them overboard into the water.

I creep forward, my toes gripping the boat. The roof is flat and stable, but I rock in panic as a shape flies toward me, its wings stretched wide. I just manage to stop myself from screaming. Bats, congregating in the dark dampness of the tunnel. When I reach the front, the light improves, and I can see around me a little more clearly. There is no one on deck, just an oil lamp sending shadows up the sides of the tunnel walls.

"Olivia." A voice reaches me, a shaking whisper.

I turn abruptly. It is Samuel; he has followed me over the top of the boat and is lying down flat behind me, his head almost disappearing in the pitch darkness between the boat and the tunnel ceiling. I am relieved to hear him, his body somehow breaking my fear.

"Can you see them?" he whispers. We both jump down onto the front decking and lean over the edge of the boat. I wince at the noise of our feet landing against the wood. He holds out the lamp, the light pooling down across the water.

"There!" I exclaim, pointing at a dark shape not far away from us. It is hard to make them out but it looks like they are struggling, two bodies expanding and contracting in the darkness.

"Wait," Samuel says, holding my arm. "We need a plan."

"There's no time for a plan. Don't you see he's drowning her? You pull him off and I'll get her out."

"Okay." He sounds unsure. I turn back to him, placing my hand on his.

"Samuel, thank you."

I don't wait for a reply. I jump into the water and start to swim toward them. The water seems to fall away from me this time. There is no tiredness, no effort. I have only one focus, and that is getting to my sister.

Samuel is right beside me. We surge forward until we are upon them. He grabs Nathan and wrenches him backward. Nathan cries out, releasing Clara as he falls back into the water.

My sister disappears down below the waterline. She is unconscious. I reach for her, but she slips below me. Taking a deep breath, I duck under the surface until I am right above her; the water is deeper here in the tunnel, just above my head when my feet find the slime of the canal floor. I kick underneath myself and lift her out, keeping her head high.

I start to swim, supporting Clara with one arm, desperately trying to stop her head from sinking. It is exhausting and slow-going, but I press on, finding my way back to the boat. I can vaguely sense Samuel to my right. He too is moving toward the boat, dragging Nathan with him, who is coughing and choking as he is heaved through the water. I reach the edge of the boat, but I don't have the strength to lift Clara over the side onto the deck. I need to do something, though; I don't even know if she is breathing.

Holding on to her with one arm, I wade to the edge of the water, wedging myself between the boat and the tunnel wall. Grasping a rope fender, I try to calm my shaking arms. I lift one leg up and over the boat, contorting my body into a position even the most flexible ballet dancer finds a challenge. My hand is wet and cold but I keep it tightly wrapped around Clara's arm as I lift my other leg over, my stomach tensing. It is a relief to find dry, stable ground once again, but it is not over yet. I lean back over the side of the boat and take Clara under her shoulders. Digging my feet into the decking, I heave, pulling her over the side and into the boat. Pain shoots through my back and legs and I collapse heavily from the momentum. She lands on top of me, her soaked tutu covering my face.

I roll Clara off me and kneel by her side, leaning down toward her mouth. As I do so she jerks up toward me, vomiting out water and coughing painfully. The light of the oil lamp reveals her face, pale and stained with streaks of black eye makeup.

"Clara," I cry. "I'm here. Are you okay?"

"Where's Nathan?" she chokes, sitting up and looking down at her hands. I can just make out red marks around her wrists, where she must have been tied with a rope. "You untied me?"

"No, the rope came loose in the water." I look down at her legs. Her ankles are still bound together. I reach down and start to unpick the knot, but it is tight from the water, the fibers stuck together.

"Where is he?" she repeats, more urgently this time. "We need to get away from here before he finds us."

"Samuel has him," I reply, concentrating on the rope. My fingers are so cold, every effort sending angry shocks through my hands.

"Samuel? What Samuel?"

"Our pointe shoemaker. There's no time to explain now. You're freezing. We need to get you out of here."

Samuel nearly has Nathan back at the boat.

"Watch out," he calls to us. "I'm bringing him up."

Samuel has no trouble lifting Nathan out of the water and heaving him onto the deck. Quickly, I position myself between Nathan and Clara, still fumbling with the rope, which is finally starting to loosen. Samuel is back in the boat before Nathan has a chance to move. He presses him to the ground, holding him still.

"What do we do now?" he says, his body pressing against Nathan, who is struggling to sit up.

I turn to Clara. "What do you want us to do?"

She doesn't speak, just stares over at him, her face stony even as she shivers.

"Clara," I insist. "What does he deserve?"

CHAPTER 36

Clara

I want to kill him. I want Samuel to throw him back into the water, to hold him down until he drowns. I want him to be afraid, like I was afraid. I look at Olivia. I can tell she wants it too. Together, we can do this. We can overcome him, just like we have overcome all our fears. I think back to that awful night when Father died. Mother hadn't even been able to look at us; our pain was too much for her. She sent us out of the hospital room, waving us away with a dismissive flap of her hand. We had to deal with it alone, sitting for hours in the gloomy hospital waiting room in Finchley, wondering whether our father was still alive. It was a nurse who finally told us, bringing us sweet tea while we sat there shivering with grief. Mother walked straight out of the hospital without even collecting us. We walked home in the dark, two eleven-year-old girls, holding hands as we avoided the drunken stares and shouts of the men coming out of the public houses. We found her at home, hours later, lying in bed in the dark with a bottle of brandy on the side table. Olivia and I knew we only had ourselves to rely on from that moment onward.

Samuel has his hand over Nathan's mouth, his legs pinning him down. He looks up at Olivia and me and shakes his head.

"I'm not killing him, if that's what you're thinking." He looks terrified, this poor boy dragged into the canal by my sister, involved in a mess that hasn't anything to do with him.

"Of course not," I hear Olivia say, but she doesn't sound convinced. I want to scream at him. Just do it, I want to shout, just press your hand around his mouth, his nose, squeeze his throat. But he won't do it, I can tell. He doesn't hate this man enough; he hasn't seen what he is capable of.

My legs are free now. Slowly, I push myself up onto my feet, Olivia getting up with me and helping as I find strength in my freezing muscles. The flower crown has fallen over my eyes and I wrench it off, pins flying out of my hair and into the water.

"I'll do it," I say, taking a step toward Nathan. Olivia follows me and we kneel either side of Samuel. Nathan looks up at the three of us, his eyes wide.

"You can get off him now, Samuel," Olivia says, starting to position herself at Nathan's legs. "We won't ask you to be involved in this."

Samuel shakes his head. "Don't you see? I'm already involved. I can't let you do this. How can I live with myself if I just sit here watching the two of you kill him, whether you think he deserves it or not? It isn't for you to decide."

I feel frustration building inside me; I could be a doll, a wind-up doll ready to explode into life. That was how Nathan saw me, only he didn't want me to spring awake. He wanted a passive, lifeless marionette. He wanted to pull all the strings.

Samuel turns to me; he looks scared, but not of Nathan. Of me. "Please, Clara," he says, almost a whisper. "Don't do this. It isn't just his life you'd be ending. None of us would ever be the same again. I don't want to be a murderer. I just want to go back to my flat, my work." He pauses, turning away from me. "And Milly." He says this woman's name, Milly, as though it is the saddest thing in the world.

"Milly?" I repeat. "Who is she?"

He shakes his head again. "I can't talk about her, not here, not right now. She is better than all this. She's just like me; I see that now. Ordinary, hard-working, wanting something but not everything. She understands me better than I've ever understood myself. I thought that this mad life you all live, always on the edge of pain and exhaustion, was somehow worth it. It was glamorous, beautiful, justified by art. But she's taught me that happiness doesn't come from producing something beautiful, something that everyone will admire and celebrate. I don't want to be celebrated. I just want to love and be loved."

Olivia has gone very still. I turn to her and see her staring across at the water, her face unmoving. In the darkness she feels far from me, as if her features have blurred and deepened into something unreadable and unknown. She turns back to me.

"Clara," she says. "Maybe he's right. It isn't up to us what happens to Nathan. We can't live with that sort of responsibility."

I sit back against the edge of the boat and put my head in my hands. There is something about what he said that hurts me; it lingers too close to the truth. And I think it hurts Olivia too. What is left when there is no love, Father dead, Mother gone before she could acknowledge what she did to us? Instead, we search for beauty and art and fame. It is the only way to hide from ourselves.

Olivia crawls over to me. "You're shivering," she says, placing her arm around me. She holds me close and I can feel the faint heat of her body, even through the chill of her wet clothes. "You know he's only partially right, don't you?" She pulls me even closer. "We may live a mad, painful life. But we do have love. We have each other." I put my head on her chest and sob, my shivering changing into deep shudders that vibrate through my ribs. "You'll go to America," she continues, "because it's exciting and new and I'd never keep you from that adventure. But you'll go knowing that you're loved and that I am loved. You'll come home one day and we will always have each other."

She stands and holds out her hand. "Let's get you inside the boat. We need to find some warm clothes." I follow her inside, and she searches in Nathan's bedroom, bringing me a towel and a blanket. It is strange to be back inside here again, the trunk still loaded with Nathan's strange memorabilia, the box of figurines lying open on the table. The music has stopped and there is just the low sound of the needle crackling against the record. The bottle of champagne is half full on the sideboard, a pot of pills lying open in a puddle of ice. I pick up the pot and read the label. The words are faded, smudged from the ice. These are what he drugged me with, I realize. They are fast-acting sedatives, sleeping pills. I can just about make out the instructions: *Take one pill ten minutes before sleep.*

"He gave these to me," I say to Olivia. "I know Samuel's right, but I wish I could crush the whole pot into this champagne and send Nathan to sleep forever."

"There's part of me that wants that too," she replies, coming over to me and putting her arm around my shoulders. Her arms are thin but taut with energy and power. "But we can't. Let's just leave him and go to the police station. They can come back to deal with him."

"And we'd tell them what? It will be his word against ours. He has no criminal convictions; he used to be a famous piano player, a golden boy. They'll take one look at us, at our mother's mental illness, me dressed in a stolen costume from the theatre, two ballet girls. No one will believe us."

"Perhaps the police don't need to believe us. He's not going to come back to Sadler's Wells now. Not after this. He won't want the embarrassment of us spreading this story. He cares about his public image more than anything."

I nod, reluctantly. But I know she is right. Nathan isn't going to be playing for ballet class now. More than anything he wants to be remembered forever as the piano-playing prodigy, remarkably talented, on a level with Constant Lambert. Already this image of him has faded; if we tell this story he will be condemned forever as a freak, a criminal, and that is what people will remember.

We go back out on the front deck. The oil lamp is still flickering and I can see that Samuel looks exhausted. Nathan has stopped struggling. He stares up at me, unable to speak with Samuel's hand still pressing down on his mouth. I gesture to Samuel, and he slowly eases his hand away. Nathan takes in a big, stuttering breath of air.

"Leave London and never come back," I tell him, trying my hardest to keep my voice firm and level. It is difficult, especially when my teeth still shake from the cold. "I will tell this story to everyone at the Vic-Wells, to Constant and the rest of the orchestra, to everyone in the Camargo Society. We have your camera with those photographs of me; and we know about the fantasy world you created about your very-much-alive mother. But more than that, the three of us will be looking out for you. And if we see you again, we're not going to let you go free again."

"I'll go now," he says, his voice high and strained. "You don't need to tell anyone. Just let me go now and I'll leave. I'll go straight to King's Cross; I'll get the first train in the morning out of London. You'll never see me again."

I think he is telling the truth. The loss of his reputation would be far worse for him than a nomadic life away from his home. What I don't know yet is whether this is enough for me, whether I will be able to resist this desire for more, for something unspeakable and horrifying, for something that reveals a power that has always been there within me, waiting, afraid. But then I see Olivia, her eyes a mirror of mine, and I know that we will not let ourselves become monsters.

Olivia and Samuel keep glancing into the dark of the tunnel, anxious that another narrowboat will appear, but it's not likely, not at this time of night. We take Nathan inside and place him in the wheelchair, Samuel still keeping a firm grip on his shoulders. He slumps forward as soon as Samuel releases him. But then he looks up and says my name, an uncertain whisper. I go over to him, taking care to keep my distance. We found the knife in his trousers when we carried him inside; Olivia threw it into the canal. I nod to Samuel, who moves slowly and cautiously back through the boat to find the engine.

"It doesn't have to be this way," Nathan says, his voice low. "Perhaps I can stay, just playing for class quietly in the corner. I'll keep out of your way." He can barely look at me, so different from the man who proudly paraded his toy soldiers across the table not long before. "I can try harder. I can start afresh. I won't ask for anything. I can be different."

"No, Nathan. You can't be different. All you want is to be special. You want to be treated like a spoiled child. That isn't just going to go away overnight. Perhaps you brought that out in me, too, made me doubt myself. You made me feel as though I wasn't good enough; I had to be this perfect doll you could parade around on your arm, shining brighter than anyone else's girlfriend. I am better off without you."

I am not sure if he hears me; his eyes have glazed over and he stares listlessly out at the macabre museum to his desires. I lean down toward him.

"If I ever see you again, I'll tell your mother what you've done. I'll tell her how leaving you was the best decision she ever made."

He shifts in the chair, his gaze fixed on a tiny toy soldier that has fallen into a puddle at his feet.

"I've found the engine controls and tiller," Samuel says, coming back in through Nathan's bedroom from the back deck of the boat. "It looks complicated, but I think I know how to get this boat to move." Samuel looks enormous in the cramped corridor of the boat, but with his neck craned to one side he seems anxious. I see him staring uneasily at Nathan.

"Are you sure he'll be all right?" he asks, though no one answers. I don't have to be responsible for Nathan any longer, not now, not after tonight.

Olivia and I watch Nathan as the engine starts running and the boat inches slowly back along the canal. He doesn't even flinch when the loud bang of the engine going into reverse announces itself, the sound vibrating and dancing between the canal walls. The tunnel is entirely straight, no side currents to take us off course, but we are all nervous as Samuel steers the boat, emerging out of the mouth of the Islington Tunnel. If anyone looked down now from the wall above Duncan Terrace, they would just be able to make out a boat moving in reverse, creeping slowly toward a mooring spot on the towpath. But the courage of Samuel and Olivia's actions remains hidden in the waters of the tunnel, a secret I'll never forget.

When we feel the boat gently nudging the side of the canal, Olivia and I run out onto the deck. I glance back at Nathan, but he is still staring straight ahead, his hands gripping the arms of the wheelchair. My legs feel suddenly light, liberated, as I make that step off the boat and onto the towpath. Olivia is clutching a bag of Nathan's belongings: his camera and a photograph of his mother that he's labeled with the date of her fantastical death. I've picked up the flower crown, too, though I don't think it's in any condition to return to Mr. Healey.

I look around me, feeling the firm ground of the path. The night sky is so dark that for a moment I am not even certain we have made it out. There are no stars, not a single ray of moonlight. And perhaps that it is for the best, I think, no one to watch as we climb out of the boat, our clothes still drenched, the tutu flopping heavily over my thighs.

Olivia is looking down into the water by the entrance to the tunnel. A large mass is floating across the surface like a swamp of algae. She kneels and tries to grab it, but I pull her away. I can see now that it is the coat, that green coat with the fur collar that I thought I could escape if I just parceled it off to my sister, silently, stubbornly, without explaining why wearing it made my body feel heavy, trapped.

"Leave it," I say to her. "Neither of us will ever wear it again." The two of us press the coat down under the water, forcing it into a bundle that sinks to join the London debris of waste and dirt and discarded memories. She stands up and takes my hand, squeezing it gently. There is no need to say anything more.

"I live ten minutes away," Samuel says to us. "Let's get there as fast as we can and get warm."

I want to leave this canal; I want to run from the suffocating walls of the boat that held me captive. But first there is something I need to do. I take two determined steps back onto the boat and push open the door. Nathan is still in the chair, his shoulders hunched forward and his hands heavy on his thighs. I go to the trunk opposite him, ripping the programs and photographs and notes from his mother down from the wall above it. They scatter, ruined, at his feet, instantly drenched in the puddles of canal water that soak the wooden floor. I watch as he reaches down to pick up the wet fragment of a photograph, his chest heaving with sobs.

But it is the dolls I am after, those rows of tiny painted soldiers and musicians and princesses. The *Firebird* ballerina has fallen into a line of soldiers, knocking them in chaotic disorder. I scoop them all up and throw them into the tin box that sits beside them.

I hesitate, my hand hovering over the final doll.

This one he can keep, a reminder of all that he has lost. I place the ballerina figurine alone on the trunk, one thin arm pointing in arabesque at Nathan.

When I get back outside, I empty the box into the canal. The miniature dolls float lifelessly on the quiet surface of the water.

I turn and look down at my body, plastered in a wet tutu with a towel wrapped around my shoulders. Samuel offers me his coat, collected from where he left it, dry, at the edge of the path. I take it gratefully. I am still in my pointe shoes, but they are soft and malleable now from the water.

"Are your feet okay?" Samuel asks me as we are dragging our exhausted legs up the slope back to the road. I look up at him and smile.

"Never been better. Whoever made these knew what they were doing." I wink at him and he smiles back.

It is late, long past pub closing hours, and the streets are still and quiet. No one would notice us anyway, three ordinary people rushing home to the warmth of their beds. But it is only when Olivia finds my hand, wraps her cold fingers firmly around mine, that I finally feel safe.

CHAPTER 37

Olivia

Samuel's flat is on Exmouth Market, a tiny one-room home. But right now it feels luxurious, safe, warm. We strip off our clothes while he lights the small fire, the room still too dark to make out its features. The coal slowly starts to glow and we huddle around it, wrapped in his small selection of towels and sweaters. He gives me his dressing gown. It is a thick wool, hugely long, and I immediately start to warm up. I have never really looked at him before, this huge man with shoulders that must be twice as wide as mine.

He boils the kettle on his stove in the corner. And I thought our kitchen was tiny. He doesn't even have a space that could be called a kitchen, just a collection of pots and plates and tankards stacked on a shelf in the corner. But the tea he makes us is delicious, just as good as any brewed in the finest London hotel, and at last I let myself relax.

As the fire builds, a warmth starts to spread through the room. Samuel lights a few candles and I look around the room as it gradually comes to life. What I see surprises me. There is a desk by the window that is covered in sketches, a leather case, rolls of paper. Pencils, chalk, a jar of scissors and rulers, a measuring tape. I look at the wall to the right of his desk. It is crowded with designs, the most detailed and intricate sketches of shoes, hats, dresses, a coat. Clara is looking now, too, both of us gazing around the room, astonished at what he has created.

We have all gone silent; Samuel seems to be holding his breath.

"You designed all these?" I ask. But of course he did. He made my pointe shoes, didn't he? The best shoes I have ever danced in, as if he understands how we move, what we need to be able to perform with power and grace.

He nods. "Yes, I'm going to start my own shop one day. These are my designs." He says it shyly, quietly, as if it is an effort to say these words. Perhaps he has never said them to anyone before.

I get up and walk across to another collection of sketches on the other side of the room. A few scraps of tulle and satin are pinned up next to them. I reach up to the drawings, not quite touching them.

There, in a series of sketches of different angles and scales, is a design for the most perfect tutu. It is white, a matte satin bodice, layers and layers sketched out for the skirt. Measurements are written out in pencil, but with a space next to waist and hips.

"Are you going to make this?" I say, turning to him in excitement.

"That's the plan," he replies, tentatively coming to stand next to me. "But I can't afford the materials without being paid to do it. And no one is going to commission me for a tutu. Not yet, while I am no one, just a pointe shoemaker's apprentice."

"But you think you could make this? If you had the materials?"

"Yes. I am sure of it. I know how I will make every cut of fabric, every stitch. Milly is lending me her sewing machine this weekend. I'm going to start with a turban hat for her mother." He points at another drawing pinned on the wall: a navy silk hat with a net butterfly pinned to the side.

"What if I asked you to make this tutu for me?" I say to him. Of course it must be Samuel, my pointe shoemaker, the man who saved my sister: he must be the one to make the tutu I've wanted for so long. An act of creation rising out of the pain of this night. "I've been saving up. I can give you three pounds. Will that be enough?"

He looks at me with an expression that I can only describe as shock.

"Samuel?" I urge. I turn back to the sketches, admiring the cut of the skirt on the hips, the delicate layers of tulle.

"Yes," he says. "I will make it for you. But I think three pounds will be too much. The material won't cost quite as much as that." He sounds uncertain. Even without looking at him, I can tell he doubts me. He doesn't trust me. After tonight, I have transformed from a ballerina into something too real, too human. I am a woman who would jump into a canal and swim in darkness to her sister; a woman who wanted to put her hands around the throat of a man; a woman who is no longer afraid of her own body.

"You'll keep the rest, though. I need to pay you for your time as well as materials. And perhaps you can start saving up for a sewing machine of your own." I turn to him and smile. In that look he knows I refuse to be in anyone's debt.

* * *

When we are dry and warm, Clara no longer shivering, we say goodbye. We look ridiculous, in clothes far too big for us and thick socks instead of shoes, but it is better than my dripping dress, Clara's tutu. Samuel tries to insist on walking with us, but we don't let him. He has done enough.

We are silent when we get home. There is no need to speak, the two of us moving as one in the cold light of our bedroom. The rest of the building is so quiet, not a single squeak of a floorboard or slam of a door; it feels as though we are the only ones awake, two sleepless sisters claiming the night as their own. Standing in front of the mirror at the sink, we brush out our wet hair so that it shines in long straight strands around our identical faces.

I look closer. Tonight my sister is different, unfamiliar, a reflection that does not quite match.

Or perhaps not. Perhaps it is what I see when I look at her that has changed. There is no comparison, no terrified weighing of myself against her. Instead, it is my own power, my own beauty, my own determination, that I see reflected back in the fierce tilt of her head as she brushes away the water of the canal.

CHAPTER 38

Samuel

Any exhaustion Samuel expected to feel the next morning vanishes as soon as he steps outside onto Exmouth Market. The street is already busy with sellers setting up their stalls. There are piles of rosy red apples tumbling over each other; carrots, tomatoes, eggplants all seem to glow like jewels. Great chunks of meat, collected that morning from Smithfield Market, are displayed on the butcher's tray, and the baker has laid out steaming rolls and buns on a bright yellow cloth. There is a chill in the air, but Samuel doesn't feel it. Not today.

The cars and buses and bicycles spread through the roads, filling every artery of the city. Watching them rush past him reminds him of a game he used to play when he was little, on the rare days his mother would take him to the beach in Norfolk when they went to visit her parents. He would dig intricate passageways through the sand and then wait to watch the high tide surging in and filling his tunnels. Today he feels part of the city, in step with the other pedestrians, all marching in time to the rhythms of London, its melody and its bass.

As he rounds the corner onto Long Acre, the energy lifts its tempo, cars jostling for space as they drive in and out of the dealers' halls, the big double doors all wide open to the street. There are people everywhere. Mechanics in their overalls, car salesmen in suits and ties, shopgirls in slouch hats, coats tied tightly around their waists. He used to think everyone looked the same, their tired eyes shadowed in the black and gray and brown of their hats and coats. But this morning they are different, or perhaps he is different. A girl with bright red shoes walks past him; a mechanic, he notices, has a floral handkerchief poking cheerfully out of his pocket; a woman on the other side of the street has pinned a silver dove brooch onto the slant of her hat, its shining tail reflected in the sunlight. He smiles and keeps on walking, imagining them all in his designs, his shoes, his colors that will bring light to the city.

Just as he turns onto St. Martin's Lane, he sees Milly hurrying down from Seven Dials. He waves to her and she joins him on the pavement; they both slow their step, walking side by side toward Freed.

"Did you get home okay last night?" she asks, smiling up at him.

He wants to laugh. It feels like a strange dream now, as though he had watched the events unfold at a distance. "Yes, eventually. A few holdups along the way. I'll tell you about it when we have more time."

"Sounds exciting."

"Yes, I suppose it was. But not as exciting as the dinner with you and your family. Please thank everyone for me. It was a wonderful evening."

"You made a very good impression," she laughs, nudging him lightly in the ribs with her elbow. "Even my brother said nice things about you, which really is saying something."

They are almost at the Freeds' shop. Samuel doesn't want to go inside, not just yet. He knows he needs to say more, be bolder. He needs to tell Milly how he feels. Last night woke him up to what really mattered, exposed those old obsessions as dangerous, false, based on a fairy-tale fiction.

He takes Milly's hand and gently ushers her into the entrance of Cecil Court, away from the busy flow of pedestrians.

"Milly, I want to ask you something." He is nervous and he can feel his hand starting to sweat. But Milly doesn't let go. Instead, she squeezes his hand and smiles at him, encouragingly. So different from Olivia and her remote, suspicious eyes. He takes a deep breath. "Meeting you has been the best thing that ever happened to me." She shakes her head, but she is still smiling. "No, I'm serious, Milly. You've made me realize so much about myself that no one has ever let me believe before. But it's not just that. I think about you all the time. Last night, for instance, when I got held up on my way home. I just kept thinking about you and how I wished I was with you."

She takes a step closer to him. "And all I think about is you, Samuel."

"I feel as though I know you and you know me." He looks nervously around him, his voice lowering as a bookseller on Cecil Court throws open his door and steps out into the narrow street. "I'm not asking you to commit to me forever, not right now. But I just want to know if we could be together, more than colleagues, more than friends I mean." He is flustered, not sure how to say what he wants to say. But it is no matter, for she rises up on her toes and kisses him.

* * *

Mrs. Freed looks up at them as they enter the shop together. She recognizes that look, the first stages of love, the moment after the connection has been made, the words spoken. She smiles at Milly, who blushes crimson as she takes off her coat and hangs up her bag.

At ten o'clock Mrs. Freed asks Samuel to deliver a new order of shoes to Sadler's Wells. The order is so big that he packs the store cart full of shoes, covering them with a waterproof cotton gaberdine. The half-hour walk to the theatre feels different now that he is wheeling a cart, avoiding the potholes and the sharp edges of the pavement. It makes him think of Nathan's journey to his boat the night before, how he must have struggled to hide Clara from view as he maneuvered the chair over the curbs and the stones that would have threatened to jam the wheels. Nathan should be on the train out of London by now, Samuel thinks. But he isn't certain he will have kept that promise. Samuel remembers the desolate look on Nathan's face when they left him there in the boat. His eyes had been fixed on that strange museum of fabricated memories, his desires stripped away and exposed.

A group of stagehands are gathered outside the Rosebery Avenue entrance when he gets there, the smoke from their cigarettes clouding his path. He hears fragments of their conversation as he wheels in his cart.

"They pulled a body out the lock. The police sent me a different way. Made me late in, it did."

"It was a barge that found it first thing this morning, drowned in Sturt's Lock. That's the third drowning this year on that part of the canal," one of the men proclaims with the air of someone delighted to be in the know.

"Suicide?" one asks.

"Probably. Or a drunken walk home gone wrong."

"Never seen so many policemen on my way to work," another adds, shaking his head. Samuel feels the cart lurching unsteadily in front of him, the shoes rolling to the side. All he can see is Nathan, that terrible expression on his face, his body drained of life. For a moment Samuel feels frustration building inside him, anger even, as he remembers how they left Nathan there, all three of them washing their hands of his sickness. As the conversation of the stagehands moves on, Samuel gives a firm shake of his head. He did all he could. And it was thanks to him that the two sisters could wake up this morning without the weight of murder forever clinging to their name.

Samuel straightens the wheels of the cart and continues into the foyer.

* * *

Wardrobe is empty, as usual, so he takes his time placing the shoes into the dancers' cubbyholes. He remembers that time a few months ago when he placed the white rose in Olivia Marionetta's cubbyhole, how he hoped she would somehow understand his love, anonymous, in the shadows. This time he has no rose. But he finds a scrap of paper from the wardrobe master's desk and a crayon. He leans over the desk and writes.

> Dear Olivia,
> If you are still interested in the tutu, please send your measurements to me at Freed at a time convenient to you.
> Yours, Samuel Steward

He takes the note and places it above her new shoes. For a moment he considers ripping it up, distancing himself as much as he can from this woman for whom he feels no love, not anymore. She has become transformed in his mind since last night, as if the woman he obsessed over has vanished, reborn into something new and strange. When he closes his eyes, he can see the two sisters crawling over to where he held down Nathan on the wet decking of the boat, the look of murder in the hard lines of their jaws. It is impossible now to imagine her in the white tutu that he has sketched with such care on the walls of his home. That obsession that dug its way into him like a worm on a sick rose, that turned the theatre into a beautiful monster: it has gone.

As he leaves Wardrobe, he sees a heap of red in the corner. He can't help but smile to think how angry Mr. Healey will be when he finds the precious Coppélia tutu wet and ragged, smelling of dirty canal water. He's a little surprised that Clara and Olivia have brought it back here; it might have been easier to destroy it. But he doesn't blame them. He, too, would find it difficult to throw away that much tulle and satin.

* * *

On his way out he goes via the Wells Room. The familiar sound of piano music greets him from the end of the corridor, and for a moment he is afraid. It can't be Nathan, he tells himself. He quickens his step anyway and hurries to the open doorway. Ballet class is in full swing, the dancers performing a *grand allegro* across the room, their legs high as they jump and turn. The room is full of the sounds of the piano, the tap of pointe shoes on the floor, the gentle thud of the men landing from their *grands jetés*, the exhalations of the dancers as they throw themselves across the room. They make it appear effortless, but Samuel knows it isn't. Even ballerinas are subject to gravity. At the piano is Constant Lambert, thumping out the notes with vigorous energy. He looks hungover, not at all delighted to have been called in to play piano for class the morning after a final night of a show, his loud playing compensation, no doubt, for his exhaustion. He will not be impressed that his protégé has failed to show up this morning.

Miss Moreton bangs her stick and the music stops. The dancers transition from performance mode into exhaustion now that there is no music to cover the pace of their breath. They wipe their brows and lean against the barre. Samuel glances anxiously into the crowd of sweating men and women, trying to find Olivia.

A shudder of panic travels through him. He sees two twin sisters, both in identical black practice leotards and skirts, the pink of their shoes scuffed gray in the dirt of the studio floor. But then he looks again. Of course he knows which is Clara, which is Olivia. Clara is on the floor by the mirror, her legs stretched out in front of her. Samuel watches as she leans forward over her legs, her back flat. He can't even touch his toes, he thinks without envy as she rocks from side to side, pressing her body further in toward her legs. Olivia walks over to Clara and reaches out her hand. Clara looks up and takes it, getting to her feet with a groan.

"We start rehearsal in five minutes," calls out Miss de Valois. Even she looks a little tired, but she hides it well, the indomitable ballet mistress who never has a hair out of place. He wouldn't want to get on the wrong side of her.

Olivia sees Samuel standing in the doorway and she waves to him. His first instinct is to think she is waving to someone else, someone just behind him. But she starts coming toward him, saying his name. She speaks in fast sentences, walking up and down en pointe, pushing her arches out over her shoes.

"Samuel, you're here." She is smiling, but there is no warmth behind her eyes. She is all efficiency and business. "We've got all the clothes you lent us. They're in our dressing room. Can you stay and watch the rehearsal? Then we'll get them for you?"

"Yes, of course," he replies, a little thrown at the invitation into this sacred room. "I just need to be back at the shop by lunchtime." It is Milly he is thinking about. They have planned to eat lunch together in Trafalgar Square, by the fountain.

"Perfect. It's just a short rehearsal. We're learning the 'Rose Adagio.' The *Sleeping Princess* repertoire. Miss de Valois wants to get everything she can out of Nicholas Sergeyev and his notation books before he decides he's had enough of us."

Clara has joined her, and the two sisters lead Samuel into the studio.

"Let me talk to Miss de Valois," Olivia says, offering Samuel a seat at the front of the room. He feels a little awkward, but no one seems to object.

"This is Samuel Steward," he hears Olivia say to the ballet mistress. "He is going to watch the rehearsal, if that's okay with you. He makes our pointe shoes with Frederick Freed."

Miss de Valois looks over to him. "Yes, I know all about Samuel. Our guardian angel." Samuel looks confused, Olivia too. How could Miss de Valois know what happened last night? But then they realize Miss de Valois is talking about his pointe shoes, the way he creates perfection with satin and paste and a welting machine. "Enjoy the rehearsal," the ballet mistress says to him, a smile just about breaking beneath her arched brows, those piercing eyes that see everything, every tiny detail.

❊ ❊ ❊

Samuel watches with a new sensation. He feels admiration, certainly, but it is different from before, when he thought ballerinas were beyond human, their dancing effortless and weightless. The "Rose Adagio" requires balance, poise, shoes that keep the feet firm and strong. Four princes, four white roses, one Princess Aurora. Miss de Valois divides them into groups, Clara, Olivia, and one other woman going first, each with a set of four men. When Olivia and Clara stand tall in an *attitude* en pointe, he sees the muscles in their legs tense. They lift their hand up into fifth position, holding a moment of balance before the next prince arrives to provide the support of his hand. Neither twin sister wobbles. Samuel is certain that if those four men vanished, Olivia and Clara would still be there, balancing en pointe, strong, powerful, complete.

The End

Historical Note

While Clara, Olivia, Samuel and Nathan are entirely fictional creations, the corridors of Sadler's Wells Theatre in *The Dance of the Dolls* are filled with dancers who would have been taking morning class, rehearsing, performing, right there in 1933. I wanted *The Dance of the Dolls* to be a story of new beginnings, twin sisters learning their strength. And so I decided to set the novel at a time of great significance for British ballet, its own new beginning.

It is interesting how many of us assume ballet has always been part of Britain's heritage, an old, established art form. However, before the work of the remarkable Ninette de Valois, British ballet was little more than divertissements in variety shows. De Valois transformed it into an art form that rivaled the contemporary cultural developments of art, music and literature. By 1933 it was firmly on its journey to becoming the successful, world-leading institution that we perhaps take for granted today.

Dame Ninette de Valois, known in the ballet world as "Madame," met Lilian Baylis in the late 1920s and the two of them worked together to transform the ruins of Sadler's Wells into a successful theatre. Lilian Baylis ("The Lady") was manager of the Old Vic Theatre; she campaigned tirelessly to find funding for the project, with sponsorship coming from many directions, including famous names such as Stanley Baldwin, Winston Churchill, John Galsworthy, G. K. Chesterton and others. When the theatre opened in

1931, de Valois set up the Vic-Wells Ballet company and moved her school into the theatre's studio. Sadler's Wells Ballet School and the Vic-Wells Ballet have evolved into today's Royal Ballet School, Royal Ballet and Birmingham Royal Ballet.

The 1930s was a momentous decade for British ballet, and I have brought many of these influential people into *The Dance of the Dolls*. In addition to Ninette de Valois, Constant Lambert was integral to the success of the Vic-Wells. He was the musical director, bringing with him his experiences of working with Diaghilev, both as a composer and conductor. Richard Shead's 1973 biography of Constant Lambert describes those years, and Antony Powell's memoir at the start of the book gives a taste of the vibrant life Constant Lambert lived.

Dennis Arundell gives a fascinating account of the early productions in his 1965 book *The Story of Sadler's Wells*. He also writes about the Camargo Society, a group which helped to fund many of the early productions. They were led by the economist John Maynard Keynes, Lydia Lopokova, the music critic Edwin Evans (for whom I have given a fictional role in his cruel review of Nathan Howell), Constant Lambert and the ballet critic Arnold Haskell. Interestingly, it was a different production of *Coppélia* (two June 1933 gala performances at the Royal Opera House) that marked the end of the Camargo Society's work; with the increased popularity of ballet, it no longer needed the funding of the Society.

Another key personality, both in *The Dance of the Dolls* and in the early days of the Vic-Wells company, was Alicia Markova. She brought the necessary celebrity excitement to the fledgling company and can be partially credited with ensuring the success of the Vic-Wells. Her beautiful book *Markova Remembers* (1986) provides photographic details of many of the performances at Sadler's Wells in the early 1930s, as well as productions at the Mercury Theatre, staged by the Ballet Club run by Marie Rambert. Ninette de Valois, in her 1957 autobiography *Come Dance with Me*, talks of those early years with great fondness. She also describes just how challenging it was to establish British ballet's reputation when both the public and press seemed determined to associate great ballet only with the celebrated Ballets Russes. She suggests that it was the death of Diaghilev in 1929 and Pavlova in 1931 that gave British ballet the space to grow.

All the productions mentioned in *The Dance of the Dolls* really did take place, including Penelope Spencer's sketch "Ladies, Sigh No More!" at the 1933 Ideal Homes Exhibition. The protest to which Clara alludes on the bus took place in July 1933, so I have moved that forward by a few months to fit into the novel's time frame. Similarly, I have taken liberties with the date of the unveiling of Boris Anrep's mosaic *The Awakening of the Muses*, bringing it forward from the actual date of July 1933. I have tried to include many of the real dancers who danced with the Vic-Wells in 1933. Robert Helpmann had just joined the company. Frederick Ashton was already creating his ballets; also appearing in the book are Beatrice Appleyard, Ursula Moreton, Hermione Darnborough, Nadina Newhouse, Gwyneth Matthews, Antony Tudor, Stanley Judson and William Chappell (whose 1951 book *Fonteyn: Impressions of a Ballerina* captures the essence of life behind the scenes at Sadler's Wells; it was my ballet teacher Valerie Hitchen who gave this book to me just before I started at the Royal Ballet School back in September 2000. She wrote that she hoped I would keep the book nearby as an inspiration. I have certainly done that, if not quite in the way she and I expected).

I danced scenes from *Coppélia* many times during the years I was training at the Royal Ballet School. It is a ballet of which I have very fond memories, and so it was an easy decision to set the novel during the rehearsals and performances of a historical performance of the ballet. The Vic-Wells Ballet put on a production of *Coppélia* in March 1933, and many of the named cast were indeed dancing in those performances. Lydia Lopokova is one of the great ballerinas of the first half of the twentieth century, and her role in *The Dance of the Dolls* comes at the end of her ballet career. She danced Swanilda for the first two performances of *Coppélia* in March 1933, after which Ninette de Valois took over the role for the remaining performances. She had a fascinating life, and the wonderful biography *Bloomsbury Ballerina* by Judith Mackrell (2008) follows Lydia from her childhood at the Imperial Theatre School in Russia to her life in London, her marriage to Maynard Keynes, and how she coped with the intellectual snobbery of the Bloomsbury Group, who felt she did not match up to their standards: how wrong they were! While Olivia and Clara Marionetta are fictional characters, I feel certain that they would have been inspired by the energy and fierce independence of Lydia Lopokova.

* * *

The Dance of the Dolls tells another story of new beginnings. Frederick and Dora Freed set up their shoe shop in 1929. From humble foundations in a workshop in the basement of his first shop in Cecil Court, Covent Garden, Frederick Freed started what is now Freed of London, the world's leading designer and manufacturer of professional dance shoes. While Frederick Freed was a quiet and ingenious creator, it was Dora Freed who helped to build the shop's reputation. She was a dynamic woman, confidently making connections and spreading the word about how different these shoes were to the previous offerings from other shoe companies. In 1933, there was just one apprentice working with Mr. Freed. Samuel Steward is a fiction, but there really would have been a hard-working cobbler down in that basement to help produce these beautiful shoes. When I started writing *The Dance of the Dolls*, I got in touch with Sophie Simpson, the senior manager at Freed of London. She fitted me for my very first pair of pointe shoes when I was eleven years old and at White Lodge, the Royal Ballet School, and since then I have worn hundreds of pairs of Freed shoes. Speaking with her about the history of Freed and the process of making a pointe shoe was fascinating and led to the creation of my character Samuel Steward.

The Freeds famously said that they would make shoes to fit the dancer, not the dancer having to fit the shoe. Individual dancers, especially regular customers, would even have their own specific shoe last created for them, molded to fit their needs. Indeed, Margot Fonteyn wore Freed shoes with a specific color of satin just for her. The discerning reader may have noticed that Fonteyn has a tiny role in the novel. She was just fourteen years old in 1933. When her mother brought her to Sadler's Wells to audition for the ballet school, she forgot to bring her ballet clothes and shoes. Ursula Moreton told her to take off her shoes and stockings and audition barefoot in her petticoat. She was enrolled in the school and quickly became one of de Valois's favorites. Fonteyn's autobiography (published 1975) gives many detailed accounts of those early years of the company, with descriptions of Nicholas Sergeyev and his pianist Ippolit Motcholov. She also writes about Madame Manya, the dressmaker. An account of the young Fonteyn visiting Madame Manya to persuade her to make a tutu inspired my fictional tale of Olivia making her own journey to Maida Vale. Fonteyn, however, was rather more successful than Olivia, coming away with a tutu that cost her £16.

* * *

The well in the basement of Sadler's Wells exists and is still used today by Sadler's Wells Theatre to source the water for the theatre. The stone cover, found by Richard Sadler's builders in 1683, is on display in the foyer of the theatre. However, the room which it inhabits in *The Dance of the Dolls* is a fiction, an embellishment of the existing well into a place for the dancers to play out their routines and superstitions. The description of the well itself is also fictional. In reality, it is a rather unglamorous hole in the ground, covered over so that it would not be possible to reach down into the water. I was inspired by memories from my years training at the Royal Ballet School: the bronze statue of Margot Fonteyn was the site of our superstitions. We would rub her finger every time we walked past, leaving that one finger highly polished and far brighter than the others. In the fictional creation of that dark storage room and its mysterious well, I hope to have recreated that same feeling of compulsion toward good luck charms and routine.

* * *

Coppélia is a joyful, comic ballet, the choreography packed with entertaining mime sequences and energetic national dances like the mazurka that Clara dances so well. The ballet is inspired by E. T. A. Hoffmann's 1816 short story "Der Sandmann," a much darker, more sinister story of a man called Nathanael who falls in love with an automaton doll, Olympia. The first ballet *Coppélia* was choreographed by Arthur Saint-Léon in 1870, with Léo Delibes composing the music. The version performed in 1933 was the Petipa version, first performed in 1884. Only the first two of the three acts were performed. In *The Dance of the Dolls* I have drawn on elements of both the comedy ballet and the gothic Hoffmann story. In fact, I took the names of Nathan and Clara directly from Hoffmann's work.

✳ ✳ ✳

While the story of the Marionetta twins is fictional, there are many true stories to be found within this novel. Frederick and Dora Freed's revolutionary pointe shoes; Ninette de Valois's wisdom and perseverance; Nicholas Sergeyev's trunks, smuggled out of Russia and filled with notation books of the great classics; Lilian Baylis's renovation of Sadler's Wells. All these people came together at the perfect moment to spark the expansion of British ballet. It is into this world that Olivia and Clara Marionetta have danced, finding love and strength together.

Acknowledgments

Thank you to my agent, Antony Topping, who has always believed in this book. I will never forget the excitement of our first meeting. His wisdom helped to shape the story and sharpen its edges. Thank you to everyone at Greene and Heaton agency for making me feel so welcome.

Thank you to Jennifer Weltz for her amazing work in bringing *The Dance of the Dolls* to the US, and to my editor Claire Wachtel at Union Square & Co. It has been such a privilege to work with Claire and I am grateful to Barbara Berger and the team at Union Square & Co. for welcoming my novel with such enthusiasm.

Thank you to my brilliant UK editor, Jenny Parrott. Working with Jenny is a joy; I know how lucky I am. Thank you to Molly Scull for her invaluable suggestions and to Sarah Terry for her rigorous attention to detail and infinite positivity. I am grateful to everyone at Oneworld for guiding me along this road to publication and for the exceptional work on the cover design. Meeting the team at the Oneworld offices was a day I'll never forget—thank you.

Thank you to Sophie Simpson at Freed of London for sharing her knowledge of the history of the fascinating pointe shoes, as well as her enthusiasm in answering my research questions.

There can be no doubt that all the ballet teachers of my youth had a profound effect on the creation of this novel. Special thanks go to Valerie Hitchen for always believing in me; Nicola Gaines for her beautiful passion for dance; to Tania Fairbairn, Anita Young, Patricia Linton, Nicola Katrak, Petal Miller-Ashmole, Hope Keelan, Irene Axon, and Brenda Last. You all taught me how to work hard and how to strive for perfection, even if it was impossible to achieve. Thank you, also, to Anna Meadmore, for her kindness and support.

Thank you to Bryerly Long, my dear friend who worked tirelessly to find opportunities for us to dance together alongside our academic studies.

Thank you to the English teachers in my life. Thank you to Suzanne Gunton and all the English teachers at the Royal Ballet School who made certain that my love of reading stayed strong even amongst the busy ballet schedules. Thank you to my A-Level English teachers for making me believe I was good enough to read English at university; thank you to my tutors at St. Hugh's College, especially Nick Perkins, for teaching me how to slow down and think deeply about what I was reading. And thank you to my fellow English teachers for sharing in my early excitement about this novel; our Byron Reading Room coffee breaks are a joy!

I am grateful to Jo Bratten for encouraging me to write and submit my work to literary journals; reading her stunning poetry inspired me to seek out publication. Thank you to my glorious book club: it is thanks to this wonderful group of people that my own reading list has expanded in such exciting directions. Special thanks must go to Natasha Bassett, who is always keen to find an excuse to celebrate: thank you for those walks along the canal—you made me fall for that little stretch of water and I couldn't resist writing it into my novel.

I am grateful to Jim Buckland: your support has been so important to me.

Thank you to my twin sister, Suzie, for her love and kindness. Thank you to my sister Jo: I don't know anyone who appreciates the joy of escaping into a story like you do. To my parents, thank you for reading every word I have ever written, and always thinking of something lovely to say. Your endless belief in me has meant I have never given up on this dream.

And finally, to Erik. You knew I could write this book. Your love made it happen.

The Dance of the Dolls
Reading
Discussion Guide

TOPICS AND QUESTIONS FOR DISCUSSION

1. Clara and Olivia are identical twin sisters and some characters struggle to tell them apart. They are also ballet dancers, working every day on a discipline that expects each dancer in the corps de ballet to move as one—identical mirror images of each other. What did you think were the differences between the two sisters? And in what ways were they similar? Did their differences get in the way of their relationship and their love for one another?

2. The twin sisters have very different motivations and desires. How did the way you related to each of them differ? Was there one sister you found yourself drawn to more than the other?

3. Samuel, the pointe shoemaker apprentice, is obsessed with Olivia. However, his feelings for her change throughout the novel. How would you describe these changes? By the end of the novel, how does he feel about her? How did your opinion of Samuel change as the novel progressed?

4. Nathan used to be a child star, praised and adored by everyone. He struggles to cope with the change in his status and feels that he is overlooked by some key members of the ballet world. To what extent do you feel his unusual childhood and his subsequent loss of fame impacts on the way he behaves throughout the novel?

5. The dancers are rehearsing for the ballet *Coppélia*. The ballet is the story of two young lovers, Swanilda and Franz, who are to be married the next day. Swanilda, however, is jealous of the way Franz appears fascinated by a beautiful young girl named Coppélia, who sits in the window of the house of Dr. Coppelius—a mysterious inventor—reading her book all day. So Swanilda and her friends decide to break into Dr. Coppelius's workshop and meet this girl for themselves. But what they see when they get inside is not at all what they expected. Coppélia is a lifeless doll, not human at all. To what extent did you see this story mirrored in the plot of the novel? How was Nathan influenced by seeing Clara dressed as the doll when she was posing for some photographs on the stage?

6. Many of the characters are obsessed with the idea of creation and art, and about whether their artistic endeavors will be recognized and appreciated. Samuel wants to make the tutu that he has designed; Nathan wants to be a successful musician again; Olivia and Clara, each in their own way, want to be famous dancers. How does this obsession impact on the decisions they all make? And to what extent are they living in the realm of fantasy rather than reality, and does this change for any of the characters during the novel?

7. Ballet provides rhythm and routine for Clara and Olivia: they go to daily ballet class, rehearse, perform, endlessly darn and sew ribbons onto new pairs of pointe shoes. However, they also worry about making enough money and finding employment out of season. What did you find most interesting about life for a ballet dancer in the 1930s? And what interested you about the historical setting?

8. The sisters' mother is sick and is a permanent resident at Colney Hatch mental hospital. How do Clara and Olivia cope with the challenge of visiting their mother, especially when she places such high expectations on them and their dancing careers? What do you think their mother finds most appealing about her daughters being ballet dancers? Or do you think she has always struggled with being a "ballet mother"?

9. All of the dancers have little routines and rituals that give them luck before a performance or help them to focus before a day of rehearsals. What did you think about their choice of the well beneath the theatre as the location for these superstitions? Why do you think so many performers turn to these types of rituals?

10. We know that Clara has an offer to go to America and pursue her dancing career in new and exciting ways. How do you think the sisters will find living apart? Do you think they will struggle or are there any ways in which they might flourish?

ENHANCE YOUR BOOK CLUB

1. Go to the ballet or watch a recorded performance of a ballet on TV or online with your book club. Can you see evidence of the toil and grit and pain beneath the poise and grace of the dancers?

2. Read the short story that inspired the ballet *Coppélia*: E.T.A. Hoffmann's 1816 story called "Der Sandmann." See if you can spot ways in which *The Dance of the Dolls* draws on elements of both the comedy ballet and Hoffmann's gothic short story.

3. Explore the skill and technique that goes into making pointe shoes. Watch the excellent videos on the Freed of London website and social media to learn more about this process.

4. Learn more about the history of the Royal Ballet. I highly recommend Dame Ninette de Valois's 1957 memoir *Come Dance with Me*, a book that tells the story of the early years of the company.

A CONVERSATION WITH LUCY ASHE

Tell us about the inspiration behind *The Dance of the Dolls*.

When I was training at the Royal Ballet School, I developed a fascination for not only the stories of ballets, but also the history of their creations. *The Dance of the Dolls* is a novel emerging out of years of research and personal experience and I sometimes feel as though I have pulled together the threads of what I love most in my life to create my debut novel.

My novel reimagines the early years of the Vic-Wells Ballet company at Sadler's Wells theatre, and the story is immersed in ballet history featuring famous historical figures such as Ninette de Valois, Lydia Lopokova, Constant Lambert, Alicia Markova, and Nicholas Sergeyev. I loved engaging with this important time period when British Ballet was starting to grow, integrating historical details into my fictional story.

How did your experience at the Royal Ballet School inform the research behind the novel?

My eight years first as a junior associate and then at White Lodge, the Royal Ballet's School in Richmond Park, had a huge influence on the novel. To spend those years living and breathing ballet, to define myself entirely as a ballet dancer, was both wonderful and challenging in equal measure. There was an intensity to those years that I will never forget.

Ballet training has much repetition and routine, and none more so than the preparation of pointe shoes. The rhythm of sewing, preparing, and replacing these shoes is familiar to all ballet dancers. It is a relentless cycle, and I found myself drawn to this when planning the novel. I always wore shoes made by Freed of London, and so I researched the company and was fascinated by the story of Frederick and Dora Freed and their pointe shoe workshop. I have worn hundreds of pairs of Freed of London pointe shoes, and I spoke with Sophie Simpson, the senior manager at the pointe shoe manufacturer, when I was researching for my novel. It was lovely to hear that she remembered when I was fitted for my very first pair of pointe shoes at eleven years old at the Royal Ballet School in Richmond Park.

Our pointe shoe fittings always took place in a beautiful dance studio called the Salon that looked out over the park. I will never forget that first fitting, how exciting it was to step up *en pointe*. The older girls taught us how to darn the ends and sew on the ribbons, as well as the best tips for protecting our toes from blisters and bruising. They taught us how to break in our shoes and how to prolong their life with shellac, though I still managed to get through two or three pairs every week; I was fortunate to have a kind sponsor who covered the cost of my pointe shoes.

Ballet is more than just the steps performed in class and onstage. There are many routines and rituals, passed down from one generation to the next. I loved recreating this world in my novel.

What drew you to setting the novel in 1933?
The early 1930s was a very important time for British ballet. Ninette de Valois set up the Vic-Wells Ballet at Sadler's Wells Theatre, the company that later became the Royal Ballet. In my research, I was delighted to see that they put on a production of *Coppélia* in 1933, a ballet that I love and that inspired the plot of my novel. I danced scenes from *Coppélia* many times during the years I was training at the Royal Ballet School. It is a ballet of which I have very fond memories, and so it was an easy decision to set the novel during the rehearsals and performances of a historical performance of the ballet.

Why did you choose to weave the ballet *Coppélia* into your novel?
Swanilda is a brilliant character, a determined, playful, and mischievous young woman who challenges both her fiancé and the mysterious Dr. Coppélius into accepting the futility of placing all their adoration onto a lifeless doll. Although *Coppélia* is a joyful, comic ballet, it is inspired

by E.T.A. Hoffmann's 1816 short story "Der Sandmann," a much darker, more sinister story of a man named Nathanael who falls in love with an automaton doll, Olympia. In *The Dance of the Dolls*, I have drawn on elements of both the comedy ballet and the gothic Hoffmann story. In fact, I took the names of two of my characters directly from Hoffmann's work.

Who are your favorite novelists?

An almost impossible question to answer, as the list would go on and on. However, I can narrow it down by talking about which of my favorite writers and books inspired my novel. There is *The Little Stranger* by Sarah Waters; *The Foundling* by Stacey Halls; *Burning Bright* by Tracy Chevalier; *The Essex Serpent* by Sarah Perry; *Jane Eyre* by Charlotte Brontë. I am drawn to novels with dark and atmospheric settings, stories where the depths of human desires can be exposed.

What are your favorite novels about ballet?

I have read *Ballet Shoes* by Noel Streatfeild so many times, and there is something timeless and magical about the relationship of the three sisters, Pauline, Petrova, and Posy Fossil. When I was a child, I read all of the Lorna Hills Sadler's Wells series. They were wonderful books and I must have read *A Dream of Sadler's Wells* about the brilliant Veronica Weston countless times. I also enjoyed *Listen to the Nightingale* by Rumer Godden, about a ballet dancer named Lottie and her King Charles Spaniel, Prince. A recent favorite is the adult fiction novel about ballet by Maggie Shipstead called *Astonish Me*. It's set in the 1970s and is all about obsession and the fear of mediocrity. Her understanding of dancers' obsessions with their body, and how their entire identity is so often based around their success or failure as a dancer, spoke very true to my own experiences of ballet.

Do you still dance?

After school, I left intensive ballet training and went to the University of Oxford to study English literature. Although it was a very difficult decision, I knew that I wasn't going to find fulfillment and success in the way I wanted it if I continued on my path as a professional dancer. However, I could not stop dancing and I trained as a dance teacher with the British Ballet Organisation. Gaining my diploma in dance teaching was hugely rewarding and deepened my understanding of ballet, the body, and the science behind the movements. I taught ballet to students at Oxford and continued to dance and perform as a freelance dancer. However, once I started working as an English teacher in a full-time capacity at a very busy boarding school, daily ballet training was simply not possible.

Now, I dance when I can, taking open class at studios such as Steps on Broadway or Ballet Arts Center in New York City, or in London I go to Pineapple Dance Studios or Danceworks. I love these classes, how welcoming they are to everyone no matter your level. Professional dancers stand at the barre next to men and women in their eighties who have never hung up their ballet shoes. Ballet is a wonderful way to keep the body strong and supple. I hope I will dance for the rest of my life.

What impression of ballet do you hope readers will take from reading your novel?

Often people think of ballet as either pink frills and tutus for little girls, or psychological horror and trauma because of the success of *Black Swan*. And yes, it can be both of these things: it is lovely seeing little girls and boys getting excited about their first ballet class or a pretty costume, and I agree that ballet provides the perfect setting for a story of obsession and pain. But it is also far more normal than that, a routine, hard work, a job that pays the bills. In the story of Clara and Oliva, I hope readers will see two young women who have desires, dreams, insecurities, and fears, just the same as everyone else, ballet dancer or not.

Most of all I hope that readers will find themselves intrigued by ballet: that my novel will provide a springboard for people of all ages to try ballet themselves, to go to the ballet, and to learn more about this beautiful, painful, magical art form.